Jake West – The Estian Alliance

(The Jake West Trilogy – Book 3)

By

M J Webb

Copyright © 2022 M J Webb

All rights reserved.

ISBN: 9798846274341

License Notes

This book is licensed for your personal enjoyment only. If you would like to share this book with another person, please purchase an additional copy for each recipient. Thank you for respecting the hard work of this author.

Acknowledgements

A series of three large novels is not penned without the help and advice of many kind-hearted souls. I have been extremely fortunate to have received support from numerous friends on this wonderful journey. Chief amongst all has to be the immensely talented A J Hateley. I am extremely proud to work with such a brilliant illustrator and I wish her every success.

I also owe a great debt of gratitude to Tanya Knapper, who has read and advised on all three novels and provided that essential independent viewpoint that every author craves.

Here's the group thanks; I'm bound to miss someone so apologies. Thanks for your understanding, encouragement, help and support... June and Graham Marklew, Simone and Brian, Mum, my best mate Wayne, Luke Thompson, Jim Smith, Vix and Brogan Mullis, Charity Parkerson, Lynn Hallbrooks and all in the Literary Guild, Lucy and Rox, Rob Faulkner, Andy Walls, Brian Norris and all at work, Sue Grier, Mike Maynard, Brian Beard, Jackie and Chloe Ward.....

Finally, an extra special thanks has to go to my wife. Not only has she had to put up with me over the last nine years and more, she has also had to contend with the writing bug that invaded my soul. I have to say that she bore the burden with varying degrees of restraint. But, she came out on top in the end and even proved to be my most valued and often used critic. Her help has been as constant as it has been vital. No words can convey the respect I have for her for that.

This is another book penned for my Jack and Sophie, my two adorable munchkins. They will be the true heroes of their own destiny, I am sure. But it is also written for all those who are young at heart and have a little imagination. I hope you enjoy the series and will help to spread the word.

Thanks for reading and the very best wishes to you all.

<u>Prologue</u>

As chronicled in the novels, 'Jake West – The Keeper of the Stones' and 'Jake West – Warriors of the Heynai', the reappearance of a Keeper changed *everything* for the long-suffering people of Estia. His was a long-awaited return which sparked the flame of resistance in their troubled land, igniting a fire which burned to varying degrees of intensity within them all. His eagerly anticipated re-emergence inspired all those who had previously been too afraid to act, as well as stirring to action seasoned veterans of the Ruddite wars, moving them to display ever more extraordinary degrees of valor. It reinforced the Estian people's belief in the prophecies of old; the legends and stories which told of the Keeper's role in their eventual liberation and their deliverance from the forces of evil which had plagued their world for a thousand years. It was a rallying sign, a call to arms for a people sick to death of living in fear, in the very depths of despair. It was *the* defining moment in a long and bitter struggle, one which until now had seemed to have no end. It was a once in a lifetime chance to do something right, to fight for a just and noble cause, to help and protect their family and friends, and secure for them all a future, one which was worth having. Moreover, the return of the latest Keeper of the Stones, 'The One' who was destined to lead them to victory and freedom, was something that had been foretold, predicted. It was always meant to be. It was fate. It was destiny.

It marked the end of innocence for some, the beginning of anarchy for most, and the restoration of hope for all.

And yet… as far as they were concerned, Jake West and his best friend, Ben Brooker, were just two ordinary fifteen year old schoolboys from Lichfield, a quaint and picturesque city in the heart of England where nothing ever happened of note. Or so they thought.

Jake West. To understand the legend, you must first understand the boy. There was *nothing* at all special about Jake West. Nothing that would distinguish him from any other fun-loving teenager. Nothing. Except for his lineage. And the rather strange and unique family history he had recently unearthed.

The life-changing role Jake had thrust upon him was an incredible burden to ask of one so young. It was one from which he *should* have been spared. The last Keeper of the Stones - his grandfather, Harry - had faked his own death and fooled everyone, on many different worlds, into believing that the precious gems and awesome weapons had been destroyed. But, a chance venture by the boys into Harry's cluttered attic would lead to a startling discovery for our two young heroes, unlocking many secrets that were meant to remain hidden and changing their lives forever.

When Jake inadvertently opened the box of stones they discovered in an old chest, he alerted everyone by his actions to the stones' survival. From that moment, a sequence of world-shattering events which could not be stopped were set in motion. Unknowingly, he had claimed his birthright. He had also placed himself and all those he loved in mortal danger. He and Ben would soon be hunted across worlds. Having unwittingly revealed one of the world's greatest secrets, he had no option now but to become a Keeper and fulfill his destiny. For like it or not, he had just been transformed from happy-go-lucky teenager to world savior and greatest hope we have in the battle against evil, in an instant.

And so their remarkable journey began. It would be a voyage into the unknown which would decide the fate of us all.

Over the next few weeks, Jake would be pursued by ferocious warriors and beasts that seemed to come straight out of his worst nightmares. Somehow, he would find the strength within him to survive and flourish, to lead a rebellion, and raise the hopes of an entire continent. Together with his new allies he'd free an army of prisoners and slaves, battle against the most powerful wizard ever known, attempt to restore the box of stones so that they might be used to defeat him, and try to find a way to return him and his friend safely home.

The boys would undertake a series of perilous missions in order to acquire the replacement gems they needed. Jake would pass trials and tests designed to defeat far better men. Together, they would fight battles, lead a newly reformed army straight into the greatest civil war in Estian history, raise a sleeping dragon, and manage to survive an onslaught from an army of the living dead, all the time keeping alive the hopes of millions for an end to tyranny.

However, the dark forces of King Vantrax would prove far too numerous and powerful to defeat. Jake, Princess Zephany and the entire

Estian force would be routed and made to retreat south, to the city of Te'oull. They escaped from the burnt-out ruins of the once mighty fortress of Dassilliak with their lives barely intact, and they had to leave behind their badly wounded king. Jake West and his allies were beaten and on the run with nowhere left to go. The final battle in the Estian wars loomed and it would be fought at Te'oull. He now placed all of his faith and trust in the four spirits known as the Heynai, the protectors of the Estian people, the ones who had bestowed upon them the box of stones. It was they who had recruited the Keepers to guard the awesome weapons, as well as the wizard, Tien, to guide them. And it was *they* who would surely come to his aid now, in this, his moment of greatest need?

If they did not, if they failed to answer the call and chose to abandon him, then Jake West and Ben Brooker, as well as Princess Zephany and the entire army of the Estian Alliance, the last great hope of their world and ours, were surely doomed…

Chapter 1
22nd September – The City of Dassilliak – Perosya

Only three of the five Lords of Srenul had managed to survive the devastating collapse of the mountain at Dassilliak. The extraordinary event which ended abruptly the battle for the city entombed forever more the remaining two knights, who were buried beneath tons of falling rock never to be seen or heard of again. The surviving warriors raised by King Vantrax from the fires of Zsorcraum knew that they had enjoyed an amazing, unbelievable escape. When the mountain began to collapse around them, they had somehow managed to throw themselves to the very edges of the tunnel, using their phenomenal speed and agility to save themselves from oblivion. Incredibly, they evaded the majority of the falling rock and narrowly avoided being crushed. And once the dust had finally settled, their far superior eyes were able to see again in the darkness. They were then able to slowly free themselves from the mountain, using their immense strength to clear a path back to the cave entrance. And once there, the enraged leader had punched his way through the rubble sending debris flying in all directions, to finally reach daylight.

Waiting to greet them at the collapsed entrance to the cave was an equally incensed and frustrated King Vantrax. Once he was informed of the events within the mountain and of the Keeper's astonishing flight, the evil wizard was aghast and infuriated. The almost impossible escape of his enemies once again when it had seemed to him for certain that he *finally* had them trapped and the war was won, was almost too much to take. He just could not believe what he was being told and he flew into yet another fit of extreme rage.

When he finally calmed down his thoughts turned toward the present. He knew immediately that he had to plan for the final pursuit; the hunting down and destruction of the remnants of the once great Estian army. For this reason, he became determined not to dwell on the intensely disappointing events at Dassilliak, even though the blood was still boiling in his veins and the whole victory his forces had achieved there, now felt like an enormous defeat. The Alliance and the rebels had been badly mauled at the great city by his invincible troops. All he had to do now was find them, bring them to battle and finish what Jake had begun.

The immense Thargw, Sawdon, stood by the king's side as he contemplated his next move, eagerly awaiting his master's instructions like a hound with the scent of fox in his nostrils. The three surviving Lords of Srenul also waited obediently to hear his command, standing alongside the sole remaining graxoth and sraine; the creatures raised from the afterlife to hunt down and kill Princess Zephany and Jake.

'Raaarr!!! Aghrast!!!'

King Vantrax suddenly roared out loud. His face was bright red with rage once more as he let out one final scream of fury. The others remained silent, sensing that no words would suffice at such a time and that it would probably not be wise to speak while their leader was in such a foul mood. The evil wizard then remained quiet for a few minutes more as he calmed himself again, breathing rapidly but gently stroking the hair on his chin as he deliberated. After a short while he stood up and strode purposefully over to the cave entrance. He remained there for several minutes, surveying the fallen debris and pondering with utter dismay what might have been, reflecting for the last time upon just how close he had come to achieving the victory he so desperately craved. Finally, he turned around to address the small crowd of warriors who had joined with the others to hear what their king had to say.

'This battle is over, but the war goes on! All of you, listen to me now and listen well. We have come too far to stop now. *This* is the final conflict, the last pursuit we shall ever have to make. The Rebellion, or Alliance, call them what you will, are defeated, having lost the best of their army here and at Erriard. They are fatigued and demoralised. We have all but destroyed them. All they have left now are a few old warriors whose best days are over. They cannot withstand our might. They run from the fight like scampering rachtis because they know they cannot win. And they have to be in dire need of rest. They need time to lick their wounds and replenish their energy. But they shall *not* have it!'

I do not know how it is that they managed to escape from us here. We *should* have annihilated all opposition put before us. However, that is what happened and in the final reckoning it will be of no real consequence. We will continue the hunt and bring them to battle again, before they have chance to regroup and regain their strength. If they continue their retreat, they will quickly run out of places to go. They will have their backs to the sea before too long and there we will complete our victory!'

'Graar! Yes, sire!' snarled Sawdon, as usual spoiling for a fight and impatient to begin, his eyes burning with fierce determination. Despite all his years of experience, he was once again displaying the eagerness and enthusiasm of a raw recruit. 'We await only your orders, my king. Though, I would ask one question, if I may?'

King Vantrax gave his warrior permission to speak. The Thargw gerada thought carefully about how to phrase his question.

'By my calculations there are now at least *two* groups of enemy to track down and kill? The escaped Falorian, Verastus, leads the tribe from Readal forest we fought outside these walls. He has with him the weaker of the two boys we found when opening the light; the Keeper's companion. We know not their destination or intent and the dragon flies above them, protecting their rear with his fire and beam of death. There is also the much larger second group to consider, *if* they have not split their force and there are only two. It contains the main prizes as far as we know; the Keeper and the stones, as well as what remains of the Estian army. They have a good start on us already and, once again, we have no way of knowing where they are heading. We *should* be able to track such a large force, but it will take...'

'Yes, Sawdon, enough! I gave you permission to ask one question. I did not invite a lecture! I know where you are heading though. You are about to say that it will take too much time to find them?' interrupted the wizard.

'Yes, my king. That being so, can we not send the graxoth?'

King Vantrax looked around the crowd as he deliberated.

'Krmmn... Yes, we could. However, I think that now the time has finally come for us to show our hand. We must risk *everything* in the ultimate quest for final victory, now that it is within our grasp. We have engaged our enemy with the full forces at our disposal. They are on the run and defeated, with nowhere to go. They are at our mercy, and they shall have none. *Now* is the time to be bold and courageous, to give everything we have in order to ensure their destruction. We must bring *everything* we own to this fight, leave nothing behind.'

'Sire…?'

Everyone, including Sawdon, looked eagerly at the evil wizard, uncertain as to what he had planned but excited by his sudden fervor, desperate to know. King Vantrax fingered the Lichtus stone which hung on the pendant around his neck. He gave an evil smile as he rubbed the reolite, delighting in the knowledge that every one of his followers was on tenterhooks, itching for him to speak. Finally, when they were almost at bursting point, he explained his plan.

'This tiny piece of rock, Sawdon, this small and insignificant stone, is far more powerful than you and I ever imagined. I know that now. And I know how best to use it. It has already allowed me to raise from the dead an entire army, warriors who are able to withstand mortal wounds from any Estian weapons and heal themselves. Do you not see? I have brought to life the beasts who served our predecessors, those who reigned victorious over this land for centuries before we came, who vanquished all before them and ruled without challenge, without mercy. If I have done all of this already, there is surely more I can do. I have not even begun to explore what is possible.'

'Yes, all you say is true no doubt, but you yourself said that the power held within the reolite stone reduces each time it is used? Be careful, my lord, there has to be a limit to what it can do. Is it wise to use all…?'

'Enough! The decision is *made*, Sawdon!' snapped the king, furiously. 'For your sake, I will consider your doubts and hesitancy as nothing more than a genuine concern for my welfare. I am fully aware of the risks, I assure you, but I will hear no more!'

The experienced Thargw commander bolted immediately to attention and bowed his head in submission, severely rebuked. Sawdon knew that he was wrong for speaking out. He was not usually so cautious, but all of a sudden something just did not feel right. He had the tiniest nagging doubt in his mind. It was something he had never experienced before and he did not like it. He tried hard to shake it off as King Vantrax continued, but to no avail.

'A solitary dragon now protects their columns, just as you say. *One* creature! He appeared on the field of battle from nowhere at Dassilliak, to thwart us at the very point of victory. Well then, it is only right that he should have company! To destroy a single dragon, we need the help of their natural enemy, the ones who defeated them and removed their kind from this land; the graxoth and revalkas. Though, I shall not send our lone graxoth against him, for that would be folly. No, Sawdon, I will send one hundred! And what is more, they shall be joined by an entire army of revalkas!'

Everyone gasped at the ludicrous statement from their wicked master. Such a thing was inconceivable, impossible?

'Can you really do that?' asked the mighty Thargw. Despite his doubts, he was now tingling with excitement and anticipation once again. 'Revalkas? I have heard of them, in the stories told by our warriors, but I...'

'*Anything* is possible now, Sawdon. Now that I have this stone. I will use it to bring forth an entire armada of flying beasts. They will be our eyes and ears, as well as the cutting edge to our battlesword. They will eliminate this dragon and destroy all those caught out in the open, whilst *we* march on to complete our victory and take what is rightfully mine; the entire continent of Estia *and* the box of stones!'

A resounding roar of delight suddenly erupted from the nearby Thargws and Falorians. Sawdon found himself howling along with his warriors, caught up in the emotion of the moment. The Lords of Srenul, graxoth and sraine remained motionless and expressionless. They did not respond to the exuberance of the nearby warriors for they were far too eager to resume their pursuits of Zephany and Jake.

The noise finally ceased. King Vantrax took the Lichtus from around his neck and placed it on the ground.

'Llaiddtreiss ufrahla hestrall ixollsalluck.

Ophranar terreghniash!'

The stone once again became incredibly bright. This time though, the light remained locked tightly within the confines of the rare gem. An unbelievably loud crack of what sounded like thunder suddenly erupted from the sky above, from behind the shattered and burning remnants of the once great city. Dassilliak was still in flames. Vast swathes of smoke were rising up to the low-lying clouds, which were tinged with red and orange, reflecting almost with sorrow the terrible scene of carnage below.

All of a sudden, the clouds began to part. Then, astonishingly, the sky beyond them did likewise!

The air was ripped in two. A vast, black, empty hole appeared before the astounded onlookers on the ground. Within seconds, screams and cries of unspeakable terror rose from within the great chasm and an army of winged monsters emerged from within almost immediately, soaring out of the blackness to hover above the evil wizard and his followers, in a scene like something from a vision of Armageddon.

Once they had all exited, the chasm immediately disappeared and the sky united once more, leaving the clouds free to return to their original positions as if nothing had happened. One hundred graxoth and nearly fifty revalkas now hovered menacingly above the ecstatic but exhausted wizard. The Lichtus had reduced in size quite dramatically. It was now no larger than the average grape and its powers were severely curtailed.

'Raar! Excellent!' Sawdon bellowed in delight. 'They can leave at once. The rebels have stolen a march on us so what are we waiting for?'

King Vantrax shook his head at the impatient warrior as he struggled to catch his breath. He wheezed and coughed. Finally, he was able to reply.

'No, Sawdon, I need to rest. I do not want these creatures flying all over this land in search of their army. I want to keep them together so they will be ready to strike. They will remain here until the enemy's exact whereabouts are known. The graxoth can find them and report back. Then, the beasts from Zsorcraum may begin their work, just as you say. We will follow behind. We will continue our hunt for this Keeper when I am rested and ready. I know the urgency, Sawdon, but I *have* to be there.

There is no telling what this boy is capable of. Besides, there is one more thing I have to do. It may not work, but I would like to try.'

'My liege?'

'Melissa, Sawdon. I may not be able to reverse the dragon's spell which has encased her in stone, for I am unsure how much of my power it will take. I may not be strong enough, but I would like to try just one time to bring back one of those he has taken from us. If it works, I can restore them all and add to our numbers. If it does not and I can only perform the spell once, I would like it to be on Melissa.'

*   *   *

Three days later on the twenty-fifth, just north of the city of Varriann and not far from Perosya's border with Siatol, Ben Brooker was riding pillion on a thoroughbred stallion. He was sitting behind and holding on for dear life to, the giant Falorian who had quickly become one of his most trusted friends. Verastus was steering the horse expertly away from the battle, as they galloped at full speed alongside Brraall's tribesmen, trying to place as much distance between them and King Vantrax' forces as they could. The mounted contingent had remained at the rear to cover the footsoldier's retreat at the great tribal leader's insistence. They were aided greatly in this endeavour by Gellsorr, the last remaining dragon on Estia. He had provided much needed cover for the slow-moving columns which would have easily been caught and destroyed without him, shadowing their every move from above and swooping down viciously upon any enemy warriors foolish enough to try to engage them, or pursue too closely. He used his fire and the beam of light he fired from his eyes, which turned to black stone any figures it hit, to keep the warriors at bay.

As the horses reached the extended columns, they slowed down and Ben was at last able to catch his breath.

'Phew! Thank God for that!' he said, talking over Verastus' shoulder. 'I don't think I'm *ever* gonna get the hang of this horse thing. Give me a bike or a nice cosy ride in a car any day.' A puzzled Verastus made to reply but immediately thought better of it, allowing Ben to continue. 'How long do you think he can stay up there?' he asked, staring up at the dragon overhead like a schoolboy on a class outing.

'I do not know,' Verastus replied. 'Remember, Ben, they are very much creatures of legend for living Estians and Mynaens like myself. They are part of our history yes, but a very distant part. They have not graced our world with their presence for many hundreds of years. We who are alive today have only heard of their like in the tales of our storytellers, or in some of the very few books we possess, for those who can read.'

'Yeah, okay. But, he's *amazing*, isn't he? How were they defeated? Why were they killed? I mean, just look at him!'

Verastus cast a glance up at the magical sight of the soaring dragon. It was an awe-inspiring image he had to agree.

'I can only tell you that which has been relayed to me, Ben. I cannot vouch for the truth behind these words. They were our greatest allies once, our closest friends. And they were a formidable opponent for any who attacked us. They fought alongside our armies with distinction, against many a foe, dying in their thousands protecting this land, for it was *their* homeland too, every bit as much as ours.'

'Yeah? Then, what happened? What changed?'

'*We* changed, unfortunately. The forces of evil grew far too strong and corrupted all those who were sworn to protect us. They spread everywhere, like an infestation of rachtis. Before long, they outnumbered the good souls who were left, the righteous. It seemed that everyone had fallen under their spell, corrupted by greed and power. There were some who stood firm and did not yield, of course there were, but they were too few. And they were powerless to prevent the chaos. Wars broke out everywhere. The land was set ablaze. Those who once lived in peace together, became intent on conquest, on destroying their neighbours and all semblance of a civilised society. In the years that followed, we ruined everything that was good, and we forgot who we were. Then, just when it seemed to our ancestors that things could not possibly be worse, when they were hanging on to survival by their fingernails, an army of even darker forces appeared out of nowhere, supernatural beasts who raised such horrifying, powerful creatures that many of those who would oppose them lost all heart. The armies, the forces of good were not enough, for they were hopelessly outmatched. *That* was just the beginning; the start of all our troubles, of a thousand years of misery and despair.'

'Wow! And we thought *we* had issues! Err... On our world, I mean.'

The giant Falorian looked up at Gellsorr again. Then, he shifted his gaze to Brraall, who was now riding alongside them both. The tribal warrior had heard the tale from the very beginning. He decided to add his own contribution to the explanation of how everything began to disintegrate.

'Gellsorr and his kind were defeated by a combination of those warriors who made an alliance with evil, and the creatures, the revalkas, demons from the blackest corners of whatever dominion they occupy. The dragons were hunted for their skin, their oil, their teeth and claws... And simply because they chose to ally themselves with us.'

'Oh, right. But that's terrible. Well, I guess we're lucky that King Vantrax hasn't managed to bring *them* back then, eh? The revalkas I mean. I don't think Jake met with any of them when he saved Princess Zephany at the bridge, and it sounds like a good job he didn't?'

Err... Hang on. One dragon isn't gonna be enough, is it? Not to defeat all the armies we face; the Thargws and Falorians, Sebantans, and those other things?'

'No, Ben,' answered Brraall. 'For my part, I think you are correct. Though, I believe that one dragon is certainly better than none? And do not forget that we have a Keeper.'

The teenager smiled at the mention of his best friend. He still wasn't used to Jake being thought of as a saviour of worlds, the greatest hope in the fight against evil, a hero to rival all others. To Ben, he was, and always would be, Jake West, his best pal. The guy he played footy with and lost to at every game they played. The friend who always had his back, no matter what.

'How far is it to Te'oull?' he asked, shaking his head to clear his thoughts.

'Another two days, perhaps,' replied Verastus.

'Right then, I'd feel a lot safer if Gellsorr had managed to persuade the other dragons to join us, but it is what it is, eh? There's nothing we can do about that now I suppose. Do me a favour? Wake me up in a few hours? And let me know when it's time for lunch? I'm starving.'

Chapter 2
27th September – The Kielth Mountains – Siatol

'But this is *madness*, Sereq! Sheer and utter folly! No! No, I say! We must not go. We *have* to stay. Who is this boy in whom you have placed so much faith? Do any of us really know him?' cried Terristor. The ancient spirit's voice and face were now more animated than they had ever been. 'We know so little, and yet you are about to sacrifice *everything* for him, in the hope that he truly is the one who will lead our people to victory? *Without us*?! Madness, I tell you. You cannot ask us to do this!'

Charr, you have that look about you, the one that tells me your mind is already made up? Then, I hope for all of our people's sakes that you are not mistaken! We have all gone along with everything you have asked of us so far, because we too want to believe in him, just as we believe in *you*. But... No, I am sorry, it has to be said. He *may* be *The One* we have waited for but even so, he cannot do this without us. He needs our help. He is just a boy. He is a stranger to this land, a novice in the art of magic, to our ways. And I need not point out to you that he is taking on the most powerful wizard we have ever faced. Please, will you not reconsider? Will you not see sense? Faith is a wonderful thing, Sereq. However, what you are proposing is way too much. Hear me, please?!'

His army is defeated. His allies too few and too weary. Ranged against them now are thousands of battle-hardened warriors, hoards of invincible Thargws! With our help, in time, he has a small chance of winning this fight. He has the very faintest of hopes. Without us though, it is already a lost cause and he will *never* prevail! Surely you can see that?'

I... I take no pleasure in saying these things to you, my friend. We have followed you faithfully for hundreds of years. You have led us well and we have stood by your side proudly. We have fought many adversaries together and there is no-one I hold in higher regard. But, in all we have done, we have *always* thought and acted as one. Spoken as one, until now!'

The dark, damp cave within the Kielth Mountains sheltered the four ghostly spirits known to Jake as the Heynai. Aided by the chosen Keepers, they and their stones had protected the Estian people for centuries. They were also responsible for rescuing the latest of them, Jake West, with their timely action at the Battle of Dassilliak. The collapse of the mountain was a stupendous feat of magic. It had ended the Lords of

Srenul's pursuit and saved the teenager's life, but it was only one of a number of spells they had cast to aid him, his friends and his cause. The Heynai were now recovering from the debilitating effects of their magnificent deeds, their energy reserves all but spent. They had done far too much in the past day or so to save the two young boys from Earth, way more than they should have done, and their astonishing feats had almost destroyed them completely. The spirits had taken way too many risks in trying to keep the teenagers alive and they knew only too well that they had been incredibly fortunate to survive. At Dassilliak, they had withdrawn from the fight through necessity, in order to rest and recover.

When their strength began to return, they took the opportunity to talk openly amongst themselves for days about the dire situation still facing the young Keeper; the boy who carried with him the hopes of millions, the ally they had met only days before. The discussion had been a long and heated one until finally, one desperate, pleading voice had cried out louder than the rest.

'I too must apologise to you, Sereq, for I am in agreement. Terristor speaks the truth,' added Lapo, feeling compelled to voice his opinion once again. 'There are too many unknowns here, too many questions you have no answer for. You place way too much confidence in the teachings, and in this boy. Surely you have *some* doubts? Yes, he has surpassed expectations so far. He has indeed achieved more than we anticipated, and in so short a time. *But*, the odds and the stakes are now far too high for such an enormous leap of faith! King Vantrax and Sawdon will descend upon Te'oull very soon with a force far greater than any ever known. They have *already* sacked the mighty city of Dassilliak; the greatest defensive fortification in the land. Never before has it fallen. They have conquered almost the entire continent. Tell me, even if this boy *is* the Keeper whose coming is foretold, what can he do against such a force, if he is alone?'

The leader of the Heynai said nothing in reply. His face was expressionless as he considered carefully his fellow spirit's words. Naught could be heard but the whistling of a gentle wind as it moved steadily through the rocks.

'Sereq!' cried Rutax, forcefully. 'Answer us! Now is not the time for silence. If we are to do this thing you ask, we must all be in agreement. And unless you can convince us right here and now, it is *not* going to happen. After all, you are talking about surrendering all we have fought for, yielding all we have worked hard to achieve and maintain throughout the hundreds of years since we died. Our very reason for existence.'

And who will protect our people when we are gone? Who will defeat the forces of evil which plague this land? Please, do not say the Keepers? They come and they go at will. They are not ever-present and most do not have the power to defeat the wizards. Not alone. I am sorry but I for one believe that this boy has yet to prove himself worthy of such high expectation.'

The dark recesses of the cave were illuminated by the light emanating from the four ghostly apparitions. The Heynai floated just above the ground, facing each other in an impromptu circle as they debated the issues, and the decision before them. With heavy hearts, they knew they were deciding upon not only their own fate, but the fate of countless millions, on many different worlds. Silence descended briefly as Sereq carefully considered his reply. The weight of the burden he had to bear was etched into his grey and weary face. He was so, so tired of living. Tired of fighting. And he knew what had to be done.

After a short while, he looked at each in turn, before responding in a soft, gentle and heavily-fatigued tone.

'We... We have given all we have to give. We are spent and we are *losing* this war. The new stone the dark wizard has found has tipped the balance far too heavily in his favour. It is now time for us to face a few unpleasant truths. The spells we cast over the past few days in order to help the Keeper and his companions have cost us dear. They have all but destroyed us. The energy and effort they took to create left us almost powerless, defenceless. We will need more of the same if we decide to stay, to fight alongside Jake. And I have to tell you now that we will not be strong enough. We will not survive to see this war won. Our fate on that path you would choose is to perish before its outcome is known. When the final battle comes, we will be unable to influence it in any way.'

'Kraas. I... I did not realise. Then, what are you suggesting?' asked Terristor, shocked by his leader's admission. 'You speak of sacrifice? But, without us here to guide him, he will be lost?'

'Yes, Sereq, what *exactly* is it you propose? We are not blind to the needs of the Keeper. Neither are we so attached to this world that we would forsake the realm beyond, if our people were helped in any way by our leaving. We will not concede defeat and betray our oaths, however. We, like you, swore to defend this land and its inhabitants, until the end of time if necessary.'

'*Time*, Lapo?' replied Sereq, seizing upon the word like a Thargw with the scent of blood in his nostrils. 'A fitting turn of phrase. That is what it is all about now; *Time*. It has finally come for us. It is also the *one* thing we can give to our friends. And it is the one thing they need most.'

'Kuh! As usual, you speak, but you do not tell,' huffed a frustrated Rutax. 'Enough riddling, please?'

Sereq smiled warmly at the wraithlike image of his aged friend.

'Very well, as you wish. Jake needs *time* to gather his force at Te'oull. Even now, thousands of fresh volunteers are making their way to the city. They are coming from all corners of Estia to join him in this fight. Our people are answering the call we made in their thousands. The war of wars is upon us. It has long been foretold and it now stands at our door. Remember the prophecy;

...A thousand-year fight is upon us, for the age of evil has come.

In the war of wars that confronts us, salvation shall lie with The One.

A Keeper to unlock the secrets, long hidden inside of a box.

A warrior chosen to wield it. The one without whom all is lost.'

This war *can* still be won. But, if King Vantrax reaches Te'oull first, with his vast army of seasoned warriors and merciless beasts, the Estian Alliance and its leaders, Princess Zephany and Jake, will be destroyed. We cann*ot* let that happen!'

They need time. Just as Ben, Verastus and Brraall need time to join them. Gellsorr protects them now. However, the dragon is about to encounter a deadly foe and I cannot predict the outcome; the effects of casting those spells linger on for me, I am afraid.'

'Yes, us too. We all feel it, Sereq. Though, given our current condition, what can we do?' pleaded Terristor.

'We can *die!* Again.'

The remaining Heynai were unmoved by their leader's deliberately dramatic choice of words. Death held no fear for them. In truth, they would all welcome the release, and the peace it promised. They had all privately grown weary of their continued existence, and the seemingly never-ending battle against evil. It was a continuous, energy-sapping fight which had taken a great toll upon them. Taken more away from their souls than anyone would ever know. In more ways than most could ever imagine.

'Srr... I fail to see how our deaths will aid the Keeper?' said Lapo.

Sereq replied, expressionless once more. 'We will use what strength we have left to cast one last spell. It will be the greatest feat of wizardry ever performed. A wall. A shield if you will. An invisible barrier of energy through which none shall pass. It will need to stretch across the entire land if it is to work, raised to separate friend from foe.'

'Sereq, what you are suggesting is *way* beyond our power,' stated Rutax. 'It would take far too much energy to create and maintain. There are simply too few of us.'

Sereq shook his head. 'No, for once you are mistaken. By willingly sacrificing our lives, such as they are, we will add to the fires our very life force. And they will burn all the brighter for it.'

Silence once again descended upon the cave. The gentle wind stroked the spirits as they considered their options carefully.

'Well? What say you all?' Sereq asked, once he was satisfied they had had long enough to decide.

It was Lapo who answered first. 'I will be sorry to leave like this, after all we have done. It will seem to many that we are deserting them in their hour of need, running away from the fight when the beast is at our door?'

'Yes. It will appear that way to some,' replied Sereq. 'Though, those who believe in us will know differently. And in time, the true reasons behind our actions will be revealed.'

'By who?' Terristor enquired.

'Jake. And Tien. I will go to them both now, very briefly, to explain. I will not be able to stay long for the pursuing forces are not far behind.'

'I see. Then Lapo and I will wait here for your return. We are with you. If you believe it can be done, we are willing to give it a try. It has been an honour and a privilege to have known you, Sereq. To have served our people alongside you all, has been by far my greatest achievement.'

Sereq nodded in gratitude at Terristor and then at Lapo. He turned to Rutax.

'And you? Are you with us in this?'

Rutax hesitated but eventually he spoke. 'I... I just do not know. It feels too much to me like a defeat, as if I am running away when there is far more I should be doing!' he rasped. 'We are leaving *everything* to chance. I have not lived like that. Is there no other way?'

'No. I am sorry but I can see none,' Sereq answered, shaking his head slightly.

'Koh. Then, I suppose it has to be. But, what of the gerada? What of Knesh Corian?' Rutax asked, realising that they would also be abandoning the spirit of the former Ruddite general, who had chosen to join with them and help his friends instead of entering the afterlife.

'He will remain here for as long as he desires. Only Knesh can decide his own fate, for he was granted the same life force we were given. It is his to surrender. He will try to save King Artrex if I know him at all. The palace at Dassilliak is swarming with enemy warriors and the king still sleeps. His wounds are severe.'

'Well, I suppose at least they will have one of us there to help them? He is a fiery, impetuous youth of a spirit, but he is a spirit nevertheless?' said Lapo.

A chorus of gentle laughter filled the cave and relieved the tension slightly.

'Then, we are all agreed?' asked Sereq. 'Good. I will go to them now. When I return, we shall begin. We will hold the enemy forces at bay for as long as we are able. It may not be enough, but once it is done, once they break through and we are gone, our people are on their own.'

Everything then, will depend upon the Keeper!'

Chapter 3
27th September – The City of Te'oull – Siatol

The Battle of Dassilliak was over. Somehow, despite the supernatural forces ranged against them, the Estian Alliance warriors and the civillians from the great city had managed to avoid what had looked like certain annihilation. Now, at the end of a long and arduous retreat, the extended lines of exhausted survivors trudged wearily through the open gates to the walled city of Te'oull. Their extraordinary escape was the stuff of fairy tales and legend. Dassilliak, or the tunnels underneath the mountains which surrounded it on three sides, should really have been their graveyard. Their final burial ground. Everyone knew it. As they poured into the city and at last had the opportunity to reflect on their astonishing good fortune, shattered warriors and civillians alike could scarcely believe their miraculous deliverance from the powerful forces of evil they had faced. Privately, when they were trapped in the deepest recesses of the mountain with no apparent route of escape, almost all had come to accept the fact that they were about to die. Hope had vanished in that moment and all had moved way beyond despair. Now they had actually achieved the impossible and reached the relative safety of Te'oull however, the survivors had a fresh glimmer shining in their eyes once again, a tiny flicker of optimism, fuelled by a shared feeling inside that they had all been saved for a purpose, or higher calling. More than anything, amongst the exhausted Estians now there was a new and growing confidence, a very real belief that even the impossible was achievable where the young Keeper, Jake, was concerned.

    The disheveled lines of fugitives cast a thankful glance at their comrades and in most cases, this natural and instinctive reaction to reaching the walled city was followed almost immediately by an anxious look towards the north, at the distressing and exasperating sight of the dustclouds gathering in the sunlit sky. It was nearly midday in Siatol. The journey to Te'oull had taken the best part of five days to complete and during that time no-one had been able to sleep. Everyone was utterly exhausted and many could barely stand. Jake, Princess Zephany, Caro and Tien were at the rear of the extended columns. The small group of intrepid leaders who were primarily responsible for the army's survival against all the odds, were therefore amongst the last to reach the gates. Once there, they too stopped to check upon the telltale signs of a lethal and determined chase. Their hearts immediately sank as it soon became clear that their worst fears were about to be realised. There would be no respite from the hunt. King Vantrax would afford the Estians no time to rest and recuperate before the next attack.

'Dragh! Well, I suppose we all knew it would not take them long?' stated Princess Zephany, bitterly disappointed.

Despite her frustration, she spoke in a matter-of-fact tone of voice that contained no hint of emotion. The young royal was now every inch a warrior princess, given all the many heroic deeds she had performed on the battlefield at Dassilliak. Zephany had fought valiantly and proven herself several times over to any who doubted her. She had led from the front, time and time again placing herself in harm's way, doing more than any other warrior or commander to ensure the survival of the Estian Alliance in its bleakest hour.

'By the look of things, they will be here by nightfall. That affords us little time to prepare.'

'No. You're right, princess, it doesn't,' replied Jake, sharply, 'but that's the position we're in and we just have to deal with it, don't we?'

He smiled warmly at her, staring wearily into her bright and beautiful eyes. Zephany made to reply but hesitated, uncertain how to take his remark and considering whether or not she should challenge him on it. After a second or two though, she decided to let it pass and smiled back.

'Srr, yes, there is no point avoiding the issue. Let us speak plainly; we cannot run any further. We have given our all. So, here is as good a place as any for what is coming. The decision has been made for us; the next battle in this war will be fought *here*, at Te'oull. On the outcome rides the future of our world, of all we know and love. I shall go now and make our preparations. Come, Caro, let us see what we have left of an army, and decide how best to use it.'

Lord Caro nodded dutifully and followed behind the impressive new Leader of the Estian Alliance as she headed purposefully into the city. Jake and Tien remained outside the city walls. When he was certain they were alone and could not be heard, Jake spoke quietly to the old wizard, all the time staring with mounting concern at the northern sky.

'Okay then, it's just you and me now, tell me the truth. It's not looking too good for us, is it? We're no match for them. They have way too many soldiers compared to ours and they are stronger, more experienced. It's... well, it's a real-life David and Goliath thing we've got going on, isn't it? Hmmph… Actually, if we're comparing, let's hope it's more like Tom and Jerry, eh? At least the mouse always wins in their fights?'

The wizard was quite obviously confused by Jake's words but he remained strangely silent.

Jake thought it odd that Tien gave no reply. He sighed deeply, before continuing. 'Err… Is this where it all ends, Tien? Have we had our chips? Are we all gonna die here?' the youngster asked, seeking a straight answer for once.

The fifteen year old was perfectly calm, speaking in the absence of fear. He just wanted to know, that's all. He was hoping to hear a pearl of wisdom from the old man of Estia which would help somehow, searching for a small nugget of knowledge or some hitherto unspoken advice, *anything* he could use to their advantage, to try to even the impossible odds they faced.

Tien though, had no words of comfort for him. It pained the wizard to speak, even though he knew that he *had* to reply. He wanted to be able to give meaningful support to this new Keeper, just as he had provided to all those he had served before. After all, that was the main purpose for his continued existence, wasn't it? He desperately wanted to be the one to bring him the smallest speck of hope, when it seemed to them all that they had already used up their full quota. In the end however, all he could do was shake his head slowly and reply to the youngster in a deeply apologetic tone.

'I am truly sorry, Jake. I have not been of much use to you since you came to Estia, have I? I wish I could have done more for you. I assure you that I have served others better. Aghh! By the stars and all I hold to be sacred and true, I wish I had *more* to give!'

'Hey, stop that!' answered Jake, sharply. 'I need you to be strong for us right now, not wallowing in self pity. And you're wrong, very wrong. You're so wrong you're off the scale in fact. You've done *plenty* for us. You're forgetting that it was *you* who made all of this possible. You who set us on this path. You who allowed us to escape. Without *you*, we would all be dead, buried under the mountains of Dassilliak. We would all have been killed in there if you hadn't opened up that tunnel when you did. Always remember, Tien, that it was you who gave us an escape route when everyone thought it was over, and King Vantrax had won.'

'Kah, yes, but in performing that spell, was I just delaying the inevitable? Did I only succeed in prolonging the agony for these people? I do not mean to sound defeatist, but the facts cannot be denied; the creatures and beasts we face now are far too powerful, too numerous and strong. I wish I could… Why can I no longer see the future?!'

Dragh! The truth of the matter, however much we try to avoid it, is that a tiny flea cannot down a dragon, even if it *does* have the will to fight. It is simply not strong enough, not equipped for the task. Some battles are lost from the very beginning, Jake, before the horns sound to begin the attack. The scales are already tipped too far in one direction. They cannot be won and it is pointless to fight. Have we been blinded by faith, you and I? Are *we* engaged in such a struggle? The army we face is…'

'Hey! Hang on just a minute!' interrupted Jake, realising all of a sudden that extreme fatigue now had the better of his normally upbeat guide. He suddenly sensed the need to take a leaf out of his best friend's book for once. 'Are you *really* calling us fleas? Ha, ha… It's a good job Ben's not here, he'd…'

He stopped himself in mid sentence. 'Oh, Tien. Ben! If they've managed to come after *us* so quickly, they have to be chasing *him*, don't they?!'

The look of pure concern which quickly spread across Jake's face was unmistakable. His emotions were all over the place, up and down like a rollercoaster, as they had been since he first found the stones. He was suddenly drained of all colour. He had already lost his best friend once and *that* experience was without doubt the worst of his relatively short life to date. The memory of the pain it wrought still burned fiercely within him, for although it seemed like a lifetime ago right now, in reality it was only a few weeks. The thought of the very real possibility that he might lose Ben a *second* time horrified him beyond measure. It was absolutely unthinkable, unbearable.

Tien's mood changed instantly as he sensed the boy's panic. He placed a reassuring hand on Jake's shoulder. 'I would not trouble yourself too much on this just now, Jake. Something tells me that young boy is indestructible,' said the old wizard, smiling slightly in an attempt to comfort the distressed teenager.

It worked. Jake seemed to immediately regain a little confidence.

'Eh? Yeah, I s'pose you're right. I mean, he's survived *this* far, hasn't he? Actually, short of being blown up, there's not much he hasn't faced, is there?'

'Ha, ha… Quite. Now, shall we rejoin the others? Even though the gift of foresight appears to have deserted me once more, for reasons I do not know, I *am* as certain as I can be of one thing; the future will reveal itself to us in time, when it is ready, no matter what we do.'

Jake nodded in agreement. The two companions began to turn in order to follow the rest of the army into the city. But, from out of nowhere, a soft echo of a voice suddenly sounded within the confines of their minds, at *exactly* the same time, stopping them both in their tracks.

'Keeper! Tien! Hear me now, my warriors… Concentrate upon my image, I beseech you. Draw it forth from your memory and I will appear. I am Sereq of the Heynai and I would come to you now, if you so wish? I have something important to say which cannot wait.'

Jake looked straight over at Tien to satisfy himself that the wizard had heard the voice too. Tien's eyes spoke for him, reassuring the young boy without the need for words that he had.

Well, Jake thought, *if the Heynai themselves think it's important, I guess this is one conversation I definitely need to have.*

They each turned back around and returned their gaze to the patch of dry earth in front of them. Clearing their thoughts completely, they concentrated in unison and gradually a faint, hazy image appeared.

'Sereq!' cried Jake. He was now an excited boy again and he responded to seeing the spirit automatically, without thinking. 'There you are! What's happening? Why did you leave us back there at the city? Where did you go? Why did you leave *me*? *Why* Sereq, when you said you would always be there?'

Tien shook his head slightly at the young Keeper, clearly disappointed in him. *That was the reaction of a child. It was immature and impulsive,* the wizard reflected.

Jake blushed immediately as his eyes met with Tien's. He knew straight away what he had said, and how it might sound. He wished at once that he could take it back, though he knew he couldn't.

'Jake, it is not for *us* to question the ways of the Heynai, nor the decisions they make,' Tien stated, softly. It was not a rebuke, more like fatherly advice, the kind of thing his grandfather might say.

'No, Tien, leave him be. He has the right to ask such questions. He has earned it,' Sereq stated, halting the conversation without delay. 'Jake, time is short. But then, this is perhaps one conversation which must be had? Yes, I will try to explain to you the best I can; in the midst of battle and also in the run up to war, there were stark choices that had to be made. Right now, with the benefit of hindsight, I am not certain that we always made the right ones. We may not have chosen the right path. The truth is, when the time came, we realised quickly that we could not help you all. We were not strong enough. So, in our wisdom, we decided to help your friends, knowing that it meant leaving you to fend for yourself. Whether we were right or wrong only time will tell, though you have to know that our actions at Dassilliak most certainly saved their lives. We also managed to bring you some respite from the onslaught, with the warriors that King Vantrax reassigned to counter the threat to his rear. So, we *did* achieve something. That cannot be denied.'

However, as I have said, we could perhaps have done things differently, chosen another way. As it was, we acted as we thought best at that time. The result was that we were left powerless for some considerable period after we intervened. We were unable to help you further and we have still not recovered our full powers. We are weak, Jake, and the situation you face is as grave as ever. I apologise if it seems to you that we abandoned you. I suppose we did in essence, but...'

'No, Sereq,' interrupted Jake, humbled by the fact he was receiving an apology from such a surreal source, 'you saved my best mate. That's *exactly* what I would've told you to do, if I was asked. I see that now. I'm sorry for my reaction, it was stupid of me. Anyway, life's too short for regrets, innit? As me granddad used to say, *there's no use crying over spilt milk.* We have to move on. So, what happens now? Ben, can you help him? And what about us? Are you gonna help us to fight?'

'Srr... Yes... And no. That is why I appear before you now; to explain our decision,' replied the spirit's ghostly image. 'Jake, prepare yourself, for you may not like what I am about to say. You may not understand.'

'What? What does *that* mean?'

Jake was not the only one present who was confused. Tien also cast a puzzled and enquiring glance at the ancient spirit. 'Yes, what are you saying? You have lost me completely. Why will he not like it? Something is wrong here, I can feel it. What are you neglecting to tell us?'

Sereq looked down upon the old man who had served him and his kind faithfully for over three hundred years. His eyes were brimming with sympathy, compassion and sorrow.

'You have been a trusted and noble ally, wizard. We Heynai thank you for all you have done on behalf of our people. Your service to us and them, your supreme sacrifice, shall never be forgotten. I am afraid that we are not destined to meet again, my friend. Our time on Estia is finally at an end. We must leave you.'

Tien and Jake were both too stunned to reply. However, it was abundantly clear that they were thinking the same thing; *The spirits are immortal, aren't they? How can they die? And how can they desert their people at such a time? Why now, when they need them most?*

Jake shook his head slightly when he failed to come up with the answers to his own questions.

Sereq felt his concern and saw his shock and dismay. 'We *must* leave you all, for good. It is not something we do gladly, for the battle is not yet won. But it is for the benefit of all of Estia, for the future of all our worlds. This decision has not been taken lightly, Jake. There has been much heated debate surrounding it. We do not wish to leave with the fight still raging, the outcome unknown, but it *has* to be this way. You have to trust me on that. Now, listen to me once more, please? Our parting gift to you all will be *time*. If all goes well, we will afford you the time you need to prepare your defences and restore the power in the box of stones. They are central to our cause and you must not be distracted from your efforts to repair the box. It will be the key to victory. Use this time we win for you wisely, Keeper, I beg you?'

'But, *why*, Sereq? You have not explained and I need to know. And *how*? How are you going to do it? How long can you give us? Whatever you're going to make happen, how long will it last?' cried Jake.

Words flowed freely and swiftly from within the youngster now, riding on waves of differing emotions that once again he could barely control.

'Keeper... We have lived a long, long time we spirits, on our journey through life and death. We have seen much that we would rather forget. In the final analysis, I am ashamed to admit that we have failed our people. As hard as we tried, and you have to know that we fought against evil with all our heart and soul, we could not protect them from the pain and suffering they endured, not as we would have wished. Those who opposed us were too strong and our powers were not sufficient. We eventually won the wars we fought, but we lost many a battle along the way. And there were casualties, many, many, innocent victims. For that, we are deeply sorry. More than you will ever know.'

However, there is now a chance to end all of the suffering. You are here with us and the final war has begun. *This* is the only way we can see to help them. They can survive without us now, for they have you and Princess Zephany to lead them, to protect them. They are frightened and lost at this moment in time but they will take comfort from the fact that they have proven their mettle on the field of battle these past few days and they were not found wanting. Their hearts are strong. They are not as helpless as they might have believed before you came. Jake, we Heynai can do *nothing* unless the advancing hoards are halted. That is the plain and simple truth of the matter. As I have said, the box of stones is the key to everything, the weapon which *will* defeat them. It is not yet fully restored, but it *has* to be! The eternal flame of energy which fuels us, that which allows us to remain with you, still burns brightly. It came closer than ever before to being extinguished at Dassilliak because of the risks we took, but it survives. That fire is the most powerful force in this land, or beyond. It is the very essence of life itself. And it is ours to give.'

Jake immediately shook his head, vigorously. He just couldn't believe what he was hearing and he determined that he had to object.

'No, no, no! *Give*? By giving, you're talking about *suicide*!' he raged, as he understood immediately what Sereq was saying. He refused outright to accept the sacrifice on offer, failing to realise that he was seeing things totally from a human perspective, looking at the problems they faced with a young boy's eyes.

But then, he *was* still a boy, wasn't he? He had his whole life ahead of him. So, why shouldn't he react like the youth he was?

It was hard for Jake; hard to appreciate the fact that the spirits were already dead. They had lived on borrowed time for hundreds of years. He was awash with emotion and it was clouding his judgment. There were lasting moments as a Keeper when he could suppress and control such feelings, but this wasn't one of them. Just as he was about to say more though, Tien placed a reassuring hand on his shoulder.

'Let him speak, Keeper. There is more, and we need to know,' he said, understanding that the leader of the Heynai was impatient to finish what he had begun, and state all that he had come to say.

'What? More? How can there be more?!'

'Keeper, you will need to remain calm and focused from here on. Though your youth and background will hinder your development, you must control your inner feelings so that they do not affect your thinking. Be assured, you *are* the one spoken of in legend. You *will...*'

'Prophecies? Yeah, I know. I've heard it all before, how I am *The One* who will make everything right. Ever since I got here it's been, prophecy this and prophecy that... That's all very well, but no-one has told me what they actually say!'

Sereq smiled a little, amused by Jake's response. 'Kah, the impatience of youth. I wish I could say that I remember it well... Listen to me, Jake. Tien will explain all to you in the fullness of time. Trust me, when you really need to know, you shall. Though, it may not form part of this particular journey; too much knowledge too soon can be... counter-productive, shall we say?'

Jake was not at all happy with that statement. He accepted though that there was probably a very good reason for all the mystery and he could see that right now, with all the uncertainty and danger that lay ahead, *his* opinion on things was not all that important. Anyway, this was one decision which had already been made, so any further debate was futile.

'Well, okay. But I don't like it, Sereq. I want you to know that right now. I need you. I don't think I can do this thing without you. Besides, you said you'd always be here with me?'

The ghostly image of the spirit nodded to acknowledge his own mistake. 'I know. I should not have... A promise is a promise. It is not something given lightly. But events can overtake us sometimes and spiral out of control. I did not foresee this. Only by leaving you now do we have any hope of stopping the wizard and his army of warriors. I am certain of that. If we stay, if we fail in our efforts to delay their march, you *will* all be killed.'

Do not be alarmed though; all is not yet lost. We will create a shield between you which cannot be breached. Be warned; we have no way of knowing how long it will last. However, I promise you now that we will hold it until our last ounce of strength is drained. You will have days at most, enough time to gather your forces and complete the quest for the fourth stone, I hope. That will then just leave the final gem; the last battle with the wizard. It is a fight you *must* win!'

'I see,' said Tien. 'Then, this is goodbye, Sereq. Or am I leaving too?'

Jake's fear suddenly intensified. The hairs on the back of his neck stood rigidly to attention as an icy-cold shiver ran down his spine. The thought of losing the old wizard as well as the Heynai was too catastrophic and terrifying to contemplate. To be left completely alone with no-one to guide him? That was his worst nightmare.

But, to his immense relief, Sereq calmly shook his head. 'No, Tien. You will remain until victory is won and the forces of evil are defeated for good. That was the vow you made long ago and nothing has changed.'

Tien nodded obediently. Then he looked straight into the eyes of the young Keeper by his side. 'So be it. I will serve you to the best of my ability. Until the end of time if I have to.'

'Err... Thanks. But I thought you were tired of all this?' replied Jake, greatly relieved to hear it. Tien did not reply to his question for he sensed that time was running out. Jake sensed it also and they both turned to the spirit once more. 'We'll all do what we can, I promise. But, what about Ben and the others?'

Sereq now looked more like a businessman who had just missed his train than a ghostly spirit. He appeared worried and anxious, but he answered nevertheless.

'The warriors of King Vantrax pursue them hard. Even as we speak they are hunting them down. Despite the dragon's best efforts to slow them, Ben is still very much in danger. He is not yet safe, though we shall do what we can for him. Now, I really have to go for I have lingered too long. If all goes well, Ben will join you soon and you will be protected from further attack until our strength fails us, until we are gone for good. If we are not successful in our endeavours, if the spell does not work, the full force of the enemy will be upon you before sunset.'

'Oh, that's just great. Cheers,' replied Jake, sarcastically. 'You really know how to raise someone's spirits, don't you? Ha, ha... Hey! Raise someone's spirits! D'ya get it? That's good that. Even Ben would be proud of *that* one. Oh 'eck, I'm turning into my best mate!'

Sereq shook his head slightly at the suddenly very immature looking 'savior of worlds', but he did not reply straight away. Jake's laughter subsided naturally and not a sound could be heard. Tien and Jake looked at Sereq, waiting impatiently for him to speak. Despite the urgency, the leader of the Heynai seemed to be taking his time deciding on what to say as his final farewell. He took one last look around at the surrounding landscape, staring with tear-drenched eyes at the land he loved and had sacrificed everything for. When he was at last ready, he spoke. His voice was calm but for the very first time since the boys had appeared on Estia, it was laced with pure emotion.

'Look after our people, Jake. Protect them, as a member of your family has done successfully since first we met with your ancestor. We were right to place our trust in you and your kind. Your family have proven to be courageous and loyal. We Estians are a good people when given a chance to prove it. We can be brave, gracious and kind, when shown that there is an alternative to war. We just need reminding of that fact from time to time. It is not our people's fault that these virtues now lie buried deep within their souls, that it sometimes takes the appearance of a Keeper from another world to unearth them, for many have known little else but conflict and pain in their lives. They have witnessed the dark magic before and they are scared. They need *you* to show them that they can prevail, to lead them to victory.'

And with that, Sereq's image vanished. The most powerful of the Heynai, the greatest ally the Keeper had, was gone.

Jake looked instinctively at Tien, waiting for the old wizard to say something, but once again Tien had nothing *to* say. He was dumbfounded and he just shrugged his shoulders, genuinely lost for words. Jake West had no such issues. Once it was clear that Tien was not going to speak, he knew exactly how to respond; in the same manner he faced all challenges put before him. He gritted his teeth and clenched his fist.

'Well, here we go again. In for a penny, in for a pound. It's game on!'

Tien couldn't help but smile at hearing the familiar turn of phrase. He still shook his head in disbelief though.

Kuh! It is hardly the awe-inspiring rhetoric of a great warrior and leader. But then, it is typical of the way in which these two young boys seem to approach every problem they face? In fact, it is the kind of frivolous response and attitude with which they seem to approach life itself. Kah! By the spirit of Nitrii-Hebul, how I envy them!

The more he thought about it, the more the wizard came to the conclusion that... *actually, those words, and that reaction, will do nicely.*

Jake spotted a faint smirk appear on the old man's face.

'What?' he asked, as they turned around and strode purposefully through the gates to the city. 'What you grinning at? Was it something I said? Yeah well, I'm sorry if you don't approve but that's just me. What good is worrying going to do? As me granddad always says; *smile in the face of adversity, deal with what's in front of you, and laugh at disaster when you can. If you do all that, you'll come out smelling of roses in the end.*'

To be fair, he's full of all kinds of crap like that, me granddad. Ha, ha...'

Chapter 4
27th September – The City of Te'oull – Siatol

Behind the walls of Taran stone which surrounded the city of Te'oull there was a frenzy of action. Hardened warriors and frightened civillians alike were rushing around everywhere making last minute, frantic preparations for the devastating attack they knew was coming. The ill-fated defenders of the city numbered in their thousands, their ranks swelled by the fresh volunteers the survivors of Dassilliak found waiting for them. The Estian army was now a sizeable force once again. However, despite the enthusiasm of the new recruits, their morale was low, affected beyond measure by the fact that they knew they had just abandoned all hope of deliverance. Everyone in the city had known for certain the moment the heavy gates were closed firmly behind their leaders, that escape was no longer an option. The decision had been made to once again stand and fight and another bloody battle lay ahead. They would face whatever the might of their enemy threw against them head on: to win, or die gloriously in the attempt.

The Estian people did not lack courage. One glance at their battle-scarred history would tell you that. Still, mothers and fathers began hugging their children closely, the sudden realisation that there was no way out this time the source of every painful tear they now shed. A few began to panic, as the gravity of their predicament rapidly became apparent. Screams and cries echoed around the city, unnerving even the most experienced warriors there. But, most ignored their innermost feelings of impending doom and faced their unknown fate stoically, nobly, refusing outright to let their shattered nerves get the better of them now, after all they had been through. Determined not to let their comrades down, the fighters of the Estian Alliance were going to wage this battle the only way they knew; with courage and honour. Even if it *was* their last.

Princess Zephany and Caro had by now organised the city defences. They had positioned their troops as best they could in the minimal time they had been afforded. The northern walls were manned with as many warriors as they could spare, for they faced the enemy directly and were the most likely points of attack. Anyone who could carry a weapon had been dispatched by Caro to man the rest of the defences. Despite this fact, a sizeable crowd remained in the main city square, as Jake and Tien joined with the rest of the Alliance warriors to plan their defence strategy. Everyone gazed longingly at the two young leaders, the young princess and the teenage Keeper, for guidance, seeking inspiration or any words of comfort they could give, looking for any sign of hope in their seemingly impossible situation.

'Jake! Nice of you to finally join us,' began Zephany with a smile. 'We were about to send out a search party to look for you. Caro and I have done our best for our people. The defences here are good and strong, the walls thick and high, so it is good ground to withstand an attack. We have a chance I think of holding out for a time. It must be said though, I am not certain for how long. I am sorry to sound so unsure, but this is no Dassilliak. Srr… I was surprised to find when we arrived in the square that there were many new volunteers waiting for us? It would seem that the Heynai were busy whilst we were fighting. By all accounts, they were spreading the word far and wide, recruiting others to our cause. And many blessed souls have answered the call. They have swelled our ranks significantly, having apparently been informed by the messengers of the spirits that *this* is the final struggle in our fight against tyranny. They have been told that the endless war we have waged will be won, or lost, right here. And they have come in their thousands.'

Princess Zephany pointed towards the exterior walls where the ramparts were lined thick with veterans, standing amongst thousands of fresh volunteers.

'Yes, Jake,' added Lord Caro, placing his hand firmly and proudly on the pommel of his sword, 'we have dispatched most of them to the northern walls, as you can see. They are fresh and eager, whereas our brave warriors are tired and in need of rest. I have though, ensured that many of my finest captains stand with them, to guide and support those who need it. Ay raas, but it is a miracle, Keeper! Somehow, from the smoldering ashes of Dassilliak, we have risen again. Do not heed the reaction of moments ago when the gates closed, for we have removed all doubt. Once they accept what is going to happen, accept that in all likelihood they are going to die, they will recover their fighting spirit quickly. And we are an army to be fearful of, I assure you. The flowers have already been distributed along the lines. Our warriors are boiling them down into the liquid poison as we speak.'

'Kah! Yes, I have been thinking about that!' shouted Tien, pushing his way to the centre of the group so that he could address Jake. 'They must be running out by now? There were not too many and the battle at the city consumed most. I believe that I may be able to be of assistance. A simple reproduction spell should do the trick. Where there were few, there shall be many. Yes, I will go now! Leave it to me,' the wizard called, as he raced away, acting like a small child who had just been handed a toy, grinning and pleased beyond measure to once again be doing something useful.

Jake laughed a little at the sight of the old man running for the walls with such exuberance. It struck the youngster as funny how their roles were almost reversed somehow. He no longer felt like a child all of a sudden. Actually, he felt as if he had lived for several lifetimes. There had been moments though, since his adventures had begun, fleeting moments when it was all he could do to stop himself from crying, or laughing uncontrollably in the most inappropriate of circumstances, like the teenager he was. He had flitted from one state of mind to another almost at random, never knowing which of his personalities would surface next and unable to control his fluctuating emotions, as the stones did their work.

Now was not the time to dwell on such things however and he soon turned his attention back to the problems at hand.

'Good, Caro, good. Thank you. There is more I have to say. I'm afraid that I have some more bad news to tell you both.'

'*More*? Jake, do you not think we have had enough ill tidings by now?' asked the princess. Jake remained silent, unsure how to take the remark and not certain how he should reply. 'Yargh! Well? What is it? Tell us.'

'Okay... I'm sorry, but we're soon gonna be on our...'

'Raise the alarm! Here they come!!!'

Jake was suddenly interrupted by a terrified, high-pitched scream. It was coming from the highest point on the northern wall. He turned immediately and looked up to see a young lookout shouting in blind panic, pointing frenetically at the northern sky. All the surrounding soldiers halted what they were doing immediately and rushed to the square, awaiting further information and orders. Their number included Queen Bressial and Lord Castrad, the Nadjan nobles still carrying the wounds they had received at Dassilliak.

'Calm yourself please, soldier?! Tell me what you see!' ordered Zephany.

'Dots your highness! Tiny specs in the sky. Hundreds of them. Something is coming, some creatures, and they are heading straight for us!'

Fear and hysteria gripped many of the civillians in the square instantly. Some began to cry and shout and many began to run, even though they did not know where they were going. Of far greater concern to Princess Zephany though, was the reaction to this news of her warriors on the walls. Many of the new volunteers simply left their posts and began running to find whatever cover they could. The intrepid warrior princess tried her best to stop them, bawling her orders to halt as loud as she was able. But, her voice was not strong enough to be heard over the mayhem. To her utter dismay and severe aggravation, she was powerless to prevent the desertion continuing, and spreading to the rest of her army.

'Hold your ground!!! Hold fast I say!!!'

A colossal, gargantuan roar of authority suddenly resounded throughout the city. It was so incredibly loud that the walls and buildings almost seem to shake, a voice stronger, louder and deeper than even that of the mighty Thargw, Sawdon. The sound was like a cannon exploding and the unbelievable din had almost the same effect; everyone stopped in their tracks, before turning their heads immediately, in unison, to determine the source of the astounding roar.

To the complete amazement of everyone there, it was not Lord

Caro or Lord Castrad who had yelled so efficiently to end the panic, or any other seasoned warrior, as they might have expected. No, the command had come from the young fifteen year old boy from another world: the Keeper.

With impeccable timing, in their hour of need, Jake West had by some means reached deep into their souls, abruptly wrenching their thoughts and attention away from the path of certain destruction they had already embarked upon. In the fullness of time, it would be this moment perhaps more than any other that would prove to be his finest hour. Seven little words. They took only a second or two to say, but on such things battles can be won or lost, wars can be decided, and heroes are made.

Jake flicked his eyes very quickly towards the astounded Princess Zephany. Then, he immediately addressed the shocked crowd, many of whom were frozen on the spot.

'You cannot run. You *must* return to the walls or we are done for. This is the work of the wizard, of King Vantrax. He has summoned these things to do his bidding, his fighting. And we *must* defeat them! There is no other way. I promise you, if you run now, they *will* kill you! We will be defeated and you will not be able to hide. Our women and children, our old and sick, have no chance unless we stand and fight, unless *we* protect them.'

Though fearful, the warriors all made their way quickly back to the walls, realising that time was short.

'Good. Thank you all. Now, this is it!' cried Jake. 'Your fathers and forefathers have warned you this day would come. You have one enemy left to defeat: one last servant of evil to vanquish. Please, do not be found wanting now? You have already proven at Dassilliak that you have the hearts of lions inside you… Err, sorry, I keep forgetting where I am. I mean the hearts of dragons.'

A ripple of gentle, nervous laughter floated on the breeze. Jake saw immediately he had convinced the defenders that there really was no other option open to them but to fight, and he relaxed a little.

'Look, we knew that King Vantrax would come, didn't we? Though we survived the fight at Dassilliak, Sawdon was never going to let it end there and give up the chase. This is the first round in this final battle and we cannot run for we have nowhere to go. The fight is here, whether we like it or not. We cannot shy away from it!'

'Jake is right!' added Princess Zephany. 'I for one will stand firmly alongside him, until the bitter end. I shall not run from such evil and neither shall my people. Who fights with me?'

A short roar of defiance and pride erupted all across the city. When it had died down Jake spoke quickly, conscious of the fact that time was running out.

'You all have to trust me now. I don't know for certain what is going to happen here, nobody does. But, I believe we are going to survive this day. We will win this war. We just have to defeat these... err, what are they?'

Jake pointed to the advancing hoards of flying monsters. He could just make out their features as they appeared over the wall, though they were still a little distance away. There were many graxoth among them. The young Keeper had narrowly managed to survive his last encounter with the deadly beasts raised from the fires of Zsorcraum. His heart skipped a beat and a surge of adrenalin swept through his body when he saw them again. Then, he turned his attention towards the rest of the aerial armada. The other creatures he saw were something else altogether: larger, far more terrifying and sinister in appearance.

'Raart! I... I cannot believe my eyes. They are... Revalkas!' cried a horrified Queen Bressial. 'But, they were destroyed, defeated?!'

'Revalkas??!!' rasped Lord Castrad, alarmed like everyone there by the very mention of their name. 'How can that *possibly* be?!'

'Srr... Begging your pardon, but I suggest to you all that it matters not now?' snapped Lord Caro. 'It is that wizard. They are here and they have to be defeated all over again, that is all we need to know. Quickly, find whatever cover you can and keep your heads down!'

The rest of the crowd dispersed, running in every direction as their leaders sprinted over to the northern wall. As they ran, Jake asked Zephany about the revalkas, hoping to learn as much as he could about his new enemy before he had to engage them in battle.

'What are they? Where do they come from?'

'Trust me, Jake, for the present at least, you do not want to know.'

Jake then looked at Tien, who had returned to the group as soon as the enemy was sighted and was now running alongside the Keeper. The old wizard decided quickly that he had time for a very brief explanation and he tried to think of anything that might help.

'Jake, this unexpected turn of events can mean only one thing; King Vantrax' powers have increased beyond our wildest imaginings. He has found a way to unlock time, to bring forth into our world the creatures who once brought it to its knees, to the very brink of annihilation. Revalkas, sraine, graxoth, the Lords of Srenul... These beasts come straight from Zsorcraum, from the darkest corners of every Estian's nightmares. Our worst fears have come true. We will be forced to confront our own demons if we are to win this war. These monsters once defeated everything we could throw against them. It is not good to be reminded just how close we came to extinction. Graxoth and sraine you have met before, but revalkas...? There is little hope against them, Jake. No Keeper has faced such adversaries. Even the dragons fell before them!'

'Tien!' snapped Jake. 'They are almost here. I will *not* accept that they can't be defeated. You did it before, all of you. There *has* to be a way!'

'I am with you, Jake. I will not stand here and do nothing!' stated a determined Princess Zephany. They had reached the wall by now and stood on the ramparts, looking out across the plain and up at the sky, at their terrifying enemy. 'Archers! Coat your arrows with the herethdar liquid. Fire when they are within range! Make every shot count, and let us pray that its potency is no myth.'

The first of the revalkas halted a little way from the city, remaining just out of range of the Estian arrows. The rest of the formidable force stopped at the same time. The creature surveyed the scene before it, deciding upon the best form of attack, allowing the defenders a good look at their newest adversary.

Revalkas were similar in appearance to a very large dragon, only they possessed two giant heads instead of one, both of which were dominated by an enormous, tooth-filled mouth. A vicious looking spike or horn protruded from each of their heads. Their strong, powerful arms were adorned with razor sharp prongs which could rip to shreds anything or anyone they touched. The claws on their hands and feet were huge and a long, thin, barbed tail whipped viciously behind them in flight, covered again in sharp spikes which carried a deadly venom.

Suddenly, the lead revalkas screamed out loudly. The remaining creatures obeyed the command and manoeuvred around until they were all positioned in one extended line, which stretched across the sky for some distance. Then, one further cry from the prime beast, an instruction or a scream of intent, launched the attack. Slowly, they moved forward, before the whole line suddenly burst into life and most of the horrifying attackers began soaring down towards the petrified defenders of the city.

The Battle of Te'oull had begun.

* * *

Ben, Verastus and the tribespeople of Readal forest had at last reached Varriann. Though the inhabitants of the medium sized city were at first fearful of the 'savages' fleeing the Battle of Dassilliak, they had by now heard of their deeds and were expecting them, news having spread quickly among the population by way of the Heynai and their chosen messengers. Eventually, the citizens left their homes and gave the weary refugees a cautious welcome. This allowed the survivors time to rest and recuperate, to recover their strength for the ordeals they knew still lay ahead.

Ben was not feeling the effects of sleep deprivation as much as most. Unbelievably, the teenage boy had somehow managed to fall fast asleep several times on their journey, even though he had been holding on tightly to the giant frame of Verastus and leaning up against the mighty Falorian as he guided their horse. Once he had dismounted and stretched his aching muscles, his brain automatically reverted to Ben mode, as usual focusing on the subject which was always uppermost in his thoughts.

'Okay then, when do we eat? I could murder a sausage sarny.'

Once again Verastus had absolutely no idea what the youngster was talking about. He presumed correctly however that a 'sausage sarny' was a hometown delicacy on Ben's world.

'Ha! Do not trouble yourself, Ben. I will go and find us something to eat if I can. Maybe these people will spare us some food? You remain here and watch the horse.'

Ben took hold of the reigns rather gingerly. He was still not used to horses, having never even been near one before entering Rhuaddan. He wasn't comfortable around them and they in turn generally picked up on his fear, and acted accordingly.

'Whooaa... Err, it's alright boy, I won't hurt you. I don't bite,' Ben said, trying to remain calm and reassure the animal as the horse shifted nervously once Verastus was gone. The stallion calmed a little and Ben relaxed. He was now able to take stock of his new surroundings.

Varriann was on a much smaller scale than Dassilliak or Ilin-Seatt, or many of the other places Ben had seen or heard about in the past few weeks. It was no more than a very large village really. The buildings were just shacks, small hovels which looked as though they were strung together with any old pieces of wood that could be found, bound by an assortment of strings, vines, nails and pegs. Most of the tiny dwellings and barns looked as though they might fall down at any moment, or collapse altogether in a strong wind. The streets and roads were of differing widths and dimensions. It was clear to any onlooker, including Ben, that this place had just evolved naturally, without any form of planning or intent.

Brraall was seeing to his people, walking among them and listening to their woes. There were numerous wounded from the battle at Dassilliak and the tribal healers were busy applying poultices of leaves and mud. Ben thought it looked like a scene from a film, a medieval re-enactment, or a depiction in a book or magazine that would have fascinated him if he was back home in Lichfield. He realised right there and then that he was lost in his own private adventure, living an impossible dream from which he could not wake up. This whole experience was a nightmare fraught with danger and uncertainty, one in which the risks and stakes were immense, and all too real. He knew that he and Jake could easily be killed at any time in this war they had waged. This was no childish game they were playing. They were fighting alongside real warriors, real soldiers, against real enemies. Ben had had these thoughts before of course, but something was different now. The extraordinarily funny thing was, to Ben at least, that he no longer wanted to wake up. He was missing home but at this moment in time, he didn't want the adventure to end.

How can I go back to my old life after all of this? Back to school? he asked himself, even though he knew he would jump at the chance if it was on offer. Like Jake, he was full of confusion and contradictions and yet at the same time, his mind was somehow clear? As clear as it had ever been in fact. It didn't make sense but he had no doubts at all. Tomorrow was another day, but right now this was where he wanted to be, and the sudden realisation shocked the life out of him.

Oh heck! It's alright for Jake. Back home he has a loving family, a decent life, something worth going home to, worth fighting for. He's gonna be a success at everything he does, I know it. That's fine though. I'm happy for him, I really am. He's my best mate and I'll always want him to do well. But me…? I wasn't born for greatness like him. I'm Joe Average. I usually get lost in the crowd. But now, for the very first time in my life, I actually matter to someone. I'm making a difference. Me! People are trusting me, relying on me, and what's more, I like it. I can actually see respect in people's eyes when they talk to me.

As he considered for a moment the implications of his own startling confession, he stared in awe at the incredibly muscular torso of Brraall before him. The great warrior and leader's frame was almost as large as Verastus'.

Huh! Alright, I suppose there is a bit of difference between him and me? I don't have his muscles, that's for sure. But, when it comes down to it, I'm not short of a brain cell or two, am I? Not when compared to these guys. And I'm fast. Then there's the sword the Heynai gave me, and the shield… Yeah, I'll be alright. Bring 'em on! Jake may have all the powers. He's the blue-eyed boy, there's no doubt about that, but I'll show 'em! And if I'm gonna die out here, I'll do some damage before they get me. It may not come to that anyway? We may win? After all, I've already been through two battles and survived, haven't I?

Ben's attempts to bolster his own self-confidence were suddenly interrupted by Verastus. The Falorian came running swiftly over to him wearing a look of real concern. Something was clearly wrong. He was joined immediately by Brraall. Verastus took the reins from Ben's hands and ushered him to the side of the nearest building as quickly as he could, out of sight. The three comrades peered around the edge of the barn cautiously, staring out to the East.

'What is it? What's a matter?' asked the youngster.

'Something is coming,' replied Verastus. 'Look! There, in the sky!'

'Raart, there are more than one of them,' stated Brraall, calmly.

'What? One of *what*?' hissed Ben. Despite his bravado of only seconds before, he was scared all of a sudden, terrified of the unknown threat they faced. His voice was trembling as he spoke, betraying his true feelings. 'Err... Where's G-Gellsorr?' he asked, realising all of a sudden that the dragon who had protected them on the retreat from Dassilliak had not been seen since they entered the city of Varriann.

'I do not know, Ben,' replied Verastus.

'He is missing. We are on our own,' added Brraall, the experienced commander understanding the importance of dealing with the here and now in such circumstances and not dwelling on matters beyond their control.

'Oh, nice one! Fine time he picked to go sightseeing!' Ben whispered, to a stern look from Verastus. 'You know,' the youngster responded to the silent admonishment, 'you're actually beginning to look a lot like Jake.'

They each drew their weapons. Brraall silently ordered his warriors to do likewise, ready to defend their people from attack. The dark, menacing shapes in the sky grew larger and larger as they approached. Before long, it became clear what they were.

'Graxoth! Two of them. And a revalkas!! But how...?!' rasped an astonished Brraall.

'Vantrax. This *has* to be *his* doing. Quickly, get everyone inside who cannot fight,' ordered Verastus. He raised his staff and a shiny blade appeared out of each end. Brraall gave his orders and everyone dispersed, leaving only the bravest warriors amongst them to face the creature's fury... and Ben.

'Bl-bloody hell! Be careful what you wish for Ben me ol' son, eh?' he said, as he saw the three beasts clearly for the first time.

'What? What did you say?' hissed Verastus.

'Ah, never mind,' replied Ben. Adrenalin was pumping wildly through his body now and it was all he could do to speak. 'I was just thinking about something I'd decided on earlier, just before you two showed up to ruin the moment, as usual. I'm glad I didn't say it out loud. If I had, you'd probably be saying that I should have kept my big gob shut! Or words to that effect.'

Chapter 5
27th September – Varriann City – Perosya

Three gruesome beasts from the fires of the underworld were now mercilessly hunting Ben Brooker and his companions down. With their far superior eyesight they easily spotted their quarry whilst still some distance away. The lead revalkas slowed his flight to a virtual standstill, hovering over the outskirts of the city below, choosing to survey their options before launching their lethal attack. On the very edge of the small city there stood many tribal warriors, all armed to the teeth with spears, knives, axes, bows and clubs. In the centre of their makeshift defensive line was an old wooden building, around the sides of which several pairs of anxious eyes were now peering. Even from such a distance with almost his entire body concealed from view the revolting creature soon spotted his main target, as Ben's shaven head gave the youngster away. The young boy from Lichfield had been marked for assassination by King Vantrax, and now his time had come!

Ben's elimination had been ordered by the evil wizard because he believed that it would serve as the perfect warning to all on Estia and beyond who would dare defy his rule. Ben was the Keeper's friend and companion. He had protected the stones when King Vantrax' warriors had attacked at Erriard and in subsequent fights and many had heard of, or witnessed, his deeds. In the relatively short time he had been on Estia, Ben Brooker had become as much of a rallying cry to the subjugated population as the Keeper himself, as much of a thorn in the wizard's side as anyone. King Vantrax had decided therefore that he *had* to die. He marked the troublesome youngster for elimination for his own peace of mind, to weaken the resolve of his enemies and instill fear once again into their hearts, to ensure that the boy no longer had the stones in his possession, and to bring one step closer the final victory he was so desperate to achieve.

A tense and uneasy standoff developed at the outskirts to the city. The three monsters weighed up their options carefully, using their highly developed brains to decide upon the best angle of attack. Ben remained crouched down low on his haunches, hidden behind the shack and concealed from view besides Verastus, who was leaning against the wooden structure and gazing around it at their attackers.

'Well? What they doin' now?' asked Ben, anxiously. His palms were sweating and he rubbed them on his shirt.

'They are doing, nothing.'

'Eh? Nothing? What d'ya mean, nothing? They must be doing something?'

'They have halted, presumably to count our warriors.'

'Oh. They're smart then, eh? Okay, that means we have some time. How are we going to kill them?'

'I do not know, Ben. Spears, arrows maybe?' replied Verastus, his eyes firmly fixed upon their foe. Still, the creatures did not move.

'Huh! Good answer. Duh,' said Ben, who just could not help but ridicule his friend. Humour was a massive part of his defence mechanism and it always rose to the fore when he was scared. He made to lean around Verastus to gain a better look at the creatures but he suddenly heard a voice sounding in his head. It was loud and clear and it arrived totally out of the blue, as if someone had just turned on a television or radio nearby.

'Ben!'

The frightened teenager halted his movement forward and immediately sat back down on his haunches, as he realised to his amazement what was happening. No-one could see him but he had a look of complete astonishment upon his face.

'Knesh? Is that you?' he asked, using only his mind to communicate, just as he had witnessed others doing. He could not believe what he was doing. It was all too much like a dream. Only, he knew that it wasn't. He was certain that it was real and the stakes for him and his friends were far too high to ignore what he heard.

'No, Ben. It is I, Sereq,' the voice replied.

'Sereq! What's happening? Why are you inside my head? Jake! Is he alright?'

'Yes, Ben, he is as well as can be expected. Listen to me now and listen well, for I have but a very brief moment with you before they

attack.'

'Err... Yeah, okay. Go on, I'm all ears.'

'We will protect the Keeper, Ben. We will give him the time he needs to restore the stones and win this war, to defeat the wizard.'

'Great! But, so you should, he's...'

'For you,' interrupted Sereq, impatiently, 'we can do little. You are too far away from our current position and we need to concentrate all the power we have on helping Jake.'

Ben gulped hard at the probable consequences of such a statement.

'Oh, I see. We're on our own then?'

'Yes, I am afraid so. Just three of his beasts face you now. King Vantrax has dispatched the remainder of his entire force to seek the main prize; Jake and the stones.'

'Three is it? Well then, that don't sound too bad, does it? I'm sure we can handle three.'

'Ben, now is not the time for such bravado. We feel your terror. There is a revalkas among them. I can give you only one thing now which may defeat it. As for the graxoth...?'

'It's okay, Sereq. I understand. Do what you must. Please, save Jake and the others? We'll be fine.'

'Kraar... You are a very courageous boy, Ben. The Keeper is lucky to have such a friend. Now, when the time comes, when the revalkas is almost upon you, tell Verastus to launch his staff at it, the weapon we gave him. He is to aim at the centre of the beast's chest.'

'Yeah, okay. I will.'

'Good. I must go. Fare thee well. And please accept our sincere gratitude for all you have done for our people.'

And with that, the voice of Sereq sounded no more. Ben opened his eyes immediately to see Verastus tightening his grip on the staff.

'They are coming, Ben,' cried the Falorian. 'Make ready!' he bellowed, to the surrounding tribal warriors, hoping that the true meaning behind his order would transcend the language barrier between them.

Ben placed a firm hand on Verastus' shoulder. 'I've just had a vision, big man, a dream or something. I've no time to explain it to you now, but you *have* to do exactly as I say! You *must* keep hold of your staff until the last possible moment, until that revalkas thing is right on top of us, okay? It's the only way we can kill it!'

Verastus was shocked and amazed to hear such words but he did not question the instruction. 'A vision you say? Just now as we were…? Raart! Ben, my friend, if that is what you command, then that is how it shall be.'

Seconds later, the three horrifying creatures flew in hard and fast. They swooped down low to kill several tribesmen on their first pass, catching them in the open as they ran for cover, incinerating them with the fire from the revalkas' nostrils and then ripping apart any survivors with tails, teeth and claws. Then, they took off swiftly, avoiding all the arrows and spears thrown at them and swinging around for a second pass. This time, all three descended upon the wooden fence which ran alongside the hut, where Ben and the others were sheltering. They fell onto Brraall and his warriors before they had chance to shift their position. The huge tribal leader fought valiantly and with great skill, fighting off his graxoth assailant bravely with sword and spear, ducking and diving, weaving violently to avoid being caught by the beast's incredibly sharp claws. Eventually, the creature withdrew a little and Brraall escaped, but not before many of his warriors had been killed.

'Raart! I cannot sit here and watch this!' roared Verastus suddenly. 'I *have* to do something!'

The mighty Falorian immediately broke cover. He sprinted as fast as he could to the centre of the open ground, just as the three beasts took off to circle around for yet another pass. His sudden and unexpected movement caught Ben completely by surprise. It was so swift that the youngster had no chance to stop him. The teenage boy suddenly felt a rush of blood to his brain and a surge of high octane adrenalin raced through his body. Though he had absolutely no idea why he was doing it, before he could think properly his short and muscular legs were already propelling him across the ground at speed, as he chased after his friend. His lips uttered words he would never have thought possible as he ran.

'Hey! Wait for me! If you're so determined to be a hero, then I'm coming with you!'

The lead revalkas immediately spotted their impulsive and reckless dash. It turned swiftly in flight and launched into an immediate dive to counter their action, intending to finish the fight swiftly and kill the young boy, to accomplish its mission.

'Oh sh...!' began Ben, as he witnessed the turn and realised that he and Verastus were now completely exposed. But, before he could finish, he caught sight of his Falorian friend and his heart almost leapt into his mouth. The freed slave had lifted his staff and he was just about to throw it at the nearest graxoth!

'No!' screamed Ben. 'Not *them*! The *other* one!'

Verastus heard the young boy's desperate cry just in the nick of time and changed the direction of his aim straight away. A shiny blade appeared out of each end of the staff, turning the long piece of wood once again into a deadly spear. This time however, both blades immediately began to glow brightly and soon they were alight. Hundreds of tiny sparks of fire surrounded them all of a sudden, reminding Ben instantly of the sparklers he'd held on every bonfire night he had known as a child.

Verastus launched the spear as the revalkas neared, delaying his throw until the last possible moment when the creature was almost on top of them and he could smell his rotten breath. The two friends ducked instinctively to avoid being hit by the oncoming beast. They did not witness the spear's effect as they both dived out of the way and fell heavily to the ground.

The Heynai's weapon flew straight and true. It sped out of Verastus' hand and towards its target. From the moment it left the Falorian's fingers, it was travelling at such an unbelievable speed, with supernatural velocity, that it passed straight through the revalkas' body and continued for some distance.

A gaping hole appeared in the creature's chest. It was smoking and the edges were on fire. Then, a fraction of a second later, the fires spread rapidly outwards to consume their host and one last awful, dreadful scream of horror filled the air. In flames, the revalkas plunged rapidly to the ground and landed with a resounding crash, not far from Ben and

Verastus. Moments later, the fires had completely devoured it and it was gone. The fearsome creature from the underworld had been destroyed, killed by a weapon and blade coated in the spirit's own fire.

However, the revalkas' companions, the graxoth, still remained.

Infuriated by the sudden loss of their powerful leader, they immediately launched a further attack of their own, directed against Ben and Verastus. Before the beasts could reach them though, a booming roar of a different kind echoed in the sky and gained their immediate attention. It came from the east and as they turned their heads they learned to their cost that it was the war cry of a solitary dragon!

Gellsorr, the last surviving dragon on Estia, suddenly burst through the low-lying clouds. He swooped down viciously and with astonishing speed to fall on the graxoth before they had chance to gain the height they needed to respond. The wizard's creatures were completely helpless, unable to defend themselves from such a swift and unexpected attack. The great dragon dispatched the first of the beasts with his fire, incinerating it in only a few seconds. Then, in the same dive, he fell upon the second beast and sank his claws deep into his shoulders, pushing him down onto the solid ground below with his momentum. He fell onto the graxoth with such force and weight that the creature's spine was broken and he was killed outright.

Ben breathed a massive sigh of relief. When he eventually stopped shaking and recovered himself, he strode over to Verastus to check on his welfare, placing a hand on his shoulder with great difficulty, given the height difference.

'Yeah! Whooaa!!! Ha, ha... Thanks, big man. You were *awesome*!'

Verastus was completely calm. He laughed a little, amused by Ben's compliment. 'You did well yourself, Ben. Though, you were very foolish to follow me. You might have been hurt,' he replied.

Ben nodded once in agreement. Then he ran over to Gellsorr. He stared down at the grizzly sight of the slain graxoth at his feet, before dismissing it in an instant and looking up to speak to the dragon. Something was bugging him. He had a question on his lips which needed an answer and, in true Ben style, despite what had just occurred, he wasn't about to let it drop.

'Err... I s'pose I'd better thank *you* as well, Gellsorr? Thanks mate. That was out of this world! Ha, ha... *Out of this world?* No? Okay, thanks anyway. But, where the *hell* have you been??!! What took you so long? We nearly died!'

By this time, Verastus and Brraall had gathered around to hear the explanation, for everyone was wondering the same thing. The remaining warriors were seeing to their dead and wounded.

Gellsorr looked severely embarrassed, which was a very great thing, because it is usually incredibly hard to discern a dragon's true feelings.

'Srr... I... I can only apologise to you all. I... I thought we were safe. I thought you were resting, that we had placed enough distance between us and our enemy, that I too could take the opportunity for some respite.'

'Resting?' replied Ben. 'That's where you were while we were fighting, having a *nap*? I've heard everything now! Gellsorr, you've been asleep for hundreds of years, for Pete's sake. The *last* thing you need is more sleep,' he said, half joking but still a little upset at just how close they had come to being wiped out because of the dragon's disappearance.

Gellsorr knew the young boy was only teasing, but he still felt like he needed to explain. 'Yes, I know. You are right, Ben. However, you must understand that this body, these muscles, have not seen action in all that time. They have suffered from inactivity and they have grown weak. I have been in almost continual flight since the battle at Dassilliak. I needed to...'

'Ha, ha, ha...'

Ben suddenly burst into one almighty fit of spontaneous laughter, to the amazement of his friends. He was in hysterics and he really couldn't stop himself. Eventually, the others began to laugh too, responding to his incredible delight more out of relief than anything else, for no-one knew for certain the source of the joke. Finally, Ben squeezed out an explanation of sorts between giggles.

'...Trust us to find the only dragon in history with gym fatigue! Ha, ha... Now then, *that* I can understand, Gellsorr. Don't worry yourself. We all have our off days. That's a very human reaction actually, and it's one which will draw no Mickey taking from *me*. Everyone, apart from Jake that is, needs a little breather every now and then. Ha, ha, ha...'

*   *   *

In the royal chambers at the palace of Dassilliak, one of the very few buildings undamaged by King Vantrax' onslaught, his chief adversary and brother, King Artrex, was *finally* coming round from the coma induced by the wounds he had received in the battle. The leader of the Ruddite Rebellion had lost a lot of blood. His arm had very nearly been severed and he had come perilously close to death. He was still very groggy and incredibly weak. And if that were not bad enough, at the moment of his waking, his eyesight and mind seemed to be playing tricks on him. Everything around him was blurred. And what's more, he actually felt as if he were floating in mid-air!

In the bleariness, he could just make out the dark figure of a knight towering over him, though he could not discern who it was, no matter how hard he tried.

'Zephany, is that you?' he whispered faintly, his voice low as he struggled to speak.

An immediate surge of excruciating pain shot through his injured arm as a rough and coarse hand was clasped tightly across his mouth. The urgency of the action could not be mistaken. Artrex could not move a muscle despite his discomfort. He lay still, imprisoned and pinned down for several minutes by the unknown stranger, unaware of his identity or intent.

His mind began awakening slowly and it returned to recent events, as he waited anxiously and helplessly to learn his fate. He pictured the battle of Dassilliak in his thoughts, the wounds he received there and his daughter's astonishing bravery, along with the courageous exploits of Lord Castrad and the rest of the warriors from the rebellion, as well as those of the soldiers from the Estian Alliance who aided his escape. The charge of the Estians had saved his life for certain, just when all had seemed lost. But, he could remember absolutely nothing after that point.

Gradually, the king's eyesight began to clear. However, the firm hand of the unknown warrior remained fixed firmly across his lips. Artrex stared at the figure above. Eventually, his vision returned and the mysterious knight's identity was revealed.

'Knesh!' the king hissed as best he could through the warrior's fingers. His heart leapt and skipped a beat at the same time. He could not believe what he was seeing. His best friend and gerada was dead, surely? And yet, here he was, as clear as anything, holding him down?

Artrex flicked his eyes upwards. The ceiling above him was barely a foot away, though the dark shadow cast all around them told him they were in the corner of the room, as far away from the candlelight as they could be. Once he realised that the darkness was deliberately intended to conceal their presence, he began to understand why he had felt as if he was floating; he *was!*

The king nodded gently to his old friend, letting him know in the only way he could that he understood what was happening and had at last regained his senses. Knesh released his hand very slowly. He placed a finger to his lips, instructing the king not to make a sound. Artrex looked down, sensing extreme danger all of a sudden. Beneath them, not twelve feet away but completely oblivious to their presence, was a party of three formidable Thargw warriors. The terrifying beasts were busy dressing themselves in their armour, preparing for battle or about to leave on some patrol.

The two old friends and rebels were both experienced combatants. They remained as quiet as possible as they waited patiently for the Thargws to leave. Artrex stared disbelievingly at the image before him, at the chiseled features of the loyal companion who had sacrificed so much so that he might live, to continue the fight against King Vantrax and restore the stones. A solitary tear rolled down his cheek. The door eventually slammed shut as the last of the Thargws left the room. Knesh then lowered his hands and Artrex' body immediately began to fall very slowly, until it finally rested once again on the bed.

'What is happening?' began the king.

Knesh placed a finger to his lips once more. He rushed to the door and placed his ear against it, listening for any sign of activity on the other side of the wood. Then, he placed his head right through it, right up to and past his shoulders. He searched the corridor outside with his eyes. Once he was certain they were alone and would not be disturbed, Knesh retracted his head and returned to the astonished king.

'Ra! That is some trick!' stated Artrex, now feeling a little stronger. 'It would have been handy when you were alive?'

Knesh laughed gently. 'Yes, sire, I suppose it would. It is good to see you again in this life. I thought you were too badly wounded, too far gone to save. We all hoped you would pull through, but we did not believe it. All except for Tien and Zephany. They never gave up.'

'Tien? *He* saved me?'

'Yes.'

'Krr... Zephany? How is she?'

'She is well, sire, for the present,' replied Knesh.

Artrex knew immediately that there was more behind his friend's guarded reply. 'Go on. I am sensing somehow that things have not gone well for us?'

'No. And yes, my king. The Battle of Dassilliak was lost. Our people have fled. They are being hunted by a powerful force of darkness. But, we are stronger now and we gain in strength with every day that passes. We are no longer alone. We have an ally in the Estian Alliance. Your daughter now leads them.'

'Zephany? She *does*?' replied King Artrex, amazed. He smiled proudly, a smile which betrayed to Knesh that he always knew she would achieve great things. He nodded his head a little with satisfaction. 'And you, my old friend? How is this...?'

'Possible? There will hopefully be a time for explanations. It is not now. In death, I serve the Heynai, but I also serve *you* still. The very moment you feel able to move, we must leave.'

'Yes, but go where?'

'I must take you away from here, out of this city. I have to get you to somewhere you will be safe. Then, we have to find some way of joining with the others, at Te'oull,' stated Knesh.

'Te'oull? In Siatol?' Artrex asked, surprised.

'Yes. That is the place, the battleground on which will be fought the last encounter in the war of wars, spoken of in all our legends and tales. Though we did not realise it, my very great friend, we have been fighting it all along. It is here. It is upon us. The final conflict will be there. We know that now. The ancient battle between good and evil which has claimed so many lives and consumed this great land of ours, is yours and mine to wage. It will be won or lost not in our realm, not in Rhuaddan as we thought, but at Te'oull. Ironic, is it not? The prophecies handed down to us are all coming true!'

Artrex was filled with a sense of destiny as he listened to his lifelong companion. His chest swelled and his eyes narrowed.

'Yes, Knesh, and *we* will play our part! We must go,' stated the king, resolutely. He tried his best to move but he could not. His arm was wracked with pain and the slightest movement sent his head into a spin. He was shocked, embarrassed, frustrated...

'I... I am sorry. I cannot move!' he cried.

'No sire, your wounds are too severe. You have been revived early with the help of the spirits, but your body cannot cope with the demands being asked of it. Your strength will return to you in a day or so and mine will fade. For the moment, we are going nowhere. Rest, my king. Sleep, and let Tien's magic do its work. You are destined to play an important part in this war yet. You will have your place in history, I swear it. It is written. You *must* rejoin the Keeper, or all will surely be lost!'

Chapter 6
27th September – The City of Te'oull – Siatol

Four of the strongest are chosen to wait for the one who will come.
To help restore that which is broken. To see that the battle is won.

Crouching behind the walls to the ancient city of Te'oull, Jake West and the warriors of the Estian Alliance awaited their first encounter with an enemy far more deadly than any they had faced to date. They were about to come under attack from an entire army of flying monsters. The impossible situation was looking increasingly dire for the beleaguered and weary defenders. And for Jake, the whole incredible scene before him was like something out of a really terrible horror film. The skies were brimming with terrifying beasts, assassins raised by King Vantrax for one solitary purpose; the complete annihilation of all his enemies. The lead revalkas were closing in on their position and the last-ditch stand, the final battle for the future of Estia, was about to commence.

Princess Zephany barked out her orders as loud as she possibly could, instructing her archers to fire at the fast and manoeuvrable creatures as they tried to descend, the very instant they came into range. A salvo of well-aimed arrows followed almost immediately. The poison-tipped weapons sped towards the aerial armada and the warriors in the Estian ranks drew a collective breath. Thousands of anxious eyes looked on in desperation, hoping and praying with all their souls that the herethdar toxin Jake had secured was lethal enough to work on the mythical creature's intent on sealing their doom. Every single warrior defending Te'oull on this day, every civillian onlooker, knew for certain that if it was not, if the vile creatures were somehow immune to its effects, then they were all about to die horrible deaths.

Meanwhile, some distance away from the epic battle which would decide the future of so many worlds, somewhere within the Kielth mountains, Sereq had finally returned to the remaining Heynai spirits. His last encounter with Jake and Tien, followed by the unplanned detour he had made to help Ben, had taken a lot longer than expected. Sereq was wracked with guilt and full of remorse. He was agonising over the thought of abandoning his people, even though he knew deep within his heart and soul they were making the right decision and really had no alternative. In the relative safety of the dark, damp cave, the four spirits had no respite from the terrible storm that was brewing. Sereq was quiet and thoughtful as he rejoined his comrades but he knew they had run out of time. He sighed and, without pausing, spoke.

'The hour is upon us,' he began, his voice calm but with an air of finality about it. 'We must act now. For the sake of our people, for the hope of all, we cannot linger.'

'We are ready, Sereq,' replied Terristor. 'We stand with you, as always. We will not falter. Know that we will follow you until the very end.'

Sereq smiled warmly at each of the spirits in turn. Then, he held out his hands. The others did likewise and a neat circle was formed. Each of their fingers were spread out wide so that the smallest digits touched those belonging to the spirits on either side. Silence descended upon the mountainside in an instant. The ferocious wind ceased to blow all of a sudden and the howling, swirling breeze within the cave disappeared. The whole mountain range fell deathly quiet, unnaturally so.

'Drea viatheluss exalem amstrallion heutt.
Etierr all krruull treothe.
Vexzienn seeall Ball hallaph praass!'

From every conceivable corner of the cavern, a mighty tempest erupted without warning. Rain, wind, hail and lightning rocked the mountain to its very core. Outside the cave the air was still and calm but inside its walls the four spirits were experiencing one of the greatest storms in Estian history. Dust, dirt, rocks and leaves began flying in all directions. Some of the airborne debris passed right through the spirit's transparent images, as they battled hard to concentrate on the task in hand. As the incredible rainstorm grew even further in its intensity, the ghostly wizards suddenly began to change form. Their translucent, lifeless figures unexpectedly began to transform into real-life, actual bodies!

'Do not be alarmed,' cried Sereq, fighting to make himself heard above the incredible noise. 'We have made our intentions clear. This was to be expected!'

The spirits were in real danger now. Having been transformed into flesh and blood, the rocks and stones being hurled violently around the confines of the cave by the tremendous wind began to hit them. Hearts which had felt no blood running through them for centuries suddenly began to beat far too rapidly. Pulse rates raced way too high and bodies newly transformed began to flinch and sweat profusely. Hands and fingers once again able to touch and feel were all of a sudden shaking uncontrollably in fear. Bruises, swellings and cuts appeared where they were hit by flying rock...

Sereq sensed that it was far too dangerous to proceed without taking action. Reluctantly, he diverted some of his own power to shield them, even though he knew that he needed every available scrap of energy he had if they were going to succeed in their task. A forcefield of invisible light spread all around the four Heynai immediately, encasing them, protecting them from the unbelievable force contained within the storm they had created. The debris continued to hit the impenetrable wall with astonishing speed and regularity but, safe within the shield, the spirits remained unharmed and while it protected them, they were able to continue their spell.

'Brruukk theus ipsillion hallthek,
apthsul zexan hinaii eckrall greu!!'

A ball of fire no larger than a tennis ball appeared in the centre of the circle. Suspended in mid-air, it floated at chest level and it did not move.

'Ulluxnell jeus achvallish neull,
ulluxnell jeus achvallish neull.'

Sereq spoke the ageless words as if the lives of every one of his people depended on them. The remaining spirits soon began chanting also, with the same levels of emotion and urgency echoing in their chorus. The lines were repeated over and over again. They rose in volume and fervor until all of the spirits were bellowing them out as loud as they possibly could. However, with each refrain, with every chant pouring from their lips, they were being drained of priceless energy. Their newly-formed bodies were wracked with more and more pain, until the agony they bore was excruciating, far greater than any mortal being could ever bear.

'Ulluxnell jeus achvallish neull,
ulluxnell jeus achvallish neull!!!'

Then, when they were at the absolute limit of their endurance, the little circle of fire began to grow and grow. Finally, when it had reached the size of a basketball, it suddenly exploded into four separate beams of fire. The flames burned brightly and they spread quickly outwards from the centre ball to enter each of the spirits' bodies through their chests, plunging straight into their hearts like an assassin's dagger.

The four Heynai rose to their tiptoes in unison as the pain intensified to an astonishing, inhuman level. They each screamed out in anguish and opened their eyes in shock and bewilderment. Sereq witnessed the disbelief and abject misery on the faces of his companions. For the first time in hundreds of years he was scared, terrified in fact. For one awful moment he was petrified that his friends and allies would not prove strong enough for what they had to do, that they would finally let him down, just when it mattered most.

'No! Hold on, my friends!' he yelled, through gritted teeth. His body was contorted in pain and covered in sweat, but still he fought valiantly to maintain the circle. 'Do *not* let it win! It means to beat us, to destroy us. It wants to escape, to be free of our influence. It does *not* want to die! But, it has *not* met our like before! We are stronger than anything it has encountered, *if* we stay focused and act as one.'

He was speaking of the fire as if it were alive. The flames before him and in each of the spirits were once part of the original source of all Estian life, the origin of *everything* that lived and breathed in his world.

The agony was now unbearable, relentless. It was absolute torture for those having to endure the sustained attack. But, the four spirits began to chant once more, straining every sinew and refusing to give in, somehow managing to withstand the excruciating pain.

After a short while, the flames grew again and then changed in colour to become a very bright red. They burned more fiercely than ever before as they battled with all their might to overcome the spirits' astonishing defiance. Finally, they reached their absolute zenith and Sereq realised they had no more to give. Despite his agony, the ancient spirit smiled. He knew right there and then that it was over, that the Heynai had actually won what he had believed to be an impossible fight.

'Now!' he cried, triumphantly, and the four spirits screamed out in unison.

'Appzelluth snairianne kraashnall truiss!!'

The ball of fire was still positioned rigidly within the centre of the circle. It suddenly changed in colour once again, from red to white. Within seconds, the four separate beams of flame left the spirit's bodies and rejoined with the ball. As they did, the sphere increased in size. Soon, it was as tall as the Heynai themselves and they naturally took a step backwards as it neared them, breaking the circle.

The agony they each felt subsided gradually and eventually it faded to nothing. Sereq was then able to address his friends calmly, without hindrance. He did so with a great deal of pride and satisfaction.

'Well done, all of you! I am extremely proud of you all. You have done what no other has managed; you have tamed the fire of life itself! You have bent it to your will. Do not underestimate the magnitude of your achievement. This is the absolute pinnacle of existence, and it is a fitting way for us to leave our world. All that is left for us now is to finish what we have begun, what we were always meant to do. *Our* journey is almost at an end, my friends. Concentrate with me one last time? Focus everything you have upon the ball of fire. Do not speak from this point, for we will need every single scrap of energy we possess, every second of precious time.'

Sereq held out his hands to either side and reached for those of his fellow spirits. Following his lead, the remaining Heynai did likewise. A continuous circle was formed again around the white fire. Together, they concentrated like they had never concentrated before, trying to picture and build an impregnable barrier, one which stretched across the entire length of their land. They visualised it in their minds, using their last remaining energy reserves and all of their considerable experience and power, willing it to happen with every fibre of their newly reformed bodies.

Quite soon, the ball of light began to shake, slowly at first, but after a few moments it began to vibrate ferociously. Then, all of a sudden, it seemed to implode upon itself. It almost disappeared completely, only to re-emerge moments later as a dazzling beam of brightness exploded from within. The incredible light raced out of the cave entrance and shot up to the sky. Then, in a flash, it vanished!

* * *

Far away on the northern approaches to Te'oull, an army of revalkas and graxoth was flying in for the attack. Thousands of arrows had already been launched towards them by the terrified defenders but, as they neared, the horrifying creatures began to take evasive action. They each manoeuvred rapidly in flight to avoid being hit, whilst somehow still managing to maintain their forward momentum. The majority of the arrows passed harmlessly by, to the intense frustration of Jake and the army of defenders below, who were now really beginning to fear the worst.

Oh no! the Keeper thought, as he tried in vain not to show his disappointment to the soldiers around him. *The Heynai are too late! Nothing can stop them now. We've had it!*

Then, all of a sudden, a bright white light appeared for no more than a second in the air ahead of him. It seemed to illuminate the whole sky and it came and went in the blink of an eye, though it distracted all those on the wall ramparts with its intensity. When the defenders immediately turned their attention once again towards the attacking beasts, the air between them seemed to have changed somehow. It was different, hazy. The fearsome creatures who served King Vantrax were still there in large numbers, only now the sinister shapes appeared a little blurred to the confused combatants.

A fraction of a second later, the lead revalkas and graxoth smashed into the Heynai's shield with thunderous force. The terrifying creatures were travelling at high speed, many were seriously injured by the near invisible wall they hit, and did not see until it was too late. They fell to the ground in a heap before the shield, some killed outright and others nursing a variety of serious wounds.

A second volley of arrows had been launched by the Estians. It crashed against the barrier almost immediately. The amazed defenders were staggered by the unbelievable sight. All across the battlefield, revalkas and graxoth began reacting furiously to the sudden and unexpected development. They raged from behind the protective screen, crying and screaming in frustration at being kept from their enemy by an unknown force they did not understand. Time and time again they tried to find a way through, fanning out and flying up and down its entire length in a desperate attempt to achieve their goal and complete their mission. But, it was no use, the spirit's deliberate obstruction was holding firm and the creatures from Zsorcraum were thwarted.

For the time being at least, the 'doomed' warriors of the Estian Alliance had won yet another, miraculous reprieve.

Inside the walls, Princess Zephany was the first to break cover. She stood up straight and proud on the ramparts, took out an arrow from her quiver and fired it at the shield. The princess wanted to satisfy herself for certain that the miracle she had just witnessed was real. The arrow hit the almost invisible wall at speed and it shattered. Zephany was content now.

She turned to Jake and smiled. '*This* is what you meant by, *trust me*, I suppose?'

Jake had the largest grin upon his face, a completely natural, boyish smirk of delight, and immense relief. 'Yeah, well, I was hoping for something, but I wasn't sure they would do it in time.'

'They? The Heynai?' asked the princess.

'Yes. This is *their* doing, but it will not last forever. We have a few days or more now to prepare. We have to make the most of it. The war is still going to come and this city is where we have to make our stand, but at least now we can plan for it properly. I have to leave. I have to go and find the fourth stone we need to restore the box, so that we can use it to defeat King Vantrax. You must stay and lead our army, prepare them for the fight.'

Princess Zephany acknowledged Jake's words with a solitary nod of her head.

'So be it. I am glad. I do not like all of this uncertainty, Jake. And, I am so very tired of running. I seem to have been doing it all my life. It feels good to stand and fight, to know those days are behind me, one way or another. Whether I live or die here does not matter. I am content to take my chances, to stand with you and my people, come what may. I will not take one more step backwards, I promise you!'

'Yes, and we are all with you, princess. Though, that is all well and good, Jake,' stated Queen Bressial, as she strode over to join the group alongside Lord Castrad, 'but, what about *them*?' she asked, pointing to the haziness of the shield on the fields outside the city walls, and the hundreds of dark, ominous shadows that lurked menacingly behind it.

'Them? They're going nowhere for the time being, are they? Just keep a close eye on them and don't let your guard down. You have to place all of your trust in the spirits now. All of you. And pray that the shield holds!'

* * *

'Right then, we've no time to waste,' stated Jake.

It was now several minutes since the shield had appeared over the battlefield. The defenders of Te'oull had recovered from the shock of what had happened and the commanders had organised which sections would man the wall. The remainder of the Estian forces were sent to gain some much needed sleep.

Jake was in determined mood. Now that the immediate danger had passed and the Alliance army was seemingly safe from attack, he knew for himself what had to be done and he was anxious to begin. The fourth of the five stones needed to restore the box had to be secured if they were going to have any hope of defeating the powerful wizard they faced. His armies were far too numerous and strong to defeat without the power of the stones. They were comprised almost entirely of battle-hardened warriors and they were used to being victorious. The same could not be said of the rag-tag force of volunteers among the ranks of the Estian

Alliance, who were surely no match for such an awesome force if it came to a conventional battle. Only around half of their number had ever seen action, and those who *had* were aged and weary. Without the powers contained within the Heynai's chief weapon, whatever they might be, this war was a mismatch of epic proportions, a foregone conclusion some might say.

Jake gazed into the faces of the commanders who had surrounded him. Lord Caro, the Perosyan champion, was as usual calm and unflustered. He was a remarkable figure of a man; an ally in whom Jake and Zephany had supreme confidence and trust. But then, even more extraordinary to Jake as he stared into all of their eyes was the fact that, they *all* were!

Holy...! This whole thing is like something from a fantasy game, or a book about King Arthur. They're all heroes. All Sir Lancelots. Princess Zephany is amazing. She's the best leader and soldier I've ever heard about. Let's face it, she really kicks ass! Queen Bressial fought off almost an entire army outside Dassilliak, single-handed. She was wounded badly, but she's never once moaned about it. She could lead this army if she wanted to, and she knows it. Everyone knows it. But, she has enough humility and grace to let King Artrex. Then there's Lord Castrad, a knight without equal in my eyes. What hasn't he done? He saved King Artrex from certain death in the midst of battle, never mind what he did at the mines, and Heron Getracht... And what about Verastus, Brraall and Ben...? Flippin' heck, I'm surrounded by supermen. Err... and women... Superpeople then. Nah, as bad as things appear to be for us right now, with friends like these, we can't fail, can we? Can I?

An almighty surge of confidence swept through his entire body and his chest swelled with pride.

'Tien, it's time now. You and I have to leave. Two stones remain from the five we seek. It looks like we'll have to take the last one off King Vantrax. I can't see any other way. So, we'll cross that bridge if and when we get to it. Right now, let's make the most of the time the Heynai have given us. Tell us, where will we find the fourth stone?'

The old wizard shifted awkwardly as several heads and numerous sets of enquiring eyes turned towards him.

'Frah, yes, well, I am afraid that it is not going to be easy.'

Everybody immediately began to chuckle at the totally predictable, ludicrous statement. After a few moments, it was Lord Caro who aired their thoughts with extreme clarity.

'Ha, ha, ha... For the love of...! Get *on* with it, wizard, before we all die from old age!'

'Krr... yes, as you desire. We have to go to where very few have ever been, and even fewer have returned from. We must travel right into the heart of the enemy's lair.'

Lord Castrad sighed heavily. He was growing impatient and he was not in the mood for more riddles. 'Aghrast! Out with it, wizard! Whatever you have to say, it will not faze us now. Speak plainly, or do not speak at all.'

Tien's expression did not change as he looked at Jake.

'We journey to the home of the Thargws, to Eratur. The continent of Mynae lies far away, over the ocean and across another country besides. It is the only place I know for certain we will find a stone made from Eratian Ore, one large enough to take the place of that which is broken in any case.'

'You... You travel to *Mynae?*' snapped Princess Zephany, hardly daring to believe the absurdity of such a notion. 'You are truly insane! You have lost your mind, Tien. Old age has finally worn you down, I fear. Mynae is too great a distance to cover in the time you have and it is a lawless cesspit of murderous beasts. I would rather walk into the fires of Zsorcraum! Surely you are...?'

'Your Highness! Please?' interrupted Jake. 'I'm sorry, but it is not *you* who will be going there, it is Tien and I. The decision is not yours to make on this occasion. And if this is what is expected of me, I must go. I have no choice. Though, I don't understand, Tien? All the original stones you said were *Estian* gems? All five were mined here on Estia, in this land? Why must we now go to Mynae to find one?'

'Yes, Keeper, you are correct in your recollection. I did not lie to you. There were stones on Estia once, though Eratian Ore is called such because of its main point of origin. Our supplies were and are exhausted, but it is still mined there, in Eratur. Even in that country it is incredibly rare. Only a few pieces are found each year, alongside far less valuable stones. Few examples have been discovered elsewhere, but there have been the odd one or two and I was hoping to find another such gem. This rarity is the chief reason for its incredible value. The Thargws covet it above all other stones and it rarely leaves their domain. They control the only two mines in existence which continue to produce small but regular supplies. I know of no other place to find the replacement we seek.'

'I see. So, that's it then. Another mine raid it is,' said Jake.

'No,' Tien answered, abruptly. 'It is not as simple as that. The task is much harder this time. We cannot take on the Thargws as though they were any normal enemy. We would be doomed to fail against such a foe. You may be assured that they will guard the stones with their lives, and we will be lucky to leave with ours intact. Do not forget, Jake, Thargws are the greatest warriors we face. They are merciless, relentless...'

'Well, *what* then?' rasped a frustrated Princess Zephany. 'What are you saying? I apologise for my outburst before, I was wrong to voice it. Tell us exactly what you are proposing.'

'Yes, Tien,' added Jake, winking slightly at the young princess in a gesture of approval. 'What is it that's expected of me? Come on, out with it. What do I have to do?'

The old wizard's face lost all expression as he replied to the young Keeper in a matter of fact tone of voice.

'It is quite simple really. I... No, *we*, expect you to fulfill your destiny.'

'Charr! What does *that* mean?' enquired Lord Castrad.

Tien looked around them all, deliberately delaying his reply for dramatic effect.

'The home of the enemy plundered. The fire of life is tamed.
A place of evil torn asunder. The stone of hope reclaimed.'

'Frah! Riddles? Is that all you speak? We stand ready to fight the greatest battle ever waged in our entire history, and you bring us more riddles?' asked Caro, angrily.

'No! Not riddles, good knight, prophecies!' snapped Tien furiously in reply. 'These things I speak of were laid down in writing over a thousand years ago, when few had yet mastered the written word. It was foretold way before any of us were even born, including the Heynai! They are the teachings and predictions of wizards far greater than *any* who came before them, or since! And so far, they have *all* come true!'

The old wizard had never been so angry. His war-weary face was now bright red and his body was shaking all over. It shocked everyone to see him this way, to witness his strange overreaction.

'He's right!' said Jake, all of a sudden. '*Everything* he has said will happen since I met him, *has* happened. There's a lot more to it as well, I know there is. There are things he has neglected to mention along the way, for one reason or another. I'm hoping in time he will explain, but for now we just have to accept it, and go with the flow. So, if not the mines, what then?' he asked, having decided that this was not the time for a long drawn out discussion.

Tien breathed in and out twice, long and hard, in an attempt to cool his anger.

'The Thargw's greatest city. We head for the fortress city of Keralux.'

'Seriously? I have listened to what you have said, but the two of you are just going to stroll right into the homeland of the greatest warring nation on Mynae? You plan to knowingly walk into a nest of... Kraullars?' asked a seriously alarmed Lord Castrad. '*And*, I do not like to be the one to point this out to you, but exactly *how* do you plan on travelling there? It is way too far for the horses, even with their wings. And time is very much against you.'

All eyes turned once again to the wizard. But, to everyone's surprise, it was Jake who responded.

'Gellsorr!'

'What?' replied Princess Zephany, surprised. 'He is too far away from us now, Jake. He could be anywhere. How...?'

'I'll call to him. I'll ask him to help, just as I did on the mountain when we first met. I can do it.'

'Yes, alright Jake. Assuming you are successful and able to secure his help, you are still talking about undertaking the most dangerous of tasks. I have never heard of such a perilous assignment. For certain, it is a walk straight into the jaws of a revalkas, a one way journey to the afterlife. You might just as well lift that shield and take your chances with *us*, right here and now!' said the highly emotional princess.

Funny thing was though, despite her heartfelt objection and concern, the young heir to the Ruddite throne was feeling slightly envious of the young Keeper. She knew that she would be more than willing to undertake such a mission herself, if asked.

'Hmmn... Yes, I hear you, princess. I can't say that the thought of what we might meet out there thrills me. To be honest, I'd much rather be playing footy with my mates at this present moment in time, I can tell you. Or maybe watching the Villa thrash United from the Holte End. But, I'm here, aren't I? If this is what I have to do to go home and see my family again, then that's what's gonna happen. Everything we have worked for, everything we're tryin' to achieve, depends on this box,' Jake replied, patting the bag draped over his shoulder gently. 'It's *this* box of stones that's gonna save us, not me. You'll see, you'll *all* see in time. When we've defeated our enemies and won this war, you'll all realise that the Heynai sacrificed all they had for you, so that we could triumph over evil and bring everlasting peace to this land.'

Princess Zephany lowered her head a little in shame. 'Yes, we believe you, Jake. You know, at times, for all my schooling, I can be a fool. Words come far too easily to me. They flow from my lips before I have had chance to think. It is one of my greatest faults. Hopefully, age and experience will rectify the problem. Go then, we will remain behind to hold the enemy at bay. We will use whatever time we are granted to train our new recruits. Call for Gellsorr, Jake. Find us a stone. Use whatever powers you... Krr... Where *exactly* is the stone, Tien? You have neglected to mention that part I think?'

'Kah, yes, so I have. It is in the Thargw Emperor's crown. We will find him in the main palace no doubt.'

'The Thargw *Emperor*?! Ay raas, but this is worse than I

imagined. It is complete and utter madness!' stated Caro. 'Jake, you know me well enough by now, I am always up for a fight if there is one to be had, I shy away from no-one and nothing, but... Thargws choose their leaders by tried and tested means, by mortal combat. If he leads them, he is their finest, be of no doubt. Please, let me accompany you on this most treacherous quest?'

Jake shook his head firmly. 'No, Caro. Thanks all the same, mate, but there will not be room for you. Besides, you will be needed here, to protect the princess and organise the defences. Tien and I must go alone, and face whatever we find there.'

Tien nodded obediently. The old wizard had served many fine masters in his time and he knew right there and then that he would quite willingly give his life for this new Keeper. This boy. Though, he was rather hoping that it would not come to that. Not yet at least.

'Okay then,' the teenager began, his mind now firmly made up, 'I think it's time that *I* spoke to a dragon?'

Chapter 7
27th September – Varriann City – Perosya

Ben Brooker was busily wolfing down a huge plate of stewed rachtis and praells. Every now and then he stopped for a very brief moment in order to wash it down with some traag's milk, though the astonishing speed at which his mug was moving to and from his lips meant that he scarcely swallowed more than a mouthful at any one time. For Verastus, Brraall and Gellsorr this was a real education, and it was one they were thoroughly entertained by. All three were fascinated by Ben's frantic eating habits, though they were more amazed by the fact that the youngster was actually able to breathe at the same time. The new friends and allies looked at one another and smiled, content to see such joy and happiness again in the eyes of one so young. The misery and strife on their own world had deprived them all of such a sight for a very long time.

Ben was at first blissfully unaware that he had become the focus of attention. He was distracted by the task in hand and concentrating solely on the need to satisfy his hunger. However, he soon felt a mild burning sensation on his neck and he realised to his surprise that he was being watched. His eyes flicked upwards and he halted his spoon arm. Then, he gazed quickly at each of his comrades, unsure what to make of their sudden interest in him and his activities. Dropping the contents of his spoon onto his plate, with great difficulty he swallowed down the large piece of rachtis meat he had in his mouth. Then he wiped away the gravy from his lips, before responding to their wide-eyed stares.

'What? What you lot gawpin' at?' he asked, feeling a little embarrassed. 'Haven't you seen someone eat before? I'm starving.'

The others laughed gently. It was Verastus who replied for them all. He thought it best to do so diplomatically, so as not to upset the humiliated teenager even further.

'Ha, ha… Yes, Ben, we can see that for ourselves. It is something of a recurring theme with you, is it not? One of your most endearing traits, if I may say so?'

'Eh? Oh come on? You're avin' a laugh,' Ben replied, recovering in an instant. 'Most endearing? You're forgetting all about my charm and good looks. Anyway, I'm a growing lad, in I? I'm *supposed* to get loads of food, to keep my strength up. It's the way of the world. In fact, by rights, I *should* get *your* share as well! Ha, ha... So, mate, from now on you'll have to give me the food off your plate.'

'Ben!'

It was Gellsorr, the old dragon, who interrupted the youngster so abruptly. His raised voice was sharp, deep and calm. It carried with it a clear warning to all, instructing them in no uncertain terms that he had something vitally important to say.

Ben halted his sentence immediately and everyone remained silent. After a few seconds without further comment though, he began to grow impatient.

'What? What is it?' the teenager asked.

'Silence, please? Someone is trying to contact me. I can feel it.'

Gellsorr closed his huge eyelids and concentrated hard upon the faint noise he had heard in his mind. He couldn't quite hear what was being said at first, so he shifted his position and tried again. The others remained quiet and watched him as the voice grew gradually louder and clearer in his head.

'*...Gellsorr! Hear me, dragon. Listen to my words, please?! I am Jake West. I am the Keeper of the Stones, and I need your help!*'

The magnificent creature's giant eyes suddenly shot open in surprise.

'It... It is Jake!' he rasped.

'Jake?' cried an excited Ben. His heart began to race, pounding in his chest. 'Well? Don't waste time, shut your eyes again and talk to him!'

Gellsorr was a little taken aback by the youngster's sudden aggression. He shook his head slightly at him to let him know that he did not approve, before obeying the rather impudent suggestion and silently replying to Jake.

'*I am here, Keeper. I have not left you. We are all here, safe and well. Tell me, what is it you require me to do?*'

'*I... No, we, need a lift. Err... Sorry, we need you to take us to*

Mynae? The horses are too slow and I'm told that they wouldn't survive the journey. Listen, we have no time, Gellsorr. The fourth stone we seek is there. We must leave straight away. Right now!'

The mighty dragon's eyes opened once more. For the briefest of moments he caught sight of a rather pathetic figure standing before him, a desperate and worried young boy from Earth, a boy who was longing for news of his best friend, to hear for certain that he was unharmed. He shut his eyelids tightly again almost immediately, to respond to the Keeper's news.

'But Jake, what of Ben and the others? Who will protect them if I leave?'

'I'm sorry but we have no choice now. They will have to look after themselves. There's no other way. Only you can fly such a distance, in so short a space of time, and return us before the attack. The forces of King Vantrax are here, Gellsorr. They are at the gates to the city. We are about to fight the final battle but, with the Heynai's help, we have secured a little time before they can get to us.'

'I see. Then conversation is futile. I am coming to you, Jake. What do you want me to tell the others?'

'They are to journey south. They are to travel to the Kielth Mountains and beyond. Not far across the border with Siatol they will find an unguarded pass. Tien has informed me of it. It leads all the way to the northern wall of Te'oull. The Heynai have created a barrier through which no-one and nothing can pass, a hidden shield to protect us from harm. It is keeping King Vantrax' armies at bay for the time being. We are safe, but it will not last long.'

'A barrier?' asked Gellsorr. 'Then, how do I, how do we, pass through such an obstruction? We will be trapped in the same way as our enemy, by the very thing that is meant to save us?'

'No, you will not, I promise you. I am not meant to, but I will contact Sereq. I will ask him to create a gap in the shield, one large enough for you to slip through. I will also ask him to do the same again when the time is right, for Brraall and his people. Approaching from such an unlikely direction, they should be able to reach the city before the *creatures know they are there, especially if we can time it right, at night time?'*

'*Creatures? Graxoth?*' asked Gellsorr. His demeanor changed and his heart became heavy all of a sudden, full of dread and hatred.

'*Yes, and revalkas. We face an entire army of them now, hundreds. You will have to fly high so as not to be seen, for you will be seriously outnumbered if they spot you... And land from the south, out of sight, with the city walls to hide you.*'

'*I understand, Keeper. Everything will be as you ask. I am leaving now. I should be with you soon.*'

'*Great! Thanks Gellsorr. With you on our side, this ridiculous plan might just work.*'

The ancient dragon opened his eyes again. A sizeable crowd had now gathered around him. In the centre of them all, was Ben. He looked like a lost child at a fairground, waiting anxiously to see if his mummy or daddy had come to collect him.

'Well? Come on then! Spill the beans,' he yelled.

Verastus shook his head. 'Raart, I will never understand the way you speak, Ben. I know you mean no harm, but please be advised that there are some in this realm who will take great offence. You are fortunate that we have come to understand that you mean no disrespect. Srr... I believe he means, tell us what was said?'

'Kah, yes. I will explain everything as quickly as I can. But then, I must leave. You have to let me go and help Jake. He needs me,' replied Gellsorr.

All eyes turned towards Ben. Everyone seemed to be expecting the youngster to voice a strong objection, or at least comment upon the dragon's statement with a heavily sarcastic repost. But, to their surprise, Ben Brooker said nothing.

* * *

The opening to the cave in the Kielth Mountains was illuminated by a strange light. Sereq and the rest of the aged spirits were concentrating hard on maintaining the power of the protective shield. The incredible focus and energy-sapping mind control techniques required to sustain it were taking their toll upon their reformed bodies. Beads of sweat were once again trickling down their brows and their hands and legs had begun to shake. An orange glow radiated from each. Every now and then, the spirit's faces would transform back into the horrid mess of flesh and bone that had scared Jake when they first met. For the Heynai, it was a clear sign that their powers were diminishing. And if they were fading so rapidly, how long could they possibly hope to keep the screen intact?

Sereq noticed the change first. His powers appeared to be greater than the others though and as yet he was not affected. The shield was holding, for now. He had recovered his faith in his fellow spirits. He was confident they would be able to withstand the relentless onslaught of pain and weariness he knew lay ahead, for several days if needed.

Everything will be fine, he thought, *just so long as nothing interrupts our thoughts and deflects our powers away from the shield.*

'Sereq!'

The leader of the Heynai was suddenly hailed. He was caught completely off-guard by it, astonished and almost overcome with shock. This was the last thing they needed, but he recognised the voice inside his mind immediately. It was Jake's and it had sounded so intensely that he knew he could not ignore it. Desperation had echoed in that one word for far longer than it ought, leading Sereq to the instant and inescapable conclusion that something had gone drastically wrong.

'*Jake! What is it? Why do you ignore my instructions and contact me now? Be very quick, Jake. Every second you distract me is a hazardous one!*'

'*I'm sorry, Sereq, there was no other way. I need you to create a hole in the wall, to let Gellsorr through to us? We need him to take us to Mynae, to find and claim the fourth stone.*'

Sereq cringed in agony as a searing burst of intense heat seemed to almost rip his mind apart.

'Raarrgghh!!!'

He screamed out loud, barely able to stand the hurt. Finally, after a second or two, it relented a little and he was able to think.

'*Frah! Very well, Jake, if we must. It will be as you ask, though it* will seriously weaken the shield for a time and King Vantrax will know of it. He will feel it.'

'It can't be helped. Good,' replied Jake. 'But, there's something else; in a day or so, you will have to create a much larger hole, one big enough for Brraall and his people to go through?'

'Jake! You realise of course that what you ask of us now could seal your fate?! If we disrupt this spell for such a time, to that extent, there is no guarantee at all that we will be able to restore it! And, while the shield is down, our people will have no protection at all from attack. They will be completely at the mercy of the wizard and his beasts.'

'Yes, I thought it might be a little risky. Oh well, it's one worth taking. This is the only way I can see to achieve our aims. I will not abandon Ben and the friends he has with him. Besides, we need all the help we can get.'

'Ay raas, but you are a stubborn one, Keeper.'

'Eh? Yes, I suppose I am. I get that from my mum. Now, I've made my decision. Do you understand what you have to do?' Jake asked, with an unmistakable air of authority.

'Yes, Jake. You are in command of everything now. The fate of this world and others is in your hands. Now go! Leave us to our work and do not speak to us again. We have fulfilled our promise to you and our people, done all we can do. I pray that we have given you hope, a small chance of achieving victory.'

'Okay, Sereq. Goodbye, again. When the time comes and the shield is lowered, we'll just have to hope that the enemy doesn't realise what we're doing.'

* * *

In the great palace at Dassilliak, King Vantrax was sitting on a very large and elegant chair. He was surrounded by warriors and servants who were tending to his every whim. Chief amongst these was Nytig. The king's personal slave was rushing around as fast as his deformed body would allow, fetching and carrying drink and food for his master, whilst at the same time attempting to remain as far away from Sawdon as he could. The Thargw gerada was seething with impatience. He wanted to depart

Dassilliak and chase his enemy down without delay. He knew the force which had been dispatched was not nearly enough to win a full-scale battle. Everything was prepared now for the pursuit. He was waiting only for the king's orders and Vantrax was just about to give them, but suddenly the doors to the large room opened and in strode the newly revived Melissa.

The Sebantan princess had been caught by the dragon's beam on the fields outside the city. She had been turned instantly into black stone, as Gellsorr's timely intervention saved the lives of Ben, Brraall, Verastus and all the tribal warriors. King Vantrax had used the Lichtus stone to successfully reverse the powerful spell. But, the energy it took to overturn the effects of such a weapon, to breathe life once again into an inanimate object, had very nearly destroyed him. The Lichtus itself had amazingly suffered no lasting damage. The king knew however, that he would never be strong enough to perform such an extraordinary feat again, not without the Keeper's stones or placing his own life in extreme jeopardy. If things remained the same, his many warriors who had fallen at the battle were therefore doomed to remain on the fields of Dassilliak, encased in stone for all eternity. And now, the evil wizard also knew that the dragon possessed at least one weapon he could not counter. It did not unduly concern him though. He was convinced that his invincible army of revalkas and graxoth were more than enough to take care of a solitary dragon.

'Kah, Melissa,' stated the king, as he caught sight of his favoured warrior. The issuing of orders temporarily left his thoughts as the Sebantan beauty approached, much to Sawdon's further aggravation.

'My liege, a thousand apologies for my unavoidable absence. You will be surprised just how tiring death can be,' said the female warrior with a smile.

The evil wizard laughed a little. 'Ha, ha…You are forgiven. Come, Melissa, let me look at you. You seem to bear no visible scars from your ordeal? You are unhurt I take it, and fully recovered?'

'Yes sire,' replied Melissa. 'Thank you, for everything. Now, I am of a mind to take me some revenge! Tell me, what have I missed?'

Sawdon stepped forward purposefully. 'You, *Sebantan*, have missed the *war!*' he roared. He moved to confront her but halted when King Vantrax raised his hand to stop him.

'That is *enough*, Sawdon! We have no time for this. We must concentrate our efforts on…'

The king was suddenly interrupted in mid conversation by an incredibly sharp pain in his chest. It was coming from his heart and the agony was excruciating. He clasped his hand tightly to it as his face was immediately drained of all colour.

'Sire?! What is it? Are you hurt?' asked Sawdon.

He rushed to his leader's side, along with Melissa and Nytig. King Vantrax said nothing. He was in shock, unable to do anything. However, the astonishing pain rapidly diminished as quickly as it had appeared and soon, it was gone altogether. Once he had recovered himself, Vantrax began searching his mind for answers, trying desperately to understand what had just happened.

What does it mean? Where did it come from?

No answers came. The evil wizard was so concerned that he made the immediate decision to use the Lichtus once more, even though he was fully aware of the risks that came with such a decision. He moved everyone aside to give himself some space to work with.

'Treibe jasskul zekrath greitre henniann mulad.'

A vision suddenly appeared out of nowhere. King Vantrax was the only one who could see it. He watched avidly as he saw his army of flying creatures outside the city of Te'oull. He was alarmed and annoyed to see that they were trapped behind some sort of shield. The blood in his veins began to boil. Then, he saw the dragon!

The barrier which had stopped his aerial armada was lowered for a short time to let the creature pass through. Vantrax realised instantly that the enormous power and energy needed to raise and lower such a shield *had* to be the source of his pain. He almost spoke to his warriors but the vision continued. Next, he saw Jake and Tien climb onto the dragon's back. It soared into the air and they flew off into the distance, before the vision disappeared and he was once again looking at the concerned stares of his followers.

'Sire, what is it? What ails you so?' hissed Nytig, feigning genuine concern as best he could. He raised a goblet of water up to his master's lips as he spoke but Vantrax knocked the chalice away with one almighty, furious sweep of his arm. He leapt to his feet.

'Raarrr!!!' he yelled at the top of his voice. 'Stop your fussing. All of you!'

'Yes, sire, of course. We are all concerned for you, that is all. What *was* that?' asked Melissa.

The king looked around the room before gazing straight into the Sebantan princess' eyes. 'I have seen... something.'

'What? What have you seen, sire?' Sawdon enquired.

Vantrax turned his head slowly to face his most trusted gerada.

'Our army of Zsorcraum is trapped. Those I raised are caught behind a magical wall of some description. There is no rush for us to join them now, Sawdon. They cannot break through to the city and engage the enemy.'

'What?!' replied the two warriors in unison, jumping forward and clenching their fists in identical displays of anger and dismay.

'Get back! I share your disappointment. It is what it is!' barked King Vantrax. 'This is not the work of wizards though,' he added. 'No, it is something far greater, not of this realm, this life.'

'A wall? Then, what of the rebels, the Keeper? What of your brother?' asked Sawdon.

King Vantrax reacted angrily. 'I have told you before and for the very last time that I have *no* brother!' he roared. 'As far as I know, the one you speak of is within those city walls, waiting for me to attack. There have been unconfirmed reports but... Te'oull is fated to be the place for the battle that will decide our destiny, I know it. It has been delayed, that is all. They have nowhere left to run. It *will* happen, and it will be there. I am certain of it.'

'Forgive me sire, but, how can you be so sure?' asked Melissa.

'The pain I felt just now was worse than any I have ever endured. It was a break in the energy of that shield, a tear in its fabric. It has to be.

The dragon was allowed through by those who maintain its power. They aid the Keeper, though I do not know to what end and for what purpose. Do you not see? If *I* felt such pain, then those who have created this force of magic will have felt it too. Only, *their* agony must surely be ten times greater than mine? Yes, I can sense it! They are struggling to hold on. They are suffering, trying to eke out every second they can before we attack, in one last gamble on which they risk everything. They will not be able to keep this wall of theirs intact for too much longer. No-one is that strong. It *will* collapse, and when it does, we will be there in such numbers that they will be destroyed once and for all!'

'Yes, sire,' stated Sawdon, 'it will be as you say no doubt. Though, what of the dragon and the Keeper? Where do you suppose they are going? And what of the rest of their army, the other boy?'

Vantrax rubbed the hairs on his chin as he pondered the questions. Eventually, he replied.

'The destination and intent of the Keeper is a serious concern. I do not know where they are heading. They appeared to be going south. It has to be something to do with the stones. But, seeing as we have no idea which stone they seek, we can take no action for the moment against them. We can only deal with what we know. As for the other boy, my graxoth and revalkas should have taken care of him by now. Besides, once we break through to Te'oull and kill anyone that stands in our way, nothing else will matter. Without an army, what can the boy do?'

Sawdon glanced briefly at Melissa. The Thargw was not happy. He had way too many questions and he knew there were too many loose ends and unknowns to be so confident. Sawdon liked to deal with facts, only facts. The great unknown was one of the few things that unnerved him.

Melissa shared his feelings but, ever the diplomat, she humoured her king.

'Once again we stand on the threshold of a great victory. Your armies are yours to command sire. What are your orders?'

Vantrax nodded smugly and replied. 'As stated, we are in no hurry now. However, we will air on the side of caution nevertheless. Sawdon will go with the entire army to Te'oull. You and I will remain here with my Personal Guard. We will follow in the morning, once we are both rested. When the wall fails, the enemy will feel the full force of my vengeance. The city of Te'oull will be wiped from the map. I am determined that no-one and nothing will survive this time. I will raise it to the ground and this Keeper of theirs will have no army to call upon. Just like the Estians, he will be crushed, never to plague us again!'

Chapter 8
Dusk – 27th September – The City of Te'oull – Siatol

Jake and Tien climbed onto Gellsorr's lowered neck. The flight from Varriann city had taken the mighty dragon a little over two hours to complete. He had covered the considerable distance in a fraction of the time it would have taken an army to march and he was far faster than the flying horses would have been. As he neared Te'oull, Gellsorr circled high around the city and approached from the south as instructed by Jake. He landed in the main square without being spotted by the enemy, who thankfully remained completely unaware of his arrival. A crowd of enthralled onlookers immediately gathered around him. Apart from those warriors and civillians present at the Battle of Dassilliak, no-one had ever seen a live dragon before on Estia. The most anyone knew about the magnificent creatures from legend were the descriptions contained in the stories passed down through word of mouth by previous generations, or snippets from fairy tales and books which relayed in dramatic prose their crucial role in Estia's turbulent history. Dragons were the stuff of myths and folklore for most on Estia and yet, a very real, very large, living and breathing beast was now standing before them. The defenders of Te'oull took great heart from the fact that he had come at their hour of need and was ready and willing to fight by their side. As awe-inspiring as the sight may have been for the many Estians packed into the square however, Jake decided quickly that they had no time for pleasantries. He immediately made his goodbyes and invited Tien to join him.

'Right then,' the young Keeper said, as soon as the wizard was settled in behind him, '*this* oughta be a blast!' Tien made to respond to yet another strange and unfamiliar statement, but Jake continued before he had the chance. 'Tell you what, if I take nothing else away from this incredible experience, this whole life-changing dream I seem to be living, I'm determined that I'm *really* gonna enjoy this!'

Tien could not see it, but ahead of him Jake West's eyes were on fire. He was suddenly alive with anticipation and his young and eager face was beaming at the prospect of what was about to come. He was taking another wild ride into the realms of the unknown. *This* was an excursion to rival anything he had done before, including travelling through the light. He couldn't be more excited. His smile widened even further when he felt Gellsorr chuckle slightly beneath him, in response to his youthful exuberance.

'Oh yeah,' Jake added, feeling like a kid again and loving every minute of it, 'Alton Towers theme park's got *nothing* on this! Ha, ha… I only wish my mates could see me now!'

The old wizard shook his head in disbelief, barely able to believe the Keeper's mood, given their current predicament. But, he soon decided that actually, he was feeling rather pleased to see some boyish enthusiasm return in Jake, if only for a fleeting moment or two. This whole new world for him, loaded with the tremendous burden of responsibility he was now shouldering, had been thrust upon the teenager without warning or choice. He had been left all of a sudden devoid of options; Jake could not object to it, or refuse the honour bestowed upon him, not really. And as far as Tien was concerned, he had dealt with it all superbly, despite his immaturity at times which often riled the old wizard. The youngster had earned the right to have a little fun if he could.

Still, though he had no wish at all to ruin the moment, Tien knew that he was there to guide him and felt obliged to point out the obvious.

'Jake, we are about to head for the very heart of our enemy's lands. In reality, we have very little hope of success. We have no plan to speak of, as far as I know? And in all probability we are journeying to our deaths. It is good to see you smiling again. However, I do not understand? I fail to see how any of this could have escaped your attention?'

Jake's expression did not alter. His smile was as wide as ever as he turned his head to reply over his shoulder.

'Yeah, I know all of that, of course I do. But, *come on?* Lighten up, will you? Look, if we're about to kick the bucket as you say, if we're gonna pop our clogs and become worm food, can you *seriously* think of a better way to go?'

Tien was unable to respond for he had no time. Realising the urgency of their mission, Gellsorr decided to leave. His huge and powerful wings unfurled without warning. They beat rapidly and the old dragon lurched forward, almost unseating his two passengers with the speed of his movement, who were left clinging onto his neck for dear life. He soared swiftly into the sunlit sky before banking immediately and heading south, in another manoeuvre which almost flung the Keeper and his guide to their deaths on the ground below. They managed to hold on somehow and the dragon headed away from the city, towards the Fetril Sea and the violent continent of Mynae which lay beyond.

They travelled for the remainder of that day and into the night. The lush green valleys of Estia beneath them soon gave way to the rough, turbulent waters of the channel which divided the two contrasting lands. At one point in the darkness, Jake began to feel very tired, exhausted in fact. Though he knew it was extremely dangerous to fall asleep in his current plight, he just couldn't help himself and his eyes began to close. He fought hard and struggled gamely to stay awake. Luckily for him, Tien somehow sensed what was happening. He performed a vitality spell he had learned from the Heynai and the young boy was immediately revived. His mind and body felt fresh once more, leaving him able to concentrate solely on the task in hand.

As they crossed into Mynae and flew low over the country of Falor, a bright and clear moon was shining, lighting up the incredible landscape below. Verastus' homeland was a mixture of baron plains and overpopulated cities, built on rough, scorched earth. It was punctuated here and there by vast mountain ranges with incredibly high peaks. These snow-covered summits had to be negotiated in flight, either by going round or by flying over them if they could. The temperature fluctuated rapidly. When they were over the plains it was pleasantly warm but the air cooled severely when approaching the mountains, so much so that it fell to well below freezing in what seemed like a matter of seconds. Jake would probably have died from exposure if it were not for another of Tien's spells.

Daylight sneaked up on them much faster than expected and as they approached the border with Eratur the sun had already risen. This was the homeland of the Thargws and Hybraddan, and it was their final destination. It was a harsh, unforgiving place. The landscape consisted entirely of rock and blackened soil. The icy wind was almost unbearable, in spite of Tien's magic. It cut right through Jake and seemed almost to enter his bones.

Eratur looked devoid of life at first glance. Closer inspection however revealed numerous small conurbations of caves and huts. They were littered everywhere, though most were obviously built to be concealed from the view of anyone at ground level.

Gellsorr continued flying for another hour or more, bypassing several cities, as well as towns of all shapes and sizes. At last, he spied his destination; a small mountain range at the foot of which was a much larger metropolis, protected on all sides by a vast wall of grey rock. It was a daunting, intimidating sight to behold. He began to descend slowly and landed behind a small hill to remain obscured from sight. Once on the ground, he lowered his neck and Jake and Tien dismounted quickly.

'We have done well to arrive safely, Keeper. The city you saw before us is Kerralux. The northern part of Eratur which we have passed through is sparsely populated. Beyond this point however, their warriors live in large numbers, in cities such as this, and in many smaller dwellings. Now, I have done as you asked, tell me your plan,' said the dragon.

Jake looked at each of the expectant faces of his new friends.

'Hmmn... Yes, a plan. I suppose it *would* be a good idea to have one of those, eh? No, I can't do it like Ben. Alright, calm down, I was only kidding. Listen in... It's almost midday I reckon. If we go marching in there now, we'll be easily spotted and killed for sure. There's way too many of them for that. We'll just have to wait for darkness. Then you'll have to glide over the wall as silently as you can and land us right next to the palace. If we're lucky, we won't be seen or heard, and we'll go from there?'

Gellsorr was astounded by the simplicity of such a notion. He was also a little disappointed. He looked towards the wizard, expecting him to say something, but Tien remained quiet and showed no sign at all that he was going to.

'I... How...? I... I admit to being taken by surprise, Jake. You mean to tell me that your *only* plan is to trust to luck?'

'Err... yeah,' replied the teenage Keeper. 'Well, no, actually, that's not quite true. I'm *hoping* we'll be lucky, of course I am. But, it's more accurate to say that I'm *trusting* in you and Tien.'

*　　*　　*

At Te'oull on the twenty-eighth of September volunteers of all shapes, sizes, creed and capability continued to pour into the southern gates. As they did, they passed by the throngs of civillians and non-combatants who were heading the other way, hoping to avoid the forthcoming battle and escape the enemy. These were led by Eyatrav, Yelena and most of the Juyen, and they left with Princess Zephany's blessing. The young warrior and her Perosyan champion, Caro, had formed a collection point in the main square for all those who wanted to fight. Here, the new arrivals were quickly assessed by army captains for their fighting ability and experience, before being assigned their new positions in the defence of the city. The princess had taken a keen interest in what was happening and she remained close by. When there was a brief lull in activity she spoke to Caro about their situation, seeking his counsel.

'By some miracle, our numbers continue to grow. But, what do you make of our new army, Caro? Can they fight?'

The veteran knight was not one for speaking anything other than the truth.

'Princess, they are *all* volunteers. They have not been coerced. They are here for you, of their own free will. I would take ten such warriors into battle with me over a hundred slaves any day. Though, to answer your question as you would like; there are many among them who have been raised like us, with sword, bow and spear in hand. We are fortunate to have them. There are also farmers, tailors, blacksmiths and saddlers in their ranks. It is yet to be seen how effective they will be in battle, but I do not believe we are in the position to be anything other than grateful? We must welcome them all with open arms and hope that we are allowed the time to train them.'

Zephany laughed at having to be reminded of a few home truths by her sworn protector. She slapped Caro on his back in a surprisingly warm show of affection.

'Ha, ha... Indeed, my friend, well spoken. What would I do without you? Thank you. Welcome!' she cried, to the crowd of fresh volunteers who now approached their position. 'You are all very welcome here! *We* are the Estian Alliance, and *this* is Te'oull, the chosen site for our stand against all those who would seek to enslave or destroy us. Fight well, and this is a story you will relay with pride in years to come!'

Lord Caro's attention was drawn suddenly towards one of the new arrivals. She looked totally and utterly out of place. He eyed her up and down, unsure what to make of her.

'Srr... you are of course as welcome as anyone here, madam. Though, forgive me, I have to ask, what is it you believe you can do for us?'

It soon became clear that Princess Zephany was equally as surprised and bemused. She looked down upon the tired and worn-out features of the old lady. Both warriors could not help but notice the scars on her face, barely hidden in amongst the many wrinkles which covered it completely. Her clothes were nothing more than rags. Shredded and faded, they looked as though they were about to fall off at any point.

'Tell us, why do you come here?' Zephany asked, softly.

The old peasant lifted her head slowly to reveal two piercingly blue eyes. They were full of kindness, even though they seemed to carry within them a lifetime of pain and anguish.

'I am addressing the princess from Rhuaddan, am I not? You *are* the Leader of the Alliance? Good, I have found you at last. I... I seek the Keeper. The one who claims that title,' she replied, with more emotion echoing in her words than most experience in a whole lifetime.

* * *

It was the middle of the night now in Kerralux. The great Thargw city was illuminated only by moonlight and a few flamed torches littered here and there to help the sentries find their way around. The inhabitants had no reason to expect an attack on their heavily-fortified capital, so a standing guard comprised of only of older Thargw warriors, the lucky few who had lived long enough to earn the honour of manning the walls, protected them.

With Jake and Tien riding upon his back Gellsorr flew high over the city using his superior eyesight to reconnoitre its defences before choosing the best place to land. Then, his wings stopped beating and he glided gently and silently down to an open patch of ground which lay just outside the city palace. He immediately made for the largest shaded area he could find, the darkest corner, where he was confident they would not be seen. It was not far from the palace doors and he allowed his passengers to dismount.

'Okay,' hissed Jake, 'so far, so good. Me and Tien are going in. Gellsorr, you stay here and protect this entrance. Try to remain undetected if you can. If anything goes wrong, save yourself. And help the others at Te'oull.'

'Do not concern yourself, Jake. I will be here when you return. You need have no fear on that account.'

Jake smiled at the dragon, scarcely able to believe the absurdity of what he was doing. He gestured to Tien for him to follow. At the large wooden door to the palace the old wizard performed yet another of his spells. He opened the lock with a single wave of his hand and they both disappeared inside. The door was shut silently behind them. Tien began to chant the same spell he had used in the vault at Ilin-Seatt, using his magic to search for the whereabouts of the Eratian Ore.

'Enuussrialle frettureieste hechniarr eratore.'

Jake looked anxiously at him once he had finished.

'Well? Did it work?'

'Yes,' Tien replied. 'Come, it is this way, I can sense it,' he added, pointing down the long corridor and up the stairs. They crept silently along the magnificent hallways until they reached the doors to a very large chamber.

'Here, this must be the room of the Thargw emperor,' said the wizard.

Jake's heart was pounding furiously now, even though he felt as calm as ever. 'So, what we waiting for? Open it, and let's get that stone.'

Tien unlocked the door, being careful not to make a sound. He pushed it ajar, but it suddenly creaked loudly. Their hearts leapt into their mouths and Jake immediately drew his sword, expecting to be confronted by guards at any moment.

Seconds later though, no-one had responded to the noise they made and the two raiders breathed a huge sigh of relief. They entered the room. It was exceedingly grand, lavishly decorated with valuable trinkets and cloths. In the centre was a huge bed and, lying on top and snoring so loudly that the very foundations seemed to be shaking, was the largest Thargw warrior either of them had ever seen. He was colossal and even the old wizard felt a shiver run down his spine at the fearsome sight.

Jake though, had only one thing on his mind. He scanned the room quickly with his eyes, looking for the emperor's crown and the precious stone they had come to collect.

'There it is!' the youngster whispered, excitedly.

It was lying on a chair beside the emperor's bed. Jake went to fetch it, but Tien held his arm and placed a finger to his lips, stressing the need for stealth. Another spell was performed and the crown lifted into the air. Then, it floated over to them slowly and silently. Jake caught it gratefully and he wasted no time in using his sword to prise the stone free. He placed it in his bag and then lay the crown down on the floor.

'Come on, we're done here,' he said, happily.

Tien nodded to acknowledge the order. 'For once, Jake, I am in complete agreement with you.' They crept away quietly and made for the exit.

Outside the palace, Gellsorr was waiting patiently in the darkness. His huge frame was partially hidden in the shadows thrown by the palace walls. He was confident he could remain there unseen for as long as it took. However, Thargw warriors possess excellent hearing and eyesight. Though the direction of his approach had enabled the dragon to avoid detection in the initial phase of the raid, a sharp-eyed lookout on the wall had spotted something peculiar and decided to investigate. Against the backdrop of the moonlit sky, the warrior could see a darker mist. It was a vapor of some sort and it was rising steadily from the walls of the palace.

The smoke was only slight, but it was rising gently from the dragon's nostrils and, unbeknown to Gellsorr, every single breath he took was betraying his position to the enemy.

The ancient dragon saw nothing untoward. He remained concealed, unaware that two experienced Thargw warriors were descending slowly down the stairs to the wall, intending to circle around and approach from both sides of his current position. The soldiers used the buildings as cover. Soon, they were staring from only yards away at the unbelievable sight of a fully grown dragon. Both carried Thargw spears and they launched them at the unsuspecting creature before he had time to react.

Gellsorr never knew what hit him. The first thing he felt was a thunderous jolt as a spear tip pierced his skin and tore into his chest. It was followed almost immediately by a second, far more deadly strike, which did him lasting damage. The spear came more from the side this time and it pinned his wing so that he could not fly. Moreover, the incredible force of the throw caused the tip of the shaft to lodge deep within his heart. He roared in pain, a resounding cry of agony that was so loud it seemed the whole of Mynae and Estia must surely have heard it. The city of Kerralux appeared to shake and vibrate with the unbelievable din. It was fully awake now and Gellsorr knew for certain that more Thargws would be coming for him.

Jake and Tien were almost at the door when they heard the awful noise. It stopped them in their tracks. A look of complete horror overcame them as they realised immediately what it meant.

'Gellsorr! Quick, we have to help him!' cried Jake.

They raced outside just in time to witness the ancient dragon taking his vengeance upon his two attackers. The Thargw assailants were incinerated by his fire. Then, he trained his other weapon upon the warriors who manned the wall, using his eyes to turn them all into black stone. This afforded Jake and Tien the brief opportunity to approach him, before the warriors of Kerralux could respond in force to the dragon's cry.

'Gellsorr, you're hurt! How bad is it?' asked Jake.

The old dragon knew his time had come. The wound to his heart was a mortal blow and he could no longer fly. His wing was damaged beyond repair, beyond healing. Even if the spear could be removed, he would not be able to take the others to safety.

'It is as bad as bad can be, Jake,' he replied. 'You *must* save yourselves. I cannot aid you now. They will be here very soon, in great numbers, to finish me.'

'No. We can't!'

'Go! You *have* to!' insisted the dragon. 'There is no other way. Take this stone and do all you can for your people, for Estia.'

Gellsorr gave the stone to the wizard, knowing full well that without it, without his life source, he was doomed. Tien thanked him quickly for his supreme sacrifice and turned to Jake.

'He is right, we have to go. We have no way of leaving this place now, but we cannot be captured. Thargws do not treat their prisoners well.'

Jake's eyes were brimming with tears. He felt totally calm, but inside, he knew his heart was breaking.

'Yes, I know. I'm sorry, Gellsorr. I'm sorry it's ended like this.'

'No need for words. I made my choices. Go!'

The two raiders ran for their lives. They hadn't gone far when they were confronted by a group of three Thargw warriors. Jake immediately drew his sword and engaged them. Tien sensed that his own intervention might not be needed and he took a step backwards. Enraged by the loss of Gellsorr, the young Keeper was on fire. Every single nerve in his body was alive. His actions were so swift and ferocious that the three beasts surrounding him could not keep up, despite their own skill and speed. Jake was ducking, diving, weaving and thrusting his sword so swiftly that his actions seem to blur into one. Before long, all three warriors lay dead on the ground and the two fugitives had resumed their flight. Soon, they had disappeared into the darkness of the city streets.

They stayed in the shadows as much as possible, moving swiftly away from the palace and into the more densely populated zones, where a thousand and one hiding places presented themselves. Thargw warriors and civilians alike appeared all around them, but somehow they managed to stay hidden as the throngs of angry beasts made their way to the palace square, where the incredible roar had sounded.

Jake led Tien into a quiet alleyway. The complete darkness and lack of life offered brief sanctuary and they stopped to catch their breath. Then, they heard the unmistakable sound of an enormous fight. The roars and screams were carried on the cool night air. It seemed to last for ages, though in reality it was no more than a few minutes. As they listened and watched the sky, every now and then it was lit up by flame. Finally, they heard the most awful cry; a dragon's death roar. Estia and Mynae had not heard it's like for hundreds of years. Piercing, intense and astonishingly severe, it resonated way above anything they had ever known.

Gellsorr had fought valiantly until his last ounce of strength had vanished. He had taken many Thargws with him to the afterlife. Though his energy had started diminishing as soon as the stone had left his grasp, he had continued to fire his beam of light and breathe his fire, even as a multitude of arrows and spears peppered his stricken body. His final cry, his last almighty roar in life, was heard far and wide, across the land.

The sole remaining dragon on Estia, the greatest living ally the Keeper had, was dead. Jake and Tien were lost and on the run in their enemy's capital. The whole city was now awake and determined to find the rest of the attackers who, they soon found out, had been spotted running away from the palace square in the darkness. It seemed to both Tien and Jake that the astonishing luck they had enjoyed to date, had *finally* run out.

Chapter 9
28th September – The City of Dassilliak – Perosya

Sawdon had already departed Dassilliak for Te'oull taking with him every warrior he could muster. Only the elite soldiers of King Vantrax' Personal Guard remained within the city walls now, besides the king himself, his servant, Nytig, and his Sebantan warrior, Melissa. The burned-out ruins told a wretched tale. Dassilliak was nothing more than the remains of an enormous ghost town, laid to waste. Inside the palace, which had somehow managed to survive virtually intact, the vast corridors and chambers that had been so full of life, now echoed with emptiness. The only room buzzing with activity was the Throne Room, where the evil wizard and his tiny entourage were entertaining themselves by devouring the food and drink they had salvaged.

In one small guest quarter situated towards the rear of the palace however, totally unbeknown to his evil brother, the severely wounded King Artrex lay recovering from wounds, still watched over and protected by his ever-faithful friend and companion, the spirit of Gerada Knesh Corian. Artrex had somehow survived injuries which would have easily killed lesser men. Amazingly, he was fully conscious and a little of his strength had returned.

'They have already begun the pursuit of our friends, my king. Sawdon leads their forces and they march on Te'oull. Though, for some reason, Vantrax and his guards have not accompanied them,' stated Knesh.

King Artrex was surprised by this news and he immediately sat upright. A searing pain in his arm and shoulder burned fiercely and almost made him faint. After a short pause to collect himself, he stood up gingerly and struggled to remain upright, as his incredibly weak legs almost gave way beneath him. A torrent of blood rushed to his healing wounds, bringing even further pain and agony. However, he refused to yield to it and bore it bravely. The Ruddite king was still weak, too weak, but his mind just would not accept the limitations imposed by his current condition. He tried to lift his sword with his good arm. He could barely hold it. The blade shook furiously as it travelled upwards no more than a few inches. The reality of their situation seemed completely lost on him in his determined and resolute frame of mind.

'My brother remains, you say? Good! With his entire army gone and with the element of surprise I presume we still enjoy, given the lack of warriors that seem to be searching for us, now is the *perfect* time to attack. I shall kill him right here and take his stone!'

Though he shared his king's desire to see the wizard dead, Gerada Knesh Corian knew immediately that what his friend proposed was impossible. Even a fit and able-bodied warrior would struggle to evade the king's Personal Guard, and Artrex could hardly walk.

'Frah! If only we could make it so. Look at us sire. You are too badly wounded. You *should* be dead. And I actually *am*! In our existing state, a small child with a wooden toy could best us. It grieves me to say it to you, but I am unable to fight this time. Raar!!!' he roared in anger and frustration.

'Sshhh! Knesh!' hissed the king. 'Be quiet, lest we be heard! If we are discovered, we will be...'

'There!' interrupted the Ruddite commander, smiling. 'Right there! *That* is the king I have served and loved all these years. Welcome back, your majesty.'

King Artrex' expression of real concern from moments before changed almost immediately to a friendly acknowledgement of Knesh's sentiment.

'Tuh. Yes, thank you. I am thinking clearly now. So, seeing as how I have risen from the path to the afterlife and am now on the road to recovery, we have to find a way to leave this wretched place and join with our army. We will be discovered sooner or later if we stay here, and I will not do nothing while others fight in my place. That is not my way.'

'Yes, sire, my thoughts entirely. I will lead the way for you. Sheathe your sword. You will have no need of it, I promise. I will use my new powers to clear our path.'

'What? How?' asked the king.

'I will deflect attention away from our flight. Those warriors who guard the exits and hallways will be drawn to other areas, allowing us to pass.'

'Koh, you can actually do that? Excellent! Then, let us go without delay. It is a long way to Te'oull.'

'Krmmn... You cannot walk far so we shall need a horse. I will secure one from the stables.'

'Another of your tricks?'

'A mind technique that is quite effective on animals, learnt from the Heynai but not yet used in anger.'

'I see. Even more impressive. Still, Te'oull is too far away. The battle will surely be over before we arrive?' said Artrex, his voice low but full of unease.

'No, my liege. King Vantrax' army of assassins will be delayed from completing their victory, by the spirits. They work for us once more. We will reach the battle in time to play our part, I assure you.'

'Grar! Excellent! Srr... What exactly do you mean by, *our part?*'

'You are a vital piece of this puzzle, one without whom it is incomplete, and cannot be solved. The Heynai have stated that there can be no victory without you, no lasting resolution.'

'Really? You know all that for certain?' asked the king. Knesh nodded once in reply. 'Then I am glad to play my part, whatever is asked of me. And, I would admit this only to you, Knesh; I am all of a sudden afraid. Strange, that I who have fought so many wars and lived the life I have, should feel that now? I expect it is fear of failure, nothing more. My subjects, my friends, my daughter... we must not let them down. We *must* prevail. Tell me, there will be a price to pay in the final reckoning, will there not? At what cost do we make this journey? Can you say?'

Gerada Knesh Corian turned to look his dearest friend in the eye. He had already sacrificed his own life, everything he had, for his beloved sovereign. He said nothing as Artrex stared deep within his soul, searching for answers.

His eyes though, revealed *everything*.

'Yes, I understand perfectly, my loyal and faithful knight. I am ready to do what must be done. Lead on, Knesh, lead on. Let us go and save Zephany and her army.'

* * *

Ben, Brraall and Verastus arrived at the great shield barring their path to Te'oull. They had journeyed long and hard with their columns of tribal warriors without rest, across the rugged countryside and through the Kielth Mountains. Brraall had made the decision to leave all those unable to fight behind at Varriann, the wounded and infirm, for their own safety and to speed their march. Now, as they exited the final pass and left the mountains behind, the only sign that a great, magical wall barred their advance was a slight haziness in the air between them and their destination; the city now visible in the distance. It was Verastus who spotted it first.

'This must be the place. The spirit's shield appears to be intact. What now, if we cannot pass through? Unless it is lowered for us, we will be trapped. And it would seem that the Heynai have not yet begun their work?'

Brraall halted the column as they approached the almost invisible partition. He jumped down from his horse and strode purposefully up to it. Taking out his sword, he thrust the tip forward. The jintan steel struck the shield and stopped abruptly, as if it had hit a solid wall of stone.

'Raart! You are correct, Verastus. There is no way through for us at present. We halt here, until we are able to continue. We can only hope that they do not take long, for we are too exposed here and vulnerable to attack. Take this time to rest!' He bawled the last part of his sentence in his own language, speaking to his warriors, before reverting back to English to continue. 'Let us hope also that these wizards know what they are doing. If we are caught here, between this wall and the mountain, in the open with nowhere to run, we will be slaughtered!'

Ben shook his head at the great warrior. 'Well, you're a cheery soul, aren't you?' he said, trying to make light of the situation, as was his way. 'Chill out. They'll do their stuff. We'll be alright, you'll see.'

Verastus raised an eyebrow at the young boy, surprised to hear such optimism from his new friend. It seemed a little out of character to the Falorian, who had witnessed a fair degree of moaning and discontent from the youngster since they met.

'What?' asked Ben.

'Nothing. I mean nothing by it. Only, did you take a knock on the head at Varriann that I did not see?' Verastus replied, with a faint grin.

Ben saw it immediately and burst into laughter. Within seconds, Verastus had joined him.

'Ha, ha, ha... That's it! By Jove, I think he's got it! Finally, you've cracked it mate. That was *actually* funny,' joked the youngster.

*   *   *

Meanwhile, in the Heynai's cave, the spirits were now in severe strife. Their faces were twisted and contorted and they were in excruciating pain. Even Sereq was shaking now and they were all sweating profusely. He tried and tried to encourage the others to hold on for as long as they possibly could. The Heynai's leader had no idea what was happening elsewhere as his concentration was employed solely on maintaining the power to the shield and keeping the spell going. But suddenly, from out of nowhere, came a real and vivid sense that he was needed. He could not ignore it no matter how much he wanted to, even though he knew only too well the dangers of tearing himself away from the circle and breaking his communication with the other spirits at this crucial time.

Despite his enormous fear, that is exactly what he did. The great protective shield shook a little and it looked as though it was going to collapse altogether for a brief moment. But, it soon stabilised and somehow it held firm.

'Ben!' Sereq rasped, inside his mind, trying to reach the Keeper's friend for the very last time.

At the shield, Ben heard the deep, booming voice immediately.

'Yes? Sereq? What? What is it?'

'Listen to me and listen well. The time is here. We will do what we can for you. We will attempt to create a hole in the shield large enough for you all to march through. It will not last long and you must not delay. Keep a sharp lookout for the enemy, for King Vantrax will sense the disruption. The sudden loss of energy will not go unnoticed. You may be sure he will dispatch the nearest creatures to destroy you, and they are close.'

'I understand,' replied Ben. 'I won't let you down. I won't let Jake down.'

'Yes, we know,' answered Sereq.

Then, as quickly as his voice had appeared, it was gone.

Back in the cave, Sereq rejoined the rest of the Heynai. Without delay, he told the others what they had to do and all four began chanting in unison, by some means managing to block out their incredible agony.

'Kruthenealin mehteus hallathe.
Vrushnien ishquall exellonne.'

The ageless words were repeated over and over again. The more they chanted, the greater the anguish they had to endure. Finally, the spirits were drained of all colour and they were shaking uncontrollably, hardly able to maintain contact with one another. It appeared as though they could not withstand it any longer, that they were all on the verge of collapse.

And then, the pain suddenly stopped!

The Heynai were astounded. To their immense relief and joy, they found that they had a brief respite from the torture and they sensed immediately that a small tear in the shield had appeared next to Ben. Taking advantage of the momentary lull, Lapo spoke urgently to Sereq.

'We cannot hold on for much longer, old friend. The agony is unbearable. We are beaten.'

'No!' replied Sereq, firmly. 'You *can* and you must!'

'Yes, we know what we have to do, but… what you ask of us is too much. It is impossible!' added Terristor.

'*Nothing* is impossible!'

'Yaargh! *You* are!' Rutax cried. His voice was raised but he was not angry. In fact, his face bore a huge smile. 'Over hundreds of years you have demanded standards from us far higher than I ever thought we could achieve. Your expectations have been extreme, madness in fact. And yet, somehow, we have always managed to do what you ask. I am resolved now to see this thing through to the bitter end with you, to outlast you on this, and prove my worth. You shall not see me fall, Sereq!'

The spirit's leader beamed with pride at hearing the robust challenge from his comrade. He gazed around him and saw that the other spirits suddenly had the same determination burning in their eyes too.

'So, that is the way of it now, is it? A contest between us all? Yes, very well then, I accept. Let us see who is the strongest amongst us. The last to perish will have earned that title. I will meet you all in the afterlife, again. Though, I fear you will all have to wait for me there. At least for a while.'

* * *

Back at the shield, the haziness suddenly cleared and everyone knew immediately that the barrier had been breached, creating a sizeable gap through which they could march to safety. The columns of tribal warriors began to move off immediately.

At precisely the same time however, far away on the road to Te'oull, King Vantrax suddenly felt another razor-sharp pain in his chest. Then, he turned a ghostly shade of white in an instant, as the air was sucked from his lungs with such speed and ferocity that they felt like they were ablaze. Seconds later, he was left gasping violently for oxygen to replace that he had lost, desperately trying to catch his breath as his vital organs refused to work for a terrifying moment or two.

The evil wizard had left Dassilliak with Melissa and the warriors of his Personal Guard some time before. He was now well on his way to an encounter with the Estian Alliance at Te'oull. When the phenomenal pain struck him however, he dismounted quickly and as best he could, throwing himself from his horse as if he had been struck by a Falorian spear. He stopped at the side of the track, doubled over and fighting frantically for his life.

'Sire!' shouted Melissa, as she rushed to his side. She looked all around for any sign of attack, but she could see nothing. 'What ails you? No wounds I can see. Is it another of the enemy's spells?'

Vantrax was still struggling hard to breathe. But, after a short while, he was finally able to force his words out between gasps.

'Yes... the ba... barrier is... down!'

'What??!! But this is excellent news. Where?' asked Melissa, excitedly.

'Near the... m-mountains... to the north of the city. The boy who came... to this land with the Keeper... is being granted safe passage through. He and the force with him... aim to join the rebels.'

'I see. Then, we must prevent them from doing so at all cost!'

'Yes, agreed,' stated the wizard, beginning to recover. 'I am well ahead of you there. Stand back... Away I said, give me some room,' he ordered.

Vantrax closed his eyes to concentrate and held out his hands. Silence reigned for several seconds as he tried his hardest to communicate with those of his raised beasts who were closest to Te'oull. Eventually, his thoughts reached the leader of the Lords of Srenul and he instructed him to immediately dispatch the revalkas. The terrifying beasts were sent without delay to intercept the fleeing column before the shield closed once more. They were also instructed to break through to the city if they could. Once there, they were ordered to attack anyone they found, to leave no survivors.

*   *   *

It was going to take some considerable time for the long columns of weary warriors to pass through the opening in the shield. Ben, Brraall and Verastus remained behind at the breach, there to ensure the safety of their warriors and to keep a sharp lookout for any enemy creatures. They were also going to ensure the hole was closed behind them, once they were all safely on the other side. Just as the end of the columns were in sight however, Verastus suddenly screamed out at the top of his voice and pointed up at the eastern sky. His superior eyesight had spotted danger.

'Aghrast! They are here! Quickly!'

He barked his orders at the top of his voice, encouraging the warriors on the northern side of the barrier to hurry, in no uncertain terms. Though they could not understand a word he was saying, the tribesmen charged through the gap as fast as they could, whilst Verastus, Ben and the rest watched anxiously as the dots ahead of them increased in number and size. They grew larger and larger until finally, the flying beasts were almost upon them.

'It's no use, they're not gonna make it in time!' screamed Ben, looking at the last of the tribal warriors who had yet to make it through the shield. 'Come on, we *have* to do something to help them!'

'Raar! No! Stay where you are! What *can* we do against such a force?' snapped Brraall, consumed completely by intense feelings of anger and frustration. 'We are caught in the open, just as I feared! We *must* get to the other side of the shield before it closes. Only once there can we make our stand, for if the spirits close it now, we will *all* be killed!'

'But they are *your* men! We can't leave them here to die!' Ben yelled, his emotions once again getting the better of him.

'We have no choice!' cried the huge warrior, barely able to contain himself. 'My heart crumbles to dust at the very thought of it. I am dying inside, can you not see? Yes, they are mine. But they will understand the choice I face. We have to survive. We have to...'

'He is right, Ben!' interrupted Verastus. 'No more words. Come, we have to go right now!'

Ben was crying openly. He was ashamed of himself and he was terrified. It felt to him as if this decision was betraying everything he believed in, everything he was. And yet, he knew that he *had* to go. So, he ran. He ran faster than he had ever run before.

The three companions sprinted through the opening but, once they knew they were on the other side of the breach, they stopped. They each turned around and tried to encourage as many of the others through as they could, before the fast-approaching beasts of King Vantrax were able to attack.

But, almost immediately, the hole before them vanished and the shield was reformed. It was as solid as it had ever been. Almost three hundred of Brraall's warriors were now trapped on the wrong side of the wall. To their utter dismay and horror, they were now completely at the mercy of the attacking revalkas!

Brraall was mortified. He approached the Heynai's barrier and placed his hand upon it. One of his most trusted and loyal warriors was the closest to him. He could just make him out through the haze and the tears that had formed in his eyes. The warrior approached Brraall quickly and placed his own hand next to that of his leader. He smiled gently and nodded his head in a last sign of respect, an honourable farewell. A solitary tear rolled down Brraall's cheek, for no words would come to him. Then, the friend he had known since childhood drew his sword, turned around and joined the hopeless fight against the ferocious beasts.

Ben wanted desperately to say something, to comfort the tribal leader somehow. He could see for himself how much the warrior was hurting. He could feel his agony and it hurt as much as anything had ever hurt the youngster, to watch such a man brought to such despair. But, he knew that *nothing* he could say or do would help.

Nevertheless, Ben needed Brraall to understand just how he felt.

'I... I'm so sorry, Brraall,' he began, placing his hand up on the warrior's shoulder. 'This is the worst day of my life. I don't know what to say. I'm sorry we ever got you into this mess.'

The veteran warrior watched agonisingly as his tribesmen died one by one. They were torn apart by the revalkas, who launched a succession of devastating, vicious attacks. Before long, they were all dead. Not a single warrior survived the onslaught. Brraall turned to Ben, wiped his cheek with his hand and looked the youngster firmly in the eye, gripped now by a fierce determination and a thirst for revenge.

'You did not get us into anything, Ben. *I* led my people to this place. It was *I* who chose to follow the teachings of our forefathers, to follow the Keeper. It is *me* who will be judged by history in the fullness of time, not you. The blame and guilt lie with me. And I will carry them with me forever, unto death. Now, let us complete our journey and join our friends. Many more of us will die before this war is won, I fear. Once the wall that divides us is down, we will *all* have to face our demons, and conquer our worst fears. I, at least, head to Te'oull safe in the knowledge that I have just met with mine.'

Verastus joined his friends. 'Then, there are at least two of us in this new army of ours who shall not fear death, my friend. Too much has happened to us in the past weeks and years for that. My own life, the things I thought were important, seem so insignificant now, almost like petty squabbles which are best vanquished from my mind. A life is such a small thing to give when the stakes are so high. If I am destined to die at Te'oull, I will meet my end bravely, I know I shall. And I promise you this; I *will* avenge the deaths of your warriors by aiding the Keeper to the best of my ability. When the time comes, I will take as many of the enemy with me to the afterlife as I can!'

He offered his hand to Brraall in a very human gesture of friendship, something he had only recently learned from Jake and Ben. Eventually, Brraall realised what was required and shook his hand. Ben immediately placed his own, much smaller hand upon them both. He choked back his tears as he spoke.

'You know, I'm only a kid, but… I used to take everything I had for granted when I was at home. To be honest, and you probably won't believe this, I was a tiny bit immature, a bit of a pain in the ass really. I was always feeling sorry for myself, wanting what others had, what with the way my dad was an' all… Anyway, what I mean to say is…'

Ben was trying his hardest to speak like an adult, and succeeding, even though his age meant he was still considered a child. But, emotion overcame him and he broke down in tears again, unable to finish his sentence.

Verastus placed a reassuring hand around his shoulder and led him away.

'It is alright, Ben. No need to go on. We know.'

Chapter 10
30th September – The City of Te'oull – Siatol

The Heynai's protective shield was now restored and holding firm, for the time being. Behind it, throngs of deadly, merciless beasts were waiting impatiently to begin their attack upon the walled city. They would soon be joined by the combined forces of the wizard king's Northern and Southern armies, led by the most feared warrior in Estian history; the mighty Thargw, Sawdon. And not long afterwards, King Vantrax himself would add to their numbers, bringing with him the Sebantan princess, Melissa, and the elite troops of his Personal Guard. The stage was almost set for the ultimate battle between good and evil on Estia. *This* was the long-awaited climax of a thousand year war and it was shaping up to be a fight which would eclipse all others. Estia's very own version of Armageddon was coming to Te'oull.

Inside the city itself, a lone sentry who was guarding one of the gates in the northern section of the wall suddenly cried out loud, as he spied Ben and his force of tribesmen approaching his position. His excited yell brought warriors running to him from all directions. Everyone it seemed rushed to greet the new arrivals at the wall, all except for Princess Zephany and her perpetual shadow, Lord Caro. The two seasoned combatants remained where they were, in the square.

'Srr... shall we not go with the others to see our friends?' asked Caro, when it became clear that Zephany was not going to follow.

Princess Zephany shook her head slowly in reply. 'No, I need a minute or two, please? That is not too much to ask, is it? I tell you, Caro, I have never appreciated silence so much as I do right now. It is bliss. Let the others greet them. They will arrive with us soon enough.'

The young royal suddenly and unexpectedly dropped to her knees. Bowing her head slightly, she whispered a short but sincere prayer of gratitude, whilst Caro watched over her.

Several minutes after she had finished and regained her feet, Ben, Brraall and Verastus joined them in the square. The intrepid group of heroes were surrounded by an excited crowd of onlookers who had followed the column all the way from the wall. At first, the leaders struggled to make themselves heard over the noise, but Caro's patience ran out quickly and he held up his hand to silence the crowd.

'Welcome, dear friends. I give thanks for your deliverance. Where do I begin, and what do I say? We know what you did for us all at Dassilliak. We will always be eternally grateful. Your effort and your sacrifice shall not be in vain, I promise you,' stated Zephany, impressively.

Never one to stand on ceremony, Ben was about to respond on behalf of all his companions, but the princess continued before he could.

'Brraall, your people have earned their place in our history books with the supreme valor they have shown. They now rank alongside the greatest Estian warriors from past and present, as defenders of this realm and as valued allies and friends. You have all served with great honour, when in my eyes we have done nothing to deserve such loyalty. Mere words scarcely suffice in times such as these, but let me try? It is my sacred vow, witnessed by all present on this day, that you and your kind will *never* be mistreated in these lands again. I swear, from this day forward, your enemies will be our enemies, your friends will be our friends!'

Everyone in the crowd began cheering wildly. The warriors of the Estian Alliance then began walking among the tribesmen, greeting them openly and behaving as though they were long-lost friends, heroes returned safely after years away from home. Though none of the tribal warriors could speak their tongue as yet, they were all carried along with the atmosphere and they responded with gratitude.

After a while Caro restored the silence once more, allowing Princess Zephany to continue.

'Now, Ben, we have much to discuss. Though you all must rest first, prepare yourselves for the forthcoming battle.'

'Err... yeah, I s'pose so. But I need to know the score?' replied the youngster.

The meaning behind his words was completely lost on the young royal from Rhuaddan. She had absolutely no idea how to respond and she instinctively looked at Verastus for guidance.

'I... I believe he means, what is happening?' the Falorian stated, amazed to find himself translating happily for his friend.

'Kah! Yes, you are a strange boy with strange ways, Ben. To answer your question; we know very little that you cannot see for yourselves. The army of evil facing us grows in strength by the hour. Though, it must be said that thankfully, so does our own. When the shield between us falls, we will have the fight of our lives ahead of us. We will have to defend these walls with everything we have, and hope that we can hold out. As for Jake, he has left and gone with Tien. They travel to the Thargw homeland. Jake hopes to steal the fourth stone away from the Thargw emperor himself. Gellsorr is with them. It is a mission unlike any other, and in truth, I do not see how it can be achieved...'

'No?' interrupted Ben. 'Well, I wouldn't count him out just yet! He's full of surprises, my best mate.'

'No, Ben, you did not let me finish and you misunderstand me. I have not, I assure you, counted him out, as you say. I did not mean to sound... I am merely intrigued as to how he will accomplish... I am counting on his success. Indeed, I am planning for it.'

'Oh, good!' said Ben. 'Sorry, I thought you were...'

The teenager ceased talking abruptly. The crowd around him had suddenly begun to stir quite noticeably, interrupting his train of thought. Their moans and grumbles grew gradually louder as somebody pushed their way forcefully through them all to reach the front. Finally, the lead ranks parted a little and through them squeezed the old lady who had spoken with Zephany and Caro earlier. She approached Ben with some hesitation and raised her trembling hand to his face. Then, her fingers began gently touching his features, as tear after painful tear rolled steadily down her cheeks.

'Srr... Yes? What is it? Can we help you?' asked Princess Zephany, breaking the awkward silence which had developed. Her soft voice was full of compassion and yet it was obvious to all that she did not appreciate the interruption.

The old lady continued staring into Ben's eyes as she replied to the question in a gentle voice of her own.

'It is all true. You... You *are* the Keeper. You have returned to us.'

Ben tenderly took hold of her hand and pulled it away from his face. He lowered it to her side, before releasing it.

'No, I'm sorry but you have it all wrong. I'm not the Keeper and I don't think I'd want to be, thank you very much. I'm his best friend. My name is Ben.'

The old lady appeared bitterly disappointed. However, her sorrow only lasted a moment or two before she spoke once more, with swiftly renewed optimism.

'I see. He *is* here though, is he not? He *has* come back to us?'

'Yes. The Keeper is on Mynae, as I have just explained,' answered Zephany, speaking for them all. 'He will return to us shortly, we hope.'

The elderly woman turned to answer the beautiful princess. 'I... I apologise for my actions, your highness. I could not hear from where I stood.'

'What is it you want of the Keeper?' asked Caro.

'I... I do not know.'

'Then, may we ask, what are you doing here? Who are you?' replied the knight.

'Yes... Yes, of course. I should have said, forgive me? I know how this must appear to you all. Where are my manners? My name is Jean. I have travelled a great distance to be with you now, to join you. I *must* be allowed to speak to the one who calls himself the Keeper. You see, the last man to bear that title, was my husband.'

*   *   *

'*What?!*'

It was an instant, natural, heartfelt reaction to the old lady's words. The ludicrous statement had shocked and stunned everybody, *especially* Ben. He had blurted out the solitary word with such power and abruptness, that all those around him nearly jumped out of their skins. Once the commotion had finally died down, it was Princess Zephany who once again took command of the situation.

'So, there is another story to be told on our journey, another twist of fate? We shall listen to your tale in more comfortable surroundings. Come with us to the tavern and there you can divulge your secrets, convince us all that what you say is true. Come, Ben. The rest of you weary souls are to relax a little while you can. Sleep, and report to Caro when you are ready for your assignments.'

Ben suddenly snapped out of the trance he was in as Zephany spoke directly to him. He was still deep in shock but his mind and body had suddenly gone onto autopilot and he followed willingly.

'Eh? Hell yeah! Now *this* oughta be good!'

Once inside the tavern, they all settled down around a large table. It was soon furnished with food and drink. Queen Bressial and Lord Castrad joined them, along with most of the Alliance leaders.

'Come on then, we're all waiting to be amazed… No? Well, I'll start, shall I? You *can't* be Jean! She's dead. Sawdon and his thugs killed her years ago, when they tried to get Harry, before he destroyed the stones, or pretended that he had at any rate,' began Ben, seeing no reason at all to mince his words.

The old lady opposite him carefully placed her cup on the table. She answered in a quiet voice which was trembling a little with apprehension.

'I… I know this will be hard for all of you to accept. But, think on it, I have no reason to lie. I have nothing to gain by deceit. What purpose would it serve?'

'But, I've seen Jean's picture, in the attic. You look nothing like her,' rasped Ben, defiantly.

'*That* was a very long time ago!' snapped the woman. 'It was taken in another lifetime completely.'

'Ben, please, let her speak? We will hear her out and we will then decide, once we have the facts, or at least, once we know what is *supposed* to have happened,' said Princess Zephany.

Ben nodded obediently and sat back on his stool, inviting the emotional stranger to continue.

'Tell us, what proof do you have of your claim?' asked Queen

Bressial.

'What proof? I... Err... I have nothing. Everything I had was taken from me. I know that sounds like...'

'That would seem a little too convenient?' stated Lord Castrad.

'Forgive me. Maybe you can tell us a little about your world, the world you came from?' said Verastus, his voice kind and gentle. The escaped slave wanted to believe her story and it showed. 'The things you can remember will help to prove your identity.'

She nodded and tried to think of what to say. 'Err... Yes, okay. Ben, if I speak to you of cars, television, radio, phones...? Does that convince you? These people here would not know of such things, would they?'

Ben was half way there but he still needed convincing. He remained a little cautious. 'Yeah, I suppose so. But you could have heard about them from the things me and Jake have said somehow? Or from one of the other Keepers?'

'Yes, I could. Though, I did not. Well, what then? What can I say that will convince you? I know, Harry! Let's see? He was in the army for years, he was away an awful lot... Err... Ah! We had a son, Graham. He would be about...'

'How?! How did you know that? No-one knows about him. They... Err, the Keepers, they have kept him out of it all along. Harry told us. His identity is a secret that mustn't be revealed, 'cos it would place him in danger if they knew... *Jean?*' asked a shocked Ben, realising all of a sudden that however improbable it was, she *had* to be telling the truth. 'Is it *really* you?'

'Yes, Ben, it is me, I assure you. I stand before you now as sure as eggs is eggs, risen from the dead I suppose? I *am* Harry's wife and Jake's grandmother.'

'But... *How?!*'

'I'll tell you, Ben. I'll tell you all. Though, you must bear in mind that these are truths which have only returned to me very recently. For years, I did not know. I could recall nothing. I had no memory at all of these events until, weeks ago now, I saw a strange light in the sky. There was a bang unlike any other, and a pounding in my head that just would not stop. It lasted for days. When it was gone, a whole new world of memories filled my thoughts and dreams, terrifying recollections of past events, heart-stopping scenes of deeds done, and wrongs suffered. They played over and over again in my mind like a bad record with the needle stuck. It took me some time to understand them, to make any sense at all of what I was seeing. Every time I closed my eyes it was as if my worst nightmares had come to haunt me all at once.'

She was shaking now, and crying hard. Ben and Zephany took hold of a hand each and it comforted her. After a short while, she felt able to continue. 'Thank you for your kindness.'

'It's nothing,' said Ben. 'The light. You must have seen it when we opened the box in Harry's attic, when we came through to Rhuaddan, to escape from Sawdon. It must have triggered something inside of you?'

'Yes, I suppose you're right.'

'But, I don't understand? How did you survive? Harry told us that he checked you in the living room, and he thought you were dead? He would never have left you otherwise. He's been wracked with guilt ever since. You should see him, he is...'

'I'm sorry? You've *seen* him? He *lives*? But that's the best news ever! Oh, praise the Lord, I thought... It does not matter now what I thought. When I heard that the Keeper was a boy and not a man, I naturally assumed that Harry had been killed, that another of our family had taken his place?'

'No. He is alive and well. Err... Well actually, that's not *strictly* true. He's not so well, he's... a bit knocked up, to be fair.'

One look into Ben's eyes told Jean that the youngster was telling the truth.

'Yes, but he *is* breathing, fighting?!' she cried with relief, as even more tears flowed. Only, these were tears of joy and elation.

'Can you go on, please? We need to hear your story in full,' stated Queen Bressial.

Jean looked at Zephany for support. The princess smiled and she continued.

'Yes, of course. I'm sorry. Where was I? When I arrived here I knew nothing of my past. For all I knew, I was just an ordinary peasant from Rhuaddan, with no memory of life before the dungeons, before captivity. I was a prisoner of no consequence, one of many held in Heron Getracht fortress for no apparent reason, just another victim of King Vantrax, that's all. I knew nothing of why I was being held there, and no-one seemed able or willing to tell me what I had done. All I knew for certain was my name.'

'That must have been awful? I cannot imagine what that felt like,' said Zephany.

'Yes, it was. But then, I knew no different, did I? I just lived from day to day, trying my best to survive. I was held for years in that fortress. Eventually, I was released from the dungeons and put to work, no longer considered a risk, if I ever was. For a time I cleaned, I cooked, washed and scrubbed... Until, one day, whilst the king was away, I escaped.'

'Escaped? From Heron Getracht? How? Few have managed such a feat. It is said to be almost impossible,' stated Verastus, who himself had been held captive there and was now seriously impressed. His own remarkable escape from the mine at Lidzenstor was considered miraculous, but *this*?

'I know. It *is* impossible, believe me. I could never have done it alone. I had help.'

'What? Who from?' replied the astonished Falorian.

'A young servant named Nytig. I never knew why he helped me, but he did. I shall never forget his kindness. I have heard that he paid terribly for it.'

'*Nytig?* Huh, I met him. He... Agh, it doesn't matter. Please, go on,' said Ben.

Jean smiled at him and continued. 'From the memories which have returned to me of late and the tales told by our people who were there at the time, the lucky few who escaped with me and heard the soldiers talking, I have managed to piece together what actually happened. It goes like this; at our house in Lichfield, many years ago now, eighteen or nineteen I'd say but I don't know for certain, I was attacked by Sawdon and two others. I had never seen a Thargw before and the sight of him turned my legs to jelly so that I couldn't stand. They tried their hardest to make me talk, asking me question after question about Harry and the whereabouts of the stones. When I refused to speak, they beat me, thrashed me to within an inch of my life. I still carry the scars of that day on my body, and now in my mind also.'

'But... Harry told us you were dead? He went back to check?' said Ben, remembering their conversation with Jake's grandfather in his kitchen, before Sawdon had attacked and been confronted by Jake.

'What can I say? I don't know what happened, Ben. I can't remember seeing him. I must have been unconscious. I would have looked dead to him I suppose, and he wouldn't have had time to check properly, would he? Not if Sawdon was chasing after him,' said Jean.

'He *was!* He told me that.'

'Well, there you go then.'

Ben was silent for a second or two. Then, he remembered something else.

'Hang on. The fire? Harry said the whole place was in flames? Sawdon had left, hadn't he? You were unconscious. So, how did you get out? And how did you end up here?'

'Yes, it's a real mystery, isn't it? Well, I was told that once the great Thargw returned to Rhuaddan, without the Keeper and without the stones he was sent to capture, King Vantrax was absolutely furious with him. He almost killed him right there and then, but he decided to use another small piece of reolite to send Sawdon straight back. Only this time, he was alone. He was told to search everywhere once again for the stones, and the Keeper, for the king refused to accept that both were lost. Don't ask me why because I do not know, but it is said that somehow, the stone and the spell didn't work properly. I guess something, or someone, interfered with them? Whatever happened though, instead of appearing next to Harry and the stones he had with him, as should have happened, Sawdon was sent back into the burning house, to the living room where I was seated.'

'That must have shocked him? It was the spirits! It *must* have been,' stated Ben.

'I... I suppose so, if you say it. I do not know anything more. Anyway, I was informed that he was only there for a short time because the fire had really taken hold by then and the heat was intense. I must have been coming round and groaned or something, because Sawdon realised to his surprise that I was still alive. He brought me back with him. I suppose it was to appease his master, or for leverage should Harry be found. Only, he never was. And when I eventually recovered from my wounds, my memory did not return. I was of no use to them at all as I could tell them nothing. I presume I was kept alive in the hope that one day I would remember. It served no purpose I guess to inform me of my real identity.'

'So, you lived all those years in that miserable place, alone, not knowing who you were?' asked Lord Castrad.

'Yes... And no. I was not alone.'

'What?' Verastus responded for them all. 'Please explain. What do you mean?'

Jean looked around the group at their confused expressions.

'My child was with me.'

'*Child?!* Wow! Back up their horsey!' shouted Ben, bewildered and amazed.

'Yes. You do not know, do you? How could you? Well, I realise that it may come as a shock to you, on top of everything else, but I was in the early stages of pregnancy when they found me. It's a full-blown miracle she survived the beating I took. I really thought I would lose her. But she did, and...'

'She? A child? Oh my God! What *happened* to her?' cried Ben, hardly able to believe what he was hearing.

Jean looked down at the floor. Her weary and gaunt face was now full of sadness, and shame.

'I do not know. I had a sweet little girl once. She was my perfect little angel. She was my entire world. She lived with me in the fortress for four years, somehow surviving the horrendous conditions. She was tough, a real fighter. Then, one day, for no reason whatsoever, she was taken from me.'

'Taken? To where?' asked Princess Zephany.

'I have no idea. To this day, I do not know for certain. I was told many months later that she had been sold on Mynae, to the highest bidder. I tried and tried to find out more but to no avail. My heart was broken and when the chance came to escape, I took it. I ran and I hid as far away from Heron Getracht and King Vantrax as it is possible to go. I eventually settled on the isle of Rawsellon, the southernmost point of Estia. It was a wilderness where no-one and nothing could bother me.'

'Yeah, okay, I understand that you needed to disappear, but a *child!*' said Ben, unable to think of anything else. 'That would make her... Jake's auntie?'

'Yes. I suppose I was a bit old for children at that point, though I am a good few years younger than Harry. It wasn't planned. I hadn't told him when I was taken. I'd only just found out myself. No-one knew.'

'Four? You said she was four?' asked Zephany. A very strange feeling overcame the princess all of a sudden, a sense of foreboding almost. 'If she survived, that would make her a young woman now. What was her name?'

Jean wiped her tears away with her sleeve.

'I don't expect that she kept it, but I named her Melissa, after my grandmother.'

'Oh hell!' screamed Ben, as a sharp intake of breath from all those around her immediately caught Jean's attention.

'What? What is it? You must tell me if you know anything!' she pleaded.

Ben looked straight at Princess Zephany.

'This is *priceless*. Are you gonna tell her, or shall I?'

The princess decided she should be the one to speak. She placed her hands on Jean's shoulders and looked her in the eye.

'Your child yet lives, Jean. In fact, I should think it highly probable that you will soon see her again. Though, it may be a severe disappointment to you if that is the case. She is a warrior to be feared, and she serves King Vantrax.'

Jean wasn't really sure what to make of the news. She was all of a sudden exhilarated, thrilled, excited, but she was also scared.

'Srr... I would not count on it,' stated Verastus. 'I may be mistaken, but I am almost certain that she was hit by Gellsorr, at Dassilliak. The light I believe has turned her to stone.'

'Oh yeah. He's right!' Ben remembered. 'Err... Sorry?' he added, as the nature of the news and what it might mean to Jean suddenly registered with him.

Jean shook her head a few times as she tried hard to process all of the information she had been given. It was an action Ben had seen his best friend perform time and time again. Silence once again fell upon the tavern. Eventually, the old lady replied.

'I feel numb. I don't think I can take much more. But then, to all intents and purposes my child was lost to me before this day, before I came to this place and found you all. I had dealt with that loss long ago. As painful as it was, I can grieve no more than I already have. I lost my little girl many years ago. The warrior you speak of would be a stranger to me now, and I to her. And if she truly serves the powers of evil, then perhaps it is for the best if she is gone?'

Oh I just don't know, I cannot think straight. Besides, all I can think of now is trying to reach my husband, to let him know that I'm still alive. Then, who knows what might happen? Maybe there is something left between us after all these years? I'm sure he will have moved on with his life though? He must have found someone else?'

'He hasn't!' interrupted Ben. 'He's still mourning you even after all this time. He's never forgiven himself. It's sad really. I never knew the whole story.'

'I see. Then I don't know what to think, Ben. A part of me feels like I should never have come here, that I should have stayed on Rawsellon. But then...? No. I have made the right decision, I know it. Tell me, how do we go home?'

'Eh? Oh, that's simple,' replied the teenager, with his customary humour. 'All we have to do is hope that your grandson, my best mate, manages to steal the fourth stone we need away from the greatest warrior in the Thargw empire, barring Sawdon of course. And that he somehow manages to escape from the enemy's lair with his life. Then, we have to defeat two great armies, countless thousands of walking zombies, and a host of unbelievably horrifying creatures, led by some horsemen from the apocalypse... Oh, and we have to kill an all-powerful wizard and take his stone... And Sawdon himself.'

If we do all that, we can then *try* to mend the box I broke. Hopefully, if we survive and we manage to restore it properly, it may just work and take us back, to exactly the right time and place... On the right world.'

'Huh! Is that all? I'm glad I asked,' said Jean.

She smiled a little and winked at Ben. In that one moment, the youngster saw the whole of the West family in her eyes. *Oh yes, she's Harry's wife alright*, he thought, and he laughed along with her.

'Well, first thing's first, let's get some food down you. Hey, tell you what, I can't wait 'til you meet Jake. Seriously, this is gonna blow his socks off!'

Chapter 11
30th September – The City of Kerrallux – Eratur - Mynae

Mid-afternoon in Kerrallux and the Thargw inhabitants of the city, who would normally be out in force on the many streets and alleyways going about their daily lives, had all shut themselves firmly behind wooden doors. There they remained, safe from harm and away from the two desperate, dangerous fugitives who had so audaciously written themselves into Thargw history books by raiding the emperor's palace. The citizens of the great fortress city had barricaded themselves inside their homes on the orders of the emperor himself, to effectively deny the escapees shelter and a place to hide. Their actions also allowed the thorough house to house search which was underway to proceed unhindered. It had begun at dawn on the twenty-ninth, as soon as the sun had risen in the sky. Hour after laborious hour had passed, hundreds of homes were turned upside down, but they found nothing. The emperor was furious, the grid was widened and the search was intensified. Every single warrior able to wield a sword now joined in the hunt. The Thargws were busily and frenetically combing every inch of the city looking for any sign of the two intruders, any clue as to their whereabouts, for they were certain they had not escaped and most just could not understand how they had evaded capture.

Beneath the heavy rock cover of a nearby drainage ditch built to remove sewerage and waste from the rows of dwellings, not far from the city centre, Jake and Tien lay in absolute silence. They were listening anxiously to the various noises coming from above. Numerous cries and shouts rang out; the signs of a frantic and exhaustive search still taking place all around their position. For the time being though, they were not concerned. The Thargw warriors would not think to search the ditch in which they were concealed, for the weighty stone which covered them was far too heavy to be lifted by anyone who did not possess a similar magic to that of Tien. No-one but a wizard would even think to attempt such a feat. As long as they remained perfectly quiet, they were safe from harm in their dark, putrid hideaway, though they knew from experience that Thargws possessed excellent hearing and had therefore decided to keep conversation to a minimum.

When he felt it was finally safe to talk, Jake whispered to the wizard in a voice as quiet as he could make it.

'Phew! Okay, they've gone. Look, we can't stay here all day, we have to get moving. Princess Zephany and the others need our help. Every moment we waste here is...'

'Jake! I am sorry but I know. I agree with you, but what can we do? Even if we *do* manage to break free of this prison unseen, we would never make it out of the city alive. Do not forget, without Gellsorr, we no longer have any means of returning to Estia,' interrupted Tien.

'Yeah, but I'm not having that. I won't give up. There has to be a way,' stated Jake, in a voice that was still hushed but now a little more forceful. 'I refuse to accept that we can't do anything!'

'Then, what would you have us try, Keeper?'

'Eh? I dunno... Can't you fly us out of here somehow? You're supposed to be the wizard. Ain't you got a spell or two for that?'

'I am afraid not. Flight is one thing I have never aspired to, or needed... Until now. I have never mastered the art for I have not tried.'

'Oh, thanks for that little gem. Ah well, never mind, just a thought. We'll have to think of something else then,' said the youngster, bitterly disappointed. 'I suppose we could fight our way out?'

'Tah! Even with all your new powers, it would take a whole army of Keepers. There are thousands of them out there.'

'Hmmn... Yeah, I guess you're right. It looks like we're stuck here then? Well, that's just great, innit? I never thought I would end up dying in a ditch of...'

Jake stopped talking and he suddenly began to snigger. He tried hard to suppress the noise by holding his hands over his mouth, but he failed.

'Ha, ha...'

'Shush, Jake! They might hear you,' rasped the wizard, his face blood red with rage all of a sudden. 'Be quiet! Quiet I say! Oh for...! And just what the darraiesh are you giggling at anyway? What is so funny, given our current plight?'

Jake's mirth halted just enough for him to speak, in-between giggles.

'Ha, ha... I'm... I'm supposed to be this big, superhero or summin', this almighty, all-conquering Keeper dude who's going to vanquish evil and save everyone. You've all been banging on about me and how special I am since the very first time we met. Ha, ha... Well, tell me this, oh great and wise one; is there *anything* in the prophecies that covers this? Ha, ha... Do they say by any chance, *the Keeper impressed all he knew, covered in muck, smothered in poo?* Ha, ha...'

'What? No, of course not! Now, stop being so *ridiculous* and help me figure out what we are going to do!' huffed Tien.

His temper was rising rapidly. He failed to see the humour and he had grown quite angry all of a sudden. Not for the first time, he was intensely disappointed by the immaturity shown by this Keeper, but on this occasion he did not attempt to hide it.

Jake saw it in his eyes immediately. He stopped laughing, calmed himself down and replied.

'Alright, alright, keep your hair on. I was only... Ha, ha...' He started laughing again, briefly. 'Oops... Sorry. I forgot, you have no hair, do you?'

Tien was now at the end of his tether. Harsh words of anger and dismay erupted from within before he knew what he was saying. Jake had pushed the right button alright, a button no other Keeper before him had even come close to pushing.

'Raargh! I am blessed by the spirits, ageless in fact, but you two boys will surely be the death of me! I do not know how you have managed to survive so far in your world, or this for that matter, but I will be *amazed* if you live to fulfill your destiny. You are...! Tah! I cannot even bring myself to say it! I used to think your ways, your methods for coping with everything that has happened, were a great asset to us. Now though, now that I am caught up in a real life or death situation...? Yargh! I am befuddled, making no sense! See what you have done? You and your friend have brought me to this! You laugh when you should be shedding tears and sweat. You smile, when you should be shaking in fear. You ridicule everyone and everything, and you just do not seem to care... I will *never* understand you.'

Jake was shamed by Tien's short rebuke. As a sudden rush of heat reddened his cheeks, he took a couple of deep breaths and accepted that the wizard had a point; this was not the time perhaps for jokes.

'Okay, okay, I'm back with you now. Relax. Kerrallux. Trapped. Thargws all around us. See? I've got it. I'm on top of things... Right, here's the plan; we can't stay here. Sooner or later they are bound to find us, or we'll have to leave to find food and water. And anyway, we have no time. Our friends at Te'oull are relying on us. So, we're gonna make a break for it tonight, as soon as it's dark. We'll head for the stables near the palace. They won't expect us to double back on ourselves, and we can try to get some horses. After that, we'll just have to revert to plan B, and fight our way out, like Jason Statham or something?'

Jake looked expectantly at Tien, expecting a response. The old wizard said nothing but he was clearly unimpressed, and a little confused.

'Well? What d'ya think?'

'Jason Stathe? Who is he? A great warrior from your world? Never mind, I... I think, that the art of planning has perhaps not proven to be where your best talents lie?'

'Ha, ha... Yeah, perhaps not,' Jake conceded, chuckling slightly. 'I wish Knesh was here. But, at least we'll be doing *something*, rather than just sitting around waiting for the end to come?'

'Indeed, Keeper. There is that. You realise though, that this probably means certain death for us both?'

Jake nodded, but he was still smiling. 'Yeah. Actually, no. No I don't. I'm hoping for a bit of that Keeper's luck we've enjoyed so far, that destiny thing everyone keeps talking about. It's gotten me out of a few tight spots already, maybe it will again? And, he's an actor, a British one at that.'

'I have no idea what that is, Jake. But, if he inspires you, I will like him. You should know that the spirits are gone. They cannot save us now. Even if they were not otherwise engaged, we are too far away from them to expect any help. We are out of reach of their power.'

'Hmmn... So, what you're saying is, we're all alone, surrounded and facing almost certain annihilation?'

'Unfortunately, yes. The odds of survival are very slim.'

'Oh. Well, that's alright then. I'm a Keeper. I would have it no other way.'

* * *

As the last remnants of daylight faded, this part of Kerrallux city was strangely silent. The search for the two fugitives continued, but by now it had spread to way past their current location. It was so far away in fact, that it was out of earshot for Jake and Tien. The city streets seemed almost deserted. Warriors had been posted all around by the military commanders, taking up positions at every vital juncture or building. There they stood motionless, straining every sinew to listen for their prey, using their powerful ears to try to detect any movement which might betray their whereabouts.

Jake decided the time was right to move. Tien cast another spell and the huge, bulky stone which had them trapped rose steadily into the air, floating effortlessly upwards until they were able to climb silently out of the ditch and move out of its shadow. As soon as they had, it fell noiselessly back into place.

'Come, Keeper, it is this way,' the wizard stated, heading towards the darkness of a nearby street.

Jake followed without a sound. His breathing was short and shallow as they crept stealthily along several side streets. They stayed in the darkness of the shadows wherever they could, sprinting across any open or moonlit areas. Their luck held. Somehow, they managed to evade detection by the numerous Thargw sentries they passed along the way. At last, they rounded one final corner and there, ahead of them, were the stables. They were next to the emperor's palace and they were guarded by two enormous Thargws. A further two warriors could also be seen patrolling up and down the nearby side streets.

'Jake, there are too many of them,' hissed the wizard. 'If you attack them now, you will surely alert the whole city. You will draw every

Thargw warrior within hearing distance down upon us.'

'Shh! Yes, alright, I know,' whispered the youngster. 'But what choice do we have? This is why we came, Tien. Come on, it's got to be done. I'll try to be as quiet as possible. You stay over there, in the dark,' he added, pointing to the shadow of a doorway which was opposite the stable doors.

Tien acknowledged the command obediently and Jake crept forward. Silently, he worked his way towards and around the two unsuspecting guards. When he was standing opposite their position, with their bodies perfectly in line, he threw his sword gently up in the air and whispered.

'Bratiq!'

Two fingers on his right hand extended to aim the strike and the sword flew rapidly towards the warriors. The bladed weapon passed straight through their bodies in turn and they fell to the ground. However, Jake's sword then continued its momentum and lodged deep within the barn's wooden wall, leaving him totally defenceless. Worse still, the noise the weapon made as it struck the wood alerted the nearby Thargws. The two alarmed warriors immediately charged towards him roaring ferociously, with their swords raised. The secret was out and everyone within miles would now know that the fugitives had been found.

Tien was still concealed in the shadows. He saw what was happening and raced over to free the sword, though he knew he would not be fast enough to retrieve it in time to pass it to Jake before the Thargws attacked.

The next few seconds passed in a blur for Jake. He acted once more without thinking, out of instinct, though it was not his own, and he knew not from where it came.

Having had no previous martial arts training or experience whatsoever, faced by two lethal and armed assailants, Jake suddenly seemed to transform into a Kung Fu legend. His arms and legs moved so fast and his body twisted and contorted so much, that he was able to evade the blades of his attackers and launch numerous strikes upon them. Somehow, the Thargw warriors, who held all the advantages, were made to look like little boys, amateurs who had no right being in his presence.

Jake was unscathed and his final two kicks landed squarely on the warrior's jaws. Both fell to the ground and did not get up. They had been struck an extraordinary amount of times in such a short period. Tien was stunned by the awesome display he had just witnessed, his mouth fell wide open as he reached the sword.

'Quick, free it and let's go!' shouted Jake, a little out of breath but no longer concerned about the need for silence.

Tien cast another spell to ease the weapon out of the wood and then he raced over to the stable doors. Jake soon emerged from within with two stallions. They were just about to mount the horses and make good their escape, when they suddenly heard an almighty commotion; cries and roars, the unmistakable sounds of swords clinking on armour, lots of warriors converging on their position, racing to do battle!

Thargws suddenly began appearing from all directions. Within seconds, they were faced by a crowd of over fifty angry beasts and more were appearing with every second that passed. Tien was aghast as he realised that it was over. They had lost. Nothing could be done against such a formidable force. He looked straight at Jake.

The young Keeper was not afraid. He should have been, he knew that. But he wasn't. His overriding emotion now was one of intense disappointment; an awful, gut-wrenching feeling that he had failed everyone.

I've let them all down. They needed a hero, and all they got was me!

'This is it, Tien,' he said, quietly. 'I'm really sorry. I'm sorry I wasn't the Keeper you thought I was. I tried my best, but in the end, I was just a boy.'

Tien shook his head at him and smiled kindly.

'No, Jake, you are far more than you will ever know. Whether in life or death, you *will* inspire our people to greater things. You will give them hope, and the courage they need to triumph.'

Jake turned his eyes to the angry mob of bloodthirsty Thargws.

'Yeah? Is that so? I don't mean to disagree with you… But, tell that to them!'

Chapter 12
Night – 30th September – Kerrallux City – Eratur – Mynae

Jake West had faced many terrifying situations since finding the box of stones and learning of his destiny. Death had only been a heartbeat away for the young Keeper at times. Too many times in fact, now that he stopped to think about it. However, despite the turbulent and world-shattering events of the recent past, he had *never* been so certain of his own demise, as right now.

He was staring at a multitude of ferocious Thargws who were armed to the teeth and clearly intent on taking his life. His only companion was the guide sent by the Heynai to help him. But, unbelievably, the old wizard seemed able to do absolutely nothing to help. The fearsome warriors were inching their way menacingly towards him, shaking with excitement, breathing heavily through their flared nostrils and yet, astonishingly, given his vast age, knowledge and experience, Tien appeared to be frozen with fear. His paralysing concern was not for himself however; it was for the fate of the Keeper and for what his death might mean for the future of his people. The future of his entire world too. Tien was genuinely petrified for the first time in hundreds of years, gripped all of a sudden by a dread of the unknown, which was the worst fear of all for a wizard used to knowing what was going to happen. He had no answers to the thousands of questions which had popped into his mind. He had seen no visions. The future was an open book, with blank pages yet to be written and words which fell drastically short of what he had expected to find, promising nothing now but disaster, destruction, and death.

When he gazed into Jake's eyes for one last time though, the qualms which had gripped him so strongly and left him almost unable to move, were suddenly eased a little, as the young boy simply winked at him to let him know he had accepted whatever fate had in store. Then, Jake went down on one knee and closed his eyes, placing the tip of his sword on the ground, as if he was praying.

The moment he did, everything around him seemed to slow to a virtual standstill. The first of the Thargws were only yards away as Jake then opened his eyes and began his attack. He launched into a frenzy of action, hurling his sword and wounding or killing scores of enemy warriors, as well as moving forward and managing to shield Tien at the same time.

It was an astonishing, miraculous display of swordsmanship, an exhibition of remarkable precision, power, speed and skill. The Thargws were amazed, but they were also infuriated. Thargws are a courageous and bold race. They live for war and they do not fear death. The incensed beasts just kept on coming at him, time and time again. Eventually, they swamped Jake through weight of numbers and he was soon at the very limit of his ability and endurance. Bodies were strewn all around him, but the fearless warriors simply stepped over them to reach the Keeper and continue the onslaught. And to make matters worse, at the head of them now was the Thargw emperor himself; their greatest swordsman.

Jake was absolutely shattered and his muscles were burning fiercely. He desperately needed to rest. He had had enough and he knew that he couldn't go on for much longer. The emperor engaged him and due to Jake's condition he soon gained the upper hand. The colossal beast was an awesome fighter. Jake was left frantically trying to block the powerful blows from the battlesword that were raining down upon him. He cried out to Tien in desperation.

'Save yourself if you can! I've had it!'

The wizard leapt forward, sword in hand. In one final act of courage, he threw himself upon the nearest group of Thargws, even though he knew that his ability with a sword was such that the fight would probably not last long.

And then, out of the darkness of night, came a thunderous roar of fury.

It was an ear-shattering cry unlike any other, full of pain and suffering, wrath, and a thirst for revenge!

Everyone in the city stopped what they were doing, including those warriors attacking Jake and Tien. The sound was so frightening, so powerful, that the Thargws all looked anxiously up at the moonlit sky.

Like Tien, Thargws were scared of nothing but the unknown, and such a cry of murderous intent had *never* been heard before.

Suddenly, a ball of fire screamed down upon them. Thargw warriors were killed in droves, disappearing instantly in a sea of flame. Then, another fireball fell from the sky, and another, and another...

Kerrallux soon became a storm of fire. The whole city was under attack!

The emperor immediately broke off his assault and ordered his warriors to find cover, forgetting all about Jake and fleeing to save his own skin. Jake was astounded. He was out on his feet and hardly able to hold his sword, astonished and amazed to still be alive. He checked Tien for any sign of wounds but there were none. Then he stared up at the flame-lit sky and saw the silhouettes of a host of dragons flying rapidly over the city, swooping down viciously upon its luckless inhabitants, taking them out systematically, setting the entire place ablaze. Every now and then he saw the flashes of light shoot from the creature's eyes, as they turned individual targets into black stone.

This battle, this seemingly endless war, had just escalated beyond measure. It was now being waged on an unimaginable scale. And this fight at Kerrallux was nothing short of a massacre, murder. It was retribution, pure and simple.

No part of the Thargw city was left unscathed, except for the stable block where Tien and Jake were standing and watching in awe as the attackers destroyed the rest of the city. The roaring flames came nearer and nearer, blown by a gentle breeze, but a solitary dragon swooped down and landed in the square not far from the two weary companions. It searched anxiously around with its eyes, looking for Thargw warriors, but the city defenders had all gone to ground by now, or been killed.

'Do not linger, climb upon me now!' the dragon bellowed.

Jake and Tien did not need a second invitation. They sprinted to the dragon as fast as their tired legs would carry them and climbed onto his lowered neck. Within seconds, they were flying away to safety, leaving behind them a scene of utter carnage, a blazing inferno, all that was left of the mighty fortress city that was the Thargw capital. Kerrallux had been reduced to nothing in a matter of minutes by the dragon's swift and deadly attack.

*   *   *

It was still the dead of a world-shattering night in Eratur. On a vast, blackened desert known as the Wrainx, the army of dragons landed. Once the lead creature had allowed his passengers to dismount, Jake and Tien found themselves surrounded by five of the awesome beasts, with their leader in the centre. The dragon shuffled backwards a little and bowed his head slightly. He said nothing. He appeared to be waiting for those he had rescued to begin the conversation.

'Err... Okay, I'll go first then,' said Jake, eventually. 'I am...'

'Please? We know who you are,' interrupted the dragon, in a strong, bold voice.

'You do? Yes, I suppose you must, seeing as you rescued us just in the nick of time? Gellsorr must have told you about me, about us?' Jake suggested.

'He has. He *did*,' corrected the dragon, the pain and hurt immediately evident in his bright, orange eyes. His despair was such that he looked as though his heart had just been smashed into a million pieces, as if he had just lost every single member of his family in one awful day. Both Tien and Jake could feel his agony deep within their souls. Another awkward silence was once again ended by Jake, who felt compelled to say something.

'I... I'm really sorry. I can't tell you how sorry we are. We... He was the bravest of us all, the most noble guy I have ever known.'

'He was. And now he is gone,' said the dragon.

Jake couldn't tell if the comment was meant as an accusation, or if it was merely a statement. However, before he could respond, Tien replied with an accusation of his own.

'Gellsorr came to you, to ask you for your help. Why did you forsake...?'

The dragon stared angrily at the old wizard. Smoke billowed from his nostrils and his eyes narrowed, halting the question before it was asked.

'He came. We did not listen to what he was telling us. And now, he is dead. The first of our kind to die in over three hundred years. His death call was heard by us all. It has brought us to you.'

Jake and Tien looked at each other, surprised.

'Death call? Really? You actually heard him, from so far away?' asked Jake.

'We did. Heard him, and felt his energy depart from us. When his life force ceased, every living dragon shared in the moment, in the pain. We are connected to one another in ways you probably will never comprehend. When one of us perishes, we all feel the anguish and desolation. For us, it is as if a part of us has left with them, and we know that we will never be whole again.'

'Oh, I see. Then, you must *hate* us for what we have done? And that being the case, I don't understand? Why did you save us? I mean, you'd already decided against helping?' said Jake.

'It was *you*,' answered the dragon. 'You are the one who freed Gellsorr and returned him to us. By doing so, you have unlocked memories and feelings which have lay dormant alongside his sleeping body, recollections of alliances forged, promises made, and vows broken. He was our eldest and wisest. His mind held more within it than any other, things which were long since lost to us. Since he returned, we have wrestled daily with our decision. Since turning him away, we have examined every inch of our conscience, searched our souls. If we had decided to return earlier, he would still be alive.'

The creature's eyes were now full of guilt and shame. He lowered his head a little, as those around him also lowered theirs. It was silent again for a few seconds, until Jake spoke once more.

'Look, nobody's perfect. You're here now. I don't know much about your history, only what I've been told, but the alliances you made with the Estians worked well once. Together, you defeated all those who stood against you. You beat off armies and wizards, everyone and everything who tried to enslave you. And you lived together in peace. It *can* be that way again, if you want it to? I will help to make it happen. However, I won't lie to you. It's far bigger than you could ever know. We're facing creatures and warriors who...'

'Revalkas? Graxoth?' interrupted the dragon.

'Yeah, and then some!' replied Jake, suddenly sounding more like his old self. 'I know they're your natural enemies and that they hunted you in years gone by. You'll have to face them again. The battles ahead will be hard-fought. If you join us, many of you may die. I think it's only fair to warn you of that, of what you're letting yourselves in for?'

A faint smile suddenly appeared on the dragon's lips.

'Gellsorr was right about you.'

'What?'

'He told us you were honourable and that you would tell us the truth, no matter how painful it might be. Though, that was maybe a little *too* honest of you?'

Jake and Tien laughed.

'Ha, ha... Yeah, s'pose so. I haven't quite mastered the art of deception as yet, or being a little more economical with the truth. I'm gonna have to work on that one,' Jake replied.

'Krrmmn... Know that when you *do*, Keeper, we shall in all likelihood leave,' stated the dragon, in a tone of voice which told everyone he was being deadly serious. 'I am Resus, the elder, now that Gellsorr has gone. Those you see around you are all that are left of my kind. We have lived in peace for hundreds of years, in self-imposed isolation. But, thanks to Gellsorr and you, we know now that we have been living a lie. We have denied our heritage and abandoned our friends, forgotten who and what we are. In such circumstances, sleep is hard to come by and peace is overrated, when you understand exactly what is missing and all you have sacrificed to attain it. We will return with you now to the days of old, Keeper. We would very much like to reclaim our place in Estian history, present and future. Lead us as you see fit. Command us and it will be done without hesitation, for as long as you stay true to yourself, to your beliefs and code of ethics. Gellsorr has opened our eyes and spoken for you. A new age has dawned. We are yours!'

Chapter 13
1st October – The City of Te'oull – Siatol

Just like the Heynai themselves, the great protective shield was growing weaker and weaker by the hour. For the present, it was holding, but the boundless hoards of monsters trapped behind it could not be held at bay forever. The time was fast approaching when they would be unleashed to attack the warriors of the Estian Alliance, free to rain down their destruction upon Te'oull and all the unfortunate souls who remained within its walls. It was a terrifying prospect, one daunting enough to make even the boldest of warriors flee. And yet, every single soldier in the Estian army held firm. In fact, their numbers continued to grow steadily and far from wallowing in the depths of despair, they were in some way gripped by a sense that something wonderful, inevitable, was about to happen. And their morale was bolstered further by Princess Zephany and Lord Caro's heroic displays of leadership, their speeches and tales of past glories or deeds.

Away from the wall, Ben and Jean spent what little time they had before the action becoming better acquainted. The youngster from Lichfield told what stories he could of his best friend, whilst Jean listened to the adventures of her grandson and his family and friends with intense interest. It was a highly emotional time for Jean, learning all about the husband and family she thought she had lost forever. For Ben, it was no less poignant. His own family was a dysfunctional one to say the least. In truth, he only had his father. He depended more upon Jake and *his* parents to get by and provide a stable family environment. Still, given all that was happening and perhaps because of the influence of Jean, he was missing his dad terribly right now. More than he would ever be able to say.

The others, Verastus, Queen Bressial, Brraall, Lord Castrad and all, had each been assigned a command by Princess Zephany on part of the wall or secondary defences. They kept themselves busy preparing their lines and organising the new recruits. Around midday, Sawdon and his vast army from Dassilliak arrived on the battlefield outside Te'oull. They were greeted by a succession of roars and high-pitch cries of delight from

King Vantrax' forces. It was an awful din which terrified the defenders of the city, who could hear every sound. However, one brave soul from Rhuaddan suddenly decided to sing. He was joined almost immediately by many others, in a scene Ben thought reminiscent of the film, 'Zulu', his favorite DVD which he had often watched with his father when he was young, before the drink and all of his troubles. The Ruddite battle songs lifted everyone's spirits and bolstered morale. Princess Zephany walked up and down the lines encouraging her compatriots to join in, singing at the top of her voice with her sword drawn, her face and demeanor the very picture of defiance.

Sawdon entered the command tent and received reports from the revalkas. He learned quickly that a full scale probe of the shield had revealed no gaps, no weak points which could be exploited. The armies he commanded were therefore unable to advance to contact with the enemy. It was confirmation of a fact he expected to find but one which still did not sit well with the impatient warrior.

'Raarrgh! So, since the wall halted your progress you have been idle? Tell me, what have you done about this situation, apart from resting while our enemy strengthens their defences?!' the Thargw raged.

The leader of the revalkas was incensed. He considered attacking the great Thargw warrior there and then, killing him where he stood for his insolence, his show of disrespect. However, he knew that King Vantrax would be furious if he did and the evil wizard's hold over the creatures was such, that they would not dare attack one of his servants.

Sawdon sensed his anger. 'Good! Turn that venom into something useful. Think. This shield must have a power source; a point of origin. It *has* to be being generated from somewhere nearby. Find the source. Kill the shield!'

The remainder of the nearest revalkas gathered around Sawdon as he spoke.

'Send your creatures far and wide, they are no longer needed here. We are more than enough to begin the fight if the shield falls. Begin a search of every hideaway, every forest, cave, dwelling you can find. Look for anything out of the ordinary, a distortion of light, a strange glow, wind, anything... Do not waste time investigating what you find. Destroy it! We are too far south for it to be an ally and these wretched rachtis before and around us are all our enemy now.'

The revalkas nodded and left Sawdon alone with one of his Thargws. The great commander was happy to once again be at the head of an army on a battlefield, free from the prying eyes and constraints imposed by his master, King Vantrax, if only for a short while. He felt alive, invigorated, invincible...

'Now we wait. There are hours of daylight left. With any luck, we will be able to attack them today. End this fight. See to it that our warriors are well rested and fed. Ready them for battle. When the time comes, I will lead the attack myself.'

* * *

Nothing was seen or heard from the revalkas for the remainder of that day and into the night. Just after midnight, an exhausted King Vantrax rode into camp alongside Melissa and his Personal Guard. The evil king took a short report from Sawdon before retiring gratefully to his bed, having forced the pace on his march to reach the battle as quickly as he could. An uneasy silence descended upon Te'oull and the valley before it.

Several miles away and not long after, over the Kielth Mountains, a lone revalkas spotted something strange in the darkness. A faint light was emanating from a cave, but this was an inhospitable, remote, uninhabited region and the fearsome beast knew immediately what it meant. It dived and swooped low overhead for a better look. The second pass was a full-blown assault. Two great fireballs were launched at the cave opening, one from each of its heads.

The Heynai spirits were almost half dead by now. Their excruciating ordeal had sapped every ounce of their energy. They had clung on to life only to gain every precious second they could, to keep the shield intact and the hopes of their people alive. Their faces had returned to a horrid blend of flesh and bone and where there was skin, it was ghostly white. They were shaking uncontrollably and all except Sereq were groaning in agony. They had not faltered or given in to the unbearable pain. The race, the contest between them, had not been won, but that did not matter now.

Sereq, the most powerful of the spirits, sensed the attack moments before it came. He broke the circle and warned his comrades, in an uncharacteristically weak voice.

'My friends, we are about to enter the afterlife together again. I will see you all on the other side.'

Before any of the other spirits could respond, the first of the fireballs smashed through the cave entrance. The flames hit the oxygen and engulfed everything. It was followed almost immediately by the second, and the great spell was broken. The shield and the Heynai were no more.

* * *

It was almost dawn at Te'oull. Ben Brooker was fast asleep, tucked up under a blanket with his thumb in his mouth as usual. All of a sudden, his sleep was interrupted by a dream unlike any other. It was so vivid and real that it was as if he was actually there.

In his mind, he saw the four Heynai standing in a circle holding hands. They looked awful, horrifying actually, *very* worse for wear. He tried to call out to them, but they could not, or would not, hear him. So, he watched and said nothing as Sereq suddenly stepped back from the others, breaking the bond between them. The old spirit began to talk briefly, but Ben could not hear what was being said. Then, almost immediately, a bright red fire engulfed everything there. The flames were so close that Ben could actually feel the heat. His arms lifted up instinctively to protect himself and he awoke, screaming.

'No!!!'

Ben realised immediately the significance of what had just happened. Within seconds, Verastus was at his side.

'What? What is it, Ben?'

Ben took a moment or two to calm himself. His heart was now pounding furiously in his chest and his breathing was heavy. After a short while, he looked Verastus in the eye.

'Oh hell!' he stated, his face full of dread. 'We're in for it now! The spirits have been cooked. They're toast. The barrier's down!'

* * *

On the other side of the valley, on the fields in front of the city and behind the Heynai's wall, King Vantrax was also fast asleep. A tremendous, heart-wrenching, searing, vicious pain woke him. He clutched his hand to his chest and screamed out in anguish. Everyone came running to see if they could help. Nytig reached him first, but the king pushed him away. He was desperate to speak but he just could not get his words out. He tried and tried to tell them what he had to say until he was blood red in the face, but the pressure on his chest was so great that it was all he could do to breathe. Everyone thought he was going to die. It was if he had had a seizure and it lasted a good few minutes.

Eventually the pain abated and he began to feel himself again, extremely relieved that his lungs were able to function normally and painfully aware that it had been a *very, very* close call. Vantrax finally looked up from his bed at Sawdon and Melissa. Where once there was a grimace of pain, there now developed an evil smirk.

'Recall the revalkas right now. That which blocks our path to glory has been destroyed. And so have those who would thwart me!'

Melissa looked at Sawdon and then back at her king, amazed and excited by the news.

'You... You are certain, sire?'

The evil wizard looked a little disappointed in her. He nodded. 'Yes, I am positive. What? Do you think I am lying? Go, go prepare for war!' Melissa left and the king turned to his Thargw gerada. 'Sawdon, I have protected you far too much of late. If this little episode has shown me anything, it is that our time is now. You are far more valuable to me commanding from the front, where your true talents can be utilised.

Though, I want you far enough from the fighting to be able to make command decisions. You must show a little constraint and learn the lessons of Erriard forest, you hear me?'

Now, you are to take this city at first light. Destroy everything and everyone you find. Wipe it from the map. We have them where we want them; trapped within the walls with nowhere to go. We have forces with us now that will ensure our victory, obliterate them all. It has been said before, but let us finally *end* this war!'

*   *   *

In the final few hours before daylight, King Artrex and the spirit of Gerada Knesh Corian had at last approached the valley before Te'oull. As they crested the final ridge, the vast armies of King Vantrax stretched out ahead of them, across the fields as far as the eye could see in the fading moonlight. Both warriors were unmoved by the daunting sight; they were experienced rebels used to facing impossible odds and they had expected to see such a force. But, Knesh Corian *was* troubled by one thing, his mind working as rapidly in death as it had in life.

'We are on the *wrong* side of them to be of any use, sire. Their armies lie between us and the princess. We will not be able to break through to Te'oull in time. If we had another few hours, maybe? We could use the darkness if that were the case and sneak through. But it will soon be light. They will see us. Well, *you* at any rate.'

King Artrex sighed heavily in exasperation. He knew his old friend was right, as usual.

'Then, how do we help?'

'There is nothing else for it. We will rest here, under the branches of that old tree. That way their beasts will not see us. Hopefully, tonight, we will have better luck. The shield should hold until then. When darkness falls again, we will make our move. After all, whilst the spirits protect them, all those defending Te'oull are safe from attack.'

Chapter 14
Dawn – 2nd October – The City of Te'oull – Siatol

'Princess Zephany... They are here!!!'

A very loud and panicked scream from one of the young soldiers on the wall ramparts interrupted Zephany's early morning stroll. She looked immediately at Lord Caro, who was as usual by her side. In a calm, decisive, confident and commanding voice she gave him her instructions.

'Sound the alarm. Raise everyone from their beds, and ensure they have enough weapons. Everything is to be coated in the poison of herethdar. Let us pray that it is strong enough to stop their beasts... And Caro!' she barked, as he began to run away. The Perosyan knight stopped immediately. He turned and awaited further orders. 'There is to be no panic, no hint of concern in our actions. I know what we face, but this is exactly what we expected to happen. It should come as no surprise to any of us. We knew it was coming so there is no cause for alarm. Remind our people of that, will you?'

The teenage princess who now led the whole of the Estian Alliance gazed up at the cloudless sky.

'Hopefully, if we all hold our nerve and become who we were meant to be, it is going to be a long and glorious day. A day that has been a very, very long time coming.'

Caro returned her smile for he knew exactly what she meant. He nodded once and then left to issue her orders.

Princess Zephany joined her warriors on the wall ramparts and looked out across the battlefield. She could see the enemy clearly, confirming immediately that the Heynai's shield had vanished. The revalkas and graxoth had begun slowly, forming up and gliding to within a few hundred metres of the wall. There, they had stopped and maintained their position. Zephany surveyed the massed ranks of enemy infantry below them, counting their numbers and noting the different factions amongst their ranks with interest. She was joined within minutes by Queen Bressial, Lord Castrad, Ben, Jean and Verastus. Finally, Brraall appeared, having taken some time to explain to his tribal warriors what was happening.

The footsoldiers of the enemy started to advance slowly, their roars, shouts and cries breaking the silence abruptly, like a chorus of thunder heralding the outbreak of a devastating tempest. Ben suddenly grew even more nervous and his stomach started doing cartwheels. He had faced a full-scale battle before at Erriard forest, but it still didn't prevent him from feeling sick. He drew his sword prematurely, his hand shaking so much that he almost dropped it.

'W-Why... Why don't they attack?' he asked, pointing anxiously at the creatures above, which were now hovering high over the city.

'They are waiting, assessing our strength. They are trying to note our weak points, anything they can use against us,' replied the princess. 'Relax a little while you can, Ben. They will be upon us soon.'

'Eh? Err... No, I mean, I don't want to hurry them if they're enjoying themselves up there. They can take as long as they want for me.'

Princess Zephany chuckled a little, along with the others. Verastus placed a reassuring hand on the young boy's shoulder, as Zephany gave one last command.

'Take your positions now. Remember, our warriors are looking to *you* for strength and direction, for courage. The example you set will win this day, I promise you.'

Ben just could not help himself. 'Oh. My section's in a bit of trouble then? And there was me thinking it had something to do with my best pal, and a certain box of stones? Well, where is he? Surely he won't miss this? Tell you what, I hope to blazes he doesn't!'

Verastus replied for them all in his deep, soothing tone.

'He will be here, Ben. He will not let us down.'

'Yes,' added Jean, who suddenly felt compelled to say something in Jake's defence. 'I can't say that I know anything about my grandson, for I haven't even met him as yet, but from what you've told me, he does seem the type to want to make a grand entrance, at the very last minute?'

'Ha, ha...' Ben laughed. 'Yeah, you're right. He's a right show-off these days, and that's just his style. But, just to be on the safe side, you stay right beside me and the big man, okay?'

Verastus reassured her with a confident smile and Jean nodded gratefully.

'Okay, Ben, I'll do as you say. My hero.'

Princess Zephany had the last word.

'This is supposed to be the beginning of the end, if the prophecies are true. Well, I hope so, I really do. Whatever happens here today, may the divine one, Nittri-Hebul, watch over you all. You are the bravest of companions. The greatest of friends.'

*   *   *

King Vantrax was at the rear of his armies, flanked only by ten of his Personal Guard and attended to by Nytig. Sawdon, Melissa and every available warrior had joined the attack. The king was taking no chances here at Te'oull. The Estian Alliance would be crushed by weight of numbers and his enemies would be destroyed in a single day. Nothing had ever been so certain. His forces outnumbered the rebels by over four to one and their ranks were full to the brim with far superior soldiers, warriors who were raised from the dead and powerful, merciless creatures who would do his bidding without question. Command had been handed to Sawdon, the greatest warrior ever to walk on Estian soil, though King Vantrax maintained control over the revalkas and graxoth. Once he received word that they were ready to commence the attack, he waited until Sawdon and his ground forces were half way towards the city, before unleashing them onto the hapless defenders. Sawdon watched the first of the graxoth begin the assault. He roared with delight and thousands of Thargws behind him joined in.

There was no finesse at all to this battleplan. The great warrior had no secret strategy, diversion or hidden surprise waiting for the Estians. Aided considerably by the aerial attack, the vast land army would launch an all out frontal assault on the main wall. The Thargws and Falorians were pulling and pushing the siege towers they had brought with them from Dassilliak, and that now dictated the slow pace of their advance. The remainder of the equipment had been left behind, Sawdon reasoning that the contributions of the revalkas and graxoth would far outweigh those of ballista, catapult, trebuchet and Retian firethrowers. The attacking throngs moved steadily but relentlessly forwards, for the distance to be covered was not great and their enemy, the Estians, were exactly where Sawdon wanted them; trapped behind the walls of Te'oull. They were going nowhere.

* * *

At the main wall it soon became apparent that the warriors there would bear the brunt of the assault. Princess Zephany ordered commanders and warriors from the other walls to assist, though she left enough in post to defend those sections if called upon. Soon, the first of the revalkas joined with the graxoth and the real battle began. The first wave dived down and struck the warriors on the wall, attacking in groups of threes and fours. It was a surprisingly co-ordinated assault and fire balls began to reign down upon the city. Princess Zephany sprinted to a section of archers she had positioned underneath the ramparts, out of sight. When the revalkas overhead came into view and slowed down to turn around, she ordered them to fire.

The arrows all hit their targets, but only two of the four revalkas fell from the sky. Zephany calculated quickly that it had taken over twenty strikes to bring them down, a worrying statistic given the shortage of archers and weapons in her army, not to mention the finite supply of liquid without Tien and his magic to call upon.

The graxoth swooped down out of the sky with alarming speed, mercilessly taking out any individual defenders on the wall who were brave enough to expose themselves in order to shoot their arrows at the approaching waves. The fire from the revalkas set buildings alight and tore into the ramparts. Within minutes, it was like a scene from hell. The dead and dying were everywhere, wounded warriors were screaming and the Estian Alliance was reeling under the sustained aerial attack, being badly mauled. It was a terrifying thought, but the land forces had still to be engaged, and the main battle had not yet commenced!

Zephany knew she had to do something, and quick. But, what could she do? Despite the valuable experience she had gained from years of fighting as a rebel, where she had grown accustomed to thinking of the unorthodox in order to save her skin and those of her followers, she knew the answer on this occasion, was *nothing*. The creature's onslaught was turning the tide of battle firmly in King Vantrax' favour before the fight had even begun. She had *nothing* in her arsenal to combat his beasts. The fight was only minutes old but the Estians were already losing the greatest battle in their history. They were dying in vast numbers and Princess Zephany was powerless to prevent the slaughter. The revalkas and graxoth were tearing them to pieces, and they were virtually unopposed!

* * *

At the eastern end of the main wall, Ben, Jean and Verastus were watching the scenes of carnage in the centre, gazing on in horror as the revalkas tore into their ranks. This was nothing short of a massacre. The warriors of the Estian Alliance were surely doomed unless something, a miracle of some description, happened very, very soon.

'Agh! Come on! There *has* to be something we can do?' screamed Ben.

The youngster's nerves had disappeared now. He was still terrified of course, but he was also feeling very, very angry and frustrated. He felt completely useless as Jean gripped his arm tightly.

'There's nothing we can do to help them from here, Ben. But, our time will come,' she said, in a soft voice which betrayed her fear and shock.

'Yeah? Well it had better hurry up!' the teenager stated, clenching his fists.

Suddenly, a single beast dropped from the sky like a stone and landed right in front of them. It was the last surviving sraine, one the evil assassins from Estian legends and history who had so nearly killed Princess Zephany and Jake in their last encounter. It had been carried to the fight by a graxoth. Spotting the distinctive shape of Verastus from up high, it had immediately decided to attack.

As it hit the ground however, two nearby Estian warriors turned to confront the savage beast. The sraine reacted swiftly and it leapt upon them with lightning speed. It sank its venom-filled fangs into their necks, administering its deadly toxin in the blink of an eye. Then it pushed off its victims to land only yards away, completely unharmed.

The courageous Estians fell to the ground instantly, never to rise again. The sraine then turned to face the three horrified onlookers who had witnessed the gruesome deaths of their comrades. Verastus moved in front of the others, drawing his sword with his right hand and shielding them with his giant frame, protecting them.

The sraine responded again and launched into an immediate attack. His powerful legs propelled him through the air and his poisonous fangs came within inches of Verastus' neck.

However, the Falorian's incredible reflexes and strength saved his life. He caught the sraine by its neck with his left hand and halted its flight, though the beast's momentum and weight toppled him and he fell backwards, onto his own sword. The sharp, jintan blade easily pierced Verastus' clothes and cut into his tough, Falorian skin. His whole bodyweight fell down upon it and the steel ripped through him to emerge on the other side, exiting his body on the right side of his stomach. He cried out in agony, but somehow he managed to keep hold of the sraine. He was now struggling violently to keep it at arm's length, to stop it from biting his neck and ending his life. But, despite his phenomenal strength, the wound in his side was sapping all of his energy. The sraine was inching closer and closer to his neck and soon its blood-stained fangs were virtually touching the Falorian's flesh.

A high pitch shriek suddenly rang out. It was not the sraine though, but Ben. In his excitement and alarm, he sounded more like a young girl than a teenage boy. He screamed for all he was worth as he raced forward with his sword outstretched and ran it clean through the horrid creature, narrowly avoiding striking his friend as the weapon came out the other side of its body.

The mortally wounded sraine took a moment or two to die. When it had ceased moving, Verastus cast it aside with one great, monumental effort and yelled again as the incredible pain returned. He tried to stand but he couldn't.

Ben was overcome by a feeling of complete and utter terror as he realised how close his friend had come to death, and seeing the terrible nature of his wound.

'Oh my God! How bad is it, big man?' he yelled.

Fireballs continued to rain down around them. People were dying everywhere, buildings were ablaze and crumbling, but Ben Brooker scarcely noticed any of that now. He just stared with extreme concern at the pained expression of his Falorian friend. Jean raced forward and took hold of his hand, sensing that he needed her support.

'It is bad enough, Ben,' answered Verastus. 'You must help me. You must pull the weapon out. I cannot fight on like this.'

'What?! Fight on? What you on about? Don't talk so daft. You can't...!'

'I can do nothing else!' interrupted the giant. 'I fight, or I die. It is as simple as that. Quickly now, there is no time to waste.'

Jean squeezed Ben's hand and then let go of it to help turn Verastus over onto his side. 'Go on, do it, Ben. He is your friend and you have to be strong for him. It is what he wants,' she said, looking deep into the young boy's eyes.

Ben gulped hard. His mind was in turmoil and his throat was parched. This was the last thing he wanted to be doing and he suddenly felt very, very queasy. But, he shook it off, took hold of the sword and breathed in hard.

'Okay mate, if you insist... Right... Ready? This is gonna hurt you a lot more than it'll hurt me.'

*   *   *

Back at the main wall, things had rapidly gone from disastrous to catastrophic for the Estian Alliance. No warriors were left manning the ramparts now, as everyone was sheltering from the fireballs and graxoth, leaving the advancing enemy footsoldiers free to take the wall unchallenged, completely unopposed.

Princess Zephany was incensed and dismayed by the way the battle was going, but she could do nothing to alter the situation and she decided against ordering her followers out needlessly, to face certain death. She gathered as many as she could around her and they waited under the stairs, ready to jump upon the first of the enemy to breach the wall. She could hear them approaching. The noise of their march grew louder and louder, until it seemed as though they were almost right on top of her.

Then, all of a sudden, a mighty roar echoed across the battlefield. It was different somehow from the shrieks and cries of King Vantrax' beasts and, unbelievably, it gained the enemy's full and immediate attention. The advancing hoards actually stopped!

Princess Zephany decided quickly that she had to see for herself what it meant. 'Caro! With me. Whatever that was, it holds their concentration, and *we* have the chance to regain our positions!'

Lord Caro responded in typical fashion. 'I am with you, Princess, to the bitter end. Lead on.'

They broke cover and the warriors around them followed. As they reached the ramparts and looked out over the battlefield, they were greeted by an awesome, incredible sight.

The entire army of King Vantrax, thousands and thousands of warriors, had halted only twenty feet or so from the wall. Their heads and eyes were all turned upwards to the sky. Zephany could see their features clearly and a surge of adrenalin shot through her body. She instinctively reached for her bow.

Lord Caro's hand stopped her however, by grabbing her arm firmly.

'Let go of me!' she screamed. 'That's...!'

'Look!' cried Caro, pointing upwards. 'Look at why they stopped!'

The princess lifted her head just in time to see an entire army of dragons launching attack after furious attack upon the unsuspecting revalkas. Fire flew in every direction and beams of deadly light painted the sky. Suddenly, there were scores of magnificent, lethal aerial dogfights of all descriptions raging over Te'oull.

The evil wizard's land forces recovered themselves almost immediately and resumed their attack, roaring with renewed rage and passion, as they realised they were too committed to halt their advance now. The Battle of Te'oull was destined to enter into Estian folklore, whatever its outcome. This was the first conflict in hundreds of years in which Estians and dragons would fight side by side. A resounding cheer suddenly arose from the defenders of the city as they emerged from their hiding places and retook their positions on the wall, just in the nick of time. With the revalkas and graxoth now otherwise engaged, they were left more or less free to engage the Thargws and their allies on the ground. The first of the ferocious beasts began placing the ladders and siege towers in position, as a solitary dragon flew swiftly down into the main square and unloaded its two grateful passengers.

Princess Zephany witnessed this and cried out to Lord Caro.

'Ra! Now, Caro! Now they will see for themselves how we *fight!* The time has come to make good on all promises, to fulfill the vows we made as warriors, and finally show our worth. Stand by me and watch me work. *This* is what I was born to. It is all I have known. In truth, I am better at nothing else. I confess to you right now that whilst I value peace above all, I am at home here, fighting and waging war!'

She looked up at the small rise at the end of the valley, where King Vantrax was standing, watching the battle unfold.

'Never, *ever*, kick me when I am down, uncle! You underestimate me at your peril. I am my father's daughter and always will be. When I rise, I shall take my revenge upon you! You will not live to rue the day you betrayed the true king, I swear it!'

Chapter 15
2nd October – The City of Te'oull – Siatol

The mother of all battles was now in full swing. An army of majestic, fire-breathing dragons had flown straight out of the Estian history books to appear over the besieged city, hoping to rescue the soldiers of the Alliance and wage war against the terrifying forces of evil threatening to destroy their new allies. Arriving just in the nick of time to stop the main aerial attack, the dragons engaged their enemy immediately and without warning. The element of surprise enabled them to kill several of the wizard's beasts in the initial assault. But, many of their awesome foe still remained and the dragons were now battling fiercely with the revalkas and graxoth in the skies above Te'oull, which had now become the battleground for a fight every bit as fierce and important as the one taking place below.

There, the massed ranks of King Vantrax' mercenaries had reached the main wall and begun to scale their ladders. Thousands of ferocious warriors of all creeds and origin stood poised to take the city. Hundreds of their comrades were waiting inside the siege towers, about to lower the ramps and storm the ramparts. The Estian archers were firing their bows for all they were worth at the enemy trying to scale the wall, sending arrow after poison-coated arrow into the attacking throngs, from almost point-blank range. However, the defenders of Te'oull had regained their defensive positions too late to inflict maximum damage upon the advancing troops and despite their frantic and desperate efforts, they were unable to stem the advance.

Sawdon watched on from below as the first of his warriors stepped off a ladder and onto the wall. The great gerada protected his own body from a hail of arrows being fired at him with the aid of a large Thargw shield, as he watched the fearless young warrior fall to a combination of Estian arrows and spears. The frustration and fury he felt within him was too much to bear and, despite his king's explicit orders that he should remain far enough away from the fighting to retain effective control, something snapped inside. He was incensed and could not contain his rage. Blood rushed through his body and clouded his judgment as his heart rate rocketed to an unbelievable pace. He raced to the nearest ladder and pulled the young Thargws waiting to ascend it away from the rungs. With his sword in one hand and his shield in the other, his huge claw-like fingers managing to hold onto the ladder at the same time, he raced up the rungs as fast as he could.

Arrow after arrow struck his shield as he held it aloft to protect his advance. When this failed to stop his incredible charge, several courageous Estian knights attacked him the moment he set foot on the ramparts. A spear thundered against his shield but Sawdon simply snapped it off with a strike of his sword and continued forward, killing with impunity as he took the rampart single-handed in an unbelievable display of courage, power and skill. He dispatched the Estian swordsmen who confronted him with effortless ease and fought his way swiftly along the wall. He was soon joined by two of his compatriots, who slowly beat the rest of the Estian defenders backwards and worked their way in the other direction, protecting his rear. Together, the three mighty Thargws suddenly halted and held their positions, showing incredible discipline and presence of mind and enabling more and more of their comrades to clamber over the ladder and onto the wall. The Thargw warriors appeared to be unstoppable. Thanks to their amazing and awe-inspiring leader, the foothold they needed to establish on the wall of Te'oull had been secured.

However, Sawdon was not done yet. With every one of his Thargw instincts now awakened and alive he felt as if his whole body was on fire, and he pressed home the attack. His eyes gleamed with uncontrollable excitement and saliva flowed from his fang-filled mouth. He began roaring loudly as he sent warrior after warrior along the ramparts in both directions. Now Sawdon and his Thargws were at their magnificent best. They excelled at close quarter combat and they tore into the Estian ranks without mercy. Their great battleswords ripped the defenders to pieces. Bodies and limbs were flung from the wall as they made their way along it in both directions. They were joined by several of the Estians, who chose to jump at the last minute rather than face the ferocious assault.

Lord Castrad was commanding this section of the wall, but along its entire length the story was the same. The enemy forces were overwhelming the Estian defenders. Isolated sections had already fallen and King Vantrax' troops were pouring into the gaps created in the Estian line. Everywhere the terrified defenders looked they could see the fearsome warriors beginning to spread out and fight their way along the wall. It soon became clear to all that the outer defences could not be held for much longer.

Lord Castrad could not see it however. The hero of Dassilliak had his eyes fixed firmly on a single warrior; Sawdon!

Ignoring the screams and shouts of Queen Bressial, who was commanding the secondary line of defence just behind him and could see everything that was happening, Castrad fought his way valiantly through defenders and attackers alike, killing and wounding several Thargws before finally coming face to face with their renowned leader.

'A knight of Nadjan!' stated Sawdon, the moment he caught sight of Castrad's tunic. Blood dripped from his sword and shield as he paused briefly amid the chaos of battle to savor the moment. 'A worthy adversary on such a day. Step forward, and I shall send you to the afterlife swiftly, with a warrior's death.'

His impressive array of teeth and fangs were exposed, enough to frighten any opponent. His eyes looked like they were on fire. The Thargw was having a wonderful day. A day as good as any he had enjoyed in a very long time, and it was just about to get even better. Each thick and rough hair of his fur seemed to stand on end increasing his already considerable frame, in an involuntary attempt to intimidate his much smaller adversary.

Lord Castrad though, was an experienced warrior in his own right. He had no fear of the terrible Thargw, despite his awesome reputation.

'Save your words and threats for those who would listen. You have taken your last step forward. This is not your land, Thargw! You stain it with your presence. It all ends here for you. Remember me and my people when you reach the other side. Let it haunt your days and nights for all eternity, how you failed in your attempt to defeat us!'

'Raarrrghh!!!'

Sawdon was enraged and he suddenly thrust his sword forward. Lord Castrad managed to parry the blow just in time and then launched several attacks of his own, all of which were repulsed easily by the mighty Thargw. They fought for several minutes whilst the battle raged around them, watched anxiously from below by Queen Bressial and her contingent of Estians. The Nadjan monarch wanted to help but she was powerless to intervene. All she could do was collect and organise those fleeing the fighting at the wall, to try and build another line of defence against the relentless hoards.

The giant Thargw's battlesword began to move even faster and it twirled and gleamed in the morning sun. Finally, one of the glints of sunlight caught Lord Castrad squarely in his eyes, distracting him for a vital fraction of a second.

And a fraction of a second was all Sawdon needed.

With astonishing speed, he feigned an attack to the Nadjan's right, but pulled his arm away when half way through the swing and switched direction, so that his sword now came from the left. The momentary loss in concentration caused by the sun's rays undid the noble knight. He was too slow in countering the move and the battlesword cut heavily into his left-hand side, inflicting a serious, mortal wound. Castrad fell to his knees almost immediately. He looked up at the Thargw warrior just in time to see the final blow, as Sawdon plunged his blood-soaked weapon deep into his neck.

Below them, Queen Bressial screamed out in horror at seeing the death of her beloved cousin. However, her cries were lost amid the tremendous noise of battle. The death of Lord Castrad devastated her. She was immediately consumed with grief and despair, but all she could do was glare helplessly at the great Thargw warrior and watch as he merely stepped over the body to continue the fight.

He was now advancing rapidly towards the steps which led down to the city itself and he would soon be upon them. He was relentless, invincible. Sawdon and his Thargws had now virtually cleared this whole section of wall. Hardly *any* Estian defenders remained to oppose them. It looked as though *nothing* could halt their progress.

*   *   *

In the centre, things were also not going well for Princess Zephany. Just as elsewhere, her archers had fired so many arrows trying to bring down the graxoth and revalkas that they had too few left with which to defend the wall. Most had already exhausted their supply and picked up a sword or axe, in order to fight on as ordinary footsoldiers. Two siege towers and several ladders had unloaded their rampaging warriors onto her section of the wall. A fierce fight had ensued as the Estians somehow managed to counterattack, led bravely by the incomparable Lord Caro. The defenders tried and tried to force the Falorians, Thargws and Retians back over the wall but to no avail.

Princess Zephany was positioned a little towards the rear with the second line, itching to join the fight but knowing that she could not, aware of her command responsibilities. After a short while, she could see for herself that the wall was lost. With a heavy heart she instructed a hornblower to sound the recall and her warriors began to disengage from the fight. The Estians fell back as quickly as they could. They converged on the outskirts of the city as planned, to establish their second line of defence. All along the length of the wall they vacated their positions and their places were taken quickly by enemy warriors. Vantrax' beasts climbed onto the ramparts and stood shoulder to shoulder with their comrades, staring down menacingly upon the ranks of beleaguered defenders, who now faced them across a relatively short distance.

The flight of the Estians had actually been so rapid and unexpected, that a short and unplanned pause in the battle followed, as the evil king's forces tried to stabilise the line and consolidate their positions.

Things were looking exceedingly bleak for Princess Zephany and her army. Seriously outnumbered and outclassed, without the Keeper, his wizard or his stones, they once again appeared to be in a hopeless position. They knew the enemy would resume the attack very soon and the battle would be over.

Lord Caro fought his way through the ranks to find the princess and stand by her side. He was breathing hard because of his exertions and he took a moment or two to speak.

'I... I am sorry, princess, there were just too many of them. We could not hold the wall as you ordered.'

'I know, Caro. I could see. You fought bravely. None could have given more. All we can do now is sell our lives as dearly as we can,' replied Zephany.

Caro looked a little stunned, and confused. 'This is it then? But, Jake? Where is Jake? I saw him land. What has happened to the Keeper?'

'He has gone. He attempts to secure the final stone we seek. We have run out of time. We need the stones and we need them now. Jake has left with our blessing and he has taken Tien with him, in the hope that he can restore them without delay. For us however, I do not think he will achieve it in time.'

Lord Caro breathed in more deeply than he had ever done. He let the air out slowly, deliberately. Then he turned to face the enemy.

'I have never feared death, princess. I will face it now with you and look it straight in the eye, proud beyond measure to serve you and be your champion. Promise me though if you will, that should the chance arise, if fortune favours us and I survive long enough, their leader, Sawdon, is mine?'

Princess Zephany raised her eyebrows in surprise.

'Such a strange request at this time, given our plight? But yes, gallant knight, I believe I can grant you that, should it fall into my hands to be able to do so. Though, I fail to see why it is of any importance to you *who* does the killing?'

'It is quite simple; he is their best. I am a professional soldier, have been all my life. There are few challenges left to one such as I.'

'Challenge?' said Zephany. 'This is *war*, Caro, not sport!'

'It is sport to me, princess. Some may consider mine a filthy, murderous occupation, but I do not, and it is all I have.'

Princess Zephany glanced up and the terrifying hoards of warriors massing on the wall for the final attack.

'We are an odd pair you and I, of that there is no doubt. Out of place in parts of this world some would say, among the more civilised sections of our society. And yet, we seem to have stumbled upon the very time and place when our kind are needed most? Farmers and tailors do not wield a sword like you and I. They do *not* win wars. Not without us to guide them? Yaar, we are here now, let us see it done! I... I cannot see the Thargw among their number?' she stated, pointing along the wall. 'I am sorry, Caro, it does not look as though you will get your wish today. I do not see Ben or Verastus in our ranks either?' she added, now searching her own lines.

'No, neither do I. Perhaps they are...?' began Lord Caro.

'Do not think it! Do not say it,' ordered Zephany, cutting him off in mid-sentence, deliberately. 'Jake left to greet them briefly before he departed, he may have taken them with him. Or we may just be unable to see them. Either way, we must look to ourselves and our people. As soon as they have formed their lines, the enemy will resume the attack... Make ready!' she cried, at the top of her voice. 'No more retreats from here! Make them pay dearly for every inch of Estian soil they take! Axes, arrows and spears to the front! Wait for my command... When it is given, send this army of beasts back to the fires of Zsorcraum from whence they came!'

* * *

Some time earlier, King Artrex and the spirit of Gerada Knesh Corian had observed from a distance as the armies of King Vantrax advanced on Te'oull. When the revalkas and graxoth began their attack and were engaged by the dragons, the two old soldiers were amazed and elated to see that the evil wizard was left standing on the small hill, guarded only by his manservant and ten of his warriors. Their delight was tempered somewhat however by the fact that all ten sentries were members of his elite Personal Guard. The two friends looked at each other immediately, both convinced their time had come and that they would *never* have a better opportunity of assassinating King Vantrax.

'This is it!' hissed Artrex, with a gleam in his eye. 'This is what you meant by my destiny, is it not? We were never meant to reach Te'oull. I have to kill my own brother. I must take his stone.'

'Yes. I did warn you. I told you that you had a part to play yet. We have no time to waste. The land between us offers good cover. We should be able to approach unseen and move to within striking distance. From there, I will draw off his Guard, leaving you free to tackle your brother. Can you do it, given your wounds? Are you up to it, sire?'

King Artrex looked down upon his injured arm. He was still very weak and it *was* his sword arm. However, he knew he had no other option open to him but to try, for the good of his people and the future of his world.

'I will not lie to you, Knesh, my friend. I would choose another time and place if I could. But, Vantrax was never good with a sword. If I can get to him quickly, before he uses his stone, his magic...? Yes, I can do it. I will take that reolite of his and end his life, for that is what has to be. I will do it, or I will die in the attempt!'

Knesh Corian's face was beaming with pride as he looked at his lifelong friend. 'You know, in this land which seems to breed heroes in abundance, I can honestly say that I know of no braver soul than you, my king. I would follow no other. Save for your daughter. If *anyone* can do this thing, it is you.'

King Artrex smiled and thanked his loyal gerada, almost forgetting that he was addressing a spirit and not a living being.

'Then let us go and steal this day. Time waits for no-one. It is the day of final reckoning, and it has already had its dawn.'

* * *

At the same time, Jake had just bid farewell to Resus, the eldest of the dragons. He watched him soar upwards into the sky and rejoin the battle, before rushing with Tien to find Princess Zephany. Their brief conversation had been short and to the point, given the dire situation and the need for haste. Jake now had four of the five stones he needed to restore the box. The powers concealed therein he still did not understand fully but he believed them to be sufficient to turn the tide of this crucial battle, and he hoped for all he was worth that he would know how to use them when the time came, in order to fulfill his destiny and defeat the vast armies of King Vantrax. Maybe even to kill the evil wizard himself. Zephany stated that he should seek the final stone without delay; to try to use them and end the war before the Estians were overrun but Jake hesitated a little. He wanted Ben by his side.

'I know the urgency, princess, but please don't challenge me on this? It has to be this way. Don't ask me why, but he *has* to be there,' he'd insisted. 'Besides, I've already lost him twice now. I want him where I can see him, and protect him!'

Princess Zephany relented and informed Jake where he could find Ben. Not wishing to delay him even further, she said nothing about Jean. Tien sensed that something was amiss, that there was more to be said, but he went happily along with Jake as they searched through the carnage of Te'oull for their friends. Eventually, they found the teenager standing beside the stricken Verastus, who was clutching his huge hand over an open wound in his stomach. An old lady stood next to them. She was ridiculously out of place in the midst of a battle but Jake scarcely noticed her as his heart suddenly leapt for joy and he raced to hug his friend. Like Ben, he was grinning from ear to ear, and crying joyous tears of relief.

'Alright, alright mate,' said Jake, when they had both calmed down a little. He pushed him away gently and looked him in the eye. 'It's been some journey, hasn't it? You don't get all this in Lichfield. And it isn't over yet. We've got to go and do battle with King Vantrax now. We have to steal his stone.'

'What?! Jake, are you certain you know what you are doing? His powers are too strong. He will kill you!' Verastus objected.

'Nah, not really. To be honest with you, I'm not sure of anything anymore, except that I have to try,' answered Jake, truthfully. He stared down with concern at the Falorian's wound. 'But then, I've been winging it from the very beginning, so that's nothing new. Err… You're wounded, and it looks bad? Shouldn't you be resting, or getting help?'

'It is nothing.'

'Liar!' cried Ben instantly, with far more force, far more emotion than he meant to show.

'Frah! You need not worry about me, I will recover. You have far more important concerns, both of you. I promise that I will seek assistance as soon as the fighting is over. Does that satisfy you?' asked the gentle giant.

'It may satisfy *them*, but it does not satisfy me. Here, let me look at it,' Tien stated, moving forward to inspect the gaping wound.

But to everyone's surprise, Verastus objected once again, this time far more strongly. 'Leave me be! There is no time. You have to get that stone. It is a thousand times more important than me. I will be fine I tell you. Now go!'

'But...' began the wizard.

'He's right, Tien. We must leave now!' rasped Jake, interrupting just as vigorously. His face had hardened all of a sudden and he was overcome by a cold-hearted look of determination. 'Come on, Ben, you're coming with me this time.'

Ben tried to argue the point but it was a half-hearted attempt and the words petered out pathetically, as the youngster realised that he really didn't know what to do for the best. Jake's sudden and forceful resolve told him that it was not a request this time. He had to go, no matter how much he did not want to leave Verastus behind. Deep inside, even though no-one seemed willing or able to explain, he knew somehow that there would be a very good reason why.

'Okay then, if that's the way you want it, Keeper. But, before we go, this is...'

Ben tried his best to introduce Jean to her grandson. She had remained in Verastus' shadow all the time, patiently waiting for her turn to speak and seemingly invisible to Jake. Tears were in her eyes as she stepped forward slightly, sensing that her time had come. However, the teenage Keeper was now in determined mood and *nothing* was going to distract him from the task in hand, or stop him from doing what he had to do.

'Sorry, time's up. We really have to go!'

Before anyone else could speak, the two winged horses reappeared from out of nowhere and landed before them, having been summoned by the Keeper moments before using the power of his mind. Jake ushered Ben quickly to the first stallion and mounted it, helping his friend to climb up behind him and ignoring all his protests.

'I don't mean to be rude, mate, but this thing can't wait. Now, no more talking. Hold on to your hat, Ben me boy. This is gonna be short and swift. We've got a date to keep you and I and it won't do to miss it. There's yet another battle to fight and my name's written all over it. Has been since the beginning of time, apparently. So, let's do this thing and then maybe we can *finally* go home!'

Chapter 16
2nd October – Outside Te'oull City – Siatol

King Vantrax' entire body was now tingling with nervous anticipation. He was like an expectant father awaiting the birth of his child as he watched the battle unfold before his very eyes. The evil wizard was standing on a small rise, situated on the fields which approached the city. His servant, Nytig, was by his side. As far as he could tell everything appeared to be going well for his legions of hired and raised beasts. It was clear that after the initial assault by the Estian archers, who had hastily retaken their positions on the wall and managed to fire several salvos of well-aimed arrows into his soldier's ranks, his relentless attackers had quickly regained the momentum of their advance. The tyrant's forces now stood on the wall itself, in almost every area he could see. Countless thousands were waiting below at the ladders to join them. To the king's immense satisfaction and relief, he saw the wall had been taken. The greatest obstacle in his way had fallen without so much as a decent fight. It would surely be only a matter of time now before the gates to Te'oull were opened and the city fell.

'Raar! They have done it, Nytig!' he roared with delight. 'They are inside the wall. Nothing can stop me now. The Alliance is defeated and Te'oull is mine!'

'Yes, my lord. May I be the first to offer my congratulations? The hardest part is over, anyone can see that. Your victory on this day is assured,' Nytig answered, tamely. His voice was flat, betraying no hint at all of emotion, no joy or enthusiasm, a fact which neither bothered nor concerned his master. The warriors of the king's Personal Guard on the other hand, began celebrating and congratulating each other as if the battle and the war were already won, though most were looking upon the remarkable scene before them with mixed feelings, and envious eyes.

'Do not trouble yourselves,' began the wizard, sensing their disappointment at missing out on the action, 'after this day, we shall go on to take the rest of Siatol and Estia. There are still forces to fight; those foolish enough to resist me. I promise you shall *all* have your fill of fighting before we are through. I will see to it.'

His words were greeted with unanimous approval but the warrior's cheers were interrupted suddenly by noises of a different kind. From within the long grass behind the ridge, they suddenly heard a very loud rustling sound. Startled a little by such an unexpected and unknown interruption, everyone turned around to search the landscape before them with their eyes, cocking their ears to listen at the same time.

There it was again! There could be no mistaking the fact that there was distinct movement in the tall grass ahead, as though a very large and clumsy creature was approaching their position. King Vantrax and his warriors scanned the entire area once more but could see nothing untoward, just grass and a few trees.

'What was that, sire?' asked a suddenly very nervous Nytig. 'What should we do?'

The king did not answer straight away. His warriors all drew their swords and closed ranks. Vantrax was certain now that someone or something was watching him. He could feel their eyes burning into his soul. Though he could not see the unknown danger, he knew for sure they were out there.

A few seconds of tense silence followed, before the unnerved wizard eventually replied to his servant's question. 'I... I am not certain what it is, but I know *something* comes. Remain where you are. We are being observed.'

Hearts began to beat a little faster as the uneasy quiet was suddenly disturbed by the sound of a large twig, or small branch, being snapped in two. The loud crack echoed across the landscape, sounding almost like thunder to those listening intently on the ledge, rising even above the noise of battle. To the experienced soldiers of the Personal Guard, it was clearly a planned, deliberate noise. That, or the foolish mistake of an incompetent warrior who had just sealed his own fate. All turned immediately to the king, awaiting his orders.

'Well? What are you waiting for, you fools?' he barked at them, his nerves now frayed. The soldiers began to run towards the unknown threat, but the king halted the nearest warrior before he had gone too far.

'Not you! *You* remain here with me. There may be others. Keep a sharp lookout and your sword at the ready.'

The remaining warriors of the Guard sprinted to the edge of the rise and ran down the slope to reach the long grass. There, the experienced soldiers halted their charge, fearful of ambush. They proceeded cautiously forward, fanning out into an extended line in order to search the ground ahead, mindful of the fact that the long grass, which reached their thighs, provided excellent cover for any attacking force. The small wooded area on the other side appeared to be deserted but the soldiers were certain that the noise had originated from there and they decided that they had to check it out. It took them some time to clear the grassland but eventually they reached the slope which led up to the trees. As they neared the first, a powerfully built knight suddenly stepped out from behind the tall, thick trunk. His sword was drawn and he looked ready for a fight. The warriors before him changed their expressions and closed up around their leader. One look in their eyes revealed what they were thinking; *This is no incompetent fool.*

'Now, if I am not mistaken, the land we walk this day is Alliance territory? That being the case, I would question what you are all doing so far south? Indeed, I would go further and offer you some advice; leave now! Go back to your fortress, and take your wizard with you. For if you remain, I will be forced to kill you all... No? None of you willing to see sense? Come now, surely it is better to live a coward, than die a courageous fool?'

The spirit of Gerada Knesh Corian was having fun. He had never appeared so menacing. He loomed before the soldiers larger than life, using all his powers of concentration to make his image look as real and as threatening as he possibly could.

Knesh had employed an old rebel trick to begin the diversion, imitating the snapping of wood vocally in order to gain his enemy's attention, the sound magnified by a power beyond his own. But, having succeeded completely with the first part of his elaborate deception, everything now depended upon how long he could hold his form. How much time he could afford his friend by keeping the formidable warriors occupied. So far, the ruse was working. The soldiers of the Guard actually believed that the threat before them was real, leaving King Vantrax virtually unguarded.

'Yah! I do not understand why you do not run away? The choice before you is as clear as can be. Tell me, are you all simpletons? Is that the entry requirement for the Guard these days? My my, the standards have fallen in recent times. Sawdon must be very proud?'

So be it then. A fight to the death it is. Now, let me see? Nine of you, is it? And one of me. Krmmn... I would consider that fair odds. What do you think? I could even fight with my weaker hand, if you prefer? Maybe place my sword hand behind my back? No? I was beginning to feel a little cold standing here all by myself. Step forward and feel my wrath. I do not know what awaits you on the other side of this life we live, but you have chosen your own trails so it is time to find out.'

The elite warriors were astonished by the lone knight's impudence. There was something vaguely familiar about him but enraged as they were by his mockery, they could just not identify what it was. They all looked at each other, at first uncertain how to respond to such an unexpected and ridiculous challenge. As members of the King's Personal Guard, they could scarcely believe that someone, *anyone*, would dare ignore their status and reputation to deliver such a suicidal affront. It was a ludicrous declaration of defiance from a hopelessly outmatched foe and a few seconds later, it was an ugly looking Retian in the centre of the group who replied on behalf of them all.

'You would like that; for us to come at you one at a time, like traags to the slaughter. You would no doubt consider it the honourable thing to do? While we hold the advantage of numbers however, it will not be that way. I know not who you are but you have dealt your last insult, and you will pay for it with a slow, agonising death.'

He gestured with his sword arm urging the others forward, as he took a step towards Knesh' position. 'Come on, we will take him together, from all sides.'

The nine hired killers advanced steadily. They spread out once they neared the ghost of the Ruddite gerada, until they had him completely surrounded and Knesh was in the centre of an ever-decreasing circle.

'That is it. Keep coming. The day is young and my blade is yet dry.'

Finally, the large Retian lunged forward and began the attack. He thrust his sword viciously towards Knesh, aiming for the great warrior's stomach. The spirit of the seasoned veteran tried instinctively to block the blow with his own weapon but, to the complete amazement of all the warriors there, the Retian's sword passed straight through the image of the gerada's blade to appear out of the other side of his body!

'Ha, ha, ha...'

Knesh roared with laughter as he stared the mystified Retian in the eye. It took less than a second for the king's guard and his companions to appreciate what had happened. The look of absolute horror on their faces as realisation dawned, filled Knesh with a feeling of immense satisfaction.

'Ha! And you are the *best* he has? We have nothing to fear, it seems. Live and learn. This lesson is on me; the cold jintan steel of a sharpened sword is an awesome weapon, but it is *nothing* without a sharpened mind, and a strong arm, behind it.'

* * *

Weak and feeble, but brimming with determination, King Artrex had worked his way around the ledge by now. He was concealed in the long grass which lay at the foot of the slope, in front of his evil brother. His heart was racing and he could scarcely catch his breath. He looked up and stared at the backs of King Vantrax and his two followers. When he judged the nine warriors of the Personal Guard were far enough away, just as they were confronting Knesh, he drew his sword and silently raised himself to his feet. Then, he charged towards his brother for all he was worth, the memory of almost twenty years of bitter conflict and hatred burning within him.

Artrex' sword was held in his one good hand. It was stretched out in front of him as he intended to run it straight through King Vantrax' body. The tip was fast approaching the evil wizard's back and there was nothing he could do. He had been caught completely off-guard and he was once again only seconds away from being killed.

But suddenly, the Lichtus stone around his neck began to glow brightly. It vibrated, warning the wizard of imminent danger, just as it had done so many times before.

'Zsabrutt!'

Vantrax felt the change and screamed the ancient word without hesitation or thought. A shield of bright white light covered him once again from head to toe, and it was not a moment too soon.

The tip of King Artrex' weapon crashed against it almost immediately. It bounced off sideways as if hitting a wall of steel, stinging the rebel king's arm and hand so badly that his whole body felt the blow, and he cried out in pain.

The noise was so loud that it immediately alerted all the warriors of the evil wizard's Guard on the plain below. But, they were at the treeline now and too far away to help. Having just discovered the shocking truth about Knesh and learned that they had been fooled, they immediately began rushing back to the small hill in a desperate effort to protect their king.

The closest of the warriors however, the one who had remained behind to guard the wizard, heard the attack and responded swiftly. He turned just in time to parry King Artrex' sword with his own, as the Ruddite leader launched his second assault upon his brother.

The almighty clash of swords devastated King Artrex. He turned with a heavy heart to engage the elite soldier, realising instantly that his efforts to kill his brother had failed.

Before he could begin the fight against the fearsome warrior though, the shield of white light surrounding King Vantrax suddenly vanished and the powerful wizard ordered the Sevitrian to halt.

'No! Wait! He is mine. Step away.'

The disciplined warrior obeyed the command immediately. He took a pace backwards but kept his sword raised. King Vantrax drew his own weapon from its scabbard and moved forward to take his place.

'Sire!' yelled Nytig, alarmed by his master's actions and thinking more of his own protection than anything else. 'What are you doing?!

There is no need to endanger yourself. Your Guard can perform this task?'

'Relax, Nytig, I am of sound mind,' replied King Vantrax, his voice now cool and calculating. The nerves of before had disappeared, now that he had his nemesis, his lifelong enemy, exactly where he wanted him. 'This is my brother before me. Though I have denounced him time and time again, he is still my father's flesh and blood. Magic and wizardry be damned on this occasion. I will see him die by my own two hands! I will prove who is the better; the one more worthy of the throne.'

King Artrex had fully expected to die when confronted by the Sevitrian warrior. He could hardly believe what was happening. He was at his brother's mercy now and he was sure that he would show none. For years, Vantrax had been hunting him down, persecuting him and his people, his army. And now that he *finally* had the chance to kill him, he was giving him a fair fight? It did not seem possible.

Though, with a little more time and thought, King Artrex began to believe that he could read his brother's mind.

'Ah! Yes, I see why you delay; you have noted my wounds?'

Vantrax smiled wickedly as he took up a guard stance and faced his sibling. He looked more than a little uncomfortable with sword in hand but he was still confident of defeating his weak and injured opponent.

'I cannot deny it. It has not escaped my attention that you are not perhaps the warrior you once were. Wounds such as those should help to even the odds and ensure a fair fight? After all, brother, it was *you* who had the schooling in warfare, and you who was given the opportunities to lead our army in battle. Come to think of it, it was you who had, *everything!*'

Artrex looked a little shocked to be discussing such things at the end of a sword point. He was absolutely stunned, amazed to be discussing anything at all.

'*Now?!* You want to talk of this now? Very well. You speak of past history, of times long gone. Look at us and what we have become. It is *you* who has everything now, because you took it. You stole it! It was not yours to take, brother. In the beginning, I sought only peace between us. *You* wanted vengeance. You wanted war! And for what? What did I do that so wronged you?'

'You... You were... First born!' the wizard raged, his face blood red in anger. His blade moved threateningly close to that of the rebel king.

'Yes, though it was hardly my fault? And for *that* you destroyed our kingdom?!' Artrex roared in reply.

'Yes! And I would destroy much more! You were handed *everything* that should have been mine, solely due to your birth date, nothing more. You had to work for *nothing*! You were weak. You wasted the power handed to you. But, I am the stronger of we two. I will take it all; the entire continent. I will raise it to the ground if I have to, and it shall be rebuilt as I command. Nothing and no-one can stop me.'

King Artrex' heart sank. He knew this brief conversation was probably his last and it confirmed all of his worst fears.

'Then, there is nothing more left to say, is there? I was right to oppose you from the beginning, to resist for as long as we did. My army will fight on. They will never surrender. So, let us finish this quarrel between us here and now. I do not care to live in this world if you are its leader. Look hard upon me, brother, for my wounds go far deeper than those you see; I am *ashamed* of you! Embarrassed to share your bloodline. If he were here, our father would...'

'Grar! Enough! You!' Vantrax bellowed, to the lone warrior from the Guard. 'As soon as the others get here, tell them to spread out and ensure that he does not escape. Keep your eyes on the fields around us for there may be others. Though, I think not? We would have been attacked before now if there were. Do not intervene in this fight, whatever the outcome!' The warrior nodded obediently. 'Good. Now, *rebel*, prepare yourself. You have thwarted my plans for the last time. The spirit world awaits.'

King Artrex raised his sword to defend himself. His whole body ached furiously from his wounds, combined with the effort of his journey. His face was a picture of determination but he was in no real condition to fight.

'At last. I pictured a different scene when I dreamt of this day, but

I am ready to die, or live, should that be my fate. Can you honestly say the same? I would give *everything* I have willingly, for this land and all who live here.'

*   *   *

Jake, Tien and Ben flew low and fast over the battlefield. The winged horses headed straight for the hill and King Vantrax. Several arrows whizzed past as the attackers below tried to shoot them down. Some only missed their intended targets by a very narrow margin and Ben became increasingly scared.

'Bl-bloody hell mate! If we *do* manage to survive this thing, which I seriously doubt, I'm never gonna let my dad make me watch another western on telly again!'

Jake ignored the comment and concentrated on weaving the horse from side to side in order to avoid being hit. Within minutes, they were clear of the army and approaching the rise. King Vantrax was standing with sword in hand at the centre of a circle of warriors, just about to attack Artrex. The rebel king looked in a very bad way. His wounded arm hung limply by his side and he was clearly in no shape to fight.

Jake couldn't believe what Artrex was doing. It seemed to be a futile gesture, though he knew it was a courageous one borne of desperation. He decided quickly that he had to intervene straight away to save the rebel king's life. However, before he could act, another voice sounded loudly inside his head. It was a strong, deep voice, and it was warning him. Tien and Ben heard it also.

'No, Jake! You must not interfere!'

Ben recognised it immediately, a fraction of a second before the others.

'Cast your eyes towards the trees. I am over here,' the voice instructed.

As they approached the hill, they looked beyond it and saw the spirit of Gerada Knesh Corian waiting for them.

'Knesh! What do you mean? What should we do?' asked Jake.

'I know you want to help the king. I can feel your desire. It is only natural that you should think that way, but you cannot. You must not. You have to come to me now, before it is too late,' answered Knesh, almost begging them to listen, desperation resounding in every single word.

'Too late? Too late for what? And what about Artrex?' said Jake.

'He buys you the time you need. He fulfils his destiny. It is what was always meant to be.'

'What?! That's no choice! That's crazy!' Ben screamed, with his thoughts. *'We won't leave him to die! It's not our way.'*

'You must trust me, Ben. It breaks my heart also. However, the king knows exactly what he has to do, and he is doing it. He understands what it means. He would have it no other way.'

Ben tried once more to object but he suddenly felt the horse veer away to the right, changing direction and heading straight for the trees.

'Hey! What the hell are you doing?!' he yelled at Jake, shouting so loudly over his shoulder that he almost burst his friend's eardrums. Tears of frustration and sorrow began falling from his eyes once more. 'Go back, go back now! We *have* to save him!'

As the horse began to land next to Knesh, Jake replied to his distraught friend. 'I'm feeling it too. But tough choices come with the territory when you're a Keeper. I can't ignore what Knesh has said. I have to believe that there's a reason for it. A reason I might not understand as yet, but one I know I can't dismiss. I've been afraid of making these choices. It doesn't come easy sometimes you know. The stone's powers, they come and go. When I'm me, the old Jake you know and have grown up with, it really scares me to death. And I don't want to grow up so quickly. Sometimes, I'd trade it all in if I could, to go back to being me again, but right now I *can't*, can I? All I know is, if Knesh tells me to walk into the fires of hell, I'm going to do it! I'm sorry, mate.'

'Yeah? Well, it's no good telling that to me. Tell *him*!' snapped Ben, pointing back towards the hill and the surrounded rebel king. 'I'm glad nobody told you to abandon *me* when I needed help, when I was dying with that Taskan's poison inside of me. What's the difference, eh?' Ben asked, his emotions getting the better of him as he attacked his friend with an immature outburst, his reaction highlighting perfectly the difference between the two young boys now.

'Me! *I'm* the difference. Every now and then I feel and act like a boy, like any normal teenager from back home, but those moments are getting fewer and fewer. I *want* to feel the way you do, really I do, but I don't. We've got to face facts, Ben; I'm not the boy I was. There'll be glimpses of him I suppose from time to time, but I'll always revert to being a Keeper, with all that goes with it... You know it's the stones, don't you?' he asked, looking his best mate in the eye, pleading for understanding. 'It's not who I am really. To be honest though, if I *was* told to leave you now, I don't know what I'd...'

'What?!' interrupted Ben, completely gobsmacked. 'You mean, you'd *actually* leave me out here?'

'Ha, ha, ha... Ah, stop your whining. I was just playin' witchya,' said Jake, winking at him. 'Now, let's see what Knesh has to say? Remember, it's not over yet. The day's still young and I can't hear any fat ladies singing, can you?'

Chapter 17
2nd October – Outside Te'oull City – Siatol

'Knesh, if we can't save King Artrex, there must be something really important you have to say? What is it you want us to do?' asked Jake, as soon as they reached the spirit of the fallen gerada.

Knesh could see the anguish in their eyes. He answered without delay and there was a great deal of urgency in his voice.

'Quickly, take out the box of stones and open it, now!' the ghost replied, motioning towards Jake's bag with his head.

'What good will that do, against such a wizard? It is not yet fixed and the stones will not work,' stated Tien inside their heads, unable to see how the gems could possibly help in their current state of disrepair. Privately, the wizard also believed that, if *he* did not have the answers, Knesh certainly would not.

The spirit of the Ruddite warrior shook his head. 'Their condition is irrelevant, trust me. I was given one final instruction by Sereq, and I mean to see it through. It is all he told me before he and the Heynai left, for there was no time to explain. Even I do not know what is about to happen. The only thing I am certain of, is that this is what *must* take place. These were my instructions. He was very clear that they *had* to be followed!'

Jake took the box from the bag and passed his hand over the crest. It opened very slowly to reveal the five stones. They did not light up this time and a disappointed and concerned Jake looked over at Tien, before shrugging his shoulders and placing the box down on the ground.

'What are you going to do?' he asked of Knesh.

'Yeah, what's the plan?' added Ben, his eyes now wide with anticipation.

Knesh Corian chuckled slightly at the youngster he had come to like enormously, in so short a time.

'My plan, Ben? I am glad you ask. For perhaps the very first time in my life, and in my death if it comes to it, I do not have one. I am following your example, and trusting my instincts. It does not come easily to one such as I but I am throwing caution to the wind, hoping that I am doing the right thing. I must leave you now, for good. I go to join with the spirits, in the afterlife. The fire which keeps me here is the only thing that will help you all, I know that now. Sereq needed no words to convince me. He simply stated that I would know what to do when the time came. And I do. I would stay with you if I could, to see Princess Zephany safe from harm and victory won, but you *need* this. You cannot win without it.'

'But...!'

The instinctive reaction, the strong, forceful objection that was about to be voiced, lodged itself firmly in Ben's throat. Despite his sudden and intense desire to air his true feelings, it almost choked him, and it would not budge. Unusually for the often-impetuous youth, he made no further sound. He desperately wanted to say more, to beg Knesh to reconsider, but he knew they were out of time and he did not believe that the soldier would wait long enough for him to speak.

As if to prove him correct, the giant warrior nodded a quick farewell and thank you gesture at the same time. Then, before anyone could say or do anything else, he threw his body head first at the box of stones!

His ghostly image diminished and narrowed rapidly as he neared the box. In a flash, he had disappeared inside.

The very instant he was gone, everything on the battlefield and in the city froze. The incessant noise of battle ceased abruptly, as thousands of warriors, creatures and dragons suddenly became living statues. Time now stood still on the whole of Estia. No-one and nothing moved on the entire continent, and probably beyond.

Nothing. Except for Jake West.

The young Keeper's body was as rigid as all the others and yet, unlike them, he was fully conscious. He tried his hardest to move but he could not budge an inch. Only his mind and his eyes seemed to be working. He realised immediately the opportunity that this unexpected development presented. He tried again with all his might to walk, hoping to free his limbs so that he might attack King Vantrax while he was unable to defend himself. He had been handed a golden opportunity to do something to save King Artrex and win this war and he was determined to make the most of it. But, apart from being able to see and think clearly, the young guardian of the stones was as powerless as everyone else to act.

Frustrated beyond belief, he tried his hardest to fathom out what was happening.

Why have you done this, Knesh? How is this going to help? Or was it you, Sereq? Have you come back to help me, despite your last goodbye? Either way, what's the point, if you're not going to let me kill him?! Come on, let me go? I can end this fight here and now!

All of a sudden, a bright image appeared before him. It took Jake completely by surprise and he would have jumped out of his skin, if only he was able to move. Instead, once the light had faded, he was astonished to find that an exceedingly beautiful woman wearing the simple dress of a peasant was standing in front of him, not six feet away. Her dress was tattered and torn, faded almost to rags, but it did not detract from her striking beauty, and her kind, caring face.

She looked around the land with sympathetic eyes, staring at the countryside for several minutes in complete silence. Jake could do absolutely nothing but watch her, for she ignored all his attempts to engage in conversation, as if she were closed to his mind and in no hurry to speak. He soon realised that she would do so in her own good time and he stopped trying. He looked her closely up and down, trying his hardest to figure out who she was in the meantime. Her eyes were now full of tears. Her heart appeared to be breaking. It was a sight which almost moved Jake to tears himself. He had never seen such a display of raw emotion, of abject sorrow and pain.

Then, for no apparent reason, Jake suddenly felt his jaw loosen. Though the remainder of his body remained stiff and rigid, he found himself able to speak, and he knew instinctively that he was actually being *invited* to say something.

'Who... Who *are* you? What is happening?' the youngster asked.

Her eyes met his slowly.

'It falls upon you, Jake West, to save this world and many others.

The time has come for you to act. The war of wars is here.'

Jake was thinking something along the lines of, *Duh! Tell me something I don't know!*

But, he decided his particular brand of cheeky humour might not be appreciated at this moment in time, by the spectre before him he did not know, the seemingly all-powerful being who had somehow suspended time itself. He chose quickly not to risk upsetting her and toned it down a little.

'Err... I'm sorry. I'd normally have a witty remark or two for that one. I mean, it is kinda stating the obvious, isn't it? I know I'm needed here, supposed to be here to help win this war. What I *don't* know, is what I'm supposed to do to bring that about? How am I going to help these people?'

The mysterious spirit smiled a little. She glided closer to Jake as she replied.

'I understand your doubts, Keeper. Though, which of us is ever certain about the path we should take in life? When faced with uncertainty and choice, the right decision is rarely the obvious one. It is often hidden from us. We have our instincts to guide us, but we are never *really* sure of which way to travel, whether we are doing the right thing, until we take that first step, are we? Even then...? If we are lucky, we are shown the way, as you were. I sent four guides to help you, Jake. They were there to help all those who fought against evil in this land. Some called them the Heynai. In their wisdom, they chose to enlist the help of a mortal. At their bidding, Tien, the wizard, also helped to keep you from harm, until such time as you were ready for what you have to do. And more recently, Knesh Corian was returned to you from the beyond the realm of life.'

'*You?!* You sent them all? But I thought...?! Well, I suppose I should be saying thank you then? But who *are* you? Please, I have to know?'

'Why? Why must you know? What purpose would it serve? Would you decline this helping hand I offer to you now, for lack of response?'

'Eh? Of course not. I just think I should know, that's all?'

'Then, if that is all, I shall answer; I am the mother of all you see. I am the one who gave birth to this land, and all of its children.'

'So... So you're a God, or something?' replied Jake, wide-eyed.

'A God? Yes, if you please. That is *your* word but it is perhaps the best way for you to understand. Some here call me Aballas. To others I am Suferra, the Wind Maiden, or Theon, the Bringer of Light... I have many names and many forms to those who believe in me. But, perhaps Nittrii-Hebul, is the one you will have heard?'

'Nittrii...? Yes, Princess Zephany and others have mentioned you. Then, you can help us? You can free me, and let me kill King Vantrax? Hey! You can restore the stones for us and...!' began Jake, suddenly growing wild with excitement at the thought of the endless possibilities if he had a Goddess on his side.

'No!' interrupted Nittrii-Hebul, forcefully. 'Understand now, that I can do *none* of those things. It is forbidden.'

'What?! Why?' fumed Jake.

'I have made that mistake already, and I am afraid that you may soon have to pay for it. I... I sent the Heynai here to help. It was wrong of me to do so and it broke every law we have. Direct intervention is strictly forbidden. These are *all* our children, good and bad, do you not understand? No, Jake, it is not as simple as you appear to think. I cannot take sides in this war. I must not. This long struggle has to be...'

'But that's *rubbish!* I'm sorry,' interrupted Jake, vigorously. His confidence was growing once again, for no apparent reason other than the stones. 'That makes no sense to me at all. You've *already* interfered, haven't you? You chose your allegiance, and you have made it known.'

'Yes, I am afraid you are correct. Though, as wrong as it was, all I did was try to even the scales. I had managed it once before and was not discovered, when I handed the prophecies to our people at the beginning of this war. So, I foolishly believed that I could do it again. I gave them hope when they needed it most. It is hard for you to understand I suppose, why I would do such a thing? King Vantrax and his evil magic had grown far too strong. They were about to defeat *everything* put before them, to destroy this world I love. Watching from afar I could not let that happen and do nothing. I tried to help in the smallest of ways, thought I could, without anyone knowing. The Heynai spirits were not supposed to meddle with fate. No-one was supposed to know of their existence. They were merely there to provide guidance, to support those who needed it, and ensure they were equipped to fight on equal terms with the wizard. I expressly forbade direct involvement. They could not fight!'

'I see... I think. But, I'm not used to Gods who make mistakes. That's gonna take a bit of getting used to... Hang on, let's get this straight? You went too far. You never meant to, but you overstepped your boundaries? Something went wrong, didn't it? Someone found out who was not supposed to know? Okay, I get that but... Well, why are you here now? What can you do for us?' asked Jake, trying to take everything in, unsure how long he might have.

The mystical deity looked thoughtfully at him as she decided how to respond.

'I did not want to come, Jake. I should not be here. I underestimated Sereq and the lengths he was prepared to go to for his people. He knew I would not stand idly by as all my spirit guides deserted you, that I would not leave you at the mercy of the wizard and his armies. I think he may love this land almost as much as I. He and the spirits have gone to the next life. It is now... Yah! I cannot watch from afar. You have no chance of winning this war. Now that Knesh has left you also, you are all doomed to die, with no hope of victory. Not without my assistance. Estia will surely be lost if I do not act. It will be plunged into a thousand more years of darkness, of despair and misery.'

Jake, I risk more than you will ever know by coming here. You were right. Others like me have discovered what I have done, sending the spirits. They are enraged and they are demanding action to redress the mistakes I have made.'

'Oh. That don't sound good? But... Good ol' Sereq! I'm sorry, again. I heard your warning, but I must say I'm a little relieved that you came to help. And it sounds as though I have Sereq to thank for that? So, it's not over yet, there's still a chance and you're here to help. What happens now?'

Nittrii-Hebul looked him straight in the eye as she took one step closer to his frozen form, until they were almost touching.

'Listen to me. The battle in the city does not go well. Despite her bravery at Dassilliak, Princess Zephany will have to prove herself all over again if they are to survive. They *all* will. King Artrex will fight this duel with his brother and he will lose. He will knowingly and willingly lay down his life for his people, for the land he loves. I can do nothing to stop that now. King Vantrax is unique amongst the Estian wizards the Heynai have faced. With the reolite he possesses, he is far more powerful than anything we have seen since the box of stones was formed. *You* have to take his stone away from him to complete the restoration. There is no other way.'

'Yes, I know! Let me go now and I'll do it!' pleaded Jake.

'Tah! As tempting as that is, you would not get close. Not now. He is wary of attack and he would have seen your approach on those horses. He would use his magic to defeat you. I would have to undo what I have done, for to free you alone and let you act individually, would be to defy the rules by which we live. I would bring down such wrath upon you and I, on all this land… No, Jake, the others like me, they would find out and *never* permit such an act.'

'Then, what *can* we do?' asked the severely frustrated youngster.

'The sacrifice made freely by Knesh has empowered the centre stone. For how long I cannot tell, but he was strong, his energy is also. You have a fully working reolite stone to use again, Keeper. Be warned though, it is not powerful enough to defeat the wizard. For that, you will need the other stones and the box restored.'

'Tien! He has the others with him. We can mend the box here and now!' Jake cried with excitement.

'You have a sharp mind. But no, you will not have time. As soon as you activate the stone on this world, everything will return to normal. The attack on the city will recommence and you will be defeated before you can complete the restoration. Replacing any of the stones in that box will result in the same outcome.'

'Oh for...! This is ridiculous!' Jake screamed in disappointment.

He wracked his brains to think of another solution. 'Okay... answer me this; with this one stone alone, is there *anything* I can do to give me the power to defeat him?'

'No. It would take three or four Keepers to combat his evil now.'

Jake's lips suddenly began to curl upwards as an idea straight out of left field formed in his mind.

'Tell me, if I used the stone to go back to my home world, would I be able to return? I mean, if the stone's power held for long enough and I was quick? And would it start things again here? Would they all come to life and start fighting again?'

Nittrii-Hebul turned her back to him and began to walk slowly away. Her image started to fade. Jake called after her in desperation several times, but she would not stop walking.

'Stop! Wait! I need to...!'

It was no use. Within seconds the spirit was gone. Jake's body immediately relaxed and he found that he was once again free to move. His first instinct was to test what he had been told, to attack King Vantrax and try to end his life. He knew it was wrong, that it was not the chivalrous behaviour of a hero, but the stakes were so high now that he ignored his doubts and turned around, drawing his sword.

One step further towards the wizard and he walked straight into an invisible shield, an impenetrable wall through which there was no possible route to get at him. Jake realised immediately that he was being prevented from taking action. Feeling slightly guilty for having even tried, he sheathed his sword, before throwing his arms upwards in a flamboyant gesture and shouting at the sky above.

'Okay, okay. It was worth a try?'

He was also a little disappointed with himself for behaving in such a fashion, but he immediately stepped up to the box.

'Cashlesh it veruq nicch leshtuq semin aresturn,
nach valiq Harry!'

A white light shot out of the centre stone and raced up to the sky in a fraction of a second. Jake took one more deep breath, looked at the frozen figure of his best friend, and muttered quietly to him.

'I know this phrase has been done to death pal, but like a Terminator, I'll be back, I promise!'

He stepped into the light, picking up the box of stones as his body disappeared.

Chapter 18
2nd October – Inside the Light

The multitude of differing sounds and images which greeted him were at first just a haze to Jake, nothing more than blurred shadows lining on both sides a seemingly endless tunnel. Nevertheless, they brought with them a strange kind of familiarity, and a soothing feeling of hope and optimism, which comforted the anxious youngster almost to the point of bliss. He had almost forgotten what it was like to be so happy. And as he continued to hurtle through the vortex at tremendous speed, the images suddenly slowed down without warning, until they were keeping pace with him almost and he could see each as they passed by, though he was looking through a kind of wave effect which distorted his view somewhat. He was astonished to find that he was able to discern what was happening and even pick out certain individuals. Unlike his previous experiences, *this* time he was completely in control and the journey home appeared to take far longer to complete, lasting a good few minutes at least. He relaxed a little and stared with fascination and wonder at the images surrounding him on all sides.

Through the unclear air he saw battles fought, weird and wonderful lands he did not know, as well as hideous creatures, warriors of all shapes and sizes, and curious beings existing somewhere between life and death. With intense curiosity and wonder, he noted that in every single vision there was a human being just like him.

They're Keepers! he deduced, his heart beating faster all of a sudden. *They're all my ancestors!*

Jake West was actually staring at a moving picture show. The sides of the tunnel had somehow become an extraordinary, unbelievable pictorial record of his family's past; the battles they had waged, the victories they had won throughout their existence, as they all fought as Keepers to protect the stones and defeat the various forces of evil they faced. The short sequence of events traced the defining experiences of each Keeper's life. Some had but a few and appeared in one or two images only. But others, like Harry, had many.

Jake's mind was now emptied of everything but the scenes before him. He tried his hardest to take in every single second of this journey, to watch and learn as much as he possibly could, in whatever time he had. Everything else paled into insignificance right now, for Jake was living an impossible dream, feeling on top of the world, and he did not want the exhilarating ride to stop.

The final image once again involved Harry. His grandfather was standing on a battlefield, next to a youthful King Artrex, who was as usual accompanied by Knesh Corian. Suddenly, a runner appeared from out of nowhere, sweat pouring from him as he fought hard to catch his breath. He appeared to deliver some devastating news. It was a report which had the King immediately distraught. The great warrior fell to knees, crying. Harry and Knesh tried to help him up, but Artrex refused to move.

Before Jake could fathom out what had happened, the image disappeared and the light ahead of him suddenly tore itself apart. Jake tumbled through the opening at speed. He fell onto a hard and shiny surface and slid along it for a split second before a solid wall brought him to a sudden and crashing halt. His shoulder took the brunt of the impact and he yelped in pain. It was almost dislocated with the force of the blow, which winded him badly.

Recovering quickly due to his Keeper's powers, he looked up. All he could see around him in the tiny room was a white toilet and a sink, besides the box of stones he had dropped in the far corner as he fell. Jake sighed with relief as he saw the light was still shining.

'What was that?!'

The startled voice sounded loudly and it came from the other side of a closed wooden door, from an adjoining room. Jake rose to his feet and rubbed his aching shoulder. The pain was leaving his body so quickly as he rubbed that it felt unnatural, but the unmistakable sound of approaching footsteps made him stop. With nowhere to go, he waited helplessly to be discovered.

For those few seconds his heart began to beat faster than it ever had, for if he was prevented from returning to Estia now, all would be lost. He found it strange that he should react that way, for he had faced far more dangerous situations and remained perfectly calm.

The door opened slowly, cautiously. A pair of nervous-looking eyes appeared and scanned the room, looking for the culprit responsible for the unexpected noise, the crash which had sounded so abruptly in a place they knew to be unoccupied.

'Dad!' Jake cried out happily. He could hardly believe his eyes, or his good fortune. 'Oh dad, I was hoping and praying you would be here,' he added, without pausing for breath.

Almost immediately, a second head appeared, looking over his father's shoulder in disbelief. 'Is that...?!' it began, shocked and amazed to hear and recognise Jake's voice. 'Jake! It's you! It's actually you! Come here!'

June West pushed her husband aside in her exuberance and rushed to hug her only son. Tears of unadulterated joy exploded from within. She held him closely, more tightly than she ever had. It seemed that she would never let him go again, and she was trembling, shaking uncontrollably with excitement and relief.

'Alright, alright, save some for me,' said Graham, when it became apparent June was not going to let go.

He stepped forward and June reluctantly passed Jake over to his father like a rag doll. The ecstatic teenager did not object though. Instead, he fell happily into his father's arms and he knew instantly that he would be perfectly content to remain there forever, if only he could.

June looked on only for a second or two before saying, 'Oh, to hell with this!' and throwing her arms around them both.

The family embrace felt like heaven to Jake but, despite his contentment, he knew that time was short and he had to act swiftly. He pushed them both away gently, with some difficulty, before he tried to explain what was happening.

'No, please? I'm sorry, there's no time. I have a job to do. This fight isn't over. Not yet. You both have to listen to me.'

Frowns of frustration and disappointment crossed his parent's brows. They obviously believed that their son had returned for good this time, and they could not hide their unhappiness. However, after all they had learned, all they knew about their son's destiny and his role as a Keeper, they understood that it brought with it dangers and responsibilities he could not avoid, or ignore.

'What is it, Jake? Tell us, we will not interrupt,' June replied, speaking for them both.

'Thanks, I was hoping you'd say that,' answered Jake, with a smile. 'Okay, first things first, how's granddad?'

'Why don't you come and see for yourself?' his father answered, a beaming smile raising Jake's hopes in an instant.

Jake followed them into the private room and immediately saw his grandfather was sitting up in his bed, a tray of uneaten food lying across his lap. He rushed over, pushed the tray away, flung himself across Harry's chest and hugged him as best he could, though he was careful not to press too hard against him, given his condition.

'Yes! Granddad, you're back!' he cried, eventually.

Harry chuckled slightly at his grandson's typical response as he gently pushed Jake away. He gave a very weak cough and then replied in a weak and feeble voice.

'Yes, Jay, I'm back. No overgrown wolf is gonna beat me. It's so good to see you. But, I think we'd better save our reunion for another time? We need to explain what has happened, why you're here. He needs to know.'

Graham instinctively knew they were talking about him. He approached the bed and retook his seat with June.

'Dad?' he asked, inviting an explanation.

Harry turned his head towards Jake as he spoke. 'Your boy has something to tell you. But, to save time, I will cut to the chase. Your mother, she is alive!'

'*What?!*' shrieked Graham, in a voice far higher than any man they knew possessed.

Jake's eyes also widened with shock and surprise for he was astounded by Harry's knowledge.

'That's impossible! How can that be?' asked June, who was equally as dumbfounded as everyone else. 'She's dead, has been for years?!'

Everyone looked to Jake. His mouth was wide open. The realisation had just dawned on him, hitting him like a wrecking ball right between the eyes. His head and eyes turned back towards his grandfather, as a sickly feeling filled his gut.

'The old woman! The one with Ben and Verastus, she was...? She is...? Oh my God! How could I have been so blind? Ben, he was tryin' to tell me summin'. I should've listened, I should have...!'

'No time for that now, Jake,' Harry interrupted, sharply. 'You have to talk and explain, and quick!'

'Err... Yeah, I know, you're right. Okay, I'll explain a little. Knesh was as strong as anyone... I've been told this stone will be strong also, so it should give us a little time. You'll all have to wait for the full version. I... Hang on! How did you know, granddad?'

'I told you before you left; I've had visions of your journey,' Harry replied, his answer kept deliberately short and sweet. He turned immediately to his son, Graham. 'You have to go back with him. You have to help.'

'Eh?!' Graham responded, absolutely astonished at the ridiculous, ludicrous statement. 'Are you *mad?* I'm no Keeper. I am not even...!'

'You are *family*. You are of our blood,' stated Harry. 'Like it or not, you carry the same genes within you as all Keepers, which means you have the power, even if you do not know it.'

'Well, thanks for bringing that up now, after all this time! But, why? Why must I go?' asked Graham.

It was Jake who answered. 'Granddad's right, dad. That's why I returned; to get you. We only have a few minutes more at best, until the light disappears forever and we are trapped here. The box is not yet fixed. It won't work unless *all* of the stones are replaced. The last is with King Vantrax and he is the most powerful of all the wizards. I have to take it from him. I'll do it, but I'm not strong enough to do it alone. Trust me, it's gonna take both of us to...'

'The *three* of us you mean,' interrupted Harry. As all eyes fell upon him once again, he had a look of complete determination. 'I am going with you!'

He pushed the tray further away and then pulled back the bedclothes, before swinging his legs over the edge of the bed, once the others had moved out of his way. Every movement was painfully slow and he breathed hard and fast. He felt as if he had just run a mile.

'You *can't*, granddad. This is ridiculous. You're not strong enough, just look at you!' said Jake.

'Yes, Harry, listen to your grandson?' pleaded June. She tried to rush to his aid but Harry held up his hand and refused her help. 'Oh, come on? You can hardly stand. What good will you be?'

Harry placed his feet down firmly on the floor. With great difficulty, he pushed down hard on his weakened legs and stood upright. He was shaking, but he was once again standing on his own two feet. The others saw something in his eyes they had never seen before; a fiery resolve which almost had them scared.

'This is not my first action. It has to be this way. There is nothing else to say. Three Keepers... at least, remember?'

'That... That's what Nittrii-Hebul said!' stated Jake, amazed once again by Harry's awareness.

'Nittrii...?' began Graham.

'It doesn't matter.' Harry cut him off before they were delayed further by the need for yet more explanations. 'The power in that stone will revive me enough to complete the task, I hope. If we succeed, the box of stones will do the rest. If not... well it will not matter too much, will it? They will come. Now, let's go, we've been here long enough. Let's defeat this wizard and save my wife! Ha! You do not know what it means to be able to say those words. I would give everything just to see her one last time, to hold her in my arms.'

'Err... *Save* her? Does she *need* saving?' asked Graham, confused.

'You will see when we get there, son,' replied Harry. 'Prepare yourself for the shock of your life. *Everything* you are about to see and experience, is something I tried my hardest to shield you from. Now at least, you may begin to understand why? Pass me my clothes.'

Harry dressed in double quick time with help from Jake. As he did, June said a quick goodbye.

'My entire family are heading off to war,' she said, as she kissed her son. Tears were streaming down her face once again. 'I never thought I'd see this day. I love you all, but I feel so, helpless.'

'I know. I'm sorry, mum. I can't imagine what it must be like for you, but can you just run interference for us please? Try to stall the nurses and doctors for as long as you can? Tell 'em granddad's on the toilet, or in the shower?'

'Yes, I'll try, Jake. You just go, and leave it to me,' June answered, wiping away her tears. She turned to her husband. 'Graham, now don't you go being a hero! Remember, it's your first time out there as a Keeper. It's going to be weird for you, but you'll have to listen to Jake for a change. He's the teacher now and you're the pupil, okay?'

'Yes, yes, I know. I promise you; it will be the first and last time I *ever* have *anything* to do with these stones. And you needn't worry; I'm no hero. I never wanted to be one.'

June kissed him tenderly on the cheek. 'You're *my* hero, and don't you go forgetting it! Always have been, always will be.'

'Okay, let's go,' said Harry, as soon as he was ready.

Jake and Graham helped him to walk to the en-suite bathroom, where the light was still shining out of the box. Harry halted them briefly before they stepped into the brightness.

'This is all that matters for us right now. Cast every thought from your mind except for this battle, this war. It's about righting the wrongs done to our family. It's about taking back what is rightfully ours. So, save any doubts you may have for another time and place. We cannot falter. We dare not fail!'

Jean, we're coming, darling. We're coming!'

*   *   *

Three generations of Keepers were now inside the light. Their combined powers were such that this journey seemed to take forever. Each of the images played out before them on the sides of the tunnel was like an individual movie trailer. They began with the first of the Keepers, Jacob West, and they ended with Harry himself. It was a glorious, living history lesson and it was being played out right before their eyes in real time. The story of all the Keepers to date was revealed in short segments. The key battles fought by every one of their ancestors who had bore the title with such dignity and bravery, the saviours of countless worlds, were shown one by one.

Harry was enthralled to once again experience the sensation of travelling through the light, though he was amazed and delighted to be travelling for so long, and to find everything so clear. In his previous time as a Keeper, Harry had taken the same journey on many occasions but his powers were nowhere near those of Jake and the images had been swift, hazy and blurred. Now though, not only could he see them clearly, he was actually able to see himself, to hear the noises and watch the action unfold, as his own memories were played out before him.

Jake managed to grab hold of his father's hand. Together, they stared avidly at the spectacular scenes. There was no need for words; the gravity of what was happening was not lost on either of them. For the very first time, Graham began to understand everything his father and those who came before him had done. He realised with disbelief and horror all his father had gone through, what he had endured, and all that he had tried to save him from. A solitary tear rolled down his cheek, a single drop of guilt, of shame for the way he had behaved. He remembered how he had blamed his father for everything that had happened and his feelings were made worse by the knowledge that *he* had been spared, when his only son had not.

Once again, the final images revolved entirely around Harry. The battles fought were many. The wars he had waged as a young man on worlds so different from our own were bloody and frequent, often on a scale that could scarcely be imagined, and the scenes of his triumphs now blew his son and grandson away. All the time everyone had believed he was away with his regiment. Jake and Graham stared at the back of Harry's head, as he hurtled through the light ahead of them. They looked at the little old man they knew and loved, the gentle pensioner who wouldn't hurt a fly if he could help it.

They would always love him, they knew that. But they would view him with very different eyes after today.

Finally, the last of the images appeared. This time it was not a battle they saw on some strange world, but the image of a house on Earth. A house that was just like any other house they might know. They each saw Jean as a young woman. She was sitting in the living room and she was bound to a chair. Standing over her was the frightening, terrifying and mighty figure of Sawdon!

All three Keepers were suddenly overcome by intense emotion. But, before they could make sense of what they were seeing and feeling, the light ahead of them opened up to reveal a host of long-bladed grass.

Chapter 19
2nd October – Outside Te'oull – Siatol

King Vantrax thrust his sword forward once again with real purpose, aiming for his brother's heart. The weapon was parried for the umpteenth time by a last-ditch intervention from the rebel king with his own blade. Artrex could barely stand at this point and yet he was somehow managing to hold his own against his unwounded sibling, using every ounce of skill and energy he possessed.

As the frustration and anger within him increased, beads of sweat trickled down the wizard's brow. He began blowing hard. He was tiring badly. King Vantrax was not used to swordfighting; he paid others to do that for him. Ordinarily, he chose not solve his problems this way and it showed. He could scarcely believe Artrex had lasted this long however, that he had not been able to complete the kill, for his brother's wounds appeared too severe. And despite the intense hatred he felt for him which had been forged over many years of rivalry and conflict, Vantrax could not help but be impressed by his brother's showing of resilience and pride, though he refused outright to show it. The fight should have ended quickly; he was far stronger at this present time than his injured and weak opponent. But it was already several minutes old and he showed no signs at all of capitulating, despite it being a largely one-sided affair with the fit and able wizard moving more freely, dominating his rival.

King Artrex, the once great warrior who had won many battles, just refused to concede defeat. He blocked, parried, thrust, swung and jabbed for all he was worth, trying desperately to find some way of beating his adversary, his nemesis. However, there appeared to be no way through Vantrax' guard. The injured king's few attacks were painfully slow due to his wounds and soon he found that he had to use all of his considerable experience and skill just to stay alive.

Before long, his wounded arm throbbed with agonising pain and his chest felt like it was ablaze. The roars, cries and shouts from the warriors of the Personal Guard around them rang in his ears, sapping his morale, like the baying for blood of an execution mob waiting impatiently for the axe to fall. They urged their evil master on to victory with untold passion, encouraging him, cheering for him, desperate for the wizard to complete the kill.

In fact, the warriors were so engrossed in the fight before them that they ignored *everything* else on the battlefield. The fight for the city no longer mattered at this moment in time, for their hearts were now filled with an incredible lust for vengeance. *This* was the rebel king they had hunted for so many years with no success. Artrex was the ruler responsible for the deaths of so many of their warriors and comrades. He *was* the Ruddite Rebellion. Without him to lead it, it would fall as swiftly as a Dzorag's axe, collapse into nothing in a very short space of time to bring about the long-awaited victory they all sought. This fight marked the end of the long war and the beginning of a new dawn. It would usher in a time of evil, where the Personal Guard and all who served King Vantrax would thrive.

Just beyond their position, in the field of long grass that lay just beneath the hill, a white light shone brightly for no more than a fraction of a second, coming and going so fast that it went completely unobserved by all those watching the fight. Three generations of the West family emerged from the brightness. They were thrown into the grass at tremendous speed, though their falls came to a rapid halt just short of the ground and they landed completely unharmed. The parting grass curiously made no sound at all and their arrival went unnoticed.

Jake somehow managed to maintain his grip on his father's hand. Together, they crawled silently over to Harry, being careful to remain as low as possible so that they would not be seen.

'Granddad, are you okay?' Jake hissed. 'How you feeling?'

'Hmmn... I've had better days, that's for sure,' replied Harry. 'Still, we're here now, and it shouldn't take long for the stones to work. Take out the box and open it.'

Jake did as he was told. The box opened very slowly and the centre reolite stone began to glow, to Harry's delight.

'Good. I was hoping as much. There is still a little power left in Knesh' stone. Nittrii-Hebul, eh? I learned of her, but I never had the pleasure myself. It would seem that she has done far more than she promised, Jake. You must have impressed her greatly. Now, if we can just... Ah, yes, I can feel it, my strength is returning to me. Ooh, that's good.'

'Great! Let's go then? We have to help King Artrex!' cried Jake.

'No, wait! I am sorry my boy, but I need a few moments longer,' Harry replied. 'We have to be at full strength if we are to do this, all of us. We must wield all our combined force and power to defeat this wizard.'

Graham was feeling a little left out, as if he'd tagged along to a party he had not been invited to and was just waiting to be rumbled. But now, he decided to speak. Despite Jake's understandable impatience, his father knew somehow that Harry was right, and he needed to say so.

'Please, Jake, listen to him? I know you want to go but he knows what is best?'

Jake was being torn apart inside and it was almost more than he could bear. Every instinct he possessed was telling him they were right and that they had to wait, that he could not intervene no matter how much he wanted to. Not yet. However, every fibre of his being *also* wanted desperately to go and help his friend, to save his life?

Meanwhile, on the ledge, an incredibly weary King Vantrax pushed his sword forcibly towards his brother one more time. Artrex attempted to block the blow, but his tired and aching muscles did not respond as they should have done. They were fractionally slower than normal and his sword arm did not react in time. The bladed weapon plunged deep into his stomach and he fell to his knees, mortally wounded.

The King of Rhuaddan and leader of the Ruddite Rebellion was done for, dying. His death would be a devastating blow for the entire continent. However, though he had no way of knowing it, his extraordinary resistance in the face of such opposition had given the young Keeper the time he needed to complete his journey to Earth, and return with the help he needed.

Artrex looked up in pain at his younger brother. King Vantrax was absolutely shattered. He was struggling to breathe and trying hard to stay on his feet. The warriors of the Personal Guard were roaring their approval, cheering loudly for their king and urging the evil wizard to finish him.

King Vantrax raised one of his hands as he approached the stricken warrior and they immediately fell silent.

'You see? You could not best me when it mattered, could you brother?' he asked, teasing and mocking Artrex in his hour of glory. He reached forward and pulled out his sword.

The rebel king gasped in pain and clutched his hands to the open wound. Blood began seeping through his fingers and a trickle of it fell from his lips.

'Oth... Others will avenge me. Mark my words. My daughter will see you defeated. You have won a fight here today, but you have not won the war!'

'You fool, you utter fool!' raged Vantrax. 'Have you no eyes in your head?! It is over! I have *won*! Your pathetic rebellion is crushed. The dragons are no match for my creatures. Soon, they will join you in the afterlife, never to curse these lands again. Your army is being destroyed en mass. The city is taken, and your little Keeper has deserted you!'

'No!' Artrex responded, fighting hard to say what he had to say, with his very last breath. He could feel his life fading fast and he spoke his final words as quickly as he could. 'He will come. It is written...'

The rebel king fell to the ground the moment the words left his lips, dead. And as the last remnants of air were expelled from his lungs, the metal chain around King Vantrax' neck, the necklace on which the Lichtus stone hung, suddenly snapped. The centre link had broken in two for no apparent reason. The chain and pendant fell into his shirt and King Vantrax instinctively dropped his sword as he rushed to grab it.

Jake reached the top of the small hill at that precise moment. He saw the wide circle of warriors from King Vantrax' Personal Guard. In the centre of them all was King Artrex. The King of Rhuaddan was clearly dead. His body was lying lifeless at the feet of his evil brother.

'No..!' the young Keeper screamed, as soon as he saw he was too late to save his friend, unable to contain himself.

It was an involuntary, stupid reaction, and it alerted everyone there to his presence.

The warriors of the Guard drew their weapons immediately and began to run towards him, determined to kill their young enemy. King Vantrax began frantically trying to retrieve the Lichtus stone in order to use it against him. Jake reached for and lifted the box of stones. Remarkably, the centre stone was still alight, though even Jake was astonished by its lasting power.

Graham and Harry suddenly appeared on either side of the ridge. As soon as they were standing upright, Jake shouted out as loud as he could.

'Traxualaet enon uufflaal acrath!'

A triangular beam of light was emitted instantly from the reolite stone. It connected all three Keepers in a fraction of a second and they immediately knew what they had to do. As the elite warriors switched direction to attack the nearest of them, the trio of Keepers threw their arms up and aimed their palms at the closest soldier's. Bolts of bright light shot out of their hands and hit the warriors in turn, turning them instantly into black piles of ash, which fell to the ground or blew away in the gentle breeze.

King Vantrax had by now retrieved his stone. He was surprised and alarmed to find that he was now faced by not one, but *three* Keepers, with only his servant, Nytig, for company. His elite warriors were gone and his manservant was cowering behind him for protection.

Jake, Harry and Graham turned their attention towards the evil wizard. Before he could use the Lichtus in anger, they each fired a bolt of light. The beams of death raced towards him so fast they were barely visible.

'Zsabrutt!'

The Lichtus stone once again threw a shield of impenetrable light around King Vantrax at his command. Only, this time it covered his servant also. The three Keeper's rays of light hit the indestructible barrier and had no effect, bouncing off the magical wall and vanishing into thin air.

Jake was aghast, mortified to find that their primary weapons had not worked. Their powers were clearly not strong enough to kill him and he looked immediately over at Harry in desperation.

'What's wrong?! Why isn't it working?!' he yelled, hoping his grandfather would have the answers.

But Harry was equally as stunned as his grandson. 'I... I do not know, Jake. The stone perhaps?' he offered in reply.

Graham looked at them both. He was horrified, but a swift reaction from their enemy prevented him from saying anything. Inside his protective shield, King Vantrax suddenly began to laugh, an evil roar of delight.

'Ha, ha, ha…! *Three* of you now? *Three* Keepers? And *still* you cannot defeat me!'

King Vantrax looked as though he was going to launch a strike of his own, to use his powerful stone against all three Keepers at once and kill them all. However, all of a sudden, everything on the battlefield suddenly froze, and time once again stood still. Nobody moved on the whole of Estia, not even Jake.

'The wizard speaks the truth, Keeper. You will not be able to destroy him on this hill, not now. Not until you restore the box.'

The gentle but firm voice inside Jake's head was loud and clear, but only he could hear it.

'Nittrii-Hebul! Then, why? Why send me back?' he asked, his frustration and anger almost boiling over. He felt like screaming, punching a wall or something, even though he knew that neither would help the situation if he could.

'Jake, now may not be the time, but I believe you will still prevail. I have broken my vows. I have broken my solemn promise not to interfere, time and time again. We are all in the hands of fate now, Keeper. Nothing is as it was, as it has been since the beginning of time. And it is all my fault.'

I have sided with you and shown you favour yet again. It is unforgiveable, and it will have repercussions, I assure you. I will not come to you again. The stone's power is almost gone. It has little left to give, but it will take you and your family away from here, as it must, back to Te'oull. Ben and Tien are close by. The power of three Keepers will help you take them with you. There is no option now, believe me. If you do not go, the wizard will destroy you all.'

'Retreat?! No. There has to be another way? We have him trapped!'

Jake's stubborn refusal to accept what he was being told was met with complete silence and it became immediately apparent that Nittrii-Hebul had disappeared. The teenager was now caught in a terrible dilemma. King Vantrax was untouchable inside his wall of light and as soon as the spell was lifted and everything returned to normal, he would be able to attack. Jake had only seconds to decide what to do. If the stone lost its power now, before they escaped, they would all be left alone to face the wizard's magic, certain in the knowledge that they were not strong enough to defeat it, to defeat *him*.

Before he had made up his mind completely, time suddenly reverted to normal and Jake felt a gentle breeze caress his cheek. The teenager made a snap decision and screamed out loud, before King Vantrax knew what was happening.

'Agh! Craasthudd velemme!'

Everyone except for King Vantrax and Nytig suddenly disappeared from the hill and surrounding areas. The evil wizard was left stunned and amazed. He lowered his shield and roared in anger.

After his initial response was over and he had a brief moment of further deliberation, he was still not sure what to think. He did not know whether he should be relieved at having survived the attack, or furious at the loss of his warriors and the chance to destroy the Keepers once and for all?

It took him several minutes to decide on the latter.

Jake and the others appeared in the city of Te'oull almost immediately. They were standing on a relatively quiet backstreet, situated behind the Estian Alliance lines. Jake was also furious, despite his relief at having saved the others from what appeared to be certain death. He had come so close to ending this epic struggle, to winning the war and going home, with his mission accomplished. But, in the end, he had failed yet again.

He was however, happy to be staring at the smiling face of his best friend.

* * *

The great defensive wall at Te'oull had fallen. The enemy forces had stabilised their lines and were now once again ready to advance, to continue their attack. Facing Princess Zephany and Lord Caro were masses of beasts and warriors from a host of different countries, across both continents. At the very last minute, their ranks slowly parted and through them all strode the Sebantan princess, Melissa. She was flanked by several of her warriors, with the entire contingent of Sebantans not far behind. Melissa identified Princess Zephany immediately.

'Warriors of King Vantrax!' The entire city seemed to fall silent upon hearing her words, even in the midst of battle. 'What is left of our enemy is before you. Give them no quarter. Show no mercy. The day is ours. Advance!'

King Vantrax' mercenaries threw themselves down from the ramparts or headed for the nearby steps and resumed the attack. Some were killed or wounded by the axes, spears and knives thrown desperately by the defenders, but before long the entire force was crashing into the Estian lines and a fierce, bloody, close-quarter struggle began.

Whilst Lord Caro was otherwise engaged, fighting numerous enemy warriors and leading the line, a curious pattern seemed to be developing. Amid the confusion and turmoil of battle, it soon became apparent to all that the attackers were doing their utmost to steer clear of Princess Zephany, to avoid her at all costs, as if ordered to do so. Only those warriors she moved to attack directly seemed to want to fight her.

Finally, the reason became clear, as Melissa fought her way through to confront the young royal.

'Yaar! A glorious day. I did not believe I would get this chance to face you. I hoped, but I thought to find your corpse on the battlefield well before I reached your position. The daughter of a king deposed. I am glad to have been mistaken. Let us fight to the death now, you and I. We are both of royal blood, both warriors and leaders, so let us see which princess is most worthy of survival?'

Before Zephany could respond, Melissa launched into a swift and lethal attack. Her sword moved so rapidly and in all directions, that Zephany found it hard to predict its angle of attack. Somehow though, she managed to block its multiple strikes with several last-moment interventions. She defended herself valiantly, but she did not seem able to move onto the offensive, and it looked as though her end was only a matter of time.

Melissa then suddenly sensed immediate danger. Two Alliance warriors attacked her, one from either side, whilst she was distracted by their leader. With astonishing speed, the Sebantan warrior withdrew a little from the fight with Zephany and countered their attack by grabbing a throwing knife from the scabbard on her shoulder blade, with her free hand. She hurled it at one warrior before turning to the other and killing him with a rapid thrust of her sword to his throat. Then she turned swiftly back to face the astonished Princess Zephany, ready to continue the fight before the rebel princess had chance to take advantage of the interruption.

'Forgive me, where were we?' she said, as she retook her position.

Despite her shock at having witnessed such astonishing skill, Zephany seized on the opportunity to delay her opponent and put her off guard.

'You... You were mistaken before. You are no princess. You are the daughter of a Keeper, your master's worst enemy!'

The battle raged on around them, but Melissa was stunned by such an absurd and unusual accusation. She was certain it was a trick, a lie designed to distract her, the desperate act of a girl who knew she was outmatched and about to die. Still, it was such an odd thing to say? In spite of the circumstances, something inside did not want to dismiss it without hearing more.

'You lie! You would say anything right now to save your skin!' she replied, her fingers tightening around the handle to her sword as she prepared to attack once again.

'And yet, you delay?' answered Zephany, smiling. 'Could it be that you know it is true? Why do you think you have such a strange name? It is not Sebantan, is it? Where do you suppose it came from? I will tell you if you like? Think!'

Melissa was angered further by Zephany's taunts. She flew into a wild rage and launched two more determined attacks, but Zephany somehow repulsed them. The Sebantan warrior then took another step backwards to catch her breath. She was trying her hardest now to block out what had been said, but the damage had been done. From out of nowhere, she suddenly saw a very brief image appear in her mind. It was a memory, long since suppressed and forgotten, a shadow of her past which had been locked firmly inside the deepest recesses of her subconscious. She saw a dungeon, a chain binding her to a wall even as a child, and a woman. Her eyes widened involuntarily and her face became a picture of surprise and amazement.

No... It is all true! she realised, horrified and stunned.

Princess Zephany noticed her reaction. 'Yes, I see it in your eyes. You see, your whole life is a lie. Listen to me; you were four years old when they took you. Somehow, you have forgotten, erased it from your mind. We have only recently learnt the truth. King Vantrax stole you away from your mother. He sold you to the highest bidder. And now you fight for him. You *kill* for him!'

'No! It is not...!'

'Yes! It *is* true!' screamed Zephany. 'However much you deny it, your mother is here to prove it to you. She is alive. She is here in Te'oull. *You* are one of us!'

Melissa was now in a state of complete confusion. A thousand different thoughts and emotions swamped her all at once. She could not think straight and she suddenly lost all focus.

Zephany seized the advantage and raced forward at speed. Melissa weaved to avoid the attack but the Estian leader's sword cut deeply into her arm. She dropped her own weapon and clutched her hand to the wound, immediately feeling a tremendous, burning pain, but refusing to scream.

Lord Caro and others rushed forward at that very moment, pushing the attackers backwards briefly as they tried to protect their leader. Melissa fell to her knees. In the tight space that had suddenly developed, she was completely at Princess Zephany's mercy. The young royal stood over her now with sword in hand and contemptuous eyes, the power of life and death resting solely with her as she towered over her enemy, ready to take her life.

Chapter 20
2nd October – Outside Te'oull – Siatol

'W-w-what happened sire?' asked Nytig, his voice trembling with fear. 'Where did they go?'

Jake and all of his companions had vanished completely. The shield which protected the king and his servant from the Keeper's attacks was gone. All the evil wizard and Nytig could see before them now, was the hill on which they stood and the open countryside beyond. The battle still raged in the city of Te'oull to their rear and the awful din of war resounded in the air, but they were now all alone on their little patch of ground, safe, and able to reflect on just how close they had actually come to being killed.

'Bah! You can show yourself now, Nytig. Come out from beneath my robes, you coward. There is nothing to fear now. They have gone,' replied the king. Nytig took a step sideways and looked around nervously. He was at first reluctant to leave the wizard's side and the protection his close proximity afforded. Another thorough, anxious visual search of the ridge though, revealed that it was indeed deserted but Nytig saw several small piles of ash lying here and there. Most had been scattered by the wind but the few that remained were fading reminders of what had just happened. Proof, if any were needed, of the awesome power wielded by Jake and his kind.

'I thought we were battling against a solitary boy? Where did the other Keepers come from? That was too close by far, sire. We were dead for certain, until you saved us. They were...' began Nytig, once he had recovered a little.

'*Insufficient!*' interrupted Vantrax, triumphantly. The self-proclaimed ruler was still incredibly angry, but his brain was now working hard to understand what had taken place. And he was seriously impressed by his own actions. 'Think on it, Nytig. Even with the powers of *three* Keepers combined, they *still* could not kill me! When it mattered, I was able to combat their spells and defeat them, to survive completely unharmed. In fact, if they had not disappeared, I would have destroyed them all! Do you realise what this means? I am... Ohh!'

King Vantrax suddenly faltered. His knees almost gave way beneath him and he nearly fell. Intense fatigue washed through his body like wildfire and his energy was drained in an instant. He felt dizzy, incredibly sick, and every one of his muscles ached and throbbed like they never had before. He was very weak all of a sudden and he dropped the Lichtus stone to the ground, as he tried his utmost to remain upright.

'Sire! What is it? You look awful. What is happening?' asked Nytig, as much concerned for his own safety and protection as anything else. He knelt down to pick up the wizard's pendant for him as he spoke.

King Vantrax was almost unconscious now and completely disorientated. The feeling of nausea was worse than any he had known. It lasted a lot longer and it was far more intense, though he was able to breathe this time without too much difficulty. He sat down on the ground, barely aware of his surroundings and what was being said, as the world around him seemed to spin uncontrollably. He remained there for several minutes as everything faded to grey. Then, his senses began to return, very slowly. At first, he was unable to move.

'Where...? Where am I? Nytig? Yes, now I remember. I... I will be fine in a moment. It will pass. I just need a little time. The life has been drained from me for a brief spell. It must have been the effects of the stone, when I fought against the Keepers. Go, fetch me some water. I have a terrible thirst all of a sudden... And be quick about it! Go!'

* * *

Inside the city, the Battle for Te'oull had descended into complete chaos. King Vantrax' warriors had broken through the Estian lines of defence in several places, whilst other isolated pockets of resistance somehow held their ground. The marauding attackers had therefore effectively surrounded large groups of Estian forces. The gallant defenders fought on with bravery and determination in the face of overwhelming odds, cut off from one another for the time being but hoping for relief, praying for a miracle. To add to their problems, more and more enemy warriors were pouring over the city walls and through the newly opened gates. However, these fresh troops were being funneled straight into the narrow city streets, where their considerable advantage in numbers was somewhat nullified due to the restricted space and the rebel forces ranged against them, accustomed to fighting lost causes, continued to give a good account of themselves.

The spell Jake had conducted to escape from King Vantrax' wrath had used the last remnants of power from the reolite stone. It had landed him and his colleagues directly behind the warriors commanded by Brraall and Verastus.

'Oh great!' Ben had moaned, when their dire situation became immediately clear. 'Nice one, Jay! Of all the places to pick! Talk about out of the fryin' pan and into the fire!'

As the enemy took the surrounding streets quickly, one by one, the Estians ahead of Jake's group fell back to form another defensive pocket, centred more or less around their current position. Jake and the others were therefore trapped in the middle and had nowhere to go. It was not long before Verastus and Brraall heard of their arrival and appeared to greet them. Following closely behind was Jean. In amongst the mass of bodies she saw Jake first and her heart leapt for joy. She immediately welled up with emotion and ran towards him, intending to give him a hug, but then she realised that he did not yet know who she was, and she stopped herself.

'Jake!' shouted Verastus, his hand now drenched in blood as it remained firmly clamped over the wound to his stomach.

'Hi'ya, big man. It's great to see you still alive. That looks nasty. Tien, do what you can for him, will you?' Jake asked.

The wizard duly obliged. He took Verastus aside and began treating his wound, his face betraying grave concern, a feeling that was obviously shared by all. He tore off part of his sleeve to use as a bandage and performed a small spell in an attempt to stem the blood loss, which seemed far too great for anyone to survive.

'Brraall, I'm sorry, but can you go back and organise the defence for us? We have to hold out for as long as we can, while we try to figure out how we can win this thing,' said Jake, looking straight into the huge warrior's eyes.

Brraall obeyed without question. He said his goodbyes quickly and left to lead the fight. Jake issued several more orders to the warriors around him and one by one they disappeared, as Jean and the others looked on. When all the necessary commands had been given and they had a moment to speak, it was Ben as usual who was first to broach the awkward subject needing to be raised.

'Oh come on, you lot! You West's are impossible, aren't you? Right, leave it to a Brooker to take charge then. Jean, meet Jake! He's the Keeper of the Stones, if you didn't know, and he's your grandson.'

Hardly able to contain herself, Jean stepped forward with tear-drenched eyes. She hugged him like they were well acquainted, family. Understandably perhaps, she had had tunnel vision ever since she laid eyes on him. Everything and everyone else around her had escaped her attention, as she concentrated solely on the grandson she had never met and waited anxiously for a chance to speak.

'Hey! Break it up, break it up. I'm not finished and we're rather pushed,' said Ben, once he was satisfied they had had enough time. 'This is... well, its bin' a few years I know, but I think you should recognise this guy?' he added, pushing Graham forward unceremoniously.

Jake's father could hardly see at this point; his eyes were filled with so many tears. He did not object to Ben's manhandling of him, largely because he could not speak.

Though he was the last person she expected to see, Jean took less than a second to recognise her only son. She nearly fainted and had to stop herself from falling over, grabbing onto Ben with both hands. Graham reached forward and took her in his arms. He pulled her close to him and hugged her so tightly she could hardly breathe. He was so deliriously happy in that moment that he didn't want to let go, but Jean's eyes opened and, looking over his shoulder, she finally caught sight of Harry.

This time, she did faint.

She fell like a stone in fact. Graham managed to hold onto her and prevent her from hitting the ground. He picked her up in his arms and looked at the others, unsure what to do.

'Here. Bring her over here,' cried Harry, pointing towards the nearest open doorway, which had been kicked in. 'It looks deserted and I'm sure they won't mind.'

The small group headed inside the abandoned dwelling and minutes later Jean came round in her son's arms. As she opened her eyes, she was greeted by the most wonderful sight; three generations of her family were looking down lovingly upon her. A family she thought she had lost forever was staring at her with concerned, enthralled, devoted eyes.

'Harry…? Is it really you? Tell me I'm not dreaming, please?'

'It's me, Jean. I'm right here beside you, at long last. I will never, *ever*, leave your side again, I promise!' Harry replied, emotionally.

He bowed his head a little and could hardly look his wife in the eye, overcome all of a sudden by intensely strong feelings of remorse, guilt and shame. As well as love. The roars, screams and shouts of an enormous battle continued all around as Harry looked down on the woman who, in his mind, he had abandoned when she needed him most.

'Oh no, no, no. Why do you look at me like that? You must not blame yourself for what happened. It was not your fault, Harry. You had to survive. You had no choice, I knew that. Your job was to protect our family, our world, and all the others I never knew about,' said Jean, softly. She reached up with her hand and placed it tenderly upon his cheek.

'Yes, but I should have…?! I could have…!'

'No. Don't think of that now. Too much has happened. Look at our son, and our grandson. Neither would be here if it were not for you, and the decisions you made. I couldn't remember a thing, for my memory was lost to me. When you do not know any better, you cannot lay any blame, so I held no grudge against you for the actions you took. I could not question what you did, don't you see? And now that I finally know the truth, I *still* think you did the right thing. If I had been in your shoes, I would have done the same. I would have done *anything* to protect those I loved.'

Harry held her closely in his arms and kissed her tenderly as if they had never been parted. They both began to sob and the others retreated to the doorway, sensing the need to give them a brief moment of privacy in amongst the turmoil.

'Well, Jay? What happens now?' asked Ben. 'I saw you on that hill fighting with Vantrax, all three of you. We both did. To be honest, when we saw him beat your weapons, we thought you'd missed the fact that we were there. Tien actually thought that you were gonna leave us.'

Jake breathed in deeply, once. 'Oh, *Tien* thought it, did he? Nah mate, leave *you*? As if. You're like a piece of bubblegum stuck to my shoe; I couldn't get rid of you if I tried.'

'Ha, ha, ha... Too right. I'm Juicy Fruit me, and I'm glad you know it,' Ben replied, placing his arm around his friend as they shared a rare moment together.

Graham's next words however, halted their laughter.

'Sorry, I hate to interrupt this touching reunion boys but, seriously now, what happened out there on that hill?! I'm not being funny, but if we can't defeat this wizard between the three of us, why the *hell* have you brought us here? I mean, far be it from me as the newcomer in all of this to point out the obvious, but we're slap bang in the middle of a war zone! And it doesn't appear to be going too well? So, how in God's name are we going to get out of this mess?!'

* * *

Nytig had been absent for far too long. King Vantrax was almost fully recovered now from the effects of using his stone to create the shield. He suddenly realised that something was amiss.

Raar! It should not take so long to fetch water, even for one such as Nytig?'

With mounting concern, he tried to stand, but the blood rushed to his head and he had to sit back down again.

'Frah! Nytig!' he screamed, furiously. 'By Hereddian's blood, where *are* you? I will roast you alive if you take much longer, you vile...!'

King Vantrax halted his outburst. To his absolute terror and utmost concern, he realised abruptly that his servant still held the Lichtus stone in his hand!

'Raarrggh!!!'

He roared his fury so loudly that the bark almost seemed to tear itself off the nearby trees. His eyes turned blood red and his fingers extended and tensed so much that they appeared to be like giant claws. The reolite stone enhanced and magnified the wizard's powers, but even without it, King Vantrax was still a powerful mage. Out of desperation and despair, he began immediately calling upon his old master; the most powerful wizard he knew, the one who had tutored him in the dark arts all those years ago. The one who had never really left his side.

'Notorold! Notorold! Venlachtreuus, expallanin iethe, Parassleugh misrall zenett srriidde qatron!'

The air ahead of the king suddenly split itself in two. A black cloud of smoke appeared within seconds and through it stepped a horrid figure; the vague semblance of what used to be a man, dressed in black rags from head to toe. Its white bones were exposed here and there beneath a thin layer of dead and rotting, grey flesh. The deep yellow of its eyes was the only other colour to be seen, apart from the brown, black and duller yellow of decaying teeth.

'Notorold!' rasped Vantrax, his rage scarcely diminished. 'How is it that I knew to summon you now, when I have never been able to before? What gave me the power and knowledge to do it? The stone is gone and without it I am...!'

'Srreeeaatt!!!'

Notorold screeched his annoyance and discontent. The black spirit's awful, ear-splitting cry stopped King Vantrax in his tracks.

'Enough! It does not matter now,' he stated, immediately reverting to a deep, sinister tone. 'Your stone is gone. It is unfortunate, but not in itself the disaster you believe it to be. The fight goes on. The battle is yet to be decided and it can still be won. There has been great disruption in the realms of the afterlife of late. You have done well to provoke such a response from those who should have known better. The chains which bound me were freed when they foolishly took action. The gates were unlocked. You felt that change. One of those who control the spiritworld and all of its domains has finally gone too far in support of a mortal. They were foolish to act. And they must now pay the price, for they have unleashed not just I, but an entire legion of spirits held in the fires of Zsorcraum! I was able to free them all before the break could be closed. I have opened up a further breach in their shield. Very soon, an army of black spirits will descend upon this world and everything within it will be destroyed. My forces wait only for the gap to widen. And widen it will, for it cannot be stopped now. The time was right, so I entered your mind. You have brought me here Vantrax seeking my help, but there are *thousands* coming behind me!'

King Vantrax was absolutely thrilled by the news that all his wishes had at last been granted, and more. He began to grow excited and started clapping his hands.

It wasn't long though before he also became impatient. 'When? When will they come?'

'Relax, Vantrax. It takes time to open a breach such as this. They are gathering at the gates as we speak. You will have your victory. It is imminent.'

'Good. Excellent. But, what of Nytig and the stone? If the boy seizes it, will he be able to destroy us?'

Notorold shook his head slowly. 'There is nothing written about us in the prophecies, for we were not meant to be here. No-one could have foreseen the thoughtless actions which have released us. No, you do not need to fear. He does not have the power to defeat us. This young Keeper is not strong enough. Soon, you will see spirits and wizards reborn who are far more powerful than you and I, more potent than any ever known. For this world, for the people of Estia and all of your enemies, today is the dawn of oblivion. There is *nothing* the Keeper can do to stop it!'

* * *

Nytig ran towards Te'oull as fast as his deformed body would allow. His heart began to beat thunderously in his chest and he was soon gasping violently for air, but he kept on running. He was convinced that he was about to die. He dashed frantically from cover to cover crossing the fields that approached the city, all the time looking up and behind for any sign of pursuit from his evil master. He was astonished to find no evidence of a chase, and convinced that it would eventually come.

'Koh no, koh no. What have you done, you stupid fool?! He will kill you for sure. Why did you do it? What possessed you to be so brave? Yarrggh! Where were your brains? Since when have you been so bold? All your life you have been a coward, so why do you decide to grow some courage today, of *all* days?!' he asked himself as he ran.

He just could not understand or believe the folly of his own action, which had surely sealed his fate. When King Vantrax had dropped the Lichtus stone on the ground before him, Nytig had picked it up immediately, without really knowing why. He was unwittingly responding to an impulse which had come to him from out of nowhere. It was an automatic reaction he had known nothing about until it was too late, and something he could not explain now. He had expected the king to see his action and immediately demand the stone's return. However, King Vantrax was too exhausted and weary to notice. He was worried about his own sudden illness and his senses were badly affected. He had given no such order. In fact, the evil wizard had not even realised it was gone, until it was too late.

The impulse to run away with the stone had come straight from the heart. It shocked Nytig more than any other he had ever experienced. It was just so unlike him, so out of character, and so fantastically weird, that he of all people should act in such a manner. Even more of a surprise as he replayed the incident in his mind and dwelled on his foolish act, was the fact that he had actually *listened* to what his heart was telling him, ignoring the vociferous protestations of his mind.

Now, as if controlled by some magical force, he headed straight towards the attacking forces and the city beyond, though he had absolutely no idea why. He did not know what he was going to do when he reached the front. Years of suffering and hardship, of serial abuse at his master's hands, came flooding back to him as he ran, ushered into his consciousness by a gentle, helping hand he knew nothing of.

The scars on my mind and body run so deep they will never heal, but the emergence of not one but three Keepers, has to be a sign that the tables have turned? Never before has the power of three been seen on this world. The days of King Vantrax are surely numbered? And if I am ever to be rid of him, if I am ever to break free, the time to act is now?!

High above Nytig and the city of Te'oull, the army of dragons were suffering terribly in their long, drawn-out fight with the creatures raised by King Vantrax. Their epic struggle against the graxoth and revalkas was still being waged furiously. Many dragons had been seriously injured or killed. Resus was leading the remaining few in a desperate attempt to turn the tide, but in a fleeting moment he looked down at the ground below, his eyes drawn away from the fight for a split second by the same mysterious and unknown force that had visited Nytig. With his superior eyesight, Resus immediately saw him scurrying across the open fields, heading for the battle within the city walls. Despite the need to remain with his fellow dragons, Resus felt another irresistible urge to investigate, instinctively knowing that he had to temporarily detach himself from the fight and help the Keeper somehow, as only he could.

Seconds later, the powerful dragon swooped down out of the sky and grabbed the luckless servant in his long talons. His giant claws cut deeply into Nytig's shoulders. Nytig cried out in pain as the dragon's powerful wings beat rapidly and he was lifted up into the air.

Resus flew low over the city and the fighting until he spotted Jake and Ben. To his surprise, they were a little behind the action and standing in an open doorway. He flew lower still and circled around, before dropping the unfortunate, pain-wracked slave upon them, like life-saving food from an eagle for her desperate, starving chicks.

Nytig landed awkwardly and with a loud cry. He rolled over several times before coming to a halt less than a yard from Jake's feet. His arms were outstretched to break his fall. In one of his hands, he had the Lichtus stone clutched firmly within his grasp.

Chapter 21
2nd October – City of Te'oull – Siatol

The razor-sharp tip of Princess Zephany's blade pushed firmly against Melissa's neck, breaking the skin and drawing blood. The young royal and Estian leader was just about to ram it home, ending the Sebantan warrior's life. And it was no more than Melissa deserved. She had killed many Estians in her relatively short life, in the service of her evil master. Princess Zephany was all too aware of that fact. At first, she was too blinded by fury and a thirst for revenge to show any mercy.

For her part, Melissa refused outright to beg or plead. She kept her hand clasped tightly over the wound to her arm and looked up defiantly at her triumphant enemy, staring Princess Zephany directly in the eye with outright hostility, almost daring her to do it.

The noise of battle was a distant distraction now for both warriors, cocooned as they were in their own little moment in time. In reality though, the fight was only a matter of metres away and they were still firmly in harm's way.

Zephany pushed a little harder with her weapon. Blood began to ooze out of Melissa's neck and trickled down her skin, beneath the blade. However, despite her incredible desire for vengeance, for some reason she could neither understand nor believe, Princess Zephany hesitated. She looked around at those who were fighting bravely for her cause. Several of her warriors had withdrawn temporarily from the fighting for a brief rest, including Lord Caro. They were now watching their leader to see what she would do.

Zephany was astonished to find that her hands were trembling a little. It was not fear making them shake, she knew that. It was rage. She was angry at herself for being so weak, for not doing what she was there to do, for wavering at the very moment she needed to be strong. More than anything, she was annoyed at herself for listening to the unknown voice that had suddenly entered her head at the vital moment; the pang of conscience that had convinced her somehow to ignore her training, and all of her warrior's instincts.

'Go on, do it! *Finish* me!' rasped Melissa. 'It is what you want, is it not? I can see it in your eyes. You know I would act if the situation were reversed, so why do you linger?'

Zephany's eyes turned once again to Melissa, burning fiercely with hatred. She wanted to take her life so badly it hurt. Wanted to gain retribution for all those rebels the Sebantan had killed over the years, or taken into slavery, the civillians she had rounded up for King Vantrax' mines who were never seen again.

But, she could not do it. She had been prevented from acting by some unknown force and the moment had passed. In any case, to kill her now in cold blood when she was captured and defenceless, was not Princess Zephany's way. Knesh Corian and her father, the King of Rhuaddan, had raised her better than that. She had been brought up as a future queen to be wise, just and honourable. And this, just did not feel right.

How will it look to my people, if by some miracle we survive this fight? Will it be seen as an act of courage if I kill her, of strength? Or will it always be remembered as the deed of a coward, a dishonorable execution which will return to haunt me in years to come?

As she pondered the decision for the briefest of moments, she withdrew her blade slightly and Melissa felt the cold steel move.

'You cannot. It is not in you, is it? You do not have what it takes.'

Zephany immediately tensed her arm in retaliation, as if to run her blade through the young warrior.

Melissa braced herself, but the rebel leader pulled her sword away at the last moment.

'You are right. I am *not* like you. I am more. Much more than you will *ever* be!' She turned immediately to Lord Caro. 'Hand me your belt.'

Caro took it off and threw away the scabbard to his sword, which was attached. 'Here, princess. Take it. Somehow, I do not believe my sword will be sheathed again, so I should have no further use for it.'

He handed the belt over and Zephany bound Melissa's hands behind her back. Melissa hissed and cursed as the pain in her arm intensified. When Zephany had finished, the Sebantan raged at her with real venom in her voice.

'Raar! *That* was a mistake! It was the decision of a weak leader, and you *will* regret it, I swear!'

Zephany turned her around and looked her straight in the eye. 'Perhaps. Only time will tell if you are right and I am wrong, and we appear to have very little of that, so we should know very soon. However, mistake or not, it was *my* decision to make!'

She handed Melissa over to one of her warriors and ordered him to guard her with his life. Then she led Caro and the rest of her followers back into the fight.

* * *

Sawdon and his huge contingent of mercenaries were continuing to fight their way relentlessly into the heart of the city. The Estian Alliance soldiers fought bravely to hold them back, but the powerful Thargw and his legions were far too skilled and experienced for them. They were relentless, ferocious, and they began making headway against the exhausted defenders of the city, capturing ground rapidly until the attack wheeled round on both flanks, encircling the Estians and pushing them back towards the main square, which had now become the centre of their desperate position.

Opposite Sawdon, Queen Bressial was in command. There was absolutely nothing that she or anyone else could do to halt the retreat. The simple fact was that there were just too many of the enemy to fight. All she could do now was organise the defences as best she could, to try somehow to delay the enemy's progress. Roadblocks were hastily erected in the narrow city streets, warriors climbed on rooftops waiting to ambush the attackers from above, trying to take them down with the few spears, axes and throwing knives they had left. In desperation, they hurled anything they could find and it became a frantic defence bordering on panic.

The Thargws in particular were relishing the hand-to-hand fighting that had developed, and none more so than Sawdon. His huge, muscular frame was clearly identifiable in the chaos of battle. Warrior after warrior from the Alliance tried in vain to kill him upon sight. Some even managed to conduct coordinated attacks involving three or four of their comrades, but Sawdon's superior senses, ability, experience and reflexes allowed him to evade their weapons and kill them all. He was like a machine and he just kept on coming, driving his Thargws forward. It seemed as though no-one and nothing could stop him.

Before long, Bressial's units met up with those commanded by Brraall. The great tribal warrior informed the queen that Jake and the others were not far behind him. Handing over command to the tribal leader, Bressial quickly detached herself from the fight to report their dire situation to the Keeper.

* * *

Nytig lay on the floor at Jake's feet. His outstretched hand held the Lichtus tightly within its grasp. Jake looked down upon it with wonder and amazement, absolutely dumbfounded at this unexpected and unbelievable stroke of good fortune. He could not imagine how or why the stone he had searched for and needed so badly was here, having fallen at his feet like a gift from the Gods.

I have travelled across worlds to fetch help, so that together we might be able to take it? I've almost been killed trying to bring my family back here in order to take on the wizard... Why? Why did I have to do that, if it was going to be this easy?!

He placed his foot firmly on Nytig's wrist, pushing down so hard that the prostrate servant squealed in pain. His fingers opened, allowing the stone to fall gently on the ground. Jake then bent down and picked it up.

'Is that...?! It is!' said Ben, as he stepped forward, equally amazed and shocked. Everyone there heard his startled response and they all gathered around Jake, including Harry and Jean.

'Kuh! I do not believe it. We have been searching all this time for the stones, braved untold dangers and given everything we have to find them, only for the last, the one we all thought would be impossible to take, to be handed to us without a fight? Something is not right here.

There is some power working for us that I do not understand, some wonderful, magical force helping you to achieve the impossible, Jake. I have said it before and I know I am right,' stated Verastus, smiling broadly at his young friend.

The Falorian giant suddenly felt a hand on his shoulder.

'Yeah, ain't it great? We'll take that helping hand any day, won't we? Look, we can ask all the questions we want later. We've more important things to do right now, like deciding on what we're gonna do with *him!*' said Ben, pointing down at the pathetic figure of Nytig, who was still lying on the ground at their feet.

'I say we kill him!' replied Verastus, immediately and without hesitation or feeling. 'He serves the wizard. He took the stones from us the last time we caught him, and he almost caused Ben's death. Besides, I think it highly likely that we are all about to die anyway? What is one more life added to all those who will perish here? If the dragon captured him, and gave him to us, that is one blessing I shall take with me to the afterlife. Any friend of King Vantrax is an enemy of mine and I will shed no tears for them as my sword enters their flesh. Listen to me; you all need to face facts. We are *losing* this fight. We can afford no warriors to guard any prisoners we take. We will need every one we have just to stay alive.'

As soon as he had finished speaking, he took out his sword and drew it back, ready to strike the servant down.

'No!'

The Falorian halted his sword arm just in time, when the tip of the blade was less than an inch from Nytig's back. A loud scream had stopped him before anyone else could object. It was a high-pitch shriek. A woman's frantic cry. It made everyone jump because it came from such an unexpected source.

Jean had all of a sudden felt compelled to intervene. She broke away from Harry's arms and rushed to Nytig, throwing herself down on the ground and covering him with her body, shielding him from further attack.

'Mum! What the heck are you doing?!' shouted Graham,

completely bewildered and concerned for her welfare.

Jean raised her head slightly to respond, as Verastus withdrew his sword to hear her words, but Jake beat her to it.

'Grandma,' he began, for the very first time calling her by the name he had always wanted to say to her, as he'd so often imagined in his dreams, 'what is it to you whether he lives or dies? Why do you care? I'm sorry, I don't mean to sound heartless, but Verastus has a point; we cannot guard him and we cannot let him go.'

'What is it to *me*, Jake? I will tell you; he is *everything* to me! He is the one who saved me, the one who freed me and gave me back my life. Without him, I would not have survived. At the very least, I would have spent my whole life in chains. I would have been kept holed up in the dungeons of Heron Getracht, allowed out in the day to wash, cook and clean, and locked in the filth and squalor of the cells by night. I could hardly bear it any longer. I was dying a little each day and praying for the end, for release, one way or the other.'

Looking on, Harry West was moved to tears by his wife's actions and words. He stepped forward immediately, determined to be heard.

'Jake, if all that is true, we owe this man a great deal. It is a debt of gratitude we can repay here and now? He cannot hurt us. He is only one amongst thousands of enemies here. And we are not cold-bloodied killers, Jake. We are Keepers, sworn to defend and protect?'

Jake turned his head to Verastus. 'Put away your blade. There will be no execution here. Nytig, stand up and look me in the eye.'

The wounded and terrified servant slowly rose to his feet. Blood was running down his chest and back as a result of the wounds he received from the dragon's claws.

'Be very brief, but explain to me why and how, I now hold the wizard's stone.'

Nytig seized the opportunity to try and describe his actions, grateful to still be alive. He spoke as fast as he could.

'I... I am not a bad man, though I know I have served a master of evil who has done terrible things to these people, to *my* people. I did a good deed once, long, long ago, and I have paid for it ever since. That single act changed my entire life. The suffering that followed robbed me of my courage and my conscience, of all my virtues. They were stolen away from me in a foolish moment, and beat out of me if they ever dared to try and return. Fear. Fear overtook them all. I have been afraid ever since, scared to take a stand. But, seeing you today, witnessing all three Keepers defying his power, his magic? I felt something different inside. I realised all of a sudden that I had found something worth fighting for, something to believe in. I do not know why, but I knew that it was something I did believe in once, before I lost sight of what it meant.'

'What? What was it?' asked Ben, surprised to find himself taking pity on the wretched figure before him.

'Freedom.'

Even Verastus seemed stirred by his words. 'Yes, all very good. It does not excuse your actions though, and how were you captured with the stone in your possession? The wizard never removes it. Tell us, for I am certain that it does not leave his sight?'

'I was *not* captured!' snapped Nytig. 'I was taken by the dragon when I was running away, on the fields outside the city wall. I had stolen it.'

'What? You took it off King Vantrax?' asked Harry.

'No,' replied Nytig, quickly. 'It fell off, and I picked it up without him knowing. I do not know why, but when he killed King Artrex, the chain suddenly snapped. It was as if he had angered those in the afterlife, and they were showing their displeasure?'

'Nittrii-Hebul!' stated Jake, speaking his thoughts out loud without realising it. Everyone turned to look at him, waiting for an explanation. 'Err... it does not matter now. There will be time later, with any luck. We have a battle to win. Right now, *you* need to restore this box!' he said, looking straight at Tien and pointing at his bag. He took out the box of stones and handed the bag and the rest of its contents to the wizard. 'How long will it take?'

'Yeah, a little hustle if you please, Tien? We're kinda on a clock, you know?' added Ben, smiling.

The wizard took no notice of Ben's comment as he took the box from Jake.

'That depends. The Eratian stone still needs to be cut to size,' he replied.

'Right, well... Hold up. Time out. It's indestructible, isn't it? You said it could not be cut, that many had tried and failed?' said Jake.

'Yes, I did. It is. But, now that I have a reolite stone of sufficient size to work with, *anything* is possible. I will begin immediately, and I will contact you when I am finished. Srr... I will need help; Jean, Graham, Harry, come with me.' Tien led them in the direction of the empty building. At the entrance, he stopped and turned to the others. 'In the meantime, while I am busy at work, you lot have a battle to wage. Keep those warriors away from me for as long as you can.'

Jake suddenly felt another surge of confidence swelling his breast. 'Okay then, you heard him,' he declared boldly as he drew his sword, 'let's kick some ass!'

Everyone drew their weapons and prepared to fight.

'What...? What of me? What shall I do?' yelled Nytig.

'You?' replied Jake. 'You are a free man now. You do as you please.'

Nytig rapidly choked up with emotion. His wounds ached and he felt completely exhausted, but he was exhilarated at the same time to be given his freedom. His first instinct was to run. But to where? He could hide, but they would find him eventually, wouldn't they? He glanced around him as he searched his soul for answers, deciding what to do. A discarded sword lay on the ground not far away. After a moment or two, he walked over to it and picked it up, just as Queen Bressial came running into the centre of the group. She looked at Jake with astonishment when she saw the servant of the evil king who had held her captive for years amongst their number.

'No time to explain now, your majesty. We need to hold them back. Use every warrior we have. Nytig here has just volunteered to serve you, of his own free will. He will fight by your side and lay down his life for you if needs be, until the battle is won.'

*   *   *

Princess Zephany was completely shattered. After an initial period of success where a monumental effort from her warriors had actually managed to push the enemy back towards the wall, they were now once again on the back foot, retreating slowly towards the main square, heading for a reunion with the soldiers fighting alongside Jake. Lord Caro and the knights of the Estian Alliance had been immense so far but the streets of Te'oull were now crammed with Vantrax' warriors, who had broken through on all sides. The large force of Estian's now falling back on the square were therefore surrounded.

'From what I can tell we are trapped, princess,' shouted Caro, as he killed yet another Sevitrian.

'Yes, it would appear that way,' agreed Zephany, her sword now drenched in the blood of the many enemies she had killed. She swung it once again to remove the head of a Falorian, before bringing it around and slicing off a Pralon's arm. Then, she thrust it into his chest to finish him and stepped back, ready to engage her next opponent. None came, and she found she had a brief respite from attack.

'We will continue to make for the square. It is the only option we have, and the only defensible area of ground. If we can establish a perimeter there, we can hold out for some time.'

'Hold out? Yes, but to what end?' asked Caro.

'Simple, Caro; deliverance. We fight for as long as we have to. To give Jake the time he needs to save our people. Hopefully, our commanders on all sides will think the same and our forces will meet there in large enough numbers to hold the lines.'

Lord Caro launched yet another attack upon an approaching enemy warrior. The Falorian sustained several nasty wounds before he fell. Once he was finally dead, Caro replied to his leader.

'As you command, princess. Your unshakeable faith in this Keeper is inspiring, if you do not mind me saying so? I do not know from where you draw your strength. Tell me, is it the legends, or the boy?'

Princess Zephany cast a quick glance in his direction and smiled slightly.

'It is a little of both, I think. The legends stated only that a Keeper would come. Beyond that, they were pretty vague, truth be told. Jake arrived here just as written, but as you say he was still only a boy to me and my people, nothing more. He was unproven, and like myself, he was so very young. How were we to pin all our hopes on him? Times have changed so rapidly that all such doubts have now been cast aside. It is not the writings we were brought up to have faith in, but his actions *right now,* that are giving us hope and making him a legend.'

* * *

King Vantrax stood with Notorold on the fields outside Te'oull, surveying with mixed emotions the great battle being fought before him. The evil spirit though, was looking eagerly in the opposite direction, staring expectantly at the eastern sky. Vantrax could not discern much from the confused scene in and around the city. All he knew for certain was that his forces were advancing far too slowly. Given their superiority in numbers and ability, the battle *should* have been over by now and he was growing increasingly impatient.

'Graar! How long is this going to take?! Where is your army? The battle will be over before they arrive!' shouted the wizard in another fit of temper.

Almost immediately, he was shocked to find that his throat was being squeezed violently by an invisible force. His windpipe constricted so rapidly that he could not breathe. He clutched his hand to it instinctively in an effort to tear an imaginary pair of hands away and save his life, as his whole body rose upwards and he was turned to face his former master. At the very point of losing consciousness, the vice-like grip was suddenly released and he fell to his knees.

'Do *not* forget who it is that you address, Vantrax! I alone have made you what you are today. It was I who gave you the chances you squandered to rule this world. I who allowed you to raid Zsorcraum for your creatures. You owe *everything* to me, for I risked everything and more to aid you!' raged Notorold, his jaw extending outwards menacingly as he roared in the wizard's face.

'No, I do not. I remember it all and I am grateful to you, I swear! I know what would have happened if you were discovered. I am fully aware what was at stake. But, you were *not* discovered, were you? I apologise for my foolish outburst; I am merely anxious to see this war won. I have waited so long for this day. I have come so close to victory before, only to see it snatched away from me at the last moment.'

Notorold withdrew slightly and his jaw retracted.

'We need not fear. It was not I who was deemed to have broken our laws. Cast your eyes to the horizon. What do you see?' he asked, his voice menacing and ominous.

King Vantrax gazed towards the east. The sky was a perfect blue and nothing seemed untoward.

'I do not see anything,' he replied, disappointed.

'Then look harder!'

The wizard looked again at the sky as instructed, staring intently at it for a good few seconds. Suddenly, the pale blue colour began to change. It turned gradually to grey, before growing slowly darker and darker, until finally it became jet black.

'Raar!' roared the wizard, excited at the thought of finally fulfilling all of his ambitions. 'At last! It is them, is it not? They are here! It is the army from Zsorcraum. You have done it. You have raised the legions of death!'

Notorold gave a wicked smile. His eyes suddenly grew brighter as he felt his powers growing.

'It is as it should be. Everything is now as we always planned. Soon, I will be strong enough to lead this fight. The power from the fires is rising to aid us, Vantrax. It is entering this world and it cannot be contained. This army of spirits I have raised will not be defeated. The mortals are finished. We will destroy everything and everyone put before us, before our enemies from the afterlife can respond. And once they are gone, it will be too late. This world is ours!'

Chapter 22
2nd October – The City of Te'oull – Siatol

The dark and sinister clouds growing on the far horizon went completely unnoticed at first by the warriors of the Estian Alliance fighting in Te'oull. Most were too busy desperately trying to stem the enemy's relentless advance to notice. The battle was now one for survival. It had their full attention and everything beyond the city walls was forgotten for the time being, as they clung on to their positions and their lives by the very tips of their fingernails. Brraall was at the head of his tribesmen, leading from the front as usual. They were involved in a fierce fight against hoards of Thargws, Falorians and Taskans, but the situation deteriorated further when the fearsome beasts were soon joined by warriors from almost every other species in King Vantrax' armies. Though his force was now considerably outnumbered, the great tribal leader was using his substantial and muscular frame to bowl over any attackers, before relying on his astonishing speed and reflexes to avoid being hit by their weapons and using his sword to deadly effect. He had sent many warriors to the afterlife this way and his followers took great heart from having him at their side.

Then, amid all the confusion, Brraall had a sudden moment of extreme clarity. His eyes fell directly upon Sawdon, the beast of King Vantrax, whose legendary skills and ferocity had the entire continent shaking in fear. The Thargw gerada had just killed two of his own tribal warriors. Brraall had witnessed the gruesome deeds and he was enraged, infuriated. He fought his way towards the colossal Thargw as quickly as he was able, determined to take revenge upon him for the loss of his friends.

As Brraall approached, Sawdon saw him coming and waited patiently for him to make his way through the crowd, smiling broadly as he eagerly anticipated yet another duel, relishing the opportunity to test himself once again against a warrior of almost equal standing.

'Kah, strength comes straight from the heart of a warrior, does it not? We do not tire from the fight, but grow stronger with each kill. And *this* day surpasses all others. Ay raas, but I must have pleased someone in another life. I must have done *something* to earn such favour. Step forward and join me in battle. Let us finish what we began at Dassilliak. You were fortunate to survive the last time we met. You will have no such luck this time. There is no place for us both in the new world we will create.'

Brraall said absolutely nothing in reply as he finally reached his opponent for he was a man of few words; a man of action. He swung his huge sword down upon the Thargw giant and immediately began a determined and ferocious attack, the likes of which had scarcely been seen on an Estian battlefield.

Meanwhile, Jake and the others had reached a different section of the front lines, not far from where Brraall was fighting. Their position was slightly elevated and as they looked out over the city, across a sea of fighting warriors, they saw the clash between Brraall and Sawdon.

Something inside of Jake snapped. All of a sudden, he knew exactly what he had to do and he reacted without thinking.

'Wait here with Verastus!' he instructed Ben. 'Keep your head down, Brooksy, and try not to get involved in the fight unless you really have to, unless you're attacked. You hear me?'

Ben nodded vigorously. He had no intention of taking any unnecessary risks and he hardly needed to be told, though he was certain he could do more to help.

'Yeah, of course I hear you. You're screaming at me from like two yards away! But, I can...'

'Ben!' snapped Jake, turning on his friend for once with an urgent, almost hostile tone of voice that was completely out of character. 'For Pete's sake! For once in your life, just do as you're told! This isn't the school playground now mate. It's a real *war*! Look, you're as hard as any boy I know when it comes to a fight. The hardest. To be fair, I wouldn't stand a chance against you in a scrap if I wasn't... well, a Keeper. But these guys are trained killers! They're in a different league altogether. Just do as I say, please?'

Ben nodded once more. 'Alright, alright. I'll hide myself away if that's the way you want it and keep out of trouble. I'll only fight if there's no other option, okay? What are you gonna do?'

'Thanks pal, that's a weight off my mind. I know that was hard for you, given your stupid pride an' all that, but it makes me feel much better about things knowing you're as safe as you can be, given the circumstances. I still think we're going to survive this day, so don't give up just yet. I'm gonna kill me a Thargw!'

Before Ben could say anything else, or try to stop him, Jake turned and sprinted away. He began working his way towards Sawdon, battling through the crowds of warriors and the packed streets to get to the fight as fast as he could, hopefully in time to help Brraall defeat the Thargw warrior who most regarded as invincible. In time to kill a legend.

Sawdon's battlesword easily parried Brraall's opening attack. Despite the ferocity and speed of the skilled swordsman's efforts, the mighty Thargw was equal to everything thrown at him. Several minutes into the fight, he began to gain the upper hand. The clashes of jintan metal upon jintan metal were so loud and frequent that all those who could actually do so, stopped fighting to watch the remarkable tussle reach its conclusion. Brraall grimaced in pain as one of Sawdon's many sword thrusts met with success and cut into his side. He tried hard not to let the wound affect him and went straight back onto the offensive, launching two more vicious attacks upon his opponent in quick succession.

To his complete dismay however, Sawdon was actually smiling as he easily fended off both attacks. Locked in a bitter fight to the death which could easily go either way, the Thargw beast seemed to be having the time of his life.

'Raar! Yes! Come on! More!' he roared, as he pressed home another attack of his own. 'This is what life is all about. Do you not feel it? We are blessed to live in such times as these. This is *war*!'

Jake could not break through the crowds fast enough, no matter how hard he tried. There were simply too many bodies in his way and he had too far to go. Every warrior he faced seemed to want to engage him, and they were all competent swordsman who delayed his progress. He used his sword like a man possessed, swiping, thrusting and eventually cutting them all down. As fast as he killed them however, others seemed to come from out of nowhere to take their place. He was only metres away when he witnessed the end of the fight.

Sawdon dropped his shield in a surprise move which fooled his opponent. At the same time, he stepped inside Brraall's intended overhead strike. It was a totally unexpected tactic, a move bordering on insanity, because it was so dangerous. Supremely confident in his own abilities, the Thargw moved so swiftly that he managed to grab the wrist of Brraall's sword arm, as it hurtled down towards him. His giant hand halted the tribal warrior's arm instantly, in mid-flight. His own sword then swiped downwards onto Brraall's thigh. The great Thargw battlesword cut straight through Brraall's leg, severing it in two. The tribal warrior fell to the ground and a second strike to his midriff, killed him outright.

Sawdon roared again in ecstasy, his teeth drenched in saliva as he celebrated the kill. He was breathing hard, but he felt unstoppable, indestructible.

'No!!!'

Jake saw the whole thing from not too far away. He screamed out loud as Brraall's body hit the ground, alerting Sawdon to his presence. The young Keeper from Lichfield felt an immense rage exploding throughout his mind and body. He had never felt anything like it before. It was much more than a feeling of intense emotion; it was controlling him somehow, invading every fibre of his being. It surpassed fury and went way beyond wrath. Before he knew it, the mild-mannered schoolboy was suddenly awash with an insatiable need to kill!

The speed and venom in his attacks intensified to an unbelievable, astonishing level. Every single warrior barring his path to Sawdon fell within a few short minutes, until at last he found himself standing before the mighty Thargw.

But Sawdon was by now fully recovered. The great warrior was grinning. Waiting for him.

*   *   *

Princess Zephany and Caro had by now fought their way to the main square. Zephany surveyed the large empty patch of open ground with extreme relief, grateful for the fact that the enemy had not yet beaten them to it, and prevented her army from regrouping. The solitary statue in the centre of the square would serve as her command post. From there she would direct the very last stand of the Estian Alliance. Zephany was under no illusions; she knew that on the outcome of this fight, rested the entire future of her world.

'Good, we are in time. Caro, tell our captains to organise the defence and set the perimeter. They are to send warriors to all four sides of this square in equal numbers. We *have* to hold out here and allow as many of our forces to join us as we can. This is it, Caro. There is nowhere to go from here except for the afterlife. Fight, or die. Those are our only choices now.'

The Perosyan champion clicked his heels as he snapped smartly to attention.

'Yes, your majesty. I will see to it. I will return to you if I can.'

Princess Zephany placed a gentle hand upon his shoulder.

'I know you will, my friend. I have been fortunate to know such loyalty in many of my warriors, but you humble me more than most. I saw the same kind of devotion from Knesh Corian and the way in which he served my father for many years. Now that it is directed towards me, I cannot tell you what it means.'

* * *

Inside the small, abandoned dwelling Tien placed the box of stones carefully down. From the bag, he retrieved each of the new replacement stones and laid them next to the box, in the order they would be needed.

'Srr... does anyone have a dagger, or a throwing knife?' he asked. Jean, Harry and Graham looked at one another but nobody had anything that would suffice. 'No matter, I will use my sword. Though, it will be awkward.'

Tien drew it from his scabbard and with some difficulty he used the tip of the blade to prize the first stone loose.

'There, that is it. Let us try to mend that which is broken, to replace these gems and rebuild the shattered hopes of our people.'

'Is that all, Tien? You just have to take them out and put the new ones in their place?' asked Harry.

'No. Of course not. That would be *far* too easy. You would hardly need a wizard if it were, would you? Watch, Keeper, and all will become clear. First, the Bloodstone, made of creine,' Tien stated, holding the new stone up for all to see. He placed it in the vacant space left by the jewel he had removed. It locked itself effortlessly into position, despite seemingly floating in mid-air, with absolutely nothing to hold it. 'As we begin the restoration of the stones and the Heynai's box, we remember the sacrifice of Lord Bierenstell at Ilin-Seatt.'

Tien then prized loose the second gem and replaced it with the new stone.

'Next, the Eye of Toganoll. Mynaen ore, won through tests of courage and wisdom by the Keeper himself in the forest of Readal. Given freely by Brraall and his tribe to the Keeper destined to hold it, the one spoken of in legend, so that good may finally triumph over evil.'

The third of the five stones did not come out so easily and Tien had to apply a lot more pressure with his sword. Eventually, it flew across the room as the force asserted suddenly dislodged it and it leapt from the box. Harry went to fetch it, but the wizard stopped him before he had taken a step.

'No! Leave it. That stone is nothing now but rock and dust. *This* is the one we need,' he said, holding up the new replacement. 'That which was taken from the Thargw Emperor himself, at the city of Kerralux.'

'Oh my...! I never realised. I never fully understood until just now, until right this second, what he has done. What he's had to do. What *you* went through, dad,' stated Graham, all of a sudden.

Harry and Jean took hold of a hand each as they tried to comfort the son who, for varying reasons, they realised now they hardly knew. Graham felt his emotions getting the better of him and a lump developed in his throat, as he was suddenly overcome by very strong feelings of regret, and sorrow.

'All those lost years. What a waste,' he said, as he squeezed their hands gently. 'I'm sorry, dad. I'm sorry for everything I put you through.

I blamed you for it all, for *everything*, didn't I? I never knew you see; why you weren't there for me, either of you. But, I do now. I know I've said it all before, but I *really* need you both to know how I feel. I need to know that you forgive me? I have to tell you how much I regret my part in what happened to us.'

'It's okay son, you were not to blame. You were the innocent victim in all of this, we know that. This whole thing was bigger than any of us. We all did what we had to do to survive, nothing more,' replied Harry, smiling warmly.

'Yes, Graham, listen to your father, please? We are together now and that is all that counts, thanks to Jake,' said Jean. 'Somehow, between the three of us, we managed to produce a remarkable young boy. He is...'

'A Keeper?' suggested Harry.

Jean nodded and they all laughed a little as they turned their attention back towards Tien, who was clearly impatient to proceed.

'Yes, thank you. Time is running out. Now for the difficult part...'

The reolite pendant lay next to the dragon's sphere. Tien removed the old stone from the box with some difficulty and held it out in front of him.

'Stand back, please? All of you. There may be some sparks.'

The others did as they were told, retreating to the open doorway, where they stood and watched as the wizard went to work.

'Rebbrell euth hineax treoll,
Verrestte prolluum neothe,
Endulae weotte neesche!'

The Lichtus in his hands suddenly began to glow, but the light being emitted was far too dim and Tien was obviously extremely concerned. Then, without warning, the stone jumped from his hands and flew across the room, halting in mid-air about one foot from the startled Harry and Graham.

The old wizard realised immediately what was happening. He smiled a little with extreme relief. 'Quickly! We still have a chance for this to work! The power of that stone is fading, but it has been drawn to you both. The mystery, the reason for your appearance on Rhuaddan, has been answered. You were both meant to be here. You were brought to this land for this very moment. It is seeking more energy. It needs the power of the Keepers. Without you, the box cannot be fully restored. Come over here, next to me. If I am right, the stone will follow.'

Harry and Graham let go of Jean's hand and walked slowly over to Tien. As soon as they were by his side and the stone had stopped moving, the wizard began to chant again.

'Heynai greesht uthreall,
Nexoll praeet vixienne,
Alltol keprarr!'

The reolite stone suddenly burst into life to emit a very bright, white light. A radiant beam then exploded from within, causing Jean to shield her eyes, even though the others seemed strangely immune to its effects. The light raced from the pendant straight up to Graham and Harry's eyes. Then it joined to form a perfect triangle. Tien reached forward without delay and threw the dragon's sphere into the centre. As it crossed the ray of light, three further beams immediately appeared, firing out of the Lichtus swiftly to fix the sphere firmly in the heart of the triangle. It remained there motionless, suspended in mid-air at eye level. Jean could hardly see now, but her heart was racing as Tien cast one last spell.

'Trendiogh kuell weppronn leeast!'

The three beams of light which held the dragon's sphere in place shifted. They moved along the orb to converge on one central point, whilst somehow continuing to keep it aloft. A faint humming noise began and the lights started to cut into the solid stone. Slowly, gradually, they carved out a smaller gem, one which would fit perfectly into the box. Sparks began flying off in all directions, covering Harry and Graham and burning their skin. The heat caused by the friction became intense, and the two Keepers began to feel the effects. They were soon in agony. They both felt as though their skin was on fire, though one frantic and incredibly relieved look down told Graham immediately that it was not. Miraculously, there were no blisters, no burns, not even a redness of the skin. Still, the pain was unbearable.

'Aaargh! Dad, I can't take much more of this!' yelled Graham.

Jean's hand shot up to her mouth and tears filled her eyes. She was horrified as she watched their suffering, afraid she might lose them both and able to do absolutely nothing to help. She could barely watch, but she knew instinctively that it had to be done, that they had to hold out.

'No! You *can* do it, son. Trust me,' she screamed out. 'My beautiful, precious boy.'

'She's right, Graham. Listen to her,' said Harry, through clenched teeth. His face was contorted now as he tried hard to block out the intense pain. 'Think of Jake. Think of all he has gone through to get us here. You are stronger than you can ever imagine.'

Graham suddenly called upon reserves of strength he never knew he had. For the mild-mannered businessman and father, it was a very real and shocking revelation. More than that perhaps, it also brought with it an awful, terrible realisation. He knew in that single moment that he was part of this dynasty, one of the chosen few, a Keeper, able to do *anything* if he put his mind to it.

Graham West was a peaceful man by nature. He was perfectly happy with his lot in life and more than content to remain in the background, where he had always wanted to be. But, he knew immediately somehow, that this event could have drastic consequences for him and his future, for the ones he loved. He knew that *his* life had just been changed forever. He was no longer on the sidelines rooting for his son. He was at the very heart of what was happening. He clenched his fists as he reluctantly accepted that fact, thought of his boy, and screwed up his face.

'Okay dad, let's do this. For Jake!'

Minutes later, the agony was over. The cutting was complete and the new stone fell from the sphere to land at Harry's feet. The beams of light retracted immediately, vanishing into the pendant as if they had never existed. At the same time, the remainder of the dragon's sphere fell and crashed to the ground.

Ignoring the replacement stone completely, Harry immediately rushed to his son.

'Graham, are you alright?' he asked, his voice full of concern.

Graham took a moment or two to collect himself, before replying in a slightly nervous, shaky voice.

'Yes, I think so, dad. I don't *ever* want to have to go through that again though! I'm sorry, I know the decision may not be mine to make, when and if the time comes, but I'm no Keeper! I don't want to let you down but it's not in me to do the things you've done, the things you've both done. I'm caught up in all of this now I guess, but truthfully, I want no part of it.'

Harry hugged him as best he could. Jake's grandfather and former guardian of the stones was barely able to control his emotions.

'That's alright, my boy. That's okay. I never asked you to be a Keeper. I tried my hardest to spare you from all of this, for I know what it entails. I love you just the way you are, and I always will. You have to know it and believe me when I say that... I promise you here and now that, if there's a way, we *will* keep you out of it. Okay?'

Graham nodded gratefully before turning back to Tien. The wizard had retrieved the new stone he had cut and placed it into the box. He was just about to place the Lichtus stone in position also, when Jean interrupted his concentration with an unexpected question.

'Wasn't... wasn't that hot?' she asked, pointing at the stone cut from the dragon's sphere.

'No, it was as cold as the snow on my mountain. Now, without further delay, time for the final piece of the puzzle. Behold, a reolite stone. This one is known as the Lichtus. It was taken from a tyrant, freed by a slave and a king, and it has been sought for a thousand years by an entire population.'

He placed the Lichtus gently into position and stepped backwards. For a while, nothing happened. Harry and the others began to grow more than a little concerned. They looked at each other and then at Tien. The wizard remained expressionless as he watched the box intently.

Then, all of a sudden, the reolite stone shone brightly. It lifted upwards to reach its highest point and each of the four corner gems burst into life.

'Close the box!' Tien instructed Harry. 'It is ready!'

Chapter 23
2nd October – The City of Te'oull – Siatol

Jake West was sweating profusely. His clothes were wet through and he was breathing so deep, fast and hard that it was really beginning to hurt. He was spattered with the blood of the warriors he had killed and he looked as though he had been dragged through the fires of Zsorcraum and back again... twice! His eyes were glazed over and he had a look of ferocious determination on his face. It seemed as though nothing could break his concentration and resolve, as he looked directly at Sawdon without any trace at all of fear.

The giant Thargw towered above him, his blood-soaked fur barely managing to hide the hugely impressive array of perfectly formed muscles that lay underneath. At first glance to all around and any onlooker unaware of Jake's powers, this was a fight that could only go one way; a foregone conclusion, an appalling mismatch. The prelude to inevitable slaughter.

However, nothing and no-one else mattered now to Jake. Caught up completely in the moment, he could not think of *anything* but the Thargw warrior he faced, not his friends or family, his life back home, not even the people of Estia he had sworn to protect. His mind was utterly consumed by this moment and this moment alone. He was like a totally different person, completely obsessed by a need for vengeance and he no longer cared if he lived or died, just so long as he took Sawdon with him if he fell.

This is what it has all been leading up to. Everything I have done so far has brought me to this; a fight to the death with Sawdon. Perhaps my one and only chance to take revenge for everything he has done to my family.

His blind wrath made him forget all about King Vantrax and the stones for a time, as well as the battle for Te'oull which would decide the fate of all.

Up until now, Jake West had behaved and acted impeccably more often than not as a Keeper, surprising and delighting many around him with an unexpected maturity. But, this time, his feelings had the better of him and his heart was now ruling his head.

He had acted on his own initiative, on a rash impulse, when he rushed into a fight with Sawdon, for it was a deadly encounter with the savage beast he had no way of knowing he could win. The small, impetuous part of him that just refused to die, that which was still very much the teenager from back home, had resurfaced just when he needed it least. He *needed* to remain calm and composed, to think and act like a guardian and saviour of worlds, to do what was best for the Estian people, even if it wasn't what was best for him. And that probably meant avoiding an impossible fight with an invincible Thargw, restoring the box of stones as quickly as he could.

And yet, here he was placing himself seriously in harm's way, jeopardizing *everything* he hoped to achieve, the future of countless worlds, just to indulge his own petty craving for revenge.

The battle raged on around them but Sawdon and Jake concentrated solely on each other. The Thargw gerada was an intelligent beast and he knew this was no ordinary Keeper standing before him. Despite his youth, the youngster he was sizing up for the kill had somehow managed to evade capture in a hostile world, making the necessary alliances along the way to further his cause. With astonishing bravery and audacity, he had raided King Vantrax' mines, in the process rallying an entire continent to stand beside him. *That* was the work of no ordinary enemy as far as Sawdon was concerned. The boy he now faced had led the whole of Estia into a war the likes of which had never been seen before.

Sawdon knew little of the prophecies which told of a Keeper's coming, but he knew enough to recognise that if the Estian's truly believed he was the saviour of their world, then the defeat of this young boy, in this fight, would destroy all their hopes and aspirations, signifying the end of their rebellion. By ensuring Jake's death in this battle, Sawdon knew he would also be killing a legend, a fairytale used to inspire revolution. And in doing so, he would bring the whole Estian resistance to his master's rule crashing down.

'Raar! I should have taken your life when I had the chance, in the home of the last Keeper,' growled the Thargw, as he flexed his muscles and prepared to fight.

Jake paced sideways, seeking a better angle of attack. Sawdon matched his every move, as Jake replied.

'Yes, you *should* have. Maybe if you had, you would have prevented all of this from happening?'

'This? The battle? This is nothing! Once we have destroyed your army here, we will go on to conquer the rest of this land as far as the sea. It will all be ours. And then, who knows? We *may* decide to return to your world and see what riches await us there, for you have proved one thing only by coming here; that your race is a weak and feeble one, incapable of combat, and ripe for the taking. There are bound to be more reolite stones somewhere on Estia, even if that box of yours is not found, or if it is destroyed somehow. We will find the means to go there if we wish, you may depend on that.'

Now, enough talk, where is the box? You are about to die anyway, so you might as well tell me? What have you done with the stones?'

'Huh! I think that's *talk*, isn't it? And wouldn't you like to know. It's safe, and it's hidden, as far away from your claws as it can be. And you should know better than to underestimate an enemy, even one as feeble as me. Though, I'm not a patch on some of the guys from my world. Plus, we have weapons far more powerful than anything you can ever imagine. So, if you think you're hard enough, you're welcome to try!'

'Really?' said Sawdon, surprised by Jake's claim. 'More powerful than a wizard? Or an army of warriors who cannot be killed? I do not think so. Unless of course you have reolite on your world? If the box is as powerful as they say and we obtain it, we will be able to send *thousands* through the light. Nothing will stop us!'

Jake gulped hard as he was forced to consider the impossible, the unthinkable. His blood boiled and he tightened his grip on his sword.

'They're just empty words, that's all. It's not going to come to that. So, are we gonna fight? Or are we gonna talk each other to death?'

'Ra! Yes, I did not expect you to yield. We have chosen our paths in life you and I, let us tread them now and see where they lead. You have been a worthy opponent for one so young. It will be an honour to send you to whatever lies beyond this life for one of your race.'

'Yeah? Well thanks, but I wouldn't count on it!'

Jake suddenly rushed forward with unbelievable speed to begin the fight. His sword actually came within an inch of piercing Sawdon's neck.

The experienced warrior's astonishing reflexes though, enabled him to swerve and bring his own battlesword across just in time to block the intended strike. Jake's momentum took him past his opponent and he came to a sudden halt on the other side of him. He turned swiftly, but Sawdon had already recovered and was waiting eagerly for his next move.

'Yes, good. An excellent attempt to gain a quick kill, fast and efficient. I believe this encounter may prove to be my toughest test so far.'

'I'm glad you liked it,' Jake replied, his eyes fixed firmly on Sawdon's blade. 'Cos' there's plenty more where that came from.'

The giant Thargw then began his first attack. His battlesword screamed down out of the sky and struck Jake's blade with unbelievable force. The bone-crunching blow almost made him drop his weapon. However, Jake's increased powers suddenly gave him an extra surge of energy, strength and speed. He moved so fast that his sword seemed to be blurred to Ben, who had now caught up with his friend and was watching anxiously from a partially concealed position just behind him. The fiery youth had ignored his friend's orders and broken his promise. The moment Jake had gone in pursuit of Sawdon, Ben had dragged Verastus after his best friend. He was now watching the fight with his heart in his mouth, as the injured Falorian and a few Estian warriors with him, fought bravely to keep the enemy warriors away.

Despite Jake's awesome and increased powers, Sawdon managed to somehow combat every single move and attack he made. The Thargw warrior was astonishing, unbelievable! He was not only holding his own against the best of the Keepers, he was actually beginning to gain the upper hand in this fight, and he quickly placed Jake firmly on the defensive.

The two young boys could not understand or believe what was happening. Having not yet mastered full control of his fluctuating emotions, Jake was shocked and stunned to find that he was suddenly wracked with fear. He was almost as distraught and dismayed as Ben, who was now beginning to really panic, as he feared for Jake's life.

How can this possibly be?! The Keeper's powers are supposed to be greater than those possessed by any living soul? So, why can't Jake kill him?!

Sawdon's sword turned and gleamed in the morning sun and a reflection caught Jake squarely in the eyes, temporarily blinding him. The Thargw attempted to take advantage by using the same move that had killed Lord Castrad. Only this time, Jake was equal to it. He sensed what was coming and blocked the attack, before immediately launching another of his own, once again aiming for Sawdon's throat.

The giant beast reacted swiftly, grabbing Jake's wrist. With his superior strength he forced it against Jake's chest and pulled him in close, so that the teenager could not move. It looked very much as though the fight was over. Jake was held in a tight arm lock that he could not break free of, and he was only a second or so away from death.

However, Jake West was not finished yet. At the very last second, just as Sawdon was about to break his arm and snap his neck, he suddenly employed a tactic which came straight from the school playground. He brought his knee up hard and fast and caught the Thargw beast straight between the legs.

The mighty warrior grunted in pain as Jake's knee connected. His hold of the boy's wrist released just enough for the youngster to break free. Jake immediately took a step backwards, mightily relieved and amazed to have survived the fight so far. It was only a few minutes old, but to his surprise and dismay he was already exhausted. However, so was Sawdon.

'Graar! That was certainly different,' the Thargw stated, in his own way complimenting Jake on his lucky escape. 'But then, I should have expected it, I suppose. I shall not misjudge you again.'

'Yeah, even us weaklings pack a punch. That one was straight from the Ben Brooker school of fighting,' Jake replied, as he raced forward again.

This time his sword was low and aiming straight at Sawdon's stomach, but as the warrior lowered his own weapon to counter it, Jake raised his swiftly upwards and to the right, then sharply to the left, hoping to cut off the Thargw's head.

Sawdon saw it coming at the very last moment. He ducked underneath the blade and it missed him by the smallest of margins, actually cutting his fur as it sailed swiftly past. His astonishing reflexes allowed him to immediately propel himself forward, whilst Jake was off-balance. He knocked his young opponent to the ground and Jake fell heavily. His sword was ripped from his grasp by the weight of the fall. Sawdon saw this and reacted swiftly. He brought his battlesword down upon the defenceless youngster in an attempt to finish him off and end the fight.

Out of sheer desperation, Jake moved rapidly to avoid the strike. But he was not quick enough and the tip of the jintan blade caught Jake with a glancing blow across his back, which easily ripped open his flesh.

Jake was now seriously wounded and completely defenceless, as Sawdon drew back his sword for one final strike. The mighty Thargw had proven by his actions in this battle and fight, why he was considered by many to be the greatest warrior who had ever lived. Now, he was at last about to take the life of a Keeper and destroy the hopes of millions.

His sword came hurtling downwards, heading straight for Jake's head. Jake saw it coming, but he could do absolutely nothing to avoid it. He had nowhere to go, no time to think, and no time to act. He was done for.

* * *

'Jake! Jake! Come to me now. The box is yours. It is fully restored.'

Tien's calm and trusted voice sounded loudly in Jake's mind, just as his sword fell from his hand and he realised the fight with Sawdon was lost. The call he had been waiting for was as clear as a bell, but it was too late.

'Oh great! You've got excellent timing, wizard, I'll give you that!'

A few seconds later, Sawdon's battlesword cut into his back. It was now only a fraction of a second away from ending Jake's life, as the Thargw warrior raised it to complete the kill.

But suddenly, a Nadjan battleaxe came flying out of the crowd. It hurtled past Jake to lodge itself perfectly in Sawdon's chest.

The great Thargw fell backwards under the weight of the blow, stumbling several feet as he fought hard to remain upright.

Jake seized the opportunity and reprieve to scamper frantically across to where his weapon lay on the ground. He turned around and stood up immediately, ready and willing to continue the fight, despite his open wound, ignoring the incredible pain which now wracked his entire body.

However, Sawdon was gone!

All that stood before Jake now were throngs of enemy warriors. Realising instantly that the fight was over, that he was wounded and needed help, Jake turned rapidly to make his way back through the Estian lines. As he did, his eyes searched thankfully for the warrior who had just saved his life with such an amazing, unbelievable throw.

But the only 'warrior' not otherwise engaged in front of him, was Ben?

His best mate was grinning from ear to ear, looking ridiculously out of place in the midst of a ferocious battle. Jake joined him and they both began running back to their own lines.

'Nah?' the young Keeper said as they ran, recognising instantly that Ben was the *only* possible candidate for the throw, however implausible it might be. 'No way! That wasn't you?! An axe? How did you know how to throw an axe?!'

'Afraid so, pal. It was lying on the ground and it was the only thing I could find. Can't throw a sword like you. Not sure where the idea came from actually. I've never even held one before, never mind thrown one. But somehow, I just knew I could do it. I don't know whether it was me, or if I was possessed or summin', but either way it worked, didn't it, eh? And you're just gonna have to face it, aren't you? It was me. I saved your bacon!'

After a short while, Jake slowed to almost walking pace. His breathing became ragged and he lost all colour. Ben looked down with grave concern at Jake's wound and he stopped.

'Oh no. Come on, let's get you to Tien,' he said, placing his friend's arm around his shoulder. He led him away as the Estian warriors around them closed the gap and covered their retreat.

'It's okay, Ben, the box is restored,' said Jake, as they rushed as best they could to find their friends.

'Great. Right, well then, let's hope the stones can help with that little scratch you've picked up?' Ben replied, as he looked once more with increasing anxiety at the gaping wound. It was deep, and it was bleeding badly. 'Huh! Some people will do *anything* for attention.'

* * *

At the abandoned dwelling, Tien sensed that Jake was wounded. He said nothing of it to the others, for a more immediate danger had suddenly presented itself. The enemy warriors had finally breeched their lines and worked their way around the Estian positions. They were now in serious danger of being completely encircled and the only option open to them now, was withdrawal. Tien explained the decision and situation to Harry, who relayed them to the rest. Whilst Harry was speaking, Tien called for a hornblower and the young boy sounded the recall.

'Everyone, back to the square! Fall back now!' Tien shouted from the doorway, in a voice louder than anything heard before. Then, they all ran for their lives, the wizard clutching the box of stones tightly to his chest.

'But, what of Jake and the others?' Graham shouted, as he helped his mother and tried to keep up. 'We can't leave him!'

Harry replied on Tien's behalf. His experience and knowledge of warfare, coming from years as a soldier, added further emphasis to the urgency of the command.

'Look, I've seen this before many times, son. We're out of time. If they outflank us, we will not survive. They will make it impossible for anyone to rescue us, believe me.'

'We do, Harry, we do. Of course, we do. We trust you with our lives. It's just that... Well, what of Jake?' said Jean, out of breath but somehow managing to speak and convey her alarm.

Harry looked at the worried and worn-out faces of his wife and son, and he tried his best to comfort them. 'He will hear the horn just like all the others. He is a Keeper. He will know what to do.'

* * *

Jake and Ben were making painfully slow progress as they tried to get back to the others. Suddenly, they heard the sound of a battlehorn ahead of them. 'What..? What's it mean?' asked Ben, startled and afraid.

'It means we are losing. We're in trouble,' Jake replied. 'Come on, we have to hurry.'

'Hey! You don't need to tell me. I'm going as fast as I can you know. You're a heavy lump to carry. Put on a few pounds recently, have we?' the youngster teased, reverting naturally to humour as usual to mask his fear.

Estian warriors of all descriptions began sprinting past them, desperately trying to save their own lives as the enemy hoards pursued them hard. Ben screamed out at a few for help, but to his dismay no-one responded. Then, to his great relief, an unknown warrior took hold of Jake's arm and his friend found himself being lifted from behind, carried swiftly away to safety. Jake turned his head and saw immediately that it was Verastus. The Falorian had once again come to his aid in his time of need.

'Oh, am I glad to see you!' he said, smiling weakly at the gentle giant. His strength was failing badly now as the blood continued to flow from his gaping wound.

'Yes!' yelled Ben, incredibly relieved and grateful to see his friend. 'Great timing! Good for you, big man. Good for you!'

However, unbeknown to the two young boys, Verastus was really struggling himself now with the debilitating effects of his own grave wound. Still, he ignored his pain and the sapping of his strength and continued valiantly onwards towards the square, refusing to give up or give in, even though he could hardly bear the weight.

'It is nothing. Consider this, my debt to you both repaid in full.'

Chapter 24
2nd October – The Main Square - Te'oull City – Siatol

The exhausted and desperate groups of retreating Estian warriors converged on the main square, where they ran straight into the waiting arms of Lord Caro and his captains. On Princess Zephany's orders they were halted immediately and sent to plug the many gaps that still existed in their new defensive lines. Before long, thousands of determined defenders were packed tightly into the small area and a strong pocket of resistance had been established; the last line of defence for the Alliance. Due to the large numbers contained therein, the Estian square spilled out on all sides with fighters who were forced to spread into the surrounding streets, creating a solid and immoveable wedge, a final barrier to the fast-approaching enemy which could be easily defended, would be held at all costs, and hopefully prove very hard to breach. The Estians were under no illusions that the battle was already as good as lost. If it wasn't a fight to the death before, it certainly was now, for they had finally run out of ground to which they could retreat.

The fighting withdrawal had been swift and orderly for the most part and, just as Zephany had ordered, the enemy legions had been made to pay a high price for each yard of ground they had taken. They had also been slow to predict the Estian's actions, failing to pursue in time to prevent their escape and prevent those fleeing the battle from organising effective defences around the square. It was a mistake borne of overconfidence and one they would surely regret.

In fact, only small sections of isolated Thargws had spotted the opportunity that had arisen to hasten the end of the battle and tried to intervene. Though, their actions had been motivated more by a sudden lust for blood, rather than an appreciation of the military tactics required. It all meant that, for the moment at least, until her enemy advanced again and closed the gap that had developed, there was once again a lull in the battle and Princess Zephany found that she had time to check on her prisoner, Melissa. She wanted to ensure that her dangerous adversary was still held captive, bound and guarded. The young royal had no idea what she should do with her. She had thought it over several times but had still not made up her mind. She only knew that she did not want such an awesome warrior running loose in the midst of battle.

A badly wounded trexonn, still has teeth and claws.

'Kah, you are still with us, I see?' Zephany stated, as she approached the statue in the centre of the square where Melissa's guard had sat her down. 'You have not managed to run off and join your comrades?' The Sebantan warrior looked up at her royal captor with venomous eyes that seemed to burn right through the princess, and immediately sent an icy shiver running down her spine. 'Ra! If looks could only kill. Have I upset you in some way? You may have murdered half my people, but that was not my intent. Forgive me?'

Melissa looked around her slowly, before reaching the inevitable conclusion once again that escape was impossible, for the time being.

'You have me bound so I am your prisoner, for now. It is therefore your right to mock me. I should have died in this battle. I would rather have my throat slit by a Dzorag, than live to bring such shame down upon my Sebantan sisters. This is no way for a warrior such as I to be treated, no matter *what* you are accusing me of. Give me a sword, and I swear I will do the job for you... No? This wound,' she said, indicating with her head towards her blood-drenched arm, 'it may finish me yet, but seeing as you are all surrounded and soon to die anyway, why not release me now and you and I can fight to the death, right here? Come on, Zephany?! You hold all the advantages. I am certain to die, and you can then bathe in the glory of my defeat, for however long you have left in this life. You can use such a victory to inspire your people in their last action? At the very least, I will go down fighting, as I deserve. Yargh! I am *pleading* with you to show some mercy to a fellow warrior, to behave with honour?'

Princess Zephany was moved a little by the impassioned appeal, but not in the way Melissa had hoped.

'Frah! You really are full of your own importance. Your days have come and gone. You have served King Vantrax and done his bidding. You sell your sword to the highest bidder. You *have* no honour, so do *not* presume to ask it of me! You and your king, my uncle, have sought to destroy this land, to tear apart everything we have built, everything we love. You may very well succeed in your efforts, for our numbers continue to dwindle and we are nearing the end, but before you do you will be forced to watch the bravery of the Estian people from up close. They stand before you now in their thousands and they will not yield, even though they know this battle, this war, is already lost. And do you know why? They fight for a cause you will never understand, but after today neither will you forget. It will be the last thing you do in this life. To sit there helplessly and watch us die, to see what freedom really means to those who have had it taken away from them. Honour? You do not know the *meaning* of the word! You would not recognise it if it...!'

'Princess Zephany!'

An excited cry suddenly rang out from a soldier on the western edge of the square, interrupting the princess just as she was about to vent her full fury at her enemy.

'Yes? What is it?' she snapped, annoyed a little by the interruption.

'It is the wizard!'

The young leader's mood changed in an instant. She smiled and turned back to face Melissa.

'Funny thing; fate. As dire as our situation may seem, things may yet be undecided here? I would not count on victory until you see your Thargws marching into this square. We may still surprise you. I must go. I may not see you again. But know this, Sebantan; you were a child once, just like any other. You were innocent, untroubled by the ways of this world. The woman who brought you into this life loved you more than anything. More than life itself. She gave you a mother's unconditional love for years, and it protected you from harm in the most horrendous conditions you could ever imagine. The child you were, somehow survived the dungeons of Heron Getracht, and it made you the warrior you are today. You survived only because of *her*! Never forget that fact. It was King Vantrax who stole you away, and it was he who took your childhood from you. He ripped you from the arms of your mother and he... He stole your memories too, it seems?'

I cannot believe you have no recollection of this?! That you feel *nothing* for what he has done to you? The wizard you call your master destroyed everything you had. And he did it for one reason alone; profit! You were sold to the highest bidder in a slave auction, it is as simple as that. It was only by chance that you became a Sebantan princess and returned to Estia alive. To *serve* him! He has no loyalty towards you. He uses you, just like he uses all of you who do his killing for him. He is a...!'

'No! You are wrong!' barked Melissa, her blood now boiling and her temper rising with every word. 'He saved me. He brought me back from the dead!'

'Farak! That may be so, but who else was going to lead your Sebantans for him?!' replied Princess Zephany. 'I really have to go, but think on this while I am fighting with my loyal subjects; if *you* did not command legions of warriors who do his bidding, without question, do you think he would have given your death a second thought? You are *nothing* to him, nothing but the hired help, a slave to his will. Look inside your soul. I tell you, your loyalty is misplaced!'

* * *

Tien, Harry, Jean and Graham made their way wearily through the Estian ranks until they reached the main square. The old wizard was holding the box of stones out in front of him for all to see, like a jubilant cup-winning captain before a capacity crowd at Wembley. The Estian warriors began clapping and cheering as soon as they saw it. The spirits and morale of the defenders were lifted immediately as word spread like wildfire in their ranks. Each and every warrior determined to fight even harder than before, if that were possible, as they all dared to believe once again that they actually might survive this fight and somehow prevail. They were clinging once more to the faintest of hopes; that the newly-restored stones and the Keeper would save them. The enemy's final assault would surely come very soon, but the Estians were going to meet it now head on, steeled by fresh resolve.

Princess Zephany rejoined the others, just as Tien walked through the lines.

'Welcome! Welcome to our little party, wizard. Tell me, is that box of yours restored at last? Will it work?' she asked as the old wizard reached her, with more than a hint of exhaustion and desperation in her tone.

Tien bowed his head to her respectfully. 'Yes, I believe it will, princess. Though, in truth, I think it only fair to warn you that only the Keeper will know for certain. And even Jake will only know for sure, once it is tested in battle.'

'Well, on that subject, where *is* he?' interrupted Graham, with some urgency. 'Have you heard anything?'

Princess Zephany was a little taken aback to be interrupted in such a fashion. She looked the bizarrely attired strangers who were accompanying Tien and Jean up and down very quickly. Her eyes had been so firmly fixed upon the box and that alone, that she had not even noticed them. Now that she *did* however, their modern clothes and unmistakable resemblance to Jake told her everything she needed to know.

'Srr, you are... Jake's father, I take it?' she asked of Graham. He nodded a firm and instant reply, behaving like a schoolboy who had just been scolded for speaking out of turn. 'Then, I understand your concern. And you must be Harry, my father's friend and the last Keeper, the one who helped my people so many times in years gone by?'

Harry bowed his head and took a step forward. 'Yes, your majesty. I had that honour. King Artrex was the greatest man I ever knew. I am really sorry to have to inform you now that he has fallen in battle. He gave his life for his people, for all those on Rhuaddan and Estia. He met his end bravely, to bring them hope.'

Princess Zephany was half expecting to hear the news, given her father's injuries and predicament. She knew his wounds were severe and that he was trapped within the walls of Dassilliak, surrounded by merciless Thargws with no realistic hope of escape. But still, it hit her hard and tears formed in her eyes as she was stunned into a temporary silence.

It lasted only a few seconds. She wanted to be able to grieve for him, to cry her heart out in fact. She wanted desperately to be able to react like any other child might respond at hearing such devastating news. But, Zephany wiped away her tears and looked around her at the faces of her friends, at all those who were depending on her to lead them. They needed their leader to stay strong and see them through this terrible ordeal.

I cannot deal with this right now. I cannot let it affect me, she realised quickly. *I have to put it to the back of my mind and focus. I am in command and my people need me.*

'No-one must hear of this!' she ordered, her voice suddenly strong and resolute. 'Do you all hear me? Not until the battle is won or lost. If we are to die here today, it will not matter, for we will all be joining my father shortly. However, if by some miracle we survive, we will mourn him in a manner befitting his sacrifice at a later date. And then, I promise you all, that we will honour his memory, his status, and his deeds.'

'Yes, we will abide by your wishes and tell no-one, Queen Zephany,' answered Tien, speaking for them all.

Zephany was a little taken aback by the wizard's deliberate choice of words. Strangely perhaps, it had not even occurred to her that she was now the Queen of Rhuaddan. It should have done she thought, but it hadn't, and she now wore a mild look of surprise.

'Queen? Yes, thank you, Tien. This... This battle is far from over, and I am resolved to fight on. Nothing has changed in that regard, except for the fact that I may just be about to become the shortest living monarch in Estian history. Take shelter by the statue in the centre of the square and prepare for the attack, all of you. Srr... Jean?'

'Yes, your majesty?'

'There is someone held captive over there. Someone I think you should all meet. You may not have much time with her, so I suggest you go immediately, without delay. Only, take my advice and do not get too close. She is dangerous.'

Everyone looked over at the prisoner who was seated on the ground. They could see only that it was a female warrior, but Jean's heart began to beat faster and she looked up at Zephany as soon as she realised who it might be.

'Yes,' Zephany said, as soon as their eyes met, 'the warrior you see before you is Princess Melissa of the Sebantah. She is a servant of King Vantrax, and she is your daughter.'

*   *   *

Jean, Harry and Graham approached Melissa cautiously, leaving Tien to discuss the box of stones and the Keeper's chances of success with Queen Zephany. The Sebantan warrior immediately raised her head as she heard them approach. Her eyes were drawn instantly to the old lady in the centre of the small group. A thousand years of pain and suffering seemed to be etched into every wrinkle on her tanned and worn-out face. And yet, she appeared gentle and kind to the seasoned warrior, loving almost?

Melissa felt certain that they had never met before. She had an excellent memory and she could not remember her face. But, Zephany's words resonated within her like an echo that just would not fade, pricking her conscience and her memories at the same time, trying hard to unlock them both. Melissa's gaze did not stray from the old woman and the captive warrior barely noticed the two males walking beside her, even when they halted their approach not two feet away.

'You, I suppose, are the one who *claims* to be my mother?' Melissa snarled.

Her hostile reaction was a typical response for any Sebantan meeting a stranger for the first time. She was still refusing to entertain or believe the fantastic story she had been told, in spite of the strange and unfamiliar sensation she was feeling inside all of a sudden. Her heart was aching and she did not know why. All she knew for certain, was that she felt a very real pain within, one that simply refused to go away.

'I do not *claim* to be your mother, child. I *am*,' said Jean, who was now shaking like a leaf on a tree. Her voice was soft and tender, even though it too was trembling and full of nerves. Her next words were laced throughout with pure emotion. 'I... I'm sorry but I hardly know what to say to you. I have dreamt of this day over and over, for many years, though inside I never thought I would live to see it. It was all that kept me alive, for I had nothing and no-one else. Now that it's here and I have found you, I can't believe that I am actually lost for words... I... I thought I would never see you again. I had given up all hope.'

Jean knelt down in front of her and tried to touch her face, but Melissa turned her head sharply away.

'Do not touch me! I am not the person you seek. You are mistaken, old woman. *I* am a Sebantan princess. A warrior!'

Jean was not deterred by Melissa's reaction. Realising she may have only a few moments to try to get through to her long-lost daughter, she was determined to have her say. She reached out and turned the warrior's face to hers, forcing her to look her in the eye.

'You *are* the child who was taken from my arms in Heron Getracht. Regardless of what you think of us, or what you might say, you *are* my daughter. I gave you life and brought you into the world. I loved you as much as any mother could, and I tried to protect you. But, you are hurt? Here.'

She ripped off her sleeve and began bandaging the wound. Melissa was shocked by her actions but she did not object. As Jean continued to work, she stared up at the two weirdly dressed males before her.

'And who might you two be?' she asked, her voice still full of contempt.

It was though, no longer filled with hatred. There was a very subtle change in tone, which was not lost upon Jean. The old lady gave a little smile, which went completely unnoticed, as Harry replied.

'I am your father. Your *real* father. Long ago I was a Keeper. Jake is my grandson, so I guess that makes us…?'

'*You?! You* are King Vantrax' sworn enemy? Seriously? *You* are the one he sent Sawdon to kill, the one who defeated his armies and saved King Artrex? But, you are…!' began Melissa.

'An old man?' asked Harry, guessing correctly at her meaning. He immediately began to laugh, much to Melissa's anger and frustration, and she rose slightly to challenge him.

'Raar! Why do you mock me now? Be very careful for I will cut out your tongue!'

'Hey! Steady on! Calm down, please? No, you misunderstand. I do not mock *you* as you suggest. Not in the way you believe anyway,' explained Harry. 'I am sorry if I offended you. I was just thinking that your reaction was so similar to one I would have expected from somebody else, that's all. I was surprised by it, and it tickled me. I apologise, okay?'

Melissa relaxed a little and sat back down. 'Yes. I will take your apology, given the circumstances. But we are still enemies you and I. Even if all you say is true, I am not your daughter now. I was raised on Mynae and I am Sebantan. I am proud of that fact and I love my people. I am not from your world. You cannot undo all that I have been taught, just as I cannot deny all that I am. No matter what you say here, you cannot change my beliefs.'

'No, you're right. We know,' replied Harry. 'However, seeing as you are held captive right now and cannot kill us, for however long it may last, we can at least *try* to explain what happened? We owe you that much. After all, you have no choice but to listen to our words, do you?'

Melissa looked up at her guard. She knew Harry was right about the last part, but the smile on his lips as he said it upset her further. Harry sat down in front of her and seemed to be preparing to deliver an intense lecture. The hardened warrior looked quickly at Jean, who was still tending to her wound. She was smiling happily, as if she hadn't a care in the world. Melissa was confused, she could not think straight. The situation was so surreal that she felt like she was being ripped apart inside.

Everything I stand for, everything I have fought for, is a lie! The only thing I have in my life which is not, are my Sebantans. They would all die for me I know, as I would gladly sacrifice my life for them. I must do what is right for my warriors.

'He's right you know,' Graham stated, all of a sudden breaking the silence, before Harry could begin his tale. He sat down next to his father. 'I can't imagine what you're thinking right now. It's a topsy-turvy world we've entered and no mistake. I'm Graham by the way. I'm your brother. That won't mean anything to you I know but, as hard as it is for you to take in right now, we *are* your true family. You were snatched from us. We were the ones who were wronged in all of this. You may see us as the enemy, but in reality, *we* are the victims here. You won't like it but it is true; you are on the wrong side in this war. You fight against your own nephew. And now, you wage war against your entire family!'

* * *

As the rest of the West family tried their hardest to explain their history and convince Melissa they were telling the truth, the youngest and most powerful amongst them was seriously wounded. He was being carried through the streets of Te'oull by his Falorian friend, Verastus. The gentle giant's strength was failing him rapidly but he refused to give up, or relax the incredible pace he had set. And it was an astonishing, remarkable pace, given his own severe injury.

Ben was leading the way, clearing a path through all the retreating Estian warriors, in his own inimitable style.

'Oi! Out of the way, you lot! Look out, will you? Make a hole! World saviour coming through!'

Eventually, they reached the square and ran straight into the section commanded by Lord Caro.

'Jake!' the Perosyan Champion shouted, as soon as he caught sight of them. Jake's complexion was now worryingly white. He looked awful, as if he might die at any second. 'What happened?!'

'He ran straight into a Thargw; Sawdon,' replied Ben.

Caro's eyes lit up when he heard the great warrior's name. 'Sawdon? Where was he when you saw him last?'

'Don't worry about it. I got him,' Ben answered proudly, as they continued to push their way through to the square.

Caro grabbed his shoulder and turned him around. 'What do you mean? You actually *killed* Sawdon?!'

'Yes, I did... That is, I think so. I didn't actually see him fall, but I hit him in the chest with an axe, and that's enough to kill anyone. It was the throw of the century actually. You should've seen it.'

'No! No. It is *not* enough, not for Sawdon!' interrupted Caro. 'I say again, where were you? Exactly!'

Ben tried to explain their whereabouts as best he could while they continued to walk.

'Excellent,' said the Perosyan knight, as soon the youngster had finished. 'Thank you, Ben, you have been a great help. Now, please inform Zephany where I have gone.'

'What?! Don't be silly!' Ben pleaded, realising with shock Caro's intent. 'He's a monster. He's probably dead anyway. And there are *thousands* of 'em out there!'

Lord Caro began to laugh at Ben's response.

'Ha, ha, ha... I know all of that. I have not lost my senses, Ben. I will not venture out alone. But, I am a warrior, a leader. I will command from the front, for it is my way and I believe it to be correct. Our warriors need to know that we share their hardship, their pain and suffering. And, if I do by some miracle come across Sawdon, I promise you that I shall finish what you have begun.'

* * *

A short while later, Verastus staggered into the main square carrying a half dead Jake in his arms. He tried his hardest to reach the spot where Queen Zephany was standing waiting for them, but he fell exhausted onto the ground before he was even half way there, dropping Jake awkwardly onto the cobbled stones.

'Verastus! Jake!' screamed Ben, as he watched on helplessly from behind, having not quite managed to catch up. Oddly, he rushed to the Falorian first.

'No, Ben, not me. See to Jake,' Verastus protested, struggling to speak in a very weak voice. His head fell backwards onto the ground almost immediately and Ben saw with great distress that his friend was unconscious. He scampered desperately around to Jake. The young Keeper opened his eyes. He was also very weak, but he managed a little smile.

'Hey, Ace. He made it then? Looks like the tables have turned, eh? It makes a change for me to be the one who is hurt.'

'Yeah, mate, but we'll be fine, won't we?' answered Ben, his voice shaky, as tears once again fell from his eyes.

'You want it straight? I'm not so sure this time,' replied Jake. 'I'm feeling really dodgy pal. My back's killing me.'

'No. No it bloody well is *not*!' stated Ben, emotionally. 'It's a scratch, that's all. A pathetic little attention seeker. Tien'll fix it for you, you'll see.' He looked up and was relieved to see the old wizard making his way towards them, along with the others. 'Oi, Tien! Come on! Get your ass over here now!' he yelled.

'Hey!' gasped Jake. 'Leave it out. That's no way to talk to a three-hundred-year-old wizard you know. Not after all he's done.'

'Eh?' replied Ben, now *seriously* concerned for the health of his best friend. He had never seen anyone looking so ill, literally like death warmed up, as if he was just about to meet his maker. 'Yeah well, that's just me, innit? If he don't like it, he can lump it, can't he?'

Ben stopped talking. His face lost all colour and he looked up helplessly at his friends, as he realised with immense shock and horror that Jake had just stopped breathing!

Chapter 25
2nd October – The City of Te'oull – Siatol

Resus and his incredible army of dragons had somehow managed to overcome tremendous odds and win their incredibly long, ferocious fight with the creatures of evil in the skies above Te'oull. Through their sheer determination and superior flying ability they had eventually succeeded in defeating a much larger, far more deadly force. It was an astonishing triumph which really should not have been possible, an extraordinary testament to the bravery and loyalty of these remarkable creatures, for the cost of victory had been incredibly high. Many of the dragons had paid with their lives for reforming their alliance with the Estians. Almost all who had survived the battle now carried wounds of some description and a considerable number had been forced to withdraw from the fight in order to find a safe place to land, realising they were too badly injured to continue but anxious to preserve their race if they could. Those who remained in the skies above the battlefield fought on with tenacity and skill, chasing the revalkas and graxoth down mercilessly until only a few of the terrifying creatures remained. Now, at long last, as the equally hard-fought battle for the city below reached its climax, Resus and his army set about the final task of eliminating the surviving beasts, determined to remove the evil plague King Vantrax had resurrected and returned to Estia, once and for all.

From the hill which overlooked the city, the evil wizard and the dark spirit who was his mentor, Notorold, witnessed with abject shock and alarm the aerial defeat. They were enraged, incensed, amazed... More than anything, they were consumed by an immediate need for vengeance.

'Baasdraexx! They will pay for this! We will destroy all evidence that they ever existed! Hold your nerve, Vantrax, the spirit army draws ever closer. Once it is with us, I will ensure the dragons share the same fate as the Estian people who resist our rule. They will *all* be annihilated!' fumed Notorold.

The ground seemed to shake as he spoke and the sky turned a shade darker all of a sudden. He turned to look impatiently at the growing bank of black smoke which now almost covered the far horizon.

Vantrax however, was still looking up disbelievingly at the dragons, who were hunting down and killing every one of his flying monsters.

'I do not understand? How could they defeat my beasts?!' he raged, his face redder than ever. 'They were raised from Zsorcraum itself?! How is that possible?' he enquired, turning to question the evil spirit before him.

Notorold did not give much for the wizard's tone and it showed. He was furious, but he shook his head slightly as he replied.

'Yagh! They were mortal creatures, reborn. They were not spirits like I. They were raised from the afterlife, summoned from the fires, so they did not have the flame of everlasting life burning within them. Remember always, that there is a great deal of difference between us. Mortals have weaknesses which can be exploited. *We* do not. They are infested with faults; those they carried in life, and cannot shake in death. They bleed, they hurt, they die. My great army has no such failings. It approaches now as surely as the end of time. The life force within my spirit warriors was forged from the fires of evil, and there is no greater flame. No weapon, no Keeper, can withstand them.'

King Vantrax calmed a little. 'Good! Excellent! Then, this is merely a setback, and the plight of my creatures need be of no concern. And, if it comes down to it for that matter, neither is that of my army,' he added, turning to look once again at Te'oull and the raging battle within its walls.

It was just a sea of black now. Thousands of the king's warriors were packed into the city streets or climbing over the wall ramparts. Their numbers were matched only by those waiting impatiently outside the city walls to join the fight. To the two interested onlookers, it appeared that only a large area centered on the main square remained in enemy hands, still to be taken, and Notorold suddenly gave a wicked laugh.

'Ha, ha, ha… Your opponents are almost defeated in this battle. This war. Victory is only a matter of time. In a few moments, I will take the greatest force this world or any other has ever seen and end this conflict. We will venture beyond those walls and crush any who stand in our way. We will descend upon them like the night, silent and deadly, kill them all before they know we are there. Fear not, Vantrax, this war is over. And when the deed is finally done, when you have everything your heart has desired since first we met, I will inform you of the price you have to pay.'

King Vantrax was shocked and stunned by the unexpected statement. He had no idea what the evil spirit meant by it and it concerned him greatly.

Price? We have never spoken of cost?

He looked anxiously at Notorold, suddenly feeling more than a little troubled as he considered what might be asked of him.

I struck no bargain with you. So, what is it you will want in return for your help?

* * *

In the main square, everyone rushed as fast as they could to where Jake and Verastus lay. Everyone that is except for Jean, who chose to remain with the soldier guarding Melissa, despite her grave concern for her grandson. The fighting had resumed by now and it was fierce. The terrible, frantic sounds of a desperate last stand could be heard from every side of the square.

As Jean tightened the bandage on Melissa's arm, the Sebantan warrior at last spoke to her long-lost mother.

'It is over you know? You are losing this fight, surely you can see that? You have no hope of victory. Soon, you will all be killed.'

'Yes,' was Jean's short and candid reply. Her voice remained calm and unruffled, the tone of someone resigned to the fact that they were about to die. But strangely, not troubled by it in the slightest.

The Sebantan warrior was amazed by her reaction and to her complete surprise, she found that she was moved to act. The words appeared from nowhere.

'Then, let me save you?!' she begged. 'We have no history you and I. We are nothing to each other I know, but if I do not help now, we will have no future either. Stay next to me and I will protect you when they come.'

Jean smiled lovingly and looked deep into Melissa's eyes as only a mother could, riding on waves of emotion, trying hard to suppress her feelings, pleased to see that their efforts to turn Melissa's opinion of them had not been in vain.

'Thank you, Lissa. It means the world to me to hear you say that.'

Melissa's eyes widened upon hearing her words.

'*Lissa?!* That was your name for me. I remember!' replied the warrior, astounded by her sudden recollection.

'I… I'm glad. It's a start. In time, maybe more memories will return to you? If we are granted any that is. At least now you know I told the truth. It changes nothing however about our situation. I'm sorry, but my place is here, with my family, alongside my husband and son. I have only just found them again. I'm not going to be separated from them. Come what may, I will share their fate, and be happy to do so. And I have finally found *you. T*oday is a day I will treasure above all others, even if it *is* my last.'

Melissa shook her head vigorously. 'No! I will *not* sit here and let that happen! Cut me free?!' she pleaded strongly, offering her bound hands to her mother.

Jean shook her head. 'No. I'm sorry, I can't! You would…'

'Cut my binds, I *beg* you?! Free my hands and give me a sword?'

'Why?'

'I can still fight! My Sebantans will listen to me, if I can but speak to them. They are not like the others who serve him; they are loyal to their princess, not to King Vantrax and his money. They follow me and they will heed my command, for we share a bond closer than any other, a union forged on the battlefield, in many wars. Please, place a weapon in my hand and let me do what I can? This is what I do best. Give me the chance to right some of the wrongs I have done? You are all doomed anyway, what have you to lose? Let me at least *try* to save you?!'

'I… I don't know… But, your wound?' Jean stated, hesitant and unsure, hardly able to believe what was happening and what was being said.

'It is deep, but I have another arm. You do not know us. We Sebantans are taught as children to use both, with equal skill. All I need is a sword?'

'I do not know! I *can't!*'

Jean was now wrestling with her emotions, in complete turmoil. She looked at the soldier who was guarding Melissa, almost begging him for advice, for answers.

The warrior was reluctant to speak at first. However, he could plainly see that Jean needed help to decide what to do. The dire circumstances negated his sense of duty he thought, and reluctantly he answered her silent plea.

'I… Forgive me, it is not my place to speak, but… I am a plain and simple warrior in the Estian army. I do not make such decisions and I am mightily glad of it. I follow orders, though you have asked so I will be honest with you. Now that we are staring defeat in the eye, I am certain of only one thing; if I am to die this day, I would choose to do so alongside my friends. I would meet my end standing with them, not here, guarding this prisoner.'

'Then go!' rasped Jean, suddenly overwhelmed by a massive rush of relief. 'Leave me your sword and join the others. There will be plenty of weapons where you are going, from the dead and wounded. We must leave nothing behind in this fight. It makes no sense for you to remain here when I can guard her equally as well and we need every warrior we have at the front. I am the Keeper's mother and *I* will assume responsibility for this prisoner. Whatever happens to her, the decision is mine and mine alone. If we survive, you will carry no blame, I will see to that.'

The Estian warrior had heard all that was said between Melissa and her family but he knew the odds were stacked heavily against survival and he needed no second invitation. He handed his sword over to Jean and left to join the fight. As soon as he had gone, Jean reached down and cut the belt that was binding Melissa's hands. The Sebantan princess rubbed her wrists. She stood up straight and proud to tower over the diminutive figure in front of her. Then, she took the sword and smiled.

'Thank you. I know how hard that must have been. I hope we will be afforded a little time to get to know each other, you and I. Though, I doubt it somehow for I may not live through this. Know that I am betraying everything and everyone I know, for *you*. Goodbye, mother.'

Jean threw caution to the wind and rushed forward to hug her daughter.

Melissa was caught unprepared by the sudden move and the embrace that followed was so firm that she gasped in pain.

She did not mind though, and she did not object to it. After a few seconds, she pushed Jean gently away.

'No time to lose. I know the best way I can help you now. My Sebantans attacked Princess Zephany's force. The majority should be at the eastern edge of the square. I will do what I can but I will need to break through your lines. I only hope that your own warriors do not kill me before I have the chance to explain.'

* * *

Jake's heart had stopped beating for a minute or so. His prostrate body was now lifeless and bizarrely, it was already going cold. A mood of shock, horror and disbelief had gripped everyone. But Tien, the old wizard, instinctively knew what he had to do.

He set to work with real purpose as the others looked on, praying and hoping he still had a trick or two up his sleeve yet. He asked Harry to open the box of stones and lay it beside his grandson's head. Harry obliged without hesitation and the corner stones lit up almost immediately. A quiet humming sound began resonating from the four gems. Then, a beam of light from each of them travelled slowly towards the centre reolite stone, at exactly the same time. As the rays of light reached it, the reolite suddenly erupted into a sea of different colours. A small triangular prism appeared over the box. Harry and the others were amazed for nobody had ever seen anything like this before. The centre stone was reolite. Up until now, it had only ever emitted *white* light. But *this* was a bright assortment of different colours?

'Something is not right. It is not working as it should, is it?' said Harry. The fear and alarm in his voice was immediately apparent and it disturbed the others. Everyone looked anxiously towards Tien for answers.

'Come on, wizard, now's your time. Do your stuff!' cried Ben.

Tien simply shook his head at the impudent young boy. 'Your unshakeable faith in my abilities is touching, Ben. However, it is not *my* stuff that is needed,' he replied. 'It is Jake's.'

'What? But he is...!' began Graham, about to point out with a broken heart that his only son was dead, even though he was praying harder than he ever had that he was wrong and that some miracle, some magical power, could save him.

'Ah, sod this!'

Ben Brooker suddenly reacted when no-one else knew what to do. In a typical show of anger and frustration, he interrupted Jake's father and before anyone could stop him, he had grabbed hold of Jake's hand and thrust it into the prism of light. His actions took everyone by surprise, including Ben himself, who had absolutely no idea where the voice inside his head which told him to do it, had come from.

Jake's palm fell down upon the reolite stone.

'Boom!'

A gigantic, ground-shaking roar suddenly erupted in the sky above. Everyone ducked as bodies almost leapt from skin. Hearts were racing as they lifted their heads and saw, to their immense relief and amazement, that Jake's eyes were now fully open. The colour began immediately returning to his cheeks, as his family and friends gazed on in awe. Graham and Harry looked at one another with tear-filled eyes. The exhilaration they shared at Jake's reprieve was greater than any feeling they had ever known. He was once again breathing the sweet Estian air.

Ben shared their emotions and he was also overcome with joy and excitement. He did not know what to do. He was beside himself and full of nervous energy, until his eyes met Tien's.

'You know, Ben, on this remarkable journey we have all undertaken, for one so small in stature, I have to admit that you have surprised everyone with your courage and your actions time and time again. You have in fact been, *immense*,' stated the wizard.

Ben's face turned bright red as he checked Jake over.

'Yeah, yeah,' he replied, 'don't let me stop you. Carry on, please? Flattery'll get you everywhere. Ha, ha... Now, let's see about those wounds.'

He rolled his best friend carefully onto his side in order to check his back. To everyone's amazement, the gaping wound inflicted by Sawdon's sword had disappeared completely! The only sign it had ever existed was the remnants of Jake's torn and blood-soaked shirt. And Jake himself had already almost fully recovered from his ordeal.

'Hey! Be careful. Go gentle, will ya? I'm not a puppet, you know.'

Ben stood up, smiling. He offered Jake his hand and helped him to his feet.

'You'll do,' he said, beaming with satisfaction. 'Welcome back from the dead, ya zombie.'

Jake smiled back at him. Then he stared with relief and gratitude at the sunlit sky. It took a few seconds only for everyone to recover from the shock of having lost him, and seeing the youngster revived before their very eyes.

Ben turned to Tien. 'Well? I've done *my* bit. It's about time you did yours, isn't it?' he stated, pointing down at the newly restored box of stones.

*   *   *

Lord Caro was now in the thick of the action. His superior skills, strength, experience and expertise had already been employed to devastating effect in this fight. The Perosyan champion of many years had killed or wounded so many enemy warriors, that bodies and body parts lay strewn all around him. He had downed such an incredible number in fact, that some of the enemy beasts attacking the Estians now, all those but the fearless Thargws, were actually avoiding him!

This rather unexpected and peculiar development had created a tiny pocket of space in an otherwise congested, fiercely contested fight. Caro was as surprised and shocked as everyone else, but suddenly he noticed that the warriors immediately in front of him were parting. They all stepped aside one by one to give way and let someone through. Caro knew immediately who would soon be joining him. He stood his ground bravely and awaited the arrival of the mighty Thargw leader, with eager anticipation.

When he finally appeared through the crowd, Sawdon was carrying a heavy wound to his upper torso. It was blackened by the effects of fire and covered in dried and charred blood. It was a monstrous gash which would have killed most Thargws without a doubt. But then, Sawdon was no ordinary Thargw. He was no ordinary warrior.

Out of necessity, he had retreated for only the briefest of moments, in order to treat his wound and stem the bleeding. Just behind the front lines he had stopped and ordered two of his fellow Thargw warriors to build a fire. This they did using anything they could find which would burn, taken from the nearby dwellings. As soon as the fire was lit, Sawdon had pulled the axe from his chest. He ignored the excruciating pain and thrust a red-hot sword onto the open wound. The bleeding had ceased immediately. Sawdon then took only a few minutes to rest, before rejoining the fight and soldiering on. Only now, he found the way ahead was blocked by a warrior whose skill in battle was so great, that those ahead of him had faltered. Seasoned campaigners and mighty veterans had already fallen to his sword. Word spread quickly and Sawdon soon learned of the holdup. With growing excitement, he strode purposefully to the spearhead of the attack. Once there, he saw that Lord Caro was waiting for him.

'Out of my way, Perosyan!' roared the furious Thargw. 'The day is ours and I have a boy to kill!'

Lord Caro did not budge. He brought his sword up to his nose and then lowered it, giving the Perosyan salute to a fellow warrior.

'I am Lord Caro, son of Truith of the house of Sirrannus, Champion of Perosya and sworn protector of her royal highness, Queen Zephany, Leader of the Estian Alliance. Today, Thargw, you join your ancestors in Kalvanaar.'

Sawdon chuckled a little, his deep, throaty laugh as menacing as his roar.

'Ha, ha... Brave words. Though words will not be enough to

defeat me, or turn back our army. And titles do not win wars. Warriors do. I am Sawdon, and death is my profession.'

Sawdon suddenly sprung into life. Without warning, he hurled himself onto Caro, ignoring the pain in his chest, blocking it out somehow so that it did not hinder him in any way. His battlesword clashed against Caro's with thunderous noise and the fight began.

The next few minutes were a frenzy of action. The two supreme combatants fought against each other at a level rarely witnessed on a battlefield. The speed and combination of different attacks was amazing to behold for any fortunate enough to see it. Sweat poured from Lord Caro's brow. Sawdon began snorting, growling and breathing so hard that the noise he made almost drowned out the roars of his warriors. His nostrils flared and steam rose from his body, and as a result of his extreme efforts, blood began once again seeping from his wound.

Caro lunged at Sawdon with yet another unsuccessful attack. His momentum took him away from the Thargw and both warriors took a moment to pause for breath.

'Ay raas! You are in a different class altogether to those who came before, Perosyan. Come and join us? King Vantrax will pay heavily for such a sword,' stated the Thargw beast.

Caro shook his head firmly at his fearsome opponent.

'I already have a queen. She is all anyone could ever want in a monarch, and I have sworn to serve her faithfully, until the end of my years. I thank you for the compliment you pay me though. I will take it gladly, just as I will take your life.'

'Frah! Words again? Many have tried. *All* have failed,' Sawdon replied.

'Yes, there is no denying your skill with a sword. And you fought against a Keeper and lived,' said Caro.

'More than one,' corrected Sawdon.

'Kah, yes. I apologise for my error. I would say that makes you perhaps the *third* greatest warrior of all time?' teased the Perosyan knight, hoping to rile his Thargw opponent.

It worked. Sawdon was enraged by the insult and he growled a scornful reply.

'Third?! *Third!?* Before I cut out your heart and feed it to my Pralon warriors, you have one moment more in which to explain yourself?!'

Lord Caro smiled. His aim had been true and he had struck a raw nerve, exactly as intended.

'You are too kind. Well now, let me see? History tells us that Lord Bierenstell was the best, before I came. His deeds are the stuff of legend, still imparted in every alehouse and tavern. In the minds of all of those on Estia, he ranks above you, and he always will.'

'Raarr!!!'

Sawdon was hurt and angry. In a rush of Thargw blood, he ran forward and resumed the fight. Only now, he was in a blind fit of rage and his fury was fuelling this savage attack, controlling him almost. He was not thinking clearly for once, not as he should have been. As he would normally be.

The momentary interruption in his concentration was all Lord Caro needed. It was what he had hoped and planned for, and he was determined to turn it to his advantage. The Perosyan champion blocked several fierce blows from Sawdon's sword. The moment he saw that the Thargw had overextended himself because of his rage and was slightly off-balance, Caro stepped forward inside his reach and jabbed the handle of his weapon underneath Sawdon's chin.

The Thargw warrior fell backwards immediately under the weight of the blow and it was all he could do to remain upright. Before he could respond to the unexpected, improvised strike, the cold jintan steel of Lord Caro's blade sliced across his throat.

The cut was deep and Caro knew he had inflicted a mortal wound. But, Sawdon still managed to launch one final attack. His huge battlesword hurtled down upon the knight from out of the clear blue sky, aiming straight for his head!

Caro saw it coming at the very last moment and, with astonishing reflexes, he managed to move his body out of the way. The intended strike whistled past him and the Thargw's giant frame crashed to the ground.

Sawdon, the mighty Thargw who had terrorised an entire continent and instilled fear into the whole of the Estian people, was no more.

* * *

Melissa reached the Estian lines and was immediately surrounded by angry warriors who had recognised her and were intent on killing their arch enemy. They hesitated only because she lay down her sword and attempted to reason with them, unarmed. In the panic and confusion of battle however, Melissa could not make herself heard and it looked as though she would be torn apart by the furious mob.

Luckily for the young warrior, Queen Bressial had observed her flight and decided to pursue. The Nadjan monarch soon caught up with the crowd and pushed her way to the front, reaching the Sebantan only seconds before an Estian blade slit her throat. Standing in the centre of an impromptu circle, Queen Bressial somehow managed to cool their hysteria and silence the crowd.

'What are you doing here?' she asked, as soon as it was quiet enough to be heard. 'Trying to make good your escape?'

'No,' Melissa stated, firmly, 'you could not be further from the truth. Believe it or not, I have come to help.'

The whole crowd surrounding her began to jeer with derision, but Melissa looked straight into Bressial's eyes.

'It is true! I have switched my allegiance, for reasons it would take too long to explain to you now. Look! I have laid down my sword and I am defenceless. Is that the actions of an enemy wishing to fight? You could have easily killed me, but I chose to take that risk. Let me through your lines? I can speak to my warriors, convince them to join with you?'

'Yagh! You would run, and they would not listen,' shouted one of the warriors from the crowd.

'Yes, he is right. And why should we trust you? You have killed too many of us in the past. We do not forget. You are at our mercy now, why should we let you live?' asked another.

'They speak the truth, my dear,' said Queen Bressial, raising her eyebrows and cocking her head slightly. 'Your past catches up with you now. I am afraid it speaks louder than any of us ever could.'

Melissa looked around the crowd and then stared Bressial straight in the eye once more.

'If you honestly believe me to be lying, strike me down! I am unarmed as I have said, so I cannot defend myself. I cannot help my past. I cannot erase the things I have done. But I *may* be able to affect the present, and the future. You *have* to take a chance on me, here and now. You *need* me!'

The Queen of Nadjan knew she was right. She had to take the risk, try to convince the crowd.

'The odds are so heavily stacked against us, my friends, that one more warrior is of little consequence, even if it *is* Melissa. If she is telling the truth, she may buy us more time. Let her through!' she ordered.

She was somewhat surprised and relieved when the Estians reluctantly obeyed her command without hesitation.

'Pass the word to give her safe passage through our lines.'

Melissa bowed her head once in appreciation and respect to the former prisoner of Heron Getracht.

'Thank you, your majesty.'

'Save your words! Prove your worth!' snapped the queen.

Shortly afterwards, Melissa reached the front line where her Sebantans were fighting against the warriors of the Estian Alliance. As soon as they saw their princess walking through the Estian lines unharmed, the shocked and stunned Sebantan women immediately disengaged from the fight. Unsure as to what the extraordinary development meant, they detached themselves from their former allies and rallied to one another, forming a defensive unit which rapidly grew in size and protected them from attack on all sides.

The swift response confused their former comrades and they could not understand what was happening. All soon became clear however, when it was followed by an immediate address from Melissa. The Sebantans quickly learned of her decision and immediately launched an attack upon King Vantrax' warriors, their former allies. They were aided by the Estians, who began cheering and roaring their approval as they rejoined the fight.

The savage nature and speed of their combined attack tore into the enemy lines, creating confusion and panic, drawing off some attacking forces and bringing some much-needed respite for the defenders of the square. Melissa led from the front. She fought bravely, with skill and determination, for the first time in her life actually believing in a cause and fighting all the harder for it.

*   *   *

The army of dark spirits had *finally* arrived on the hill which overlooked Te'oull. The dense clouds of black smoke had evaporated to reveal legions of undead beasts. All were hideous to behold and every single one possessed a heart of pure evil.

The Guardians of Zsorcraum were the custodians of the fire. It was their job to oversee the wicked domain and control its beasts. The spirits were trapped there by the laws of the afterlife; the spells cast by the higher beings or Gods, and the gates which had been kept locked and secure since the beginning of time. However, the spells had been weakened by Nittrii-Hebul's actions. The walls of the prison had cracked and the chains on the gates could now be broken. She had acted of her own volition and pushed the boundaries too far by interfering in the affairs of mortals far too many times, on behalf of Jake. Time and time again she had come to the aid of those who needed her, more often than not without their knowledge, and now the true consequences of her foolish deeds were about to become clear!

The army of death lined up in front of Notorold. The once great wizard gave one last evil smile, before turning with renewed vigor to face Te'oull.

Chapter 26
2nd October – The City of Te'oull – Siatol

Jake had by now fully recovered from the wounds he received in his fight with Sawdon. His mind and body felt rejuvenated, alive and fresh, revitalised by the power contained in the newly restored box of stones. In fact, he felt much better than he ever had; pumped, psyched, confident, full of energy, and extremely focused. He had no doubt at all that in another situation, on another world, he could quite easily go out and run a marathon. And what's more, he knew that he would scarcely be out of breath at the finish line.

The finish? he thought. *Yes, I have to get going!*

He thanked Ben with all his heart for his bravery and quick thinking, for saving his life. But he did not linger and he turned quickly to Tien and Harry.

'This ends now! Everything we've done so far has been leading up to this moment. Fingers crossed, eh?'

Tien had absolutely no idea what that meant and, when he cast a quick glance at Harry for an explanation, Jake's grandfather was simply smiling at him, in no mood to oblige.

'Go on, Jay, do it! Become the person you were always meant to be. Make us proud son, as you have always done.'

'Yes,' added the wizard, determined to end all conversation, 'do as Harry says. But whatever you are going to do, *hurry!*'

Jake lifted the box of stones and held it out in front of him. He concentrated hard upon the centre stone for a second or two, before taking his hands away to leave it unsupported.

The box remained motionless, floating in mid-air. Then, as Jake increased the power of his concentration, the light from the four corner stones grew steadily in intensity, until at last they were shining as brightly as they ever had. The centre reolite stone then began to rise. Once it had reached its apex, the prism of light disappeared and the centre stone reverted back to bright white light once more. A fraction of a second later, the light raced up to the sky. This time however, the light bounced back down to the small crowd immediately and hit the Keeper squarely on his chest.

It struck Jake with such astonishing force that it lifted his entire body off the ground. He was raised about four feet into the air and moved slowly through the beam until he was positioned directly over the box, trapped in the centre of the light. As the others looked on with grave concern and anxiety for several seconds, nothing happened. But then, all of a sudden, he was lowered gently to the ground. The light disappeared and the stones returned to normal.

'Err... is that it? Or is something else gonna happen? Jake, are you okay?' asked Ben, as usual the first to speak.

Jake sat upright. He began rubbing his head hard, as if he had the world's worst headache. When he lifted it up, his eyes had lost their pupils and were completely white.

'Yeah, I think so. Wow! Bit of a kick to that.'

He stood up as if nothing had happened, aware that everyone was staring at him.

'You ain't wrong there, mate,' Ben replied.

'Eh?'

'I suppose you could do with a mirror or something. You look like something from a horror film,' Ben explained. 'Your eyes pal, they're all white. You look like an extra from Scooby-Doo.'

'Forgive me, but it matters not,' said Tien, before Jake could answer. 'They will return to normal soon enough. What has happened, Keeper? Tell us, how do you feel?'

'Like... Like I've just been run over by an express train, if you must know,' replied Jake. 'That's a real shame that, 'cos I *was* feeling really great, like some sort of superhero... No, wait! Yeah, it's okay. It's going. Wow, this is something else! I... Yeah, it's done. I'm back to normal, just like you said.'

'Huh! *Normal?*' said Ben, sarcastically.

'What? Oh yeah. Well, you know what I mean,' Jake replied. 'Look, I know what I have to do. It's all suddenly become so clear to me now. Resus, I need Resus!'

He closed his eyes and called the dragon, once again using the power of thought. Within seconds, Resus had answered the call and moments later he landed in the square. He bore several nasty wounds. Scorch marks and gashes of all shapes and sizes covered his body, some of them trailing thick green blood. His huge wings were torn in places and he appeared to be exhausted. Nevertheless, despite his fatigue, he remained silent and awaited the Keeper's command.

'Resus, my new friend, are you ready? You and I were born for this day. We are the only ones who can save these people now. This entire world is relying on us to end this war. I know that you have given so much already, much more than I ever hoped or could have expected, however, I must ask for even more from you. Are you with me?' asked Jake.

'How can you ask that of me now, after all we have done? Lead on, Keeper. Whatever you require of me, it will be done. Though, you must act quickly, for there are forces approaching which terrify me and my kind.'

Jake cast a quick glance towards the far horizon and everyone present did likewise. All were horrified by what they saw. The warriors of the Estian Alliance had been too busy fighting, too engrossed in their own private battles, to see what was happening beyond the wall. The army of black spirits was now absolutely immense. It covered the sky as far as the eye could see. And it was coming straight for them.

A sudden and extreme fear gripped everyone, and several cold tremors ran down numerous backbones.

'*Holy cow!*' Ben screamed, when he caught sight of their new opposition. 'I tell you what, Jay, I'm gonna have to *seriously* re-evaluate our friendship when we get home! Hangin' around with you is getting to be a little dangerous. You must have killed every single black cat we know? You're jinxed!'

Jake's grandfather was the only one to respond. All his years as a Keeper had taught him many things, but none more important than the advice he was about to impart to his only grandson, to his true heir.

'Jake, if I can teach you one thing and one thing only, let it be this;

you cannot do everything all at once. You must take one fight, one battle at a time.'

Without delay, Jake nodded at Harry and ran straight over to Resus. He climbed up onto his neck as fast as he was able.

'Ha!' he yelled, as soon as he was ready, and the mighty dragon soared into the sky once more.

* * *

All around the main square the Estian warriors were fighting with fierce determination, trying to hold the warriors of King Vantrax at bay. It was a desperate struggle, a last-ditch battle for survival. They were outnumbered and outclassed, and they soon began slowly losing ground to the hired killers they faced. The large defensive pocket began shrinking on all sides. Even the awesome Sebantan warriors were now falling back to join their new allies, as weight of numbers and fresh reinforcements forced Melissa and her excellent force to retreat, in order to avoid becoming encircled. Queen Zephany's army was drawing upon its very last ounces of energy and strength. Her warriors had performed miracles so far to keep the enemy hoards at bay, but they were clinging on desperately to their positions, holding on by their fingernails to life itself.

Above them, Jake and Resus passed over the scenes of carnage and chaos until they were flying directly over the centre of the square. Once there, the mighty dragon stopped his forward momentum and hovered at Jake's command. The Keeper's eyes suddenly reverted to normal. His pupils returned in a flash and he began to shout, bawling out loudly in the ancient Ruddite dialect.

> 'Eesgrinall allavruud vinneroll mathuus,
> Sennarr presstriolle Te'oull akraall,
> Exolonne rechranne zsabrutt!!!'

Jake's attention was focused entirely upon the defenders of the square. His eyes suddenly changed once more, becoming bright red in colour before erupting almost immediately into a fiercely bright, white light, which raced down towards the ground at phenomenal speed. It came to a sudden and abrupt halt when it was about thirty feet from the cobbled stones below. A second later, it spread out rapidly on all sides to form one giant, continuous dome, changing from dazzling brightness to an almost invisible shield, as soon as it was formed. A slight haziness of the air was the only sign that it existed.

The impregnable barrier was similar to the one employed by the Heynai to protect Te'oull and it fell over the Estian warriors wherever they were fighting, separating them from their assailants in an instant. Where the fighting was at close quarters, the beam of energy hit the enemy warriors and cut them in two, right before their astonished and extremely relieved opponents.

A huge protective wall of shimmering air now surrounded the warriors of the Estian Alliance. Within its confines, for the time being, they were all safe from harm. The enemy forces of King Vantrax were incensed. They tried everything to break down the indestructible barrier, but with no success.

The beam of light retracted back into Jake's eyes and once again they returned to normal. A spell of unbelievable power and epic proportions had just saved the Estian Alliance from defeat, but for how long?

Resus was amazed, and seriously impressed. 'Draas! We were right to side with you, Keeper, for so many reasons. The threat still remains though. How long will it hold?'

'Not long. We have to work fast,' Jake answered. He immediately placed his hands upon the dragon's neck and chanted again.

'Gerestvol arrunslarr mennieth.
Raatreonne ebulat pathradde!'

Jake looked down upon the swarms of enemy warriors who were now massing at the edges of the shield as he spoke. They were chomping at the bit, regrouping and waiting for it to fall so that they could complete their victory.

'Now, Resus. Your time has come!' the young Keeper cried. 'Your eyes. Use your eyes!'

The exhausted dragon was a little shocked by the sudden suggestion and with a little hesitation, he pointed out the obvious.

'But, there are too many of them, Jake?' he protested. 'I would not have enough time before the army that approaches falls down upon us?'

'Just trust me. Together, we are a deadly combination you and I.'

Resus took a deep breath and shot a bolt of light from his eyes, aiming instinctively at the large concentration of warriors in front of Queen Zephany. The ray of light hit the air just above them and it immediately dispersed over a wide area, turning every single warrior underneath into black stone.

The elderly creature was astonished to see the awesome and devastating effect of his strike, but he kept on firing at large sections of the wizard's army, taking them out in droves. Strike after strike reigned down upon the warriors of King Vantrax, every bolt of light transforming into useless rock any enemy within a hundred feet or so, but miraculously leaving the isolated pockets of Estian warriors nearby, *completely* unharmed.

Resus swooped down and circled around the square, continuing to fire until he was certain all of King Vantrax' troops and beasts had been destroyed. Before long, every warrior inside the city walls had been accounted for and the dragon turned his attention towards those outside, but they had seen his deeds by now and having bore witness to his extraordinary power, were fleeing for their lives.

The Estians inside the protective dome began cheering and roaring their approval, celebrating their unexpected deliverance and liberation with such fervor, that their cheers and screams of delight could be heard for some distance across the land.

However, many soon lost their high spirits as they cast one eye towards the dark and sinister army that was still approaching. The mood changed rapidly once again in Te'oull as the news spread and realisation dawned. An anxious and nervous silence returned to the square. In a matter of minutes, thanks to the power contained in the newly restored box of stones, Jake West and his dragon had destroyed the armies which had conquered almost the entire continent of Estia. The teenage Keeper had lived up to every expectation. He had proven beyond doubt that the prophecies and legends were true, and he had fulfilled his destiny.

But, Jake's work was not yet done. Having just defeated the

greatest war machine Estia had ever known, a new and far more deadly force now confronted him.

*   *   *

A vividly intense, unexpected and mysterious light had appeared over Te'oull without warning. It had then disappeared in a flash. Watching from a short distance away, the unexplained phenomenon soon had King Vantrax very concerned. It disturbed him greatly because it brought with it an unknown threat, one which gave the wizard an immediate and uneasy feeling of uncertainty, where moments before he had felt nothing but supreme confidence. To his horror, it quickly transformed into a wretched sense of impending doom. He was all of a sudden wracked with a fear he could neither shake nor explain, for to his eyes his forces were *winning* the battle, and just about to complete a long awaited, momentous victory. Despite all he could see, his forces surrounding and just about to crush the last of the Estian resistance, it was an awful, invasive sensation.

'Kalleist!!! What was that?!' he yelled, looking at his former master, hoping he would supply the answers he desperately sought all of a sudden.

Notorold did not know for certain what had caused the light, but he swiftly became aware of a new presence on the battlefield, one which had not existed earlier, or at least was concealed from him if it did. It worried him greatly, because it seemed to carry with it immense power, an almighty force of energy that was so great, he could sense it. And his silence did nothing to calm the wizard's fears.

'Yaarrgh! What is it? What is wrong? Why do you delay your answer?' Vantrax yelled.

'It... It is not right. Something is wrong here. They... They have not come?' the evil spirit replied.

King Vantrax was furious now. He could not understand what was happening and his frustrations were boiling over. His warriors and beasts were fighting hard to take the city, giving everything they had to hand him the victory he sought, and the great army of black spirits appeared to be doing absolutely *nothing* to help! He was on the verge of an historic achievement which would eclipse all others in Estian history. So, Notorold's cryptic reply to his urgent need for answers enraged him even further.

'Who?! What are you talking about? The city is ours for the taking!' he screamed in frustration. 'Unleash your spirits now and finish what we have begun!'

Notorold moved his head slowly and deliberately to look King Vantrax in the eye.

'*It did not work!* Why did it fail? We were supposed to draw them out into the open, where they could not hide, where they were not protected. This was the battle we planned all along, one we could fight on our terms, one we were certain to win, and could not lose.'

'Draw them out?!' fumed the wizard. 'The spirits? You planned all of this to wage war upon them?!'

'Yes! To destroy them all.'

'Raarrgh! You used us as bait. You used *me*!' Vantrax screamed, incensed by the deceit and treachery of his mentor. His fists clenched tightly and in his rage he instinctively moved a little towards the dark spirit.

Notorold however, immediately gave him a threatening look which suggested he was just about to strike the wizard down. King Vantrax saw this and backed off, withdrawing a little even though he was still seething.

'Yes, is the answer you seek. I used you, but why are you so surprised? You would have done the same to me, if the situation were reversed. You forget that I know you too well. You and your armies were the enticement we needed to set the trap. Nothing was left to chance. Though it has not worked? They have not come. I do not understand. Where *are* they? Why have they forsaken him, abandoned him? It is not their way and it makes no sense?'

King Vantrax was still absolutely livid and conscious of the fact that he needed to direct all of his attention towards winning the battle, but he wanted to understand what had happened. He needed to know.

'Him? The Keeper?'

'Yes, of *course*, the Keeper, you imbecile! Who else?' raged the spirit.

Before King Vantrax could reply, a solitary dragon and rider suddenly appeared over the city square.

'There he is!' cried the wizard, surprised and alarmed. 'Quickly! Attack!'

Notorold was just about to give the order, but it stuck in his throat as he witnessed another light shining down upon the defenders of Te'oull.

King Vantrax was suddenly filled with a further sense of foreboding, only this time it felt as if his whole world was just about to crash down around him, as if everything was slipping away from him slowly and he could do absolutely nothing to prevent it. He felt as if he were dying inside.

'What...? What is happening *now*?!' he screamed, as his heart began racing and sweat started to pour down his brow.

Notorold was just as horrified and exasperated, dismayed by the sight before him. He roared his answer in the deepest of tones, with all the energy he could muster.

'The day, the battle, has turned! The teachings of old. They are all coming true!'

He looked straight at King Vantrax. His eyes were on fire now and his ghostly face was a picture of grim determination, of desperation even.

'We have shown our hand. They know we are here. So, we have no choice now but to act. We *have* to stop that dragon! We *must* kill that Keeper!'

The black spirit immediately waved his army forward. It was very much to King Vantrax' relief. However, Resus and Jake had already begun attacking the wizard's warriors who were trying to take the city. The spirits would not intervene in time and they would be powerless to prevent the intrepid pair from completing their work. Notorold and his great spirit army had left it too late. As Resus and Jake switched their point of attack to those on the surrounding fields outside the wall, King Vantrax could only sit and watch his vast armies being destroyed, massacred before his eyes. All he could do now was hope that Notorold and his supernatural force could prevail and save the day, destroy his enemy and do what his legions of hired killers and raised beasts had failed to do.

* * *

The joyous celebrations of most of the Estian warriors inside the protective shield were halted, as some of their more observant comrades drew their attention to the army of spirits bearing down upon them. Some of the defenders panicked at the sight of such an enemy and they began running for any kind of cover they could find. But, most of the Estian warriors did not panic, preferring to stand their ground and trust that the shield above them would hold. Resus and Jake had ensured that the survivors amongst King Vantrax' armies were too few and in too much disarray to return to Te'oull and continue the fight. The shattered remnants of King Vantrax' army of mercenaries were in full retreat, and they would trouble the Alliance no more.

'Jake!' Resus shouted all of a sudden, as they flew over the battlefield looking for more targets. 'We have company!'

Jake looked over his shoulder in the direction of the dragon's gaze and saw immediately that the mighty creature was right. An entire army of hideous, black spirits was approaching rapidly. The youngster had only seconds to act or they were certain to die.

In true Keeper style, he did not hesitate, instinctively knowing what to do.

'Inqsurramm!'

Jake turned his head towards the nearest spirit and lifted his right hand, using his left to hold on tightly to the dragon. His two fingers extended quickly to aim his strike and a beam of bright white light shot out of the tips. The light hit the first of the spirits and passed straight through to hit another, and another, and another… until a spirit in every rank of the vast army had been struck. Each one it touched was immediately vaporised, disappearing with an ear-splitting, high-pitch wail never to be seen or heard from again.

The army of spectres from the hellish fires of Zsorcraum however, was too large for one Keeper to destroy, and now it began fighting back!

Several bolts of deadly black light whizzed past Jake's head, only missing him by the faintest of margins because of the swift evasive action taken by Resus. The dragon weaved violently, soared and dived furiously in flight, as he tried his utmost to anticipate and react to each of the many strikes launched by the fast-approaching spirits. The merciless wraiths were now close to swarming around them. Jake was trying in vain to keep them at bay, firing beam after beam of light to kill as many as he could, as fast as he could. His new powers were allowing him to stay on the dragon and keep firing despite the creature's erratic movements, but he knew he was outgunned and outmatched. He could not kill all the spirits around him and they just kept on coming. It was only a matter of time before they were hit.

'I can't hold them off. There's just too many of them!' he yelled, as he continued to fire.

'I know. You can only do your best. Look out, Jake! This one is not giving up!' Resus suddenly shouted, glancing over his shoulder at a more determined spirit he could not shake, no matter how hard he tried.

Infuriated by the failure of others and sensing the need for immediate action, Notorold had latched onto the dragon's tail. He was firing multiple bolts of death from his eyes for all he was worth. He watched with increasing fury and frustration as one by one they narrowly missed destroying their target. But he was getting closer and closer all the time with each shot, and he knew it. He was encouraged and became more determined than ever to shoot the dragon and the Keeper down.

Jake tried his hardest to fire back, but each time he turned his head to see where he was and get off a clean shot, the evil spirit anticipated it and crossed to the other side of Resus' body, out of sight. And behind Notorold, bearing down upon them also, were vast numbers of black spirits with equally deadly intent.

'It's no use, I can't get him. We've had it!'

* * *

Inside the walls of Te'oull the remainder of the spirit army from Zsorcraum began attacking the defenders of the square. The protective shield was still holding, but the spirits attacked it with real force, intent and venom. Some flew straight into it and came to a crashing halt. Others fired their beams of death at the hazy air and scored numerous direct hits. Many landed and tried to prize it open with spells, and even brute force. Eventually, the evil spirits realised that only their collective action would work. They all took up a position directly over the square and bombarded the shield from above, with concentrated fire from their eyes. They began aiming at one central point in an effort to weaken it and create an opening. The rays of lights crashed down upon the shield with deafening force and frightening intensity, as the Estian warriors below covered their ears and shook with fear, helplessly awaiting their fate.

As the shield began to weaken under the weight of the combined attack, so did Jake. He suddenly began to shake and sweat. Within seconds, he felt very weak and his eyesight began to blur, but he still maintained his concentration and kept up his fight against the spirits pursuing him.

For minutes, the bombardment continued with little effect as far as the attackers and defenders could see. But, after a while, it became clear that the shield was losing its power. The hazy air was turning into white and yellow light, as each new strike hit the area being attacked. For a fleeting moment the shield was down, but after each strike the barrier quickly mended itself and immediately reverted back to its original state. The terrified Estians below the dome witnessed this and they looked on with increasing concern, powerless to do anything and afraid that they were all about to die. They knew the shield could not take much more. The spirits were relentless and there were so many of them.

The Battle of Te'oull had entered a new and deadly, final phase. Once again, despite their astonishing bravery and all they had been through, the tide of battle had turned and the Estian Alliance seemed to be doomed. Their saviour, the Keeper, was far too busy fighting for his own life to aid them. It was Jake who was somehow maintaining the power in the shield, the only thing which now stood between them and oblivion. The Estians knew this and they also knew that if he fell, so would the shield.

* * *

Notorold's last intended strike came closer than any other to hitting the dragon and killing the Keeper. Only a last-ditch swerve from Resus had saved them both. Jake's powers meant that he was not at all afraid. However, he could see no way out of his predicament and he was just beginning to really accept that escape was impossible. Any second now it would all be over. He was going to die.

This has to be it. There's no way out this time. I've been here before but this really is a battle too far. I've tried, but there's nothing else I can do, is there? Tell me someone, please?! Where have you all gone?! What else can I do?!

'Look!'

Resus continued to swerve and dive to avoid being hit. However, he was now looking straight ahead of him, towards the hill where King Vantrax stood watching the battle unfold. Far behind the wizard, unbeknown to him, a giant cloud of white smoke had appeared from out of nowhere. It was travelling fast and moving in the same direction the army of Zsorcraum had taken on its way to the battle, heading straight for them!

'What is it?' asked the magnificent dragon, as he soared upwards to avoid yet another beam of light.

Jake could see nothing but white smoke. It looked like an enormous bank of white cloud and he replied more in hope than anything else.

'Err... don't quote me, mate, but I *think* it's the cavalry!'

* * *

Notorold had gained on Resus now. He was almost on top of him and he could not miss with his next strike. Confident that he could take the dragon out with one more shot, he lined himself up directly behind his tail and prepared to fire.

Suddenly, from out of nowhere, a bolt of pure white lightning hit the evil spirit squarely in the chest. His body contorted in flight and an awful scream filled the air. Within seconds, he was gone.

Jake saw the light flash by. He turned his head rapidly and watched it hit its target, recognising immediately that the timely intervention had just saved his life. Despite still being pursued by the rest of the dark spirits, he looked up to see where it had come from.

Flying towards him like a blessed vision of a host of angels, was an entire army of white spirits from the afterlife. And, as they neared, he saw that they were being led by several figures he knew.

'It… It's Sereq!' he cried, ecstatically, shocked and hardly able to believe his own eyes. 'Resus! It's Sereq and the Heynai! They've come back to save us somehow! Oh my...! I can't believe it! Knesh! Knesh is with them!' he screamed, barely able to control his excitement.

The white army passed by swiftly before the dragon could reply. They fell upon the hoards of dark spirits and another almighty battle in the skies above Te'oull was underway, watched by the enthralled and amazed Estians below. The ferocious fight took several minutes to win, but eventually every single evil spirit had been destroyed, all mercilessly hunted down and killed by their white counterparts. And, whilst all of this was taking place, Jake West decided that he had one final task to complete.

'Resus, put me down on that small hill over there,' he instructed, pointing at King Vantrax.

Resus obeyed without hesitation. He landed not far from the evil wizard and stared at him with venomous, hate-filled eyes.

'Say the word, Keeper, and I will turn him to ash for you.'

'No! He is mine,' cried Jake, as he jumped down and approached his arch enemy.

The teenager from Lichfield was alert, ready to act, to counter any move King Vantrax might make against him, or his dragon. He was confident that his new powers would protect them both, and that he would know what to do when he needed to.

'It's over. You've lost. It's all gone; your armies, your Thargw, the creatures you raised, your crown... Everything! These people are free now. They are finally rid of you.'

'Not quite!' Vantrax replied, suddenly yelling his response and acting so swiftly that even Jake was caught unprepared. He raised his arms in a flash and shouted out a solitary word.

'Harrujj!'

The air beside the evil king suddenly ripped itself apart with astonishing speed. Through the gap created rode the remaining three Lords of Srenul, astride their magnificent stallions. Their huge swords were drawn and pointed at the Keeper, as they thundered down upon him at breakneck speed.

Jake responded once again without hesitation or thought.

'Bratiq!'

Fuelled by the power of the restored box of stones, the young Keeper roared the command like never before. His hand switched from King Vantrax to his new targets and three bolts of lightning fired from the ends of his fingers. They struck each of the dark knights and passed straight through them, ripping out their insides.

The dark Lords continued their momentum however. At first, it looked as though the light would have no effect. But, when they were almost upon Jake, they each suddenly vanished into thin air with an awful cry of anguish and pain.

The Lords of Srenul who had once ruled the whole continent and terrorised the Estian people for hundreds of years, had been destroyed once and for all by a boy destined for greatness.

Jake West could hardly believe it. He let out a huge sigh of relief.

Chapter 27
2nd October – The City of Te'oull – Siatol

A sudden and dramatic surge of energy and power swept through the whole of Jake's body as the last of the Lords of Srenul was destroyed. It was accompanied by an enormous swell of anger and fury the likes of which he had never experienced before. In the blink of an eye, he was filled with another overwhelming desire to kill, only this time it was a feeling so intense, so incredibly severe, that he could barely contain himself. An insatiable thirst for vengeance which the young boy from England could hardly control, as if he could feel the combined pain and anguish of the countless thousands of Estians who had suffered at the hands of King Vantrax over the years. The agony endured by his innumerable victims was tearing at Jake's heart, almost ripping it apart. The powerful emotion coarsed through his body quickly and eventually reached his throat. The teenager seemed to be possessed and he suddenly roared like a demonic Thargw. His eyes were bulging and his muscles contracted, growing in size at the same time, sending his entire body into spasms and lifting him onto his toes. He struggled viciously to contain the mighty force within, for it was a violent, dangerous and unexpected strength which threatened to devour his very soul.

For the two astonished onlookers, Resus and King Vantrax, it was an unbelievable and terrifying sight which had them both frozen on the spot, for differing reasons. Jake's whole body seemed to almost double in size and in no time at all, he was transformed from an ordinary teenager, to a muscle-bound freak. The need and desire to exact revenge upon the wizard had consumed him and fuelled the fire. He lifted his right arm and pointed his fingers towards his arch enemy, ready to shoot his beam of light and send the sorcerer to whatever awaited in the afterlife for one as evil as he.

King Vantrax was still reeling in shock. He had witnessed the awesome power of the Keeper and his fascination had the better of him. He watched in awe as the unknown force invaded the young boy's body, when he really should have been taking action. *This* was the very thing he craved most. Though he knew he had to do something quickly in order to save his own skin, he just could not tear his eyes away from what was happening. And as he looked on, he wasted the small window of opportunity he had to take advantage of the Keeper's momentary vulnerability.

Now that it was over, he was completely at Jake's mercy.

However, despite the raging torrent of emotions still burning within, Jake West inexplicably hesitated. The wizard before him was the tyrant who had brought Estia to the very brink of the abyss, the man he knew for certain he had to kill. If *anyone* deserved to die, it was him. But, something inside the youngster began fighting the almost irresistible urge to take his life. A second or two passed by and Jake's hand and fingers began to shake a little, as a battle between two opposing forces raged inside his mind.

Sensing the Keeper's struggle, Resus tried to encourage him to act.

'Do it, Jake. Kill him!' the dragon cried.

Resus had more reason than most to want the evil wizard dead. Many of his dragons had been lost in the fight for Te'oull. Those who *had* managed to survive all carried wounds of some description. Thanks to King Vantrax and his ruthless prosecution of the war, the dragons were now on the very brink of extinction.

'Why do you hesitate? It is a just killing, if ever there was one. A fitting end for one such as him. He has wrought destruction wherever he has been. Finish him, Jake. End this now!'

Jake's eyes did not move from the evil mage as he replied. His arm and fingers were still trembling but they remained poised to strike. He understood completely what Resus was saying. Heck, he agreed with him entirely! But he still could not bring himself to do it. And he didn't know why?

Believing that he might yet enjoy an unlikely reprieve, King Vantrax decided to speak.

'He cannot do it. He is afraid.'

Resus was incensed by the wizard's taunt and he moved forward threateningly, as he decided to act.

'That may be so, but *I* have no such concerns! I will...!'

'No!' roared Jake. He did not move a muscle, but his instant command was enough to stop the dragon in his tracks, just as a bolt of light formed in the creature's eyes, ready to strike the wizard down. 'I am the chosen Keeper, the guardian of the stones. I ask you to stand down for me now, Resus? Let me finish what I have come here to do?'

Smoke oozed from his nostrils as the dragon took a reluctant step backwards. 'As you command. We follow you, so I will do as you wish,' he stated, bowing his head slightly to Jake, but unable to conceal his disappointment.

King Vantrax shifted his eyes back to the young boy who had him cornered.

'It is not so easy to kill someone in cold blood, is it?' he snarled. 'I do not imagine you have faced such a thing on your world? And this is your first encounter, your first full-scale battle. I can tell,' he added, trying to engage Jake in conversation to buy more time. 'You are not to blame. Yours is a natural reaction, a perfectly understandable fear.'

Jake swallowed hard to suppress a lump in his throat. 'If I was any ordinary boy, I'd probably agree with you. It *is* incredibly hard to kill anything, and it does not come easy for most, thank God. That's the way it should be. But I am no ordinary boy, am I? I guess I never have been. Though I never knew anything about it, the ability to take a life was always inside of me. I have wrestled with my conscience now and it is clear. It is for the greater good. When I kill you, know that I will feel no guilt, no shame or fear. You see? You were wrong, King Vantrax; I am not afraid to act. What you saw in me just then, was not fright. Your death is what has to happen. It is the end of a terrible journey. And it is my duty to the people of Estia.'

'Kah! And yet, you delay?' replied the king, sensing with concern Jake's sudden change of heart and surprised by the gleam of determination now in his eyes. The wizard's right hand worked its way unseen into his pocket and began searching for one of two pieces of reolite stone he had concealed there. The pair of reolite shards were the last known stones of their kind on Estia which were not in the Keeper's possession. The tiny gems were so small that Vantrax had trouble locating one.

'I have resolved any issues I may have had. I think it was nothing more than curiosity which prevented me from taking action before, for there is an unanswered question which is troubling me, nothing more,' Jake said, completely unaware of the warlock's actions.

'I see. Then, ask away, young Keeper,' the king retorted, as his fingers finally located the stone he was searching for. 'I will answer you truthfully if I can.'

'The horsemen... where did they come from? How did you open the rift from which they appeared, when you have not been able to before?'

King Vantrax smiled a wicked smile. 'Kuh! Have not been able to? Or, have not *chosen* to? You are the Keeper, do you not know?'

Jake thought about it very briefly, before the truth suddenly dawned on him.

'Reolite! You had another stone!'

King Vantrax nodded. 'Yes. For years I searched these lands, looking for other gems. I found only a few. With more such stones I could have ruled the world, ruled countless worlds. Though it was not meant to be, so I have had to be more creative!'

The wizard king acted so swiftly that Jake was unable to stop him. He threw the shard of reolite onto the ground and shouted out one solitary word as it fell.

'Treveq!'

Another hole opened up immediately in the air right beside the sorcerer. Vantrax rushed into the gap with unbelievable speed, just as Jake fired his beam of light in an attempt to stop him. The tear in the atmosphere closed the very instant the light disappeared inside.

Jake and Resus did not see what happened. Vantrax was gone and nothing remained ahead of them but thin air. Both were too stunned to speak. After a short while though, the horrified dragon asked the question that was weighing heavily on both of their minds.

'Did... Did you hit him? Is he dead?'

Jake shook his head in despair, as he realised what he had just done. Or rather, what he had *failed* to do.

'I don't know. I couldn't see. Oh, why didn't I kill him when I had the chance? What came over me? I should have...!'

He was too angry to continue, too distraught to finish what he was saying. His entire body was shaking with rage and he hardly noticed as it slowly reduced in size. It stopped diminishing when he was just larger than he had been before he confronted the evil king.

Though he was equally as disappointed, Resus stepped forward to stand alongside the Keeper.

'It may be of no consequence now, Jake. I am certain he is dead. The light was far too close to him. He could not have survived.'

'Yeah? You think?' asked Jake, hoping and praying that the dragon was correct. 'Okay, but what if you're wrong? What if he *did* survive, and he finds a way back from wherever he's gone?'

'In that case, he has lost his power, his entire army. He no longer has any wealth to speak of, for we will ensure that the mines are run for the good of all on Estia from today. I give you my word on that. So, without warriors, or the money to buy them, what damage could he do to our cause now?' asked the dragon.

'...Though, if I may offer one word of advice? I think it best that this news remains just between us?' he added, as an afterthought. 'The people of Estia need not know what happened here, Jake? They have been through too much, suffered too much heartache and pain to have this victory tarnished by such news. It will be our secret. One I will take with me to the afterlife if I must?'

Jake turned to look the dragon in the eye. 'No. Thank you, my friend, but I will not lie to them. I will tell them the truth, for they deserve nothing less. They must know that I failed them, failed to kill the one responsible for all of this; King Vantrax. Despite the anger and disappointment they may feel, I have to be honest, and inform them that I let them all down.'

The mighty dragon suddenly began to laugh for no apparent reason. It soon became a thunderous roar of delight. When it became clear that Jake was mystified and was not going to join in, he stopped laughing slowly and tried his best to explain why he had responded in such a fashion to the Keeper's statement.

'*You* have let them down?' he said, in a tone of voice that openly mocked the teenager's choice of words. He lowered his neck so that Jake could climb on as he spoke. '*That* is perhaps the most *ridiculous* thing I have ever heard!'

* * *

Queen Zephany and the defenders of Te'oull looked on with relief and excitement from under their protective shield as the army of white spirits destroyed the dark forces from Zsorcraum. It was the most exhilarating, stupendous sight they had ever seen. The short but incredibly vicious battle was being waged right before their eyes.

As the last of the hideous spectres was destroyed, an enormous roar of delight erupted in and around the square. It swept through the Estian ranks rapidly, until it seemed the whole city had just sprung into life. The surviving warriors of the Estian Alliance began celebrating and congratulating each other like never before. Some wept openly at their miraculous deliverance, whilst others hugged and kissed any member of the female persuasion they could find, particularly the Sebantans. The fearsome warriors would normally kill anyone acting in such a manner without a second thought, but on this occasion they shared their ally's relief and joined in the festivities willingly. Songs and cheers rang out everywhere. Zephany and Lord Caro were lifted high onto the shoulders of their warriors and carried triumphantly to the centre of the square, where it seemed the whole Estian army had converged. Once there, they were lowered to the ground and they hugged each other warmly, to another crescendo of exuberant cheers.

However, the merriment soon stopped when their attention was suddenly drawn to the shield overhead. For a split second, the air above had suddenly been transformed into a white and yellow light. Then, as rapidly as it had formed, it became crystal clear. The great protective shield had disappeared.

Everyone in the city who had not already done so began

converging on the square. The vast army of white spirits encircled the city and closed in to hover just above the buildings, forming a perfect circle numerous ranks deep. Five ghostly figures then floated out of the crowd. They weaved their way through and over the Estians to halt at the centre statue, where Lord Caro and Queen Zephany were standing waiting for them, having by now been joined by the others. Jean was holding onto Melissa's hand as they talked to Nytig. Queen Bressial was congratulating Tien, Harry and Graham on their exploits. All were smiling and laughing, and anxious to hear what the spirits had to say.

Zephany silenced the crowd when she saw the figures approaching. They were all as white as the driven snow. The young queen smiled with delight when she realised it was Sereq and the rest of the Heynai. Then, her smile grew even wider and her heart leapt for joy when she saw they were accompanied by a far more youthful spirit; the ghost of her friend and teacher, Gerada Knesh Corian.

'I... I have quickly become accustomed to making speeches. It goes with the territory I suppose. On this occasion however, words fail me. I can only say what I feel; we owe you our lives. And we will be eternally in your debt,' Zephany began, speaking to them all, but looking straight at Sereq. 'We shall *never* forget this day. Neither shall we forget those who came to our aid.'

Sereq bowed his head once as a sign of respect. 'You seem to have found your voice as easily as you found your courage, and your calling? All of Estia should be grateful for it,' he replied.

Then he raised his voice so loud that the entire city could hear his words.

'Queen Zephany! You and your warriors are responsible for the victory won here today, not we! Our world is safe again because of you. All of you!'

That was greeted by thousands of cheers and the jubilant Estians celebrated once more. Once the incredible noise had finally subsided, Sereq spoke again.

'This is a time like no other. We are all in uncharted waters, uncertain of our own future, and with no-one to guide us. Those who reigned in the afterlife were moved by your actions Zephany, just as *we* were moved by you at the river and compelled to save your life. Your courage, your faith, inspired us all. And beyond this realm, where the dead live on, one among many is all it took. One solitary soul decided to ignore the constraints imposed by others and obey her conscience, in spite of the dangers and incredible risks she knew she was taking; Nittrii-Hebul,' he stated, pointing to the statue of the Goddess which stood in the centre of the square, 'fought for us all. *She* is the sole reason we have been allowed to live among you. Why we are able to come to you now. It will never happen again. Be under no illusion though, good queen, we stand victorious on this hallowed ground only because of *your* deeds.'

'Me? I... I do not understand?' said Zephany, humbled and shocked to hear such praise.

'Yes. *You!* First, the Keeper appeared and moved us to greater things. He upset the natural laws of existence, threw this world and the next into turmoil. That is what needed to happen and it is what was written; the climax to the war of wars. Then, one supreme being, acting on her own, out of nothing more than a sense of injustice, risking everything to protect the mortals of this land, released the forces of evil and set in motion the events which followed. Without you and your army, they would have won an easy victory here. And if Te'oull had fallen…?! Your strong leadership and resolute defence of this place meant that others *had* to act. We spirits had already given all we had. We were done. Spent. In no position to help. We stood at the gates of the afterlife seeking entry to the hereafter, fated *never* to return. But, when it became clear what was needed, she called out to us again and offered us a reprieve. In their determination to defeat the dark ones, the rulers of the realm beyond reached out to others, to *us!* An army of spirits was raised and...'

'We kicked ass, as Ben might say,' interrupted Knesh, rudely. He was looking straight at the youngster and smiling.

Sereq cast a very stern glance in his direction and Knesh stepped obediently back into line.

'Srr... do forgive the young one, please? He has a lot to learn still, but he will, in time. Though, I suppose that turn of phrase will do. After all, it *is* what the Keeper might say?'

Tien was watching and listening intently. He took a step closer to the spirit leader, before asking the question which was on the tip of his tongue, burning his lips.

'Sereq, what happens now? Is it over? Have we finally won?'

'Yes, wizard, it is over. The final war, spoken of in legend, has ended in victory, and Estia is once again free to chart her own course. Her future belongs to Queen Zephany and her descendants now. We spirits must leave once again for the afterlife. We depart safe in the knowledge that our enemies are vanquished, that the armies of Zsorcraum have been brought to battle and been soundly defeated. It will take *hundreds* of years to replace what they have lost. They will not plague this land again for a very, very long time. If ever. You, my friend, have earned your rest. You have shouldered your burden heroically and you are welcome to join us?'

Tien was overwhelmed by the sudden and unexpected invitation. The old wizard was exceedingly tired all of a sudden, feeling every one of his three hundred plus years. He gazed over at his friends. Harry and Ben nodded to him, letting him know they understood and that he had their permission and approval to go, even though they knew very well that he did not need it.

'Thank you,' Tien whispered. 'Please say goodbye to Jake for me? There is so much I wanted to tell him, about the prophecies, and all he will become and achieve.'

'I will,' answered Ben, with a tear in his eye and a very large lump in his throat. 'Take care of yourself... Hey! If you're ever haunting Lichfield or thereabouts, pop in for a cup of tea and say hello?'

Tien laughed a little at his young friend, only then beginning to understand just how much he would miss the teenager and his ways. Then, he stepped forward to stand beside Sereq. As he reached him and turned around, his body suddenly dropped and fell to the ground. The lifeless corpse remained there for a few seconds. Then, a white spectre rose from within and Tien took his place alongside the rest of the spirit army as they began to fade, slowly. Before their images had disappeared completely however, Gerada Knesh Corian suddenly yelled out one last time.

'Zephany! I can see your father! He is with us now and he is going to be alright. Remember, child, we will love you until the end of time!'

Chapter 28
2nd October – The City of Te'oull – Siatol

Jake West flew into the main square at Te'oull on the back of a magnificent, battle-scarred dragon, over the heads of thousands of exuberant and triumphant warriors who greeted his arrival with unparalleled joy and wild excitement. The full extent of the many wounds Resus bore only became apparent when the young Keeper dismounted and turned to thank his new ally. Everyone was horrified when they saw the rips, gashes and tears in his flesh. None more so than Jake, who thought it a miracle he was still able to fly. They covered his entire body. In fact, Resus had sustained so much damage that Jake realised even the mighty dragon had to be close to collapse. Tears of extreme gratitude flooded his eyes as the full impact of such an awful sight tore straight at his heart. He immediately began apologising for not seeing it earlier and for asking so much of the splendid creature. Resus reassured him that he would be fine and stated it was his duty to help the Keeper, but his words did little to diminish the guilt Jake felt. The youngster hugged his neck in appreciation and the massed crowds of hushed onlookers erupted once again into more cheers of delight.

Once the great noise had eventually died down a little, the rest of the leaders approached and Queen Zephany silenced the crowd. Jake then addressed the dragon officially in the loudest voice he could muster, speaking in his capacity as a Keeper, and for the benefit of all.

'Together we have defeated our common enemy. Together we have stood firm and proud, made stronger by the friendships we have forged. The threat posed by King Vantrax and his armies has gone. Thank you, Resus. From the hearts of everyone here, thank you for *everything* you have done for us! We would not have defeated anyone without you and your dragons. I want you to know that I know that, and I will not forget it. We *all* know it.'

More resounding shouts and screams of delight followed. Resus bowed his head slightly to acknowledge Jake's gratitude and the cheers of the Estian warriors. Zephany then stepped forward as Leader of the

Alliance and everyone fell silent once more to hear her words.

'Hear ye all! We would like to add our sincere gratitude and appreciation to those of the Keeper. Resus, it shall be known throughout this realm that you and your noble kind are welcome anywhere, at any time. You need no invitation. Please, say that you will return to Estia and live among us? Share our lives once again? Help us to rebuild that we have lost; our cities, and the bonds of comradeship we once treasured above all? Help us to make this land a better place for our children? Teach us your values, those you have demonstrated so readily these past few days; your honour and integrity, your loyalty and courage? For henceforth, I swear that for the rest of my years, we shall be the very best of friends.'

The crowd was heaving now and it exploded with howls of approval. Resus once again bowed his head in gratitude, before letting the cheers subside and replying to the queen and Jake in his deep, gentle voice.

'Thank you both. Thank you all. The courage you have shown here has justified our decision to stand with you a thousand times over. I must leave you now to go and tend to my dragons. We have many wounded and we will need time to recover. Though, I believe I can speak for them all when I say that we accept your invitation to return gladly. It means more than you will ever know. Estia is our home. It is the land of our ancestors. We have proven we can co-exist and thrive. So, I look forward now to the future, with renewed hope and confidence. We will be strong, united. And we will use that strength to ensure we live in peace and harmony forever more.'

As the crowd roared their approval for the umpteenth time, Resus suddenly unfurled his wings and soared high into the sky. He left the Estians behind to find his dragons, with tear-laden eyes and their resounding cheers and cries ringing loudly in his ears.

Jake watched him leave and then immediately rushed over to his family. He hugged his father like there was no tomorrow. Then, he embraced Harry as best he could, given his wounds, before doing the same to Ben.

'Hey! Steady on, mate. There's people watching, you know,' joked Ben, feeling more like his old self again.

'Yeah, but you know what, Ace? I couldn't give a...!' replied Jake, deliberately stopping short of finishing his sentence. Ben knew exactly what he meant nevertheless. 'We *did* it, bro! We actually *did* it! I never thought we would you know, not really. To be honest, I didn't think we had it in us.'

Ben was suddenly overcome with emotion. He had kept himself pretty much together so far, but when Jake referred to him as his brother, something inside of him just snapped, and the tears began to flow. He knew in that instant, right there and then, that the family he longed for, the family he had always dreamed of, was right in front of him. Or at least, most of it was. And he realised all of a sudden that even if he did not share their surname, it always *had* been. As he hugged Jake again, he looked over the Keeper's shoulder and stared at the West family members before him.

Hmmn... we're an odd-looking bunch I suppose, he thought, as he looked Jean, Harry, Graham and Melissa up and down. *We're not really Joe Public, are we? But then, I'm no oil painting myself, a little rough around the edges...? We're not gonna win any beauty pageant, that's for sure... Well, actually, Melissa probably could? Ha, ha... You know what? I don't care. They're mine, all mine!*

Jake pushed Ben gently away and then embraced his grandmother tightly, saying a few heartfelt words to her before staring with shock and surprise at the Sebantan warrior he had hardly noticed in all the commotion.

Melissa was still holding Jean's hand. She had not let go of it since the battle was won. She said nothing as Jake eyed her up and down, uncertain as to how the Keeper would react to seeing her and too ashamed of her past deeds to speak. Rather surprisingly perhaps, it was Jake's father who broke the awkward silence.

'Err... yes, I see you've spotted our new addition? *That* is going to take some explaining I'm afraid. We need to talk, son. But the short version is that she's on our side now. She's one of us. It's going to take a while for you to understand, but then, we have all the time in the world now, don't we?'

Jake was still confused but he smiled. Then he laughed a little, more out of relief than anything else. The others joined in with him and the laughter spread until Ben interrupted them all, as he suddenly thought of something.

'Hey! Wait a minute! Stop! *All the time in the world*. Jake, the box is fixed! We can *finally* go home!'

Jake took the box out of his bag immediately and placed it down on the ground.

'Yes, mate, I suppose you're right. We've been waiting for this, so no time like the present. Time to go,' he said, as he stood upright. He walked up to Queen Zephany and gave her a big hug, followed by a tender kiss on the cheek. 'What can I say to you, after everything we've been through together? It's never going to be enough I know, but thanks for all you have done. You've been... awesome! I couldn't have done any of this without you or your father. We would have been nothing without your people, and the astonishing valor they've shown.'

Zephany shook her head firmly. 'Jake, your words are like my sword I think; they cut both ways. You have proven to be much more than a protector of worlds. You have powers in you that defy all logic. And you have been a trusted ally and friend. I hope we shall see you again, from time to time? You have achieved the impossible here and restored the stones, so it is now within your power to go wherever you wish to go.'

'Yeah, it is, isn't it? I'd like that,' Jake answered, smiling warmly. He moved on quickly to say farewell to Queen Bressial, Lord Caro, Nytig and the rest, before his eyes suddenly fell upon a much larger figure standing out in the crowd.

'Verastus!' he cried, overjoyed to see his friend alive. Jake ran over to where the giant Falorian stood. The crowd parted as he ran and he was soon joined by Ben, with the others not far behind.

'Big Man, you're alright!' Ben yelled, as they reached him.

But Verastus smiled weakly and shook his head. 'My friends, it is so very good to see you free from harm. I am sorry to bear such news on a day like this, but I am not alright, Ben, as you put it. I am afraid I am dying. I can feel it. My strength is failing and I can barely stand. I just wanted to say goodbye to you both, and thank you for restoring my honour. Please, shed no tears for me when I am gone, for I would not have missed this whole fantastic adventure for... Uuurgh... Apologies, the wound will not stop bleeding,' he stated, looking down at his stomach as a tremendous, searing pain interrupted his farewell.

Everyone gasped in horror at the sight of such a horrendous injury, but Jake suddenly felt the blood tingle in his veins. The faint voice of a woman sounded in his head once again. He could not hear her clearly over the sound of the crowd but somehow, he knew immediately that he could help.

Without delay, he placed his hand over the wound and closed his eyes. When he opened them again, they were lit up brightly by a white light locked within. Then, the light travelled through his body and exploded out of his hand, entering Verastus and seeping through the gaps in Jake's fingers, so that everyone around could see.

The Falorian's wound healed in a matter of seconds and the surrounding warriors took a sharp intake of breath, amazed to behold such a miracle. They were joined by Ben.

'Jake! What the hell did you do?!' cried the youngster. 'Oh yes! Get in there, my son! I don't believe it. You're like Jesus or summin' now?! This is just getting way too weird. You can't be. You'll be walking on water next. Err... you're not going to, are you? What's happened to you? You're my...? Ah, whatever! Just do your thang!'

Hang on, *this* is fantastic! I... Err… I think you've got your work cut out? There's plenty more where Verastus came from, and you can help them all. The dragons for a start, not to mention the wounded here, and in the streets, on the wall...?'

Jake looked up, staring around him at the shocked and stunned faces. Then, he nodded in agreement.

'Yeah, I suppose you're right for a change. Oh, I can't really say that to you now, can I? I mean, being right is beginning to become a habit for you, isn't it, Cleverclogs. We're gonna have to think of a new way of taking the mickey out of each other. It's all your fault you know; you've upset the natural way of things, so you only have yourself to blame. Look, I'd better get started, healing so many is going to take some time, and there's shed loads of 'em. So, I suppose we'd better get you guys home first? And then I'll get to work, eh?'

Despite the fact he would be leaving Jake behind, Ben did not object. Now that there was finally a realistic chance of actually returning, he was missing home, more than he ever thought he would in fact. For a fleeting moment he'd considered staying on Estia, reasoning that he had nothing to go back to. But he knew deep down that this was not his world, and something inside the youngster told him that things would be different now, that Jake would need his help in the days and weeks to come.

Ben looked over at Verastus as he realised that, *this is it*. In such a short space of time the Falorian had captured his heart to become one of his dearest friends. They had shared in so much together, and he had saved Ben's life on more than one occasion.

'I suppose we'd better go?' the teenager said, with mixed feelings, as he offered his hand in friendship.

Verastus took hold of it and shook it gently. 'Yes, Ben, I will never forget you. I do not think anyone will *ever* question your courage or honour again. However, should you find that they do, send them to me!'

'Ha, ha... Thanks,' Ben replied. 'This is my very last quest though, believe me. I'm gonna go back home and retire to my pipe and slippers. Not really, it's just a saying. No, I think I'll be content to stay in the background from now on, in a sort of advisory capacity. I've had more than enough adventure to last a lifetime. If I make it back home, they can call me whatever they want to. I'll know the truth and that's all that matters, isn't it? I'll just be content to watch from a distance. But, what about you? What are *you* going to do?'

'Well, now that King Vantrax is no longer a threat to my people, I believe I will return to my homeland. Or rather, I will go back to what is left of it. Their king has been missing for far too long.'

'*King?* Did you say, *King?!* You sly old dog! You never said?'

replied Ben, shocked and amazed to learn the truth.

Verastus smiled broadly as he looked his young friend in the eye, confident and happy that he had finally beat him at his own game.

'Koh, did I not? Kuh! Strange, that I should neglect to tell you something so important? But then, you never asked, did you?'

'Err... I think we did!' snapped Ben.

His face was serious for a second, but his voice was light-hearted and an even broader smile soon covered his face. The three friends laughed a little before they turned to rejoin the others.

Jake walked his family back over to the box of stones. 'Right, it's time. Let's get you lot safely back home.'

Harry stopped Jake before he could open the box however, by putting his hand firmly upon his arm.

'Wait, Jake. Just a minute, please? There's something I have to say first.'

'What? What is it, granddad?'

Harry reached for Jean's hand. Jean was as surprised as anyone by his actions but somehow, she knew immediately what he was going to say. She nodded at him and smiled, to let him know she agreed with his decision. They both turned to look at Graham and Melissa, and Harry spoke directly to his only son.

'I'm sorry, but we won't be coming with you. We're not going home this time. We've decided to stay. I don't expect you to understand, son, but it's something we have to do. We've just found each other, and we've just discovered that we have a daughter. Second chances don't come very often in life, especially at my age. This world, it's all your mother and Melissa know. I may not have many years left, but I think... No, I *know*, that we can be happy here?'

Harry was almost pleading, praying that Graham would understand and forgive him. Graham looked stunned at first, horrified in fact. But, it soon passed. He looked at Jake briefly, before holding out his hand and inviting his son to join him. Jake stepped into his father's arms and he turned within them to face Harry. With his arms draped lovingly around his only boy's neck in a fatherly show of affection, Graham replied in a soft but emotional, sympathetic tone.

'I… I'm having real problems imagining the life you have led. What does that say about me and our relationship? I wasn't there for you when you needed me, but I think I understand now, dad. Stay with my blessing. I'm going to miss you though, really I am. I was looking forward to getting to know each other again, to making up for all those wasted years of stupidity. You must do what you have to do though. I'll survive. I will be… Oh my…! June! She's going to be *devastated* by this! Christ! She'll *kill* me!'

Ha, ha… No, seriously, she's not going to take it well. Though, I think she'll understand too, once I explain it to her… I think! Promise me that you will look after each other?' he asked, his eyes now firmly fixed upon Melissa.

The young Sebantan warrior had remained silent throughout. It came as a major shock to her when the parents she had only just met, said they were staying. She did not know them at all, and she certainly had no expectations of them. Still, her heart had leapt for joy when she heard the words, and she was still too stunned to speak. As Graham's comments struck home however, she found herself replying to him without thinking, and with words laced throughout with a totally unique feeling of raw emotion, of unbridled joy.

'I will protect them, brother, with my life. You have my word of honour as a Sebantan warrior. It is something we do not give lightly. I know that I do not deserve this chance at happiness, but now that it is here, I am *determined* to make the most of it. I have done many terrible, wicked things in my life,' she said, hanging her head in shame, 'but I mean to try and make amends, to be a better person from this day forward.'

Jake suddenly felt compelled to speak. He stepped free of his father's embrace to address the crowd.

'Listen to me, all of you! We must put history behind us now and move forward with our lives. This is a new day, a new beginning, for all of us!'

The Battle of Te'oull will long be remembered as the day when evil was *finally* vanquished on Estia. In this fight, you took back your freedom and your right to determine your own destiny. King Artrex has gone and many of your finest warriors have fallen in battle, but many more of you still remain! If Estia is to flourish and once again be what it was, you *all* have to work together, regardless of the differences you may once have had. They must be forgotten and consigned to the past. You must unite behind one leader, for the good of all. I'm not talking about countries or borders. You can keep your kings and queens if you wish. But, chief amongst them when it comes to leadership and decision making should be a just and fair ruler who is acceptable to all, someone who will settle any disputes you may have before they come to war, someone who will act on your behalf, fairly and with compromise. There is only one person strong enough and brave enough for the task and she stands before you, a living symbol of all that is best in this world. Show your support for her now. I ask you to kneel and show your allegiance to Queen Zephany, the true and rightful Queen of Rhuaddan, and of Estia!'

The square was crammed full of thousands of warriors. Every single one of them fell down immediately on bended knee. They were joined without hesitation by Queen Bressial and every noble there.

Zephany was almost overcome by a rush of very strong emotion but she managed somehow to control herself and stepped forward to address the crowd again.

'Rise, all of you, please?' she shouted. Her voice was now strong and commanding, despite the butterflies which had just appeared in her stomach.

'Much has already been said here, so I will be brief. I thank you for the tremendous honour you bestow upon me. I swear that I will discharge my duties faithfully and remain true to our beliefs. I will act in the best traditions of my father, King Artrex, and of Gerada Knesh Corian and all those who came before them. We have a lot of work before us and we have to begin without delay. First, we must take care of our wounded. Bring them all here to the square so that the Keeper may heal them, for we will have great need of such heroes. Our new friends must depart for their own world. We wish them well and thank them for their help in winning this war!'

The crowd cheered again and the din almost toppled the nearby buildings. Then the Estians began to disperse, as they set off in search of their wounded comrades.

Zephany turned to Ben one last time. 'Goodbye, Ben, I have really enjoyed meeting you. I think perhaps that we may have been great friends you and I, more than we had the chance to become, in a different place and time?'

Ben gave a cheeky smile. 'Yeah? Friends, eh? And then some?' he answered, winking at the beautiful young royal.

Zephany blushed slightly and everyone laughed. It was Jake who spoke next.

'Right then, let's try again. It looks like it's just you and dad going home for the present, pal. Are you ready?'

'Ready? I was *born* ready!' said Ben, uttering a phrase he'd stolen from some film or other and used a million times before back home. 'Too right! Let's do it. I wonder what time it is back home? With any luck, I'll be back in time for the footy. Ha, ha... I... I suppose it's gonna be pretty boring after all of this? Then again, I've always thought boring was completely underrated, you know? And, something tells me that if it *is* a little tedious, I'll manage.'

Jake opened the box of stones. The others looked on as he cast his spell and the bright white light shot up to the sky. Graham took hold of Ben's hand. Together, they stepped into the light and disappeared.

Chapter 29
Dead of Night – 2/3ʳᵈ October – The City of Te'oull - Siatol

Inside the very same dwelling that Tien had earlier used to restore the box of stones, all was quiet. The celebrations and partying in Te'oull had lasted well into the dying hours of the glorious night. But, for two weary souls anxious to make up for so much lost time, the effects of their exploits and the rollercoaster ride of emotions they had experienced, meant that the festivities were merely an unwanted distraction, and one of which they wanted no further part. Melissa and her mother, Jean, were blissfully content just to be in one another's company. They had therefore made their excuses quite early on and left the bustling square in order to find somewhere quiet to talk. Jean had remembered the empty house and suggested it as a good place to hold their remarkable reunion, and then to gain the much-needed sleep their bodies craved. Inside the relatively quiet solitude of the four walls, behind a makeshift door made from an upturned table, mother and daughter talked happily for hours. They conversed safe in the knowledge that the battle and war had finally been won, that they had all the time in the world to renew their relationship, to get to know one another, confident they would not be disturbed.

'The future can wait and the past be damned,' Jean had said to begin the discussion. 'I only want to deal with the present tonight. I will listen to the stories of your life gladly, however much you would like to tell? Or not. *Whatever* has happened before today means nothing. The only thing that truly matters to me is right here and now. I have found you at last and I do not want to *ever* let you go.'

In the early hours of the morning, both sets of eyes began to inform their hosts that their shattered bodies desperately needed to sleep. Melissa offered Jean the only bed in the back room. She settled down under a blanket she had found, her head resting on the pillow from the bed, which Jean had insisted she took. The Sebantan princess lay down on the cold, hard floor and closed her eyes, as contented as she had ever been. Sleep came quickly despite her excitement, for she possessed at last an untroubled mind.

Sometime later, when all was deathly quiet and it seemed the whole of Te'oull had joined them in slumber, the air near to the sleeping Melissa suddenly began to part. A tiny tear in its fabric widened slowly and silently. Before long, it was large enough for a person to step through and out from the hole appeared a wary King Vantrax.

He looked around the room to ensure he had not been seen and then quietly approached the sleeping warrior to stand over her with knife in hand. For a second or two he just stood there, as if he was deciding on a method of attack, the best way to assassinate the Sebantan princess in her sleep, without being discovered and before making good his escape. But then, the evil wizard put away his dagger and bent down to shake her shoulders gently.

'Melissa!' he hissed, as quietly as he could. He glanced once more around him to ensure his presence has not been detected. 'Melissa! Wake up!'

Melissa stirred slowly and opened her extremely heavy eyelids. She blinked several times and then rubbed them hard, having been awoken from the depths of a deep and blissfully happy sleep. The experienced warrior had never before slept so soundly. She would normally have heard such an approach and responded to it like the trained soldier she was, so she was in uncharted territory now, confused and somewhat dazed.

'King Vantrax!' she stated, shocked and amazed to see her former master alive and standing before her. 'But I thought you were dead?!'

'Shh!' Vantrax replied instantly, placing a solitary finger up to his lips. 'Be quiet, they might hear you. Come with me, we have to go now.'

'Go? Go where? Why are you here? And where have you been?'

'I escaped to Mynae, to the only place I could think of that was safe. I have been in a cave, not far from Herashtuk,' said the wizard.

'What? How?' asked Melissa.

'It is not important. I had to leave Estia before that boy could use his powers. It has afforded me some time to think. Listen to me, I know of a way we can take back *all* we have lost! I sensed your survival. The bond we share is strong, and I have returned for you now.'

Melissa slowly sat upright as she tried to take in all that was happening.

'You... You came back for *me?*'

'Yes. Now let us go, before the guards outside hear us talking!' Vantrax urged.

Melissa's mind was still not working correctly in her confused state. Perhaps it was tiredness, or the effects of the battle and everything that had happened, but she was not herself and she knew it. She *did* however pick up on the fact that the king obviously believed she was being held captive, against her will, that she was a prisoner of the Estians. She looked him in the eyes for a brief moment and the memory of her conversations with Jean and the rest of her family came flooding back. All of a sudden, she felt a rising and intense anger swell in her breast, though she tried her hardest not to let it show.

This is the true enemy, the one who ruined all of our lives! she thought.

Still, he had come back for her in the most dangerous of circumstances, and that fact played on her mind. She did not know what to make of it. She had to know why.

'Do not worry, the guards will not come. The walls are thick and we will not be disturbed. Answer my question. Why have you come for me? And what happens now?' she asked.

'Raar! I do not understand why you hesitate? We *must* be going!' rasped Vantrax, in a much stronger tone. 'I have had to use my very last piece of reolite to save you, is that not enough?!'

Melissa once again looked him squarely in the eye. She replied in a cool, calm voice, all the time working her hand slowly under her pillow, without it being noticed.

'It *would* have been, once. But I am not the same as I was before this fight. I have grown a little since we parted. Tell me, why have you come for me? The truth!'

King Vantrax was growing more and more impatient. He became more furious with every single second they delayed their escape, but he knew that he had no choice but to answer honestly, for Melissa seemed intent on staying where she was unless he revealed why he was there. It was a reaction he had not planned for, totally unexpected, and he just could not believe what he was hearing.

'Aghrast! Very well. Reolite! It is all about the reolite. Do you not see? Always has been. I need more stones, more shards. And *you* will help me get them.'

'So, there we have it. You are *using* me once again? Just as you have used me all of my life!' Melissa cried, her voice raised now to a very strong and forceful whisper.

King Vantrax was stunned by her insolent tone and her impudence. He could not understand where it came from, and he *definitely* did not like being spoken to in such a fashion.

'What has happened to you, Melissa? Why do you speak to me so, after all I have done for you? You ungrateful...!'

'*Ungrateful?!*' interrupted Melissa, angrily. 'Tell me then, what do I have to be grateful for? You return here only because you need me. Tell me I am wrong? You mean to raid the mines of Eratur, to take from the Thargws that which is rightfully theirs, to steal what few stones they have. I am no fool, Vantrax. To take on the Thargws you will need an army, one capable of such a feat. There are few better than my Sebantans. Yes, your true motives are revealed; you came back solely because you know that they will only follow me!'

King Vantrax smiled a wicked smile, aware that he had just been rumbled.

'Kah, I always said you had a keen mind to match your beauty. You are right, Melissa. But what of it? What choice do you have but to leave with me now? Come quickly, before my powers wane and I am able to keep the hole open no longer, before this opportunity is gone. You are their prisoner here. I offer you freedom, and a chance to lead your beloved warriors in battle once more. So, why are you not moving? Why do you delay? Think of it. With more reolite, I will raise a much greater army, one full of Mynaen warriors, taken from the dead and the living. We will return very soon to this land, before these Estians can recover, to crush their armies and take their stones. I offer you a chance for glory and adventure. Here, you will be nothing but a slave!'

'No!' Melissa responded, forcefully. 'You are mistaken. I am no slave. I am no captive.'

'What?' said the wizard, confused.

'Look outside. You will see no guards at my door. I am as free as anyone here.'

King Vantrax could see in her eyes that she spoke the truth. His blood was boiling now and his face was red with rage. He wanted to kill her where she sat, on the floor. But he knew he needed her.

'Yagh! Enough of this! We must go now. I will take you by force if I have to!'

'If those words were said by anyone else...?! Use your magic all you like. You have taken from me for the last time. Yes, I know! I know what you did.'

Vantrax' mouth dropped open for a second, as he saw with amazement that she was telling the truth.

'Srr... you know *what*, exactly?'

'Everything. I have been told everything,' replied Melissa.

'I do not believe you. By who?'

'By my mother! She is alive, Vantrax. You failed to cover your tracks. But then, you are no warrior, are you? It scares me to think how much we are alike, of the things I did in your name. What kind of beast takes a child away from its mother? How could you look me in the eye all these years, knowing what you did? And now that I know, how can you *seriously* expect me to go with you, to help you? No, I will not. Do your worst! Cast your spell and strike me down. I will *never* serve you again!'

King Vantrax raised his arms to launch his attack. However, at exactly the same time, Melissa's fingers tightened around the handle to the knife she always kept under her pillow and...

'Melissa? Who are you talking to out there?'

Jean suddenly appeared in the doorway to the back room, having been awoken by the sound of an unknown conversation. She was wiping the sleep from her eyes in an attempt to clear her blurred vision.

Despite his shock and surprise at being interrupted, Vantrax realised immediately who it was and he reacted swiftly, turning his body in Jean's direction. He began saying the two words which would end her life and his fingers extended to aim the blow.

'Ferrein heeuss...!'

A split second before he uttered the final part of the last word, Melissa jumped up with phenomenal speed and plunged her knife deep into his heart.

King Vantrax stumbled backwards, the blade still embedded fully within in his body. His face wore a look of deepest horror as he watched the hole in the air disappear immediately. Everything began to go dark for him and, as he took his final breath, his eyes turned towards Melissa.

'That is for my family!' the warrior stated, her eyes brimming with hatred. 'Take on *them*, and you take on me!'

Melissa and Jean watched as King Vantrax' lifeless body dropped to the floor. Then, Jean rushed over to her daughter and flung her arms around her.

'Oh, Lissa, thank you! You saved my life. You saved all of us.'

Melissa pushed her mother away gently so that she could look her in the eye.

'No, mother, thank *you*. It is you who has saved mine. Now, help me move him outside. He has gone now and he can hurt us no more. It is finally over!'

*   *   *

Four weeks later, Jake West was sitting in his usual seat at the rear of a rather boring history lesson. Everything had returned to almost normal as far as the two young boys were concerned. The excitement of their adventures on Estia had died down somewhat and they had settled back into their everyday routine. School life had its highs and lows, but no more than that of any youngster. The police had *finally* given up asking questions about their whereabouts and were concentrating now on the fate of Harry. Everyone had reluctantly accepted the boy's version of events surrounding Jake's grandfather's sudden disappearance. In the absence of further evidence or proof, they really had no choice. The story they had told that he had decided to discharge himself from hospital and chosen to visit an old army buddy in Australia was a little far-fetched perhaps, but however unlikely it seemed to the police, their efforts in trying to track him down had met with no success, meaning that it was the only plausible explanation they had. And it certainly succeeded in diverting any unwanted attention away from the boys. Jake and Ben had been left pretty much alone for a week or so now and they were extremely grateful that the seemingly endless questions had stopped. In fact, life had actually become quite tedious for them both, almost as boring as Mrs Binley's class on the Industrial Revolution, which they now had to endure.

Almost!

There *were* one or two changes however. Frightened to death by his son's disappearance and the fact that he had almost lost his only boy for good, Ben's father had *finally* decided to quit drinking. The ex-soldier was now fighting a very different battle of his own, and he was winning. He was making a real and determined effort to turn his life around, working hard to remain sober and trying to make up for lost time with Ben. He was attending lots of support meetings and because of this, he had moved into his parent's house in Birmingham temporarily whilst he was undergoing treatment. That meant that for the past month or so Ben had lived with Jake at the West's house. There, he was treated as one of the family, but he was due to move back home this coming weekend, when his father was expected to return. Finally, after several turbulent years of pain and heartache, they could actually start to rebuild their lives together. Having been changed a little by his experiences on Estia and having come to realise just how precious life and family are, Ben was looking forward immensely to trying. There was a definite spring in his step now which had been missing for some time, before he had entered that attic, and found that box.

For Jake, the return to the relative monotony of everyday life had come as a major disappointment, given all he had done and accomplished since learning of his incredible destiny. He had expected to be whisked away to lands far and wide at a moment's notice. He was excited by the prospect of further exploits in different worlds and he had been frustrated when nothing happened. Just like Ben, he was no longer the same boy who had entered that attic. Despite the uncertainties and peril associated with being a Keeper, he actually longed for action, for mystery, for danger. His Keeper's instincts and feelings were now fully awoken and they fuelled this desire. He needed *more* in his life than just school and sports, more to focus on, more to believe in. He felt incomplete, as if he was cut in two somehow. It was as if he didn't really belong in Lichfield anymore and he was just passing time until he was needed, until somebody summoned him, or called out to him for help.

More than anything else, Jake absolutely hated the waiting!

Mrs Binley gazed at her class over the golden rims of her spectacles, checking as she always did that her pupils were still paying attention to what she was saying. She was in the middle of explaining all about the 'wonders' of the Industrial Revolution and what a massive turning point it was in history, trying hard to fill her students with enthusiasm. As she paused and stared at them, every pupil tried their hardest to look as though they were paying her their undivided attention, including Jake.

But, just as her eyes met his, he became distracted, as he suddenly heard a very faint voice inside his head. He was shocked by it at first, but he tried his hardest not to show his feelings. He waited for Mrs Binley to continue, before closing his eyes to concentrate harder upon what it was saying. The voice grew steadily louder and louder until at last he could hear it clearly. There seemed to be real urgency in the tone and it was clear that the caller was desperately trying to reach him. The problem was, the language being spoken made no sense to him at all.

Arrggh! They might as well be speaking Swahili!

Jake opened his eyes in exasperation and threw his rubber at Ben to gain his attention. His best friend was busily daydreaming at the next desk. The eraser hit Ben on his shoulder but he did not stir. For a while, he remained completely oblivious to his friend's numerous and ever more frantic, but silent, attempts to gain his attention. Then, Jake suddenly realised why.

Ben's eyes were fixed firmly on Louise Underhill's legs. The petite beauty was sitting at a desk several rows ahead of him. Ben had fancied her since the first year of secondary school and his infatuation had not waned. She was for him the best part of Mrs Binley's class. In fact, she was the *only* reason for his so far one hundred per cent attendance record.

Jake's frustration grew and he tried again. This time, he lobbed his open pencil case at his best mate so hard, that it hit him on the head and the contents fell onto the floor, resulting in a loud crash that made everyone jump.

A furious Mrs Binley immediately scoured the room looking for the culprit. When she could not identify the offender, her eyes followed the direction of the noise and they fell upon Ben. The innocent teenager was rubbing his head and staring with confusion at the pencil case on the floor.

'Ah yes, I might have known! Ben Brooker, the usual suspect. Pick up your things and stay behind to see me after class, Ben. We can have another little chat together, and you can explain to me what that was all about? Now, settle down and let's move on! Where was I?'

Mrs Binley quickly regained her train of thought and she launched once again into her tutorial, ever the consummate professional. For a second, Ben was about to voice an objection to her unwarranted command and accusation, but he thought better of it. The words stuck in his throat as he realised that if he did, suspicion would immediately fall upon Jake. He said and did nothing. Once he felt it safe to do so, he looked over at his friend and whispered to him.

'Thanks! What the hell was that all about?'

Jake replied in a voice kept as low as he could manage, all the while trying to conceal his actions from the rest of the class, and his eagle-eyed teacher.

'It's happening again. The voices, they're back!' he hissed.

'What?!'

Ben didn't know what to think. His automatic reaction was to place his head in his hands and give it a shake. Almost immediately however, he lifted it back up again.

'Well? Go on then, spill the beans. Who is it? What do they say?'

'I dunno. I can't make them out,' answered Jake, shaking his head slowly. 'Hang on a minute! There they go again,' he added, as the same message replayed once more in his mind.

**'Brettsalp inkaroth preeenett ddrreea alph,
Menneeett saak wroophajj treelp me… I seek the Keeper!'**

Jake caught the final part of the last sentence. His heart began racing and his complexion turned white all of a sudden. He had a familiar dry sensation in his throat and his fingers began trembling with excitement. He did not recognise the voice or the language initially spoken, but it was definitely a female and she sounded scared. She sounded *petrified* in fact.

'What's a matter?' asked Ben. 'You look as though you've seen a ghost?'

Jake looked over at Mrs Binley to make sure she wasn't watching. Then, he turned his attention back to his friend. His face lost all expression as he whispered to him in a deadly serious tone.

'I've got to go. I'm needed.'

Ben was absolutely stunned. However, he replied in typical fashion.

'Go? Go where? Don't talk wet, Jake! You're in school. You can't just get up and walk out.'

Despite the irresistible urge he felt to race to the box of stones and use his powers, Jake knew his friend was right. However, he also knew that this was something he could not ignore. It was something he had longed for, been waiting for. He made up his mind quickly and tried to stand up, but Ben reached over and put his hand on his arm, stopping him before he was fully upright.

Mrs Binley couldn't fail to notice what was going on now and she halted her lesson.

'You two boys! Sit back down and be quiet!' she instructed, in a harsh, unyielding voice.

'Let go of me!' cried Jake, pulling his arm away from Ben. He tried to keep his voice as low as possible, even though the whole class had turned around by now and were watching him. 'I haven't a clue what it means, but someone out there is in trouble, so I guess I'm about to find out.'

Ben's eyes shifted to the rest of the class, telling Jake in no uncertain terms that they were being watched.

Jake reacted without thinking, suddenly knowing exactly what he had to do. He realised all of a sudden that somehow he possessed a new power, one he had not been able to call upon before this point. He responded quickly to the abrupt and unexpected realisation and he shouted out a solitary word.

'Ecrravisstte!'

The entire classroom was instantly suspended in time. Everyone was frozen on the spot and the immediate silence was deafening.

Jake did not know it yet, but the whole planet was frozen. At Jake's instinctive command, time on Earth now stood still. It was a spell of unbelievable power, one which had never before been attempted by a mortal, and one which up until now had been the sole preserve of those who ruled the afterlife, the ones considered to be Gods. Even the spirits and wizards had not been powerful enough to stop time.

Jake's mouth fell open in astonishment. He could not believe it had worked, and he was genuinely amazed by his own extraordinary feat of wizardry. However, he was too concerned for the welfare of the sender of the message, too eager to contact them and help, to dwell on it. He shook his head a little and whispered one more command.

'Likkraash!'

Ben immediately awoke. He took a deep breath and gazed in shock and bewilderment at the seemingly lifeless figures around him. He very quickly accepted however, that it was just another of Jake's surprises, something else he had to accept and get used to. He replied to his friend's last remarks, though he could hardly believe what he was about to say.

'Alright, alright! Hold your horses, cowboy. If you're determined to do this thing, if there's no way I can talk you out of it, I'm coming with you! No arguments, okay? I know I said I wouldn't, but I have to. You're my brother and I'd never forgive myself if something happened to you.'

After all, *someone* has to watch your back?'

The Jake West Trilogy

Jake West – The Keeper of the Stones

Jake West – Warriors of the Heynai

Jake West – The Estian Alliance

Thank you for reading this book. I love hearing what people think so please review it and help to spread the word.

Best Wishes,

M J Webb

Also by this author

A Child of Szabo – Adult Thriller.

Printed in Great Britain
by Amazon